T.A. WHITE

Dawn's Envoy

An Aileen Travers Novel

T.A. WHITE

To Cianna

PROLOGUE

Liam's bright blue eyes danced as he gave me a fierce grin, the sort of happy expression a dragon might make right before it chomped on you. It was all the warning I got before he swept my leg out from under me. I hit the mat with a grunt, surprised and startled at his speed.

When would I learn?

I sat up, frowning, even as I rubbed the offended spot on my backside. It was the exact same butt cheek on which he'd dumped me three times so far.

"What were you saying about old men?" he asked, not showing an ounce of repentance for my pain.

I grumbled as I leveraged myself to my feet again, debating the odds I'd land a worthwhile blow before this session was done. Not good, I was thinking.

In the two months since these training sessions had become a regular occurrence, I'd only landed a legitimate punch—not glancing or blocked—a handful of times. Worse, was the suspicion he was still holding back with me.

"They should know when they've become fossils and find a deep dark hole to crawl into," I fired back.

His grin flashed. "When the children prove they're good for blowing more than hot air, maybe they will."

I couldn't help my amused snort.

Much to my surprise, I was starting to enjoy these weekly sessions with Liam. He was growing on me—like fungus.

He knew it too and took full advantage whenever he could, pushing my boundaries just a little bit more each time, making his interest obvious.

It was an interest I returned, enjoying the flirting and banter these nights inevitably brought.

"Have you given any more thought to my proposal?" he asked as I started stretching out my kinks.

He hadn't yet indicated the match would resume. Until he did, I was going to give my poor, abused muscles the care they deserved.

"Let me think. Being at your beck and call with a bunch of enforcers—half of whom dislike me—as my bosses. Not sure how I feel about that," I said, wincing as a particularly tight spot protested the movement.

"Becoming part of a team and getting paid a living wage. Not really sure what the issue is," Liam shot back.

I frowned at him. He'd gotten good at finding arguments that would have the best chance of influencing me. It demonstrated an understanding of what drove me and was slightly disconcerting, given his inclination towards manipulation.

Much as I hated to admit it, he had several valid points. The money especially, would be welcome.

"I'm still waiting for you to show me the bright side in all this," I complained.

"Be here Friday night and I will."

Oh. A field trip—that sounded interesting.

"Will you make it worth my while?" I asked, a playful note entering my voice.

His smirk turned seductive, his eyes half-lidded as he gave me the look a man gives a woman he's attracted to. "Show up Friday and find out."

I couldn't contain my small laugh, choking it back before he took it as a sign of encouragement. Until I knew which direction I wanted to go, I found it best not to give the vampire any bright ideas. He took every opening as an invitation to push harder, displaying a distinct resemblance to a battering ram.

Avoidance and ignoring the charge between us wouldn't work much longer. I needed to make a choice.

I frowned at him as I remembered all the reasons he and I were not a good idea—starting with the fact his loyalty to the vampires would always outweigh anything he felt toward me.

Then there was his age. He wasn't just a few decades older than me. He was centuries. Three to four hundred years older, at least. Some of the things he'd let slip made me think he could be even older. Thinking about it was enough to make my teeth hurt.

His gaze flickered as his attention fastened on something behind me. I turned to see Eric standing at the edge of the gym, the normally reserved enforcer appearing even more intense than normal.

That was odd. Liam's enforcers didn't typically interrupt during our training periods.

Whatever message he brought must be important.

"We'll end here for the night," Liam said.

My eyes lingered on Eric for a beat longer as I tilted my head in question. Yes, whatever this was about, was very important.

Curiosity took hold. I shook my head, mentally rejecting the urge. As tempting as it was to ask questions and pry into matters that most likely didn't concern me, that was a good way to get drawn deeper into vampire politics. I wasn't sure if I was ready for that step yet.

"And here I thought vampires were supposed to have stamina for days," I said as I bent to grab my shoes from the edge of the mat.

Liam stepped closer and trailed a stolen touch across my shoulder. Goosebumps skated down my spine. I stilled.

"I would be glad to show you just how long my stamina can last," he said, a seductive smile edged with sly humor taking over his face. "On the mats, of course," he added as an afterthought.

Amusement invaded and I cocked my head, taking pleasure in the game. "Another time—perhaps when dreams become reality."

Appreciation at the jab passed over his face as he inclined his head.

I sauntered away, saying over my shoulder, "See you Friday."

*

I bounded up the steps of the clan's mansion Friday night, anticipation and eagerness giving me urgency. I had a good feeling about tonight.

Drinks with Caroline had cleared my head and given me much needed perspective when it came to what I wanted out of life. I'd been stuck in survival mode for so long that sometimes I forgot the other things in life. Maybe it was time to loosen up and live again.

Liam could be the beginning of that, starting with my taking him up on his proposal of a field trip.

Afterwards, we'd see where the night led. Either way, I was tired of fighting this attraction between us.

I walked into the gym with a smile on my face. "I've thought about what you said and I'd like to take you up on it. You were right."

Nathan straightened from his stretch, looking up in surprise. "What am I right about?"

I ground to a halt and frowned. "What're you doing here? Where's Liam?"

"He'll be gone for a while. He asked me to take over your training in the meantime."

Everything in me went still. "For how long?"

Nathan shrugged. "Don't know. The mission is hush-hush. Until then, you've got yours truly."

My nod was slow. Liam had left.

All the anticipation I'd felt moments before drained away, leaving

3

behind ice.

"Something wrong?"

I was quiet.

"Nope." I gave my head a slight shake.

Nothing. Nothing was wrong. Liam had a job. He didn't owe me any explanations.

"What was Liam right about?" Nathan asked, his eyebrows climbing in question.

I jerked my attention back to Nathan. It took a second for me to form words. "He said my form needed work and my endurance was still lacking."

Nathan pursed his lips, as he gave me a slightly disbelieving look. He shrugged his broad shoulders a second later. "Don't you worry, cupcake. I'll get you into top shape. He won't ever complain about your endurance again."

My smile was strained. "Sounds good."

When he returned to stretching, my smile faded, and I rubbed my forehead. My excitement had turned to ash in my mouth. I should have known better.

I was alone in this. Liam and Nathan felt a duty to help someone who'd gotten a rotten start. That was all. They were free to come and go as they pleased. It'd be best not to forget that or form attachments that wouldn't last.

CHAPTER ONE

A bag full of donut holes, five giant chocolate bars, and three cases of Diet Coke were going to be the death of me. Not literally—we vampires were a little more difficult to kill than that—but emotionally? Financially? Definitely.

I looked up from the assortment in front of me to the customer radiating impatience.

"The sign said free snacks with purchase," the woman explained again.

My gaze shifted from her to the sign—the bane of my current existence. I don't know how it got out of the storage room—again—but I was going to take a pair of very sharp scissors to it as soon as I got rid of this woman.

It did indeed say, 'free snacks with purchase', but it wasn't meant to be used the way the customer intended. The deal only applied to one free item, not eight. My only saving grace was the date tacked on the bottom.

"Ma'am, that deal expired at midnight." My cheeks hurt from the polite smile I kept pinned on my face. It had been stuck there, becoming increasingly strained, for the last five minutes as we went over the same argument again and again.

The sign's promise expired two hours ago, which was when I'd moved it to the storage room, thankful to be done with it. It had caused nothing but trouble since I'd come on shift. Whoever wrote the stupid thing made it needlessly vague. All night I'd had to explain its true meaning so customers didn't succeed in clearing out the store of all valuable merchandise.

I was done with the whole issue. Done. And one annoying woman who didn't know when to quit wasn't going to force me to surrender.

"Then why is the sign still out?" she argued. "That's false advertising."

I kept my frustrated sigh internal, the polite smile turning even more strained. "I'm so sorry for the confusion, ma'am. We haven't had time to

5

take it down."

That was a lie. I'd already taken the stupid thing down. Twice. Each time it somehow found its way back into the front of the store. At this point, I knew there was someone or something messing with me. As soon as I got rid of this customer, I planned to hunt them down and show them exactly why irritated vampires should be left alone.

The woman's mouth pursed in a frown as she looked around the empty gas station as if to call me on the lie, her expression clearly stating she thought laziness had more to do with my predicament than anything else.

"Whether you had time or not, the fact remains that you have a sign promising me these things for free. I expect you to live up to that promise." Her expression soured and she lifted one perfectly groomed eyebrow as if daring me to argue.

Unfortunately for her, I could outstubborn even the most persistent of customers. My sire would be only too happy to inform her of the depths to which I could sink.

The woman was a few inches shorter than me. Her youth was far behind her and the years had softened her middle and face. She compensated for that with hair styled into a sleek bob, not a strand out of place, and a perfectly made-up face, complete with foundation and blush, despite the sweats she wore.

She was a study in contradictions, not the least of which was her passion to get twenty dollars' worth of junk food for free. It baffled me. You would think it was a supersaver deal worth hundreds of dollars, given the amount of grief she'd heaped on my head since walking into the gas station ten minutes ago.

It might have been different if I thought she couldn't afford it, but I'd seen the car she'd driven up in—a tricked out MDX, not an inexpensive car. There was no way she couldn't afford twenty dollars, not when she was riding in a car that could have been a down payment on a house.

"I'm sorry, ma'am, but I can't give you the reduced price. The system won't let me," I said, my smile stretching my cheeks. I tried to infuse it with some sympathy, a token of empathy—hard to do when I made minimum wage and didn't have twenty dollars of my own to waste.

It was quickly becoming clear this job was not for me. When I lost my position with Hermes Courier Service, I'd known it would be difficult. I'd known things would be tight. I just hadn't known how difficult and tight they would be.

Working at a gas station hadn't been part of my five-year plan. It wasn't the worst job I'd ever had, but it was definitely not where I thought I'd be at this stage of my life. It had quickly reinforced the knowledge that I wasn't cut out for customer service. I needed a place where I could be my grumpy, antisocial self, not somewhere I had to smile on command and pretend I didn't want to whack people on the back of the head sometimes.

Hermes had given me a certain autonomy that I very much missed. Employees were left to do a job unsupervised as long as pickups and deliveries were accomplished. Not quite the case at my current place of employment.

Despite that, I was lucky to have anything. Jobs that let you work only at night were few and far between, and since most of the spook world wouldn't touch me with a five-foot pole given my status as a clanless vampire who'd been fired by Hermes, it meant my options limited.

I reminded myself that I needed this job. Rent was due in a week, and I was down to the last of my nest egg. If I wanted to keep a roof over my head, I couldn't afford to alienate customers and risk getting fired.

"I want to talk to your manager," the woman proclaimed in a ringing voice.

That's what I was afraid of.

"Unfortunately, I'm the only one here right now," I said in as polite a voice as I could muster.

This shift was the least busy, and as a result, the owners only staffed the gas station with one person. Me. The manager wouldn't be here until mid-morning. That meant I was flying solo and all customer complaints went through me.

Lucky me.

The woman's face turned cruel as a self-satisfied smirk twisted her lips. "How fortunate for me."

I stiffened, the smile slowly falling from my face. Some instinct had me switching to the othersight of my left eye. I'd gotten better at controlling it, seeing the magic overlaying the world when *I* wanted, as opposed to when my eye felt like it.

Sure enough, the woman had a haze surrounding her, beautiful lights that twinkled and flared.

She definitely was not what she appeared. This was no housewife on a midnight binge or a mom desperate to get last minute supplies for a child's party. She belonged to the same shadow world I did. A dangerous place, full of things that often posed as their more harmless counterparts.

I let my hand drop from view below the countertop and inched it toward the gun hidden by a "don't look here" charm, even as I glanced up at the cameras pointed in our direction. Surely, she wouldn't be so stupid as to try something in a place where normals could see and record the evidence.

There weren't many rules in this shadow world, but one of the biggest was "don't let the humans find out there were more things that went bump in the dark than they'd ever imagined." It was the quickest way to earn your way onto a kill list.

Before I could do more, her hand flashed up as she threw something at me. My eye saw it as a dark blur that filled me with a sucking feeling of dread. I flinched instinctively, a shield of white flashing into existence between me and whatever it was. The dark blur struck it and boomeranged back to the woman, hitting her in the chest.

She staggered back with a grunt as the darkness slowly absorbed into her chest. She touched the spot where it had disappeared with an uneasy look on her face.

I don't know which of us was more surprised over the turn of events. I blinked dumbly at her chest, grateful whatever she'd thrown hadn't touched me.

Pain tightened the corners of her mouth and eyes as she glared at me over the chaos of the rebound. One of the cases of Diet Coke had exploded while the candy bars had melted into a pile of goo, escaping their wrappers to pool on the counter. The change dispenser was now on its side and the newspapers kept in a rack by the door were strewn everywhere.

"You need to go." My voice was strong and rang with an authority I didn't necessarily feel. "Now."

She straightened, her back ramrod straight as she shot me a glare worthy of a grand lady from a period drama, one filled with haughty scorn and dislike.

She snatched her purse off the counter in an abrupt movement, tucking it under her arm. I watched her gather her stuff, my hand still on the gun, which was now aimed at her under the counter.

"Leave it," I ordered when she tried to grab the donuts and the remaining intact cases of Diet Coke. My smile turned nasty. "Unless you're planning to pay full price."

Her expression grew livid. "You'll get what's coming to you, parasite."

She lifted her gaze to the same cameras I'd glanced at earlier. Her smile turned sinister. She didn't wait for my reply before turning and flouncing out of the gas station.

I released the breath I'd been holding and set the gun back into place. Things could have been worse. They could have been better too, but at least I was still alive.

I cast a resigned glance over the mess. I had quite a bit to clean up before dawn.

Not for the first time, I said a prayer of thanks for the charm Dahlia had given me to protect me against such unsavory encounters. I lifted the necklace with its thumb-length pendant from under my shirt.

To my left eye, it gleamed with a soft silver glow. That same glow was infused along the entirety of my own faint aura. This wasn't the first time it had saved me from a magical attack, though it might be the last. A hairline crack ran through the middle of the stone.

I dropped it back under my shirt with a sigh. Jerry, the owner of Hermes, hadn't been kidding when he said I'd become the number one target in town once he withdrew his protection. Over the last two months, it had become evident how many spooks had an axe to grind with vampires.

As the youngest vampire in the area, and the only one I knew of without the benefit of a clan's protection, I was considered an easy mark. Where they wouldn't dare challenge the vampires who were both stronger than me and possessed the full might of a clan at their back, they seemed to think killing me would settle whatever score they had, while resulting in the least amount of danger to themselves.

I'd like to say they were wrong, but they weren't. Not entirely. As a baby vamp, I had very little personal power, except for a strange ability to see magic and a frustrating talent for finding trouble in the least likely of places. All things considered, I was significantly weaker than the weakest of spooks and all alone with no one to watch my back or avenge me should I fall. Not a good place to be when you were part of a species both envied and hated.

I sighed and looked up at the camera again. It had caught the entire confrontation on its recording. I'd have to watch it and see if the magic had shown up. Sometimes it didn't. Magic was tricky. It didn't always act the way you expected. If it did show up, I'd have to figure out an explanation for why an entire night's recording was deleted.

But, first things first, I needed to deal with the dratted sign, in a way that meant it wouldn't come back to cause me problems later.

I groped around under the counter, pulling out a box cutter before heading to the sign. It wasn't a pair of scissors but would hopefully get the job done.

I rounded the counter and only made it a few steps before the lights flickered, the world around me darkening as if a thundercloud had invaded the postage stamp-sized store.

The dry rustle of old paper surrounded me. I realized with a start it was laughter. "Poor little vampire. Such trials you face. What's she going to do now, I wonder?"

"Cry."

"Surrender."

"Bleed."

"Die."

Other voices echoed as they threw out their guesses.

"Perhaps we should put her out of her misery," another voice suggested.

The theatrics were meant to be ominous, to inspire dread and fear. I remained unmoved, my expression unchanged. It seemed my tormentors had decided to make themselves known. Finally.

It was all very dramatic and might have worked had I not known an expert at this type of intimidation. The sorcerer was many things, showman included. Now there was a guy who could work a room. These punks were amateurs compared to him.

I focused, taking a look at the magic around me. Sure enough, the sign had little red prints all over it. Ones that appeared to be a cross between a small animal's paw and a hand. That at least was vaguely creepy.

In the aisle, the shadows under the shelves deepened, becoming more dense than they should be under the fluorescent light. A normal would ascribe the shadows to a trick of the light. I knew better. Especially since I caught the impression of eyes and pointed teeth in the depths of some of those shadows.

Goblins.

I suppose it could be worse. Goblins weren't typically considered dangerous, not unless they were part of a swarm or one of the higher goblins. These weren't.

Thank all the gods.

I counted only five, three of whom were no bigger than my hand. Annoying but not deadly.

Sometimes it was the small wins that kept me going.

"I suggest you move along," I told them, my smile widening to show my fangs. "My patience with your antics is fast disappearing."

"Stupid vampire. We know you're bluffing. You're too weak to scare us."

One goblin grew bold, drifting out from under the shelf and dropping some of its glamour.

The creature was no bigger than a house cat, slinking forward on all fours, its back rounded. Its skin had a dark green bordering on black tint to it.

I expected its form to be grotesque, as many folktales depicted it, but the little goblin wasn't. It was sleek and streamlined, its face containing some human characteristics as well as something alien—something that made it all the more interesting to look at.

Its eyes were large pools of black, and sticking out of its forehead were tiny protrusions that might have been considered horns had they been a bit longer.

Like me, goblins were denizens of the night, even more susceptible to damage from the sun than a vampire.

There were many types of goblins, some powerful, some not. These looked to be minor goblins, the kind that could irritate and annoy but weren't really dangerous.

I had to wonder if their presence here was a crime of opportunity or if someone had pointed the little assholes my way. Vampires weren't really

DAWN'S ENVOY

their preferred targets and I hadn't done anything to draw their ire that I knew of.

"Are you sure about that?" I asked with a bravado I didn't necessarily feel. "Because I know a couple of harpies who enjoy trying adventurous new foods. I've heard goblin blood is considered a delicacy among some circles."

The goblin reared back as cries of "monster" echoed from the rest.

I leaned forward and gave them a sinister smile. "You leave me alone, and I'll do the same for you."

There was a dry rattling hiss as the goblins slunk away, the shadows they'd used for cover fading, until only the one who'd dropped his glamour remained.

"You're more like your kind than you pretend." The words were not a compliment.

"You think so?" I asked. "I don't. Had another vampire been here, they would have killed you all without giving you the nice warning, just because you irritated them."

I turned toward the sign. "Now me, I don't think it's unreasonable to expect peace in my place of business. I've got a lot of patience, but I won't stand for you lot putting my job in jeopardy."

I turned back to where the goblin should be, only to realize I was addressing an empty store. I sighed. Figures. At least I'd earned a little peace. That threat should keep them away for the rest of the week. After that, we would see.

I set about returning the store to its normal state of untidy orderliness. The first thing to go was the sign. I unhooked it from its stand and dragged it outside. The thin poster board was about the same height as me. It was awkward more than anything, as I carefully carried it around the side of the building.

Cutting it into small, jagged strips was harder than I'd thought. The box cutter didn't want to slice through the thick paper, the blade dull and useless. Eventually I tossed it aside after checking to make sure there were no prying eyes or cameras watching. Finding myself alone, I grasped the sign in my hands before ripping it apart piece by piece.

Having a vampire's strength came in handy sometimes. This was one of those times.

After reducing the sign to about twenty small pieces, I threw it in the dumpster and turned back to the interior of the station. I'd like to see them reassemble that, I thought with an evil smile.

Next, I gathered up the burst soda cans and carried them to the dumpster along with any other un-salvageable items.

I tried to save what I could, tidying the newspapers strewn about and returning the change dispenser to its normal position. A stray case of Diet

Coke and a few candy bars probably wouldn't be missed. Much more than that, and the owners might try to take some of the damaged goods out of my paycheck. I couldn't afford the loss of income. I just had to hope and pray no one did inventory for a while.

The rest of my shift was uneventful. Only two more customers ventured inside—both human—both content to pay and go about their business without even a grunted word of greeting.

After an interminably long time, five a.m. finally rolled around.

My replacement dragged in muttering, "Good morning," around a wide yawn.

"Tough night?" I asked Josie as another yawn cracked her jaw.

"The best kind," she said, before making a beeline for the coffee machine.

For a gas station with ninety-nine cent coffee, its flavor wasn't half bad. At least, that's what I'd been told. Food and I were on a break at the moment, and beverages like coffee were one of the many things I couldn't have.

Josie had dark circles under her eyes that said she'd probably been out partying until the early morning. Her hair was a snarled mess, barely restrained in a messy bun at the top of her head.

"Any problems?" she asked.

I shook my head. "Pretty quiet."

By some miracle, the cameras hadn't caught anything from my earlier encounter that might reveal the spook world. I looked mildly crazy at one point talking to myself, but that was about it.

"I don't know how you stand that shift. I would go insane," Josie said with a shudder.

I shrugged. "It's not that bad. I get to catch up on my reading at least."

Josie did a faceplant on the counter. Her words came out garbled, but I thought she said something like, "Books, bleh."

I revised my earlier opinion regarding the dark circles being a result of partying.

"Studying not going well, I take it."

A muffled response came along the lines of, "Studying sucks."

Josie was in college, studying to be a nurse. She worked here for rent and spending money.

She raised her head off the counter, a crease mark on her cheek. "It's pretty dead in here. I don't think we'll pick up again until closer to rush hour. You're welcome to take off if you'd like."

I hesitated, glancing outside and calculating how much time I had left until sunrise. It was early September and the sun wouldn't be up until nearly seven. Plenty of time to bike home and be under the covers of my own bed before the pesky ball of fire in the sky put me out for the day.

As a baby vamp, my tolerance to the sun was a lot less than a vampire a century or so older. It meant I had to be careful, always keeping one eye on my watch. The sun probably wouldn't kill me, not as long as I was topped up on blood. Death from sun exposure was a myth, one created after a few starved, weakened vampires caught fire after exposure. For vampires at their peak strength, it was a pesky irritant capable of giving you the worst sunburn of your life. For me, it would put me into a coma-like sleep—the kind you didn't wake up from easily—no matter how much someone shook and slapped you.

Still, I was torn. The extra money would be nice. Summer was killing my wallet. Reduced hours of dark meant limiting my working hours, leaving me to get by on the bare minimum. I was looking forward to winter and increasing my hours and paycheck.

Accurately reading my hesitation, Josie propped her cheek on a hand and gave me a sleepy smile. "Here's a tip. If you check out at the forty-minute mark, you still get paid for the entire hour."

"Really?"

She nodded. "I'm not supposed to share that because they don't want people taking advantage. Owen let me do that a few times when I was prepping for finals."

Somehow that didn't surprise me. The manager, Owen, had a huge crush on Josie and let her get away with things the rest of us couldn't.

"Alright, I'll stay until then," I agreed.

She slapped the counter and straightened, her face brightening. "Great, now I don't have to suffer through the next hour by myself."

The remaining time passed quickly. Josie, it turned out, was pretty funny and made a good work buddy. She kept a running commentary on the customers who stopped to pump gas or come inside.

Before I knew it, I was clocking out and wheeling my bike from the storage room. I took a moment to look it over, not trusting the goblins had left it alone. Surprisingly, they hadn't touched it; something I was grateful for.

As my only means of transportation, I was serious about the bike's care and upkeep. Had they messed with it, I might actually have made good on my threat.

Or maybe not.

There was still an hour before I needed to be home. Plenty of time to bike there. The stars were beginning to fade as the sun prepared for its ascent. First light, which typically began half an hour before true sunrise, was still thirty minutes away.

The normal lethargy that plagued me during first light was still absent, but it wouldn't be long now. It was a reminder of my limits. I could feel the sun in my chest as it lingered just under the horizon. The sensation would

13

steadily grow stronger as sunrise approached.

Home was a second story walk-up on the outskirts of the university district. It was a plain, two story brick building composed of townhome style apartments. Mine was on the second story. I'm not sure if my place had originally been intended to be a one room apartment since the rest of the units were 2 story units, or if someone had gotten greedy for extra rent and turned the second floor into a stand-alone apartment.

When I'd first settled here, the entire complex had been little more than a slum. Since the new owner had taken over, they'd begun renovating the place, bringing everything up to code.

You'd think I'd be happy about that. Unfortunately, the new owner happened to be my sire, Thomas—a vampire I would gladly avoid for the rest of my undead life. Such was not to be, given his propensity for interference.

The cracked, unusable parking lot had been replaced and was now smooth, with sharp white lines delineating parking spots. One of them held the black Escalade my sire had given me as a gift. I still hadn't touched it or figured out what I was going to do with it. Not that it mattered anymore, since I couldn't even afford the gas it would take to fill it.

Gifts from vampires, I'd learned, always came with a set of strings attached to them. My sire seemed determined to get his hooks into me by any means possible, and I was just as determined to steer clear of them.

Everything to do with my sire involved hidden agendas and things not always being what they appeared. I couldn't trust anything he did or said. I didn't like being used, and I preferred to control my own destiny. It left me in a precarious predicament.

It didn't help that he wasn't afraid to use his power as my landlord to fuck with me either, as evidenced by the partially completed set of stairs to my unit.

It was not lost on me that construction on them halted right around the time I refused to use the mansion as my temporary lodging. I liked having my own place. Say what you will about the building's condition, but I'd turned it into a home. I wasn't willing to give that up. Not even for the opulent lodgings of the mansion.

Thomas thought by taking away my stairs he could force my hand. Not the case. As with everything in life, I adapted, and I overcame. Granted, it wasn't easy and was growing increasingly annoying, but until my sire bored of this game, I was stuck finding new and inventive ways to access my own apartment.

I pulled a harness out of my backpack and slid into it. Once done, I shifted my backpack to my front before attaching the hooks in the back of the harness to the bike. I would have loved to leave my bike down here, but a couple of the college kids liked to play pranks. I couldn't trust it would be here when I got back. That left me in the unenviable position of having to lug it upstairs every night.

I set one hand on the wall and began my climb, taking advantage of the easy handholds formed by the half-built stairs.

"You're just making things worse. He'll find another way to get to you until you stop being so stubborn," a voice said from below.

CHAPTER TWO

I stilled. I knew that voice. Liam.

I shifted my weight, putting most of it on one foot and in my arms as I peered down. Liam's impossibly blue eyes stared up at me.

I caught my breath, suddenly feeling like I'd been punched in the chest. He always did that to me. He had the sort of charismatic presence that eclipsed any notion of beauty, the sum of his parts totaling to much more than what each feature would be if taken separately. Not to say he wasn't handsome. He was. His face possessed the strong lines and rugged features you'd imagine on one of those billionaire CEOs featured in romance books.

But a pretty face wasn't the only reason he drew women like a moth to the flame. No, it was the power he wore like others wore clothes. It was the confidence in his movements, as if the world only existed to please him. Nothing and no one would ever successfully thwart him, at least not for long.

The sight of him, hearing his voice after several month's long absence caused an avalanche of conflicting feelings I didn't want to deal with. Not now or at any point in the future.

He wasn't quite smiling as we stared at each other. My expression had gone blank.

"So, you're back."

He dipped his chin once.

"I won't keep you," I said before turning back to the wall and climbing again. "I'm sure you have many important things waiting for your attention."

There was a small sound behind me, then a powerful force lifted me up, yanking me from the wall. My stomach dropped.

Seconds later, I was set on my feet in the middle of my living room.

I blinked. If I'd ever needed a demonstration of the difference in power between the two of us, the speed, agility, and strength he'd just demonstrated would have brought that point home very nicely.

My lips parted, whether in rebuke or something else, I'll never know. In the next moment, Liam yanked me to him, his eyes glowing with an otherworldly power, his fangs denting his lower lip.

His mouth descended on mine, forestalling any comment. Passion rose, threatening to swamp my better judgment. Someone's fang, I don't know if it was his or mine nicked flesh, and suddenly the rich decadent copper of his blood filled my mouth.

Just like that, the whirlwind feelings his presence had caused disappeared, leaving me consumed with need.

A moan filled the air, I wasn't sure it if was his or mine. Our bodies pressed together as if we were trying to climb inside the other.

His hands were on my back even as mine fisted in his hair. With a little hop I jumped up, his hands going to my ass to support me as I wrapped my legs around his waist.

Our bodies became a tangle of limbs as each second pushed us higher. My skin felt flushed with need.

I panted as he broke the kiss to rain small pecks down my neck and shoulder. I tried to grab hold of a thin thread of logic, but his lips covered mine again.

Several minutes passed where only the small breathless sounds we made could be heard.

He was fire and fury against me. I was the push and pull of the ocean against him. Tangling and dueling, each of us exalting in the battle of desire.

A crash in my bedroom brought me back to the present. Reason cascaded down on me like ice cold water, reminding me of why this, me and him, was a horrible idea.

He'd left without a word of warning. Just picked up his things one day and was gone, like a ghost. There wasn't one word of goodbye.

He didn't owe me anything. We hadn't embarked on a relationship. I knew that. Still, I thought we'd been heading down a certain path. To have him up and disappear like that had brought the cold grip of reality back.

Liam was vampire. Not just clan, but an enforcer for their council. His agenda was not mine. I couldn't trust him or his reasons for taking an interest in me.

For that, I was grateful he'd left the way he did. It reminded me of the facts of life, before I got too invested.

I lifted my head and stared down at him, noting the otherworldly glow, the slightly unfocused eyes, the softened expression. The sight made me waver in my decision. He looked at me with the single-minded focus and intensity of a man who hadn't had a drink in a year, and I was a cool glass of water taken from a mountain spring.

I pushed away, my body suddenly stiff as I unhooked my legs.

He was slow to let me go, his expression fierce and watchful.

His hands lingered as he helped me down. I stepped back, avoiding his gaze. I turned and saw the bike he'd somehow unlatched from the harness without me even noticing. It lay half on the couch.

I headed to it, lifting it up and wheeling it over to the bike rack I kept near the front door.

"So, you're back," I said in as steady a voice as I could. I'd said it before, but it was worth repeating, as I busied myself with getting the bike situated on the rack.

He watched me, his expression closed off, the passion of moments before gone. "Yes, my business finally wrapped up."

"That's good," I said. I was grateful he was willing to gloss over what just happened, but it still galled me that it seemed so easy for him.

"I thought we'd made progress," he finally said.

I could feel the weight of his stare on my bent head.

"I'm still attending my weekly lessons," I responded, choosing to misunderstand.

Frustration flickered on his face. "I know. Nathan's kept me informed of your progress. That's not what I meant."

Ah, so someone in vamp headquarters had been able to keep in touch with him. Good to know.

He stared at me for a long minute. I kept my head down, intent on fiddling with the bike as I fought to keep my face bland, every emotion that might give away my turmoil carefully hidden. The fluttering in my belly and slightly unsteady feeling didn't make it easy.

I didn't know what he expected of me, but I was determined not to give it to him.

His sigh was long and angry. He rubbed one hand through his hair before he nodded and straightened.

His mouth tightened and he drew himself upright, his face settling into authoritative lines. "Why are you back here?"

I stood up. "This is my home. It's normal to live in the place you call home."

He arched one eyebrow, turning his attention to the still open door, his message clear.

I shrugged in answer. The lack of stairs was a nuisance, but I hadn't let that stop me.

"I know Thomas offered you a place in the mansion until the renovations of this building were complete," he said.

That was true, and I'd even taken him up on it for the first month. Very mature of me I know. However, once I learned the extent of the renovations and calculated just how long I would be away from my apartment, I decided to rethink that plan. You see, Thomas had so many things he planned to do to this place, and my apartment in particular, I would have been out of my home for a year or more.

Liam would know that. Or he should. He was more versed in Thomas' shenanigans than I was.

"It was taking too long." There, that was diplomatic enough.

He was quiet, his gaze thoughtful as he looked over my apartment. I struggled not to feel defensive over what he might see. My home wasn't filled with name brand stuff. It was mostly things I'd gotten at yard sales or hand-me-downs my family had grown tired of. As a result, it was a mishmash of a dozen different styles. Despite that, it suited me. The rooms felt lived in, like they'd seen endless amounts of joy, pain and sorrow.

I was very aware after staying in the mansion, that it looked a little threadbare and worn, in no way comparing to the magazine quality rooms there. Still, it was mine. My first home post-military, and something I'd created through my own hard work.

He seemed to come to a decision, his gaze piercing as it shifted to me. "Be at this address tomorrow night," he said, pressing on the screen of his phone.

From my backpack, my phone chimed with a text. I made no move to pick it up or look at it.

I stiffened, some of my natural antagonism at being ordered around rearing its head. With effort, I forced it back down.

This man had a habit of getting under my skin. He could do more with a simple shift of expression than most could with carefully crafted barbs. The only other people capable of inspiring such reactions in me were my family.

In my head, I knew I should be an adult. Mature. Act my age. Not let him see how he got to me.

What came out was. "Nope. I have work."

"Call off."

"Can't." I didn't bother explaining my money issues or the fact rent was due in five days. I needed every hour of work I could get. Even if that hadn't been the case, I probably still would have refused. Half of it was due to my genuine hurt over his disappearance. The rest was just the primal need to battle it out until I came out the victor.

"I'll pay you triple what you would make there," he said with forced patience.

That wasn't the incentive it should be. I made an idiotically low wage for a night's worth of work.

"It's not about the money," I told him.

I needed this job. Yes, I could call off. Josie did it all the time. I would probably keep my job, but the risk wasn't worth it. A higher paycheck tomorrow night might be nice, but what about in a week or a month? I needed steady paying work, not to dance at some vampire's whim.

"You'll be there," he said, his expression smug.

"That's an arrogant assumption."

He sauntered closer, stopping with the barest of space between us, forcing me to look up to see his face. I wasn't a short woman, just over average height at five feet seven inches, but Liam made me feel petite.

He leaned down, cheek sliding against mine as he whispered into my ear. "You owe me."

His message delivered, he straightened and gave me another lazy smile, one that widened as he caught my fulminating look. "An hour after sundown. I expect you won't be late."

I didn't answer as he slid past me, too busy glaring at the wall. His exit was silent.

Sneaky vampires and their stupid games.

I'd be there, whether I wanted to be or not. Because he was right. I did owe him. Ten nights to be exact.

Guess he was calling in the first of those.

I stalked over to the door and slammed it shut, turning the locks and hooking the chain into place. Not that it would do much good, considering he'd already gotten past a locked door once tonight, but it made me feel better.

Turning back to the room, I was brought up short at the sight of my two roommates perched on the edge of the kitchen countertop, tiny feet swinging as they watched me. Inara and Lowen were pixies and had settled in the apartment despite every attempt to force them out. They'd ignored my repeated protests. I'd grown used to them now.

Each no bigger than my hand, their wings fanned behind them in a bright display. More beautiful than any butterfly wing, they were as distinctive as the pixies themselves.

Inara tended to be the bolder of the two. A pixie queen, she could be mercurial and autocratic, but I'd seen moments of softness, especially when she addressed her consort, Lowen.

Her wings were an iridescent green and yellow, the pattern unlike anything I'd ever seen in nature. When they moved, it was like watching tree leaves rustling in the wind.

Her skin had a slight greenish tinge to it, and her eyes were overly large in her face. People often equated pixies to bugs because of those eyes, but I'd always likened them closer to a doll. In miniature, her features were delicate and fierce.

Lowen, on the other hand, was often the calming voice of reason, advocating restraint where Inara would leap into battle without considering the consequences. He could be just as fierce as she, but it took more to get him to that point.

I'd learned just how deadly he could be when a family of brownies had tried to move in. He'd dispatched them with a skill and precision that would be chilling in a creature any bigger than he was.

Where Inara was clad in the shades of the forest, Lowen more closely resembled a field of flowers. His skin was burnished copper and his wings the most vivid blues and purples I'd ever seen.

"That crash was very well timed," I told them.

It was as close as I could get to saying thank you. It was never wise to thank the Fae outright. They could use it as a way to enslave you, calling in debts likely to mean the end of you.

"That vampire has an agenda," Inara said. She didn't wait for my response, leaping off the counter and fluttering back down the hall.

I sighed. I couldn't argue with that.

"What are you going to do?" Lowen asked.

"There's not much I can do. I owe him ten nights. If he's calling in one of those nights, I have no choice but to answer." It didn't make me happy to admit that.

You would think after the first time someone called in one of the debts I owed, I would stop handing them out like candy. Not the case. I had more debts floating out there than I liked to think about, including to my two permanent house guests.

Lowen lifted into the air, his wings a purple-blue streak behind him. "Sun's coming up. You should get ready for bed."

He flitted off, leaving me standing in my living room, first light already making its way across the sky.

*

Opening my door to head out, and hearing a startled *mrph* as a stranger teetered on the thin ledge next to it was not my ideal way to start off my night.

My hand snapped out, grabbing a well-muscled arm, before the person could fall the ten feet down. It was awkward, trying to keep from being pulled out of my apartment as I juggled the person and my bike in the opposite hands.

Somehow, I managed to pull my visitor inside with me. He sprawled at my feet, his eyes slightly wide as residual adrenaline kicked in.

There was a riot of golden hair around his face as he remained on all fours, breathing heavily at the close call.

Inara and Lowen flitted near, landing on a pair of shelves near the entry way. We all stared down at the unexpected visitor.

"A sphinx," Inara said. "What is one doing at your door?"

I shook my head. I had no clue.

21

I'd only ever met one sphinx, and that was a brief encounter.

I gave the man at my feet another moment to compose himself, waiting until he looked up. His bright green eyes were lined by thick, dark eyelashes. The golden hair on his head was the biggest clue to his species.

He was young, not more than twenty, his face lean and narrow. The last sphinx I'd encountered had pointed ears—this guy's were as rounded and human as mine.

He gave me a strained smile. "Hello."

I arched an eyebrow and gave him a look, one that said he'd have to do a lot better than that.

"What were you doing there?" I asked.

"Ah, well," he said, climbing to his feet and brushing off his pants. He seemed uncomfortable, glancing around with furtive glances.

"Speak, sphinx," Inara ordered, her voice every inch a queen's. "We don't have time to waste."

Lowen buzzed toward the sphinx, veering close enough that the man shied back from the razor-sharp thorn he held in his hand like a sword.

"I heard this was where the clanless vampire lived," the man stuttered.

That caused me to straighten. My home's location was no great secret. Both the vampires and the wolves seemed to feel they had an open invitation, but I hadn't realized it was common knowledge to the rest of Columbus.

I didn't like the thought of every spook out there knowing where I lived.

Inara and I shared a glance, our thoughts mirroring each other's.

"And you thought you'd earn a name for yourself?" Lowen snarled.

The sphinx flinched back, the smaller pixie intimidating even me. Lowen's face now appeared murderous and cold. He might be small but right then it didn't seem to matter.

"No, I need help. The harpies said the vampire was my best chance," he said quickly.

Harpies? That was interesting. I shook my head before Lowen could do something drastic—like stab the sphinx.

"Which harpy specifically?" I asked. I had several contacts among the harpies. To my knowledge none of them hated me enough to set assassins on me.

The sphinx didn't look like an assassin, but you never knew. He seemed harmless, maybe just a bit desperate. Could be a ruse designed to lure me off my guard. Appearances were often used to deceive. I knew that better than most

"Natalia," he blurted out.

I'd done her a favor a couple weeks ago involving a kobold, so his story was plausible. I doubted she would be quick to set an assassin on me. I could picture her sending someone in a similar predicament my way, especially if she knew him.

"What's your relation to her?" I asked.

"Her mom used to babysit me," he said. It seemed to occur to him how tenuous his position was and his expression turned uncertain, fear and uneasiness filling his face.

I wasn't used to inspiring those emotions in others, and I wasn't sure if I liked seeing them now.

I fought the urge to put him at ease. There had been more than one attempt on my life in the last month. I couldn't afford to be careless.

"And why did she point you to me?" I asked.

I folded my arms across my chest, my right hand dipping down to brush the weight of the gun in its holster under my light jacket. If Liam was intent on dragging me into whatever was going on, I wasn't going unarmed. Physically and magically I was weaker than most, even this sphinx in front of me, but I'd found a gun helped level the playing field very nicely. It was filled with ammo of my own recipe—one that incorporated silver nitrate— lethal to vampires and werewolves, along with several other creatures.

His expression grew uncomfortable as his eyes flitted to my two roommates. "I don't suppose we could have this conversation in private."

"No." My response was flat and brooked no argument.

He jerked and looked at the two again. It was clear he wasn't comfortable speaking in front of them. Too bad for him. I had no intention of kicking them out or going off alone with this guy. Not when we'd caught him skulking around. He could just suffer or get out.

"You have one minute to start talking before I carry on with the rest of my night," I said, not bothering to check my watch.

The threat was enough. The guy stood, shifting from foot to foot as he took in the three of us. "I was given the honorable task of protecting an item."

That made sense. Sphinxes were often considered guardians and protectors in many myths. From what I'd heard, they tended to either make a name for themselves in places of learning, became excellent puzzle crafters, or took on the duty of protecting items of great worth.

"I think it was stolen yesterday," he confessed, looking slightly ashamed.

"You think?" I asked.

"What kind of sphinx lets their treasure be stolen?" Inara scoffed.

I sent her a quelling gaze.

"It's not like I spend all day watching it," the sphinx defended. "I have a life, you know."

"I bet whoever it was cracked his riddles and puzzles," Lowen snickered.

The sphinx rolled his eyes, the pair's mockery returning some of his confidence. "Please. That's so ancient history. We now use vaults and state of the art technology coupled with the most advanced magic. I've never had anything given into my protection stolen."

"Until now," I observed in a dry voice.

The words seemed to have an impact and his shoulders rounded as he winced. "Yes, well, I'm hoping you can help me with that."

I stared at him, nonplused. "And how exactly am I supposed to do that?"

He shrugged. "I don't know. Do what you did for Natalia?"

My eyes got wider and I'm sure my expression looked as startled and discombobulated as I felt.

I couldn't do what I did for Natalia. For her, I'd simply had a conversation with the kobold to understand what he really wanted before finding him a new, willing home owner for him to practice his household magic on. I doubted this would be so simple. It sounded way beyond anything I could ever do.

"This sounds like a matter for the police," I observed.

He shook his head. "No normals. The item is a scroll that can't fall into their hands or be brought to their attention."

"Why do you think I can track it down for you?" I asked. It's not like I'd ever done anything like that before.

"Your reputation. They say you'll help anyone because you don't care what they are," he said, his expression avid.

"Who says?" I asked. Of everything he'd said today, that seemed the closest to a lie.

"Everyone. People have been talking all summer about how you found that werewolf who'd been missing, and how you're the reason we no longer have any trouble with the draugr." He sounded enthusiastic as he listed off the events of the past few months.

I shifted, his words making me uncomfortable. It was true I'd been involved in all that, but I hadn't been the only one.

Inara chortled. "You want her to be a detective for you."

He nodded.

I sighed. This had been a waste of my time.

"I can pay," he blurted out as I turned toward the door.

I hesitated, interested in spite of myself.

"Natalia said your rates were very reasonable. A hundred dollars per hour," he said.

I kept my surprise hidden, watching the stranger with a cool expression. I hadn't charged Natalia for the kobold. Interesting that she'd given him made up rates. Not that I was arguing. That sort of money could do a lot for me. It was way more than I'd ever make at the gas station.

Still, I had no experience and wouldn't even know where to start.

"What's your name?" I asked.

"Fred."

I paused, the utter simplicity of the name throwing me.

"Alright Fred, I don't know why Natalia pointed you to me, but I can't do what you're asking. I'm sorry." I ignored the crestfallen expression on his face and grabbed the door, opening it.

"Please, I don't know where else to go. If it gets out that my vaults were breached, I'll lose everything," he said.

I sighed. His desperation tugged at me, making me feel guilty when I knew it shouldn't. "Try Jerry with Hermes Courier Service. He's expensive, but he should be able to help you."

While Hermes was primarily a courier service, it also accepted jobs like this sometimes. If Jerry could, he'd help the man—for a fee, of course.

Surprise crossed Fred's face. "Haven't you heard?"

"Heard what?"

He looked between Inara and me. "He's shut down the shop."

"Bullshit."

"Impossible," Inara said at the same time.

I spared her a glance before glaring at Fred as he tried to make himself as small as possible. "I don't know what game you're playing, but that's not possible. He wouldn't do that."

He held up his hands placatingly. "I'm not lying. Check around. Everyone is talking about it. They're saying he got picked to join a court of the High Fae."

Inara's wings stuttered and she dipped momentarily, sinking about a foot toward the floor before she caught herself. "Which court?"

Fred flinched back from the pixie. Inara suddenly seemed much larger than the length of my hand as she stared menacingly at the sphinx.

"I don't know their names. Several have been spotted around Columbus over the past few weeks. Most of the Fae in the city have made themselves scarce, so it's hard to get much information," he blurted out.

Inara processed this before zooming out of the room without another word.

I watched her go with concern. My pint-sized roommate was prone to odd behavior, but this seemed out of character even for her.

"Please, just think about my request. Here's my card."

I reluctantly took his card, a simple white piece of paper with the words Sphinx Vault written in gold lettering. The body of a lion was etched on the back of it.

"I'll be waiting for your call," he told me as he stepped past. He dropped to the ground below with little effort, landing lightly. He turned and waved before walking away.

"That was weird," I said softly, pulling my head back into the apartment.

I frowned at the open door for several minutes, feeling slightly off-balance after the sphinx's visit. Worry niggled at me over Jerry.

Closing Hermes was out of character. In all the time I'd worked for the courier service, there hadn't been a single day that I could remember where Jerry's business wasn't open. Not one. Even on holidays, during rain storms, and winter blizzards. He always accepted jobs. Always.

I grabbed my phone out of my pocket and dialed the number from memory.

It rang and rang. After twenty more rings, I hung up. The feeling that had started with the sphinx's news changed from slightly concerned to outright worry.

I tapped the phone against my lip as I considered my options. There weren't many. Jerry had fired me, effectively ending our relationship. I owed him nothing and there was no reason to stick my nose where it probably wasn't wanted.

"Where are you going?" Inara's voice rang out as I started for the door.

My silence answered for me.

There was knowledge on her face as she flew closer. "You have a date with the vampire."

"But—"

"Leave the half-blood to his business." Her words were harsh. Her face softened. "Jerry wouldn't want your interference on his behalf anyway."

For half a minute I thought about arguing, or at the very least ignoring her. In the end, I sighed, conceding she was probably right. I'd gotten in trouble more than once by sticking my nose where it didn't belong.

"Are you going to help the sphinx?" Lowen asked, changing the subject. More than once he'd acted as peacemaker, smoothing over the rough spots when Inara and I butted heads.

"I don't see how I could," I said, letting the matter go for now. "I'm not a detective, and Hermes has services similar to that."

The last thing I wanted to do was set myself up to cross him. I had to believe whatever his reason for closing the service, it was temporary.

"Similar, yes, but not the same," Inara said. "I doubt your former boss would take you to task should you choose to find the sphinx's lost scroll."

I gave her a questioning look. "You think I should do this? Aren't you usually the one telling me to keep my nose out of other people's business."

She gave me a haughty look. "He's offering to pay you. Those others never did. We both know you could use the money to keep this roof over our heads."

I suspect it was worry over the supply of hummingbird nectar I'd been providing them drying up that motivated her rather than the threat of losing the apartment. They were small and easily overlooked. They could live here for months with no one the wiser.

"The job at the gas station is beneath you. At least this will be more in keeping with your status," she observed, her chin tilted up.

"What status?" To my knowledge, I had none. I waved a hand before she could answer. "Never mind. This is all pointless until I find out what Liam wants."

Inara shook her head and rose from the shelf, her wings moving impossibly fast as she flew back the way she'd come.

I grabbed my bike, using a rope wrapped around its frame to lower it to the ground.

"I'll pull the rope back up and make sure to lock up," Lowen said from the doorknob. He balanced on it as I prepared to descend.

"Thanks, I'll be back soon."

"We'll see," Lowen said. "Don't worry about this place. Inara and I will protect it until you return."

I nodded and stepped out. The ground rushed up to meet me. I landed with a thump, not nearly as lightly or gracefully as the sphinx. Still, I was in one piece and nothing was broken. I'd take that as a win.

I unwrapped the bike, then waited as the rope slithered back inside. I didn't know how the pixies managed to pull it up, considering it weighed much more than them. I never asked. The door swung shut in the next moment.

My home as safe as I could make it, I rolled the bike to the street, pulling up short at the sight of the man waiting for me there, his long, rangy frame leaning up against the twin of the black Escalade in the lot at my back.

"What are you doing here, Nathan?" I asked.

CHAPTER THREE

Nathan gave me a lazy smile, lifting one of the two take-out cups he held and handing it to me. I took it with a frown, balancing the bike against my hip.

"I'm your chauffeur for the night," he said, stepping away from the Escalade. He matched the car, dressed in black jeans and a tight black shirt that outlined his wide shoulders and muscled arms.

Nathan was one of Liam's men, and also the vampire who'd been responsible for my lessons over the past few weeks. He was the opposite of Sir Grumpy Pants in many ways. Blond and handsome, it was rarer to see him frowning than smiling. His lips always seemed to be tilted in a half-smile, as if in response to a joke only he knew.

He liked to push people's buttons, but he was also a big kid in many ways, I'd discovered.

"I should have known he wouldn't trust me to come on my own," I said in a sour voice.

Nathan gave a charming shrug. "You can't really blame him, given your track record. Besides, I'm not here at his behest."

I gave him an interested look. "Oh?"

He gave my bike a significant glance. "I figured you would try to bike there, which meant you would never make it in time. Decided I'd save you the trouble and the inevitable ass chewing."

"I could have made it," I responded defensively. I could have too. As a former bike messenger for Hermes, I was used to such trips.

He scoffed. "Maybe, but then you would have been sweaty and out of sorts by the time you arrived. This puts you there ahead of schedule and in a presentable state."

My frown deepened. "Do you know what this is for?"

He shrugged. "You'll see when we get there."

"Does that mean you know?" I asked, already considering ways I could get him to reveal his secrets.

His mouth curled in a secretive grin. "Oh no, little student. You won't get that information so easily."

I sighed and held up the cup with straw he'd handed me. "And this? Or are you keeping it a secret too?"

"It's a blood smoothie," he said smugly.

My face wrinkled with distaste as I looked at it.

"Don't be proud," he said when it looked like I'd try to hand it back. "You can use the nutrients. I know you're not getting all you need because you won't drink live blood. This'll top you off."

That might be, but the thought of sucking down the smoothie made me feel slightly nauseous. Lately, bagged blood made me feel sick to my stomach, and it could be difficult keeping it down. That hadn't always been the case. At one point, I'd lived for it, craved it with the same passion I craved black raspberry ice cream.

Those days were long gone. Ever since Liam had given me some of his super-charged blood, it had gotten harder and harder to satisfy myself with the pale imitation I insisted on sticking to.

Nathan knew some of my troubles, but not all of them. I'd kept the particulars carefully hidden. It was harder to keep the weight loss from him, especially since he headed up my combat training. Who knew vampires could lose weight? I guess that's what came of not getting enough blood for weeks on end.

Surprisingly my grip on the bloodlust had not faltered. Not even once. It was strange, but because of my control I decided the risk was worth it, until I could figure a way out of this that didn't involve turning humans into slurpy straws.

Nathan believed my troubles stemmed from the taste of rot that seemed to permeate bagged blood. I needed to keep him thinking that, if I wanted to keep some control of my life and not lose the last pieces that made me feel human. Not drinking from humans might seem like a strange place to draw my line as a vampire, but emotions didn't always make sense.

"If you have an episode, our fearless leader will make you drink from a live donor," Nathan said. His expression turned sly. "That donor might even be himself."

I gave him a dirty look. It was a reference to the few times Liam had fed me from his own wrist. His blood seemed to be catnip to my vampire, turning me into a brazen hussy who threw caution and good sense to the wind, becoming a hedonistic creature who couldn't get enough of the grumpy vampire.

To say the weakness was embarrassing was putting it mildly.

In defiance, I lifted the straw to my mouth and took a sip, making a pleased expression at the taste.

"That's good," I told him, impressed.

"I know." He gave me a wink. "It's my own special recipe. All the nutrients and vitamins a growing baby vampire might need."

I snorted, my laugh muffled.

"You can call me master any time you want," he said, referencing an ongoing argument as he stepped to the back of the Escalade and opened the trunk.

He took the bike from me as I shot him an acerbic stare.

"I'm never going to call you that," I told him.

"How about sensei then?"

"No."

"I'm the teacher of all things mystical and vampire. I should get a cool name," he complained, slamming the trunk shut.

"Not happening."

I slid into the car and buckled my seatbelt, before chancing another sip of the smoothie. It tasted surprisingly like strawberries and chocolate. Decadent and refreshing all at the same time.

I'd have to ask him what was in it before the night was over. This just might be the answer to at least one of my problems.

"Did you know he was coming back?" I asked with studied nonchalance.

Nathan shot me a look out of the corner of his eye before pulling onto the road. "You mean why didn't I give you a heads-up."

I shrugged.

"He didn't tell us of his arrival," Nathan said. "Just showed up last night."

"I hear you've been giving him reports of my progress," I said.

His lips quirked up. "That is true."

I made a *harrumph.*

"Come on, you didn't really expect me to do anything else, did you?"

I suppose not. Liam was Nathan's sire in truth, not to mention his boss. Nathan's loyalties would always lie with him.

"There are things going on that you don't understand," Nathan said, his face turning serious.

"There are always things going on that I don't understand." I propped my chin on my hand and stared out the window.

"I'm just saying maybe you shouldn't be so prickly about it."

My head snapped toward him as I gave him a glare. "Prickly?"

"If the shoe fits."

I grunted and went back to staring out the window. I wasn't prickly. Okay, maybe a little.

"You've been a very grumpy porcupine since he left."

I gave him a look. "Thanks, Dr. Phil. I really appreciate your armchair psychology."

"You know I have a degree in psychology, right?" he asked.

It was just strange enough to be true. Vampires were long lived. It meant they had more than enough time to pursue anything that interested them. They had vampires who'd attended medical school, why not vampires who'd attended shrink school as well? If nothing else, having a better understanding of a human's psychology would make them more effective hunters.

Nathan might seem easy-going, like a really energetic puppy at times, but he was every inch the vampire that Liam was. He might hide it behind a charming smile, but at his core he was a killer. We all were. It's why I fought my instincts as hard as I did.

"You have hidden depths," I told him seriously. I would do well to remember that.

"As do we all, baby vampire," he said with a meaningful glance.

The drive passed in silence after that, the city sliding past the window. In the end, I was grateful Nathan had stopped to retrieve me. It would have taken me forever to bike this far north of the city, past the outer belt to one of the suburbs. The road curved and winded as the flatter part of the city was left behind in favor of the dips and bumps of small hills.

The houses got further and further apart until we mostly drove on tree-lined roads. We had to be up near Galena or Westerville. I didn't know the area well enough to tell which it was.

I had only been here a few times since returning home, preferring to stick closer to the heart of Columbus. When you're reliant on getting places through your own pedal power, it meant your travel radius was smaller than if you had a car.

Nathan turned down a small, easily overlooked road, one that didn't see a lot of traffic. The street sign was barely visible, the overgrowth from trees mostly shielding it from view.

The tires of the Escalade crunched as he turned onto a gravel driveway lined with tall trees on either side. These weren't the overgrown bushes we'd seen on the drive up. They were mature, standing tall as their limbs arched overhead, forming a canopy over the driveway.

"Woah," I said, getting my first look at the house.

It looked like a turn of the century farmhouse, only about three times the size of most that I'd seen. It boasted a large wraparound porch and loomed over the surrounding grounds. Three stories tall, it had a dramatic roof and the large windows characteristic of that period.

I got out, stilling when I noticed a family of deer across a long stretch of grass from me. Their heads came up, ears alert, as we watched each other.

31

A rustle of branches distracted me, and I glanced over, my heart thumping as a large form stepped out of the shadows. His coat was silver in the moonlight, while antlers jutted from his head in a proud rack.

There was a crash as the other deer took off, dashing back into the woods surrounding the house.

I looked back at the stag, to find him gone as well. The place he'd stood empty as if he'd never been.

Nathan came around the car, his face questioning as he looked from me to the place I was staring.

"What's wrong?" he asked.

I finally shut the door I'd been holding open for the last few seconds. "There were deer staring at me."

He rolled his eyes, some of tension in his body leaching away. "There are always deer around here."

He could afford to be unworried about such things. I'd fended off twenty assassination attempts in the last three months—most of which came from unexpected quarters. It had made me a bit more paranoid than usual.

Deer might not seem suspicious, but I'd never seen a stag with a rack that impressive anywhere near humans. Maybe in some remote wilderness, but here? In Columbus? Not likely.

"Maybe," I said, turning toward the house and following Nathan as he mounted the stairs.

There was a porch swing in one corner and a few rocking chairs. Pots of flowers were everywhere, their pretty colors obvious even in this dim light.

"What is this place?" I finally asked, curiosity getting the best of me.

"Liam's house. He just bought it," Nathan said over his shoulder.

Liam did? Why?

Nathan held the door for me, letting me precede him inside.

The interior matched the outside, charming and stately while still managing to seem warm and inviting. Once upon a time, this was the type of place I'd seen myself settling in long-term. Not a farmhouse exactly, but what this place represented. A home. Somewhere to come back to after a long day, where you could feel safe and warm because of the people who lived inside. A sanctuary against all the dark things in the world.

Eric stood to my right in the living room, his face impassive as he waited, his back straight and rigid.

I shouldn't have been surprised to see him. He'd disappeared at the same time as Liam, and probably accompanied him on whatever super-secret mission the two had undertaken. It made sense now that Liam was back, Eric was too.

"Eric, I'm glad you're back." I meant it too.

The normally reserved enforcer had grown on me. A force in his own right, he tended to hang back in any situation, taking on the role of silent observer. It meant he saw more than most.

His dark eyes lightened with surprise and he inclined his head.

"I never did thank you for that tip."

"I hope it helped," he murmured.

"It did. Working at the Book Haven keeps Caroline occupied. I think she might like it better than working at the university, but she'll never admit it," I told him with a small smile.

"If only someone else would learn from her example," Liam rumbled from behind me.

I turned and gave him a sardonic look. "And what exactly am I supposed to have learned?"

"That there can be a bright side if you simply quit being so stubborn," he said.

That was true. Most things had a silver lining, even this. Being turned into a vampire against my will and then abandoned wasn't in my plans, but it had worked out. Or at least, it had been heading that way until I lost the job with Hermes. Now I was struggling to find my feet again.

"I'd say Caroline's situation is a bit different from mine," I observed in a mild voice.

She'd found a balance with the pack and a job she found fulfilling. I was working at a gas station for minimum wage and still struggling to keep the vampires from trying to control every aspect of my existence.

"I've offered you a job. You're the one who refuses to take it," Liam returned, the slightest hint of frustration in his voice.

Yes, he had, hence his having to use the debt to force my presence tonight.

The problem was, I didn't want to work for the vampires, not even Liam or any of his enforcers. The way I saw it they'd already wiggled their way further into my life than I liked.

It seemed every time I gave them a small window, they used it to force their way deeper in. The latest issue with my sire taking over as my landlord was just the beginning.

I was determined to stay in control of myself and my life. It'd be easier to give up and toe the line like a good little flunky, but the antisocial grump inside wouldn't let me. I'd done that in the military, but it had felt like being rubbed by sandpaper the entire time. I had no intention of that being my eternity.

"How long before you tried to use that against me?" I asked. Because he would have. It seemed that was the modus operandi of vampires.

"Instead you're here without the leverage you would have had if you'd simply been reasonable," Liam observed. "Smart, Aileen."

The words burned, especially since they were true. I should have considered all the angles before rejecting his original offer. My only defense is I hadn't expected such an enthusiastic greeting from him. It upset my emotional balance, forcing me to react rather than plan, something I couldn't afford with vampires.

He made a small sound, something close to a sigh. He seemed tired, his skin pale and drawn, circles around his eyes.

Now that the surprise of our first meeting was past, I realized he'd seemed just as exhausted last night.

I hesitated, wanting to ask what was wrong. I stopped myself. A true friend might have, but we weren't that. His disappearance had made that clear.

Instead I looked around his house. "Nice place. What made you decide on it?"

There was a guarded expression on his face. "I'm looking to make a few changes in my life. I decided having a permanent base of operations here in Columbus was a good place to start."

I frowned. "Sounds like you're thinking of sticking around."

I'd always kind of thought he was here short-term. The council, no doubt, had need of him all over the place. While this territory was an important hotspot with a new master, I was sure there were other places throughout the world that could use a badass enforcer keeping things in line.

He inclined his head, hands clasped behind his back as he stared at me, his thoughts veiled. "I've been assigned to this territory full-time."

I moved around the room, looking at everything. For all that he was probably older than the country, it was surprisingly modern. It had an old-world charm but it had touches of today's world as well.

I left the topic of his house and now extended residence in Columbus alone. I wasn't ready to touch the implications of what either might mean.

"You have me here. What is so important that you were willing to use one of your nights and necessitate my missing work?"

He didn't respond, his gaze flicking to Eric and Nathan in dismissal. The two excused themselves without a word, leaving the room and heading further into the house.

"That's kind of a pointless gesture. They'll hear every word we say even from the other side of the house," I said.

Vampire hearing was far superior to that of a human. It still surprised me how the rooms at the mansion were as private as they were. The soundproofing in each apartment must be topnotch. It would have to be. You wouldn't want to live right on top of each other for long if every statement or move you made could be overheard. Imagine, waking up in the middle of the day to hear the person in the room above you having a bit of private time in the shower.

"They won't listen," he decreed, his voice autocratic.

I scoffed. Sure, they wouldn't. Curiosity was part of human nature, and vampires were no less prone to it.

He observed me with an impenetrable expression, my disbelief not phasing him.

"You've lost weight."

"I don't know what you mean," I lied. I didn't like that he knew me well enough to be able to tell that at a glance when people I was around everyday hadn't.

"I didn't notice yesterday, but it's obvious," he continued, not paying attention to my denial.

I gritted my teeth and narrowed my eyes at him. "Is this why you called me here? To criticize my weight?"

"We'll get to that. First, I'd like to know why you look like a stiff breeze could knock you down," he said, not taking the bait.

"I'd prefer to get to it now."

"Anticipation is its own reward," he murmured, his eyes running over me critically. "When is the last time you ate?"

I gave him a smug smile. "On the way over."

I didn't even have to lie. The blood smoothie had gone down easily and I'd finished it before I realized it.

"You should not be so thin," he said, still stuck on the subject.

I shook my head at him. "You're not my father, my boyfriend, or even my friend. My health is no concern of yours."

The skin of his face tightened and he gave me a look bordering on insulted. He seemed to withdraw, a mask settling into place. It was like a stranger stood in front of me—one who reminded me of the Liam from our first meeting. A cold bastard who thought nothing of breaking someone's ribs simply because they were in the wrong place at the wrong time.

I hadn't realized how much he had softened with me—how much of himself he'd let show past the facade until he withdrew—the flash of vulnerability he'd shown me earlier, disappearing.

It made me second-guess my last words. Perhaps I'd been needlessly harsh. Liam had somehow made it past my walls and become a friend of sorts. Granted, it was the type of friend who needed to be held at arm's length and watched at all times.

"Very well then. If that's how you want things," he said.

I should have been relieved we were back to business, but I wasn't.

"I have need of your eyes," he said brusquely.

By that I took it to mean he needed my ability to see magic with my left eye.

"I thought you wanted me to keep that little secret under wraps." I stuffed my hands in my pocket and cocked a hip as I frowned at him.

It was a simple enough request. Surprisingly painless even.

The request eased some of my nerves. This, I understood. It was all the emotional crap that tripped me up.

"I do. That's why I had you come here," he replied.

I watched him with reservation. It still surprised me he'd told me to keep the fact I could see magic from Thomas, my sire and the master of the city. Also, Liam's friend, a man he considered a brother since they were made by the same master.

"Alright, what do you want me to look at?" I asked.

Despite my earlier reservations, I was a little excited by this. I couldn't help but wonder what was so important that he needed my eye. Perhaps it was an ancient artifact that had been cursed or an arcane object whose purpose he needed me to decipher. Either possibility was enough to spark my interest.

"Me, I need you to look at me." His face was cold and remote, his gaze piercing as I frowned in surprise.

He didn't look happy about admitting that, and the tight press of his lips warned me from asking questions—though I wanted to. Badly.

"Can you give me an idea of what I'm looking for?" I asked.

I needed somewhere to start. I was too new at this and didn't have enough of a handle on it to know how to do what he wanted.

"If it's there, you'll know it when you see it," he said.

Well, that wasn't cryptic or anything. Typical vampire.

I shrugged. If that was how he wanted it, I wasn't going to argue. I took a deep breath, centering myself.

I glanced away from Liam, turning my attention to the rest of the world. Sometimes, looking at a powerful source of magic right away disoriented me. It was kind of like looking right at the sun, blinding, with odd halo effects afterward. I'd found it was easier to start small and ease into looking at something powerful.

It was hard to describe to others exactly how I used the othersight. I'd tried before with Liam, once we'd figured out the mechanism. It wasn't like a switch in my head that could be flicked on and off. It was more like I relaxed a muscle that I kept constantly flexed, allowing the magic in the world to filter into my senses.

I blinked as I looked around. The world was the same yet different. Everything was a touch out of focus, hazy and indistinct.

Certain cultures in the world believed all things contained a spirit or essence. Whether animate or inanimate, they had a spark, oftentimes so small as to be barely present. Looking at the world through my left eye, I could see why they might believe that.

Most items I viewed had a soft glow. I wouldn't go so far as to call it a spirit, but there was a speck of something. A presence, even if I got the sense the essence wasn't entirely sentient.

An antique lamp in the corner was rimmed by such a glow, its light warm and comforting, as if the lamp sensed its purpose and was happy to fulfill it. The painting above the mantel displayed an essence considerably stronger than the lamp's, and much darker, as if the painter had been in turmoil when he'd created the piece, or perhaps the painting had witnessed some horrible event that had steeped it in darkness.

Both thoughts might have been fanciful, but without someone available who understood this power and could explain it to me, I was left with instinct.

I turned to Liam, keeping my gaze to the right of him. I stared at a speck of space, not seeing it, as I let my peripheral vision get a sense of him. Slowly, I looked at him full on.

His power clung to him like finely honed armor. He shone brightly, a well of strength at his core surprising in its depth and intensity. He'd gotten considerably stronger since the last time I'd done this. Maybe not quite as strong as Thomas who was nearly blindingly bright, but close. This power was more controlled, answering eagerly to his call. A sleek jungle cat waiting to pounce, more interested in slipping in unseen and unchallenged rather than barging in like a battering ram.

As I scanned him, I got the briefest sense of wintry ice and biting wind. It should have stung my senses, repelled me. Instead it brushed along them with an almost physical sensation as it purred in contentment.

To my eye, he looked the same as always, only there was more of it. The power flickered around him, a small strand reaching out to where his mark tingled on my forearm, not quite touching before it dissolved.

I moved around him to make sure, scanning him twice in case I'd missed something the first time.

Nothing. No tell-tale signs of other magic, no shadows lurking within. There was zero indication as to why he'd felt the need for my presence.

"I don't know what you thought I'd find but you look much the same as always," I told him.

His shoulders relaxed and I thought I saw a faint flicker of relief, though his expression remained grave.

"I'll need you to perform the same task with Eric," he ordered.

I gave him a dour look but didn't argue, waving my hand to indicate my consent. Might as well. It wasn't like I had anywhere to be tonight.

Liam fell silent, his focus turning inward. Eric appeared in the entry to the room. He moved forward on quiet feet, his attention going to where Liam waited, hands clasped behind his back.

Liam looked at me with expectation, eyebrows raised, arrogance stamped on his face.

I didn't bother arguing before focusing on Eric. I didn't know the quiet enforcer's power signature the way I did Liam's, so I couldn't say for sure, but to my inexperienced eye it looked no different than I'd expect.

Where Liam's power felt like the coldest of nights during the deepest parts of winter, Eric's was an electric blanket that crackled and rumbled, the distinct opposite of the way he presented himself to the world.

It made me wonder just what went on behind the quiet, imperturbable facade, and if beneath the surface there was a volcano of feeling and emotions just bubbling away.

I shook my head at Liam. If there was something there, I couldn't see it.

Liam lifted his chin at Eric, dismissing him without a word spoken. Eric spun and walked out of the room without a backwards glance or even a question to ask why he'd been called in the first place.

I couldn't help but be impressed. Most individuals wouldn't have been able to suppress their curiosity or annoyance at being summoned and then dismissed without a word. Either Eric knew about my abilities despite Liam's assurance to the contrary, or he trusted Liam on such a profound level that something like this didn't bother him.

Liam's expression grew contemplative as he considered what I'd told him.

I waited, tapping my finger on my thigh. Curiosity burned inside me as I wondered what exactly he thought I'd find. I held my questions back.

"Nathan will see you back to the city," Liam said into the silence.

I started, my attention spinning back to him. What? This little jaunt had taken up all of twenty minutes of my time. That couldn't be all he wanted.

"That's it?" I asked, not believing him. "That's what you wanted?"

"It is," he said. He moved past me, his smell wrapping around me. "Now, don't you wish you'd accepted the money for this request instead of having me force your compliance?"

I stiffened, my feet stuck in place, and fought to keep my expression emotionless as a cold feeling invaded. I wasn't getting paid. That should have occurred to me. For some reason, it hadn't.

That was just ducky. My chances of making rent were getting smaller and smaller. I might have to take the sphinx's job after all.

His smile widened just a touch as if he could sense my thoughts.

I gave him a superior look as I sauntered past him. "I don't know. Twenty minutes to knock a night's debt off doesn't seem like too bad a trade to me."

I didn't wait for his response, heading for the foyer. The loss of a night's income burned, but redeeming one of the nights I owed for such a small price was almost worth it.

My victory was short-lived as my stomach clenched painfully. My steps hesitated as I fought the urge to double over. Pain and nausea swamped me.

Nathan's concoction had lasted longer than the normal blood I drank, but not long enough. My body was getting ready to purge it from my system.

I gritted my teeth, touching the wall for balance. Not if I could help it.

I breathed slowly for several seconds, conscious of Liam at my back, watching, learning. If he'd been concerned before, I didn't want to think how he would react if he knew how much trouble I'd been having keeping blood down. I could kiss any autonomy and my non-biting days goodbye.

He seemed to have appointed himself my keeper/guardian, and he took his duties very seriously.

"Something is wrong," he said, coming around me and peering at my face.

I forced myself to straighten and gave him a cocky smile. Everything was fine and dandy. If I kept telling myself that, maybe one of these days my body would actually listen.

"Nothing wrong here. I just got myself a free night," I said, moving around him.

Nathan was waiting for me in the foyer when I got there.

"Let's go," I said, moving past him.

His gaze lifted above my head.

"Aileen." Liam's voice held a note of warning.

My hand was already on the doorknob and turning it. I fought to keep from groaning even as my stomach cramped again. In retrospect, taunting him had probably not been my best idea. Had I let him have the last word, he might have never witnessed that moment of weakness in the hall.

The door creaked open as I turned and gave him an expectant look. His attention locked above my left shoulder as an emotion crossed his face that made the breath in me still. It was full of a naked yearning, the breadth and intensity of which was scorching.

I turned to see what had caught his attention outside and caught the briefest glimpse of white before it disappeared into the dark.

To Eric, he said, "Go."

Eric moved past me, disappearing into the trees almost faster than I could see.

I turned back, a question on my lips. Liam's closed off expression stopped me.

"See her home," Liam ordered Nathan, his focus already returning to the trees.

It wasn't lost on me something had just happened. He'd heard or seen something that had stopped him from saying whatever was in his mind.

This was Liam. Badass vampire. Dangerous enforcer. He could kill more easily than most people breathed. What had caused that reaction?

I didn't bother asking, knowing he wouldn't answer anyway. I stepped onto the porch, scanning the grounds and immediate woods one last time before heading to the Escalade.

For Liam to ask me to use my magic-seeing eye to scan him, it had to mean he was worried about interference of some sort. Either a curse laid on him or a mental suggestion perhaps?

What sort of creature would be able to do that to a vampire? That was the more important question.

And what was in the woods that could cause that look of naked hope?

CHAPTER FOUR

The ride back to the city was a quiet one. I was busy trying to keep the contents of my stomach where they were while Nathan seemed lost in thought.

We were close to the city when the pain and nausea finally receded. I mentally checked Nathan's smoothie concoction off the list of things that might help solve my little problem.

I turned toward Nathan to watch as he stared at the highway in front of us with intent focus.

It was tempting to pepper the enforcer with questions, but ultimately it would no doubt prove useless. As his sire and master, Liam commanded the entirety of Nathan's loyalty.

I sighed and leaned back. There was something going on and the curious person in me wanted to know what. Still, involving myself would no doubt backfire. It would be smarter and probably safer to stay out of it.

"Get off here," I said as we approached the exit for Henderson.

He glanced at me, his face startled. He looked back at the road and kept driving.

"Nathan, come on. I have a free night. I don't get a lot of them and it seems a shame to go back to the apartment," I argued.

"Liam ordered me to take you home." He glanced over his shoulder and changed lanes. We weren't far from the exit now. A few more minutes and we'd be past it.

"We both know that won't keep me there," I said. "Five minutes after you leave, I'll be out the door again. At least this way, you'll be able to give Liam a place to start if he decides to track me down."

Nathan exhaled and shook his head. The car shifted lanes, moving to follow the exit ramp. I felt a thrill of victory and sat back.

"Why here?" he asked. "There are much better places in the Arena district or Short North."

That was true, but that part of the city saw a lot of traffic by other spooks, especially those who preyed on humans. Both areas were heavily frequented by humans looking to have a good time. The presence of alcohol often resulted in humans with lowered inhibitions who were less wary. It made them easy pickings for creatures looking to use them as a food source.

I preferred to stay out of both parts of the city whenever possible. It was a lot easier now that I wasn't a bike messenger.

"Turn right," I told him as he stopped at the light.

"You don't even have any friends here," he complained.

"You don't know everyone I know."

He raised his eyebrows as if to say 'that's what you think'.

It made me pause. I gave him a searching look as I narrowed my eyes. The vampires had proven more than once their skills at ferreting out the minor details of my life. I had few secrets at this point. The ones I did I protected with a fierce zealotry.

"Some people would say such a statement indicates you're a stalker," I said in a calm voice.

He choked on a laugh.

Before he could respond, I leaned forward. "Pull over here."

"There's nothing here," he said with a frown.

We were on Henderson, right next to the bike path. Normally, I would never attempt a stop on this road. It was one of the main veins of traffic, connecting the two sides of the river. This late at night, the street was empty. All the humans were tucked safely in bed dreaming about unicorns or monsters.

"That's the point." I unbuckled my seat belt, giving him a challenging look. "You didn't think I'd make stalking me easy, did you?"

I didn't wait for an answer, getting out and heading around to the back of the Escalade. Nathan got there before me and popped the trunk, reaching in and hauling my bike out before I could.

He set it on the ground, his hands hesitating on the handlebars. He frowned at me, his eyebrows pulling together. It was clear he was second-guessing the decision to drop me here.

I stepped forward and took the bike from him.

He sighed. "Liam is going to have my ass for this."

"You could always not tell him."

He shook his head. "He'd know. He always knows. You're the only one I've ever seen challenge him and not get punished for it."

I pulled the bike onto the sidewalk. "It's part of my charm."

"That's one word for it," he said, running his hand through his hair.

I stood on the curb, my bike propped against me and gave him an expectant look. He waited, staring back at me blankly.

I shifted my eyes to the vehicle, a silent signal he could go now.

He folded his arms over his well-defined chest, the muscles bulging under the thin fabric of his shirt. "You're kidding."

I shook my head, my expression not quite making it to regret.

He grunted in frustration before he headed back to the car. I watched him, waiting as he started the car and drove off. Even then I remained in place, knowing he'd most likely have to double back if he wanted to return to the highway.

Sure enough, minutes later he cruised past me, glaring out the window.

I gave him a cheery wave and waited as he pulled onto the entrance ramp. Only then did I throw my leg over the bike and ride it across the street into the neighborhood.

My route was not direct. It would have been simpler to head to High Street and use the straight shot it would have given me, but I liked the peace of the neighborhood. I liked seeing the old houses, big half a million-dollar homes side by side with their smaller companions, cottages that were probably not much bigger than my apartment, where the yards were as unique and distinct as the houses they led to.

This was an old neighborhood, the streets not laid out in neat grid patterns. They dipped and swerved, with hidden ravines and wooded paths popping up out of nowhere, only known and frequented by locals familiar with the neighborhood.

I approached a charming bridge, one that looked like it belonged on a postcard—the stonemasonry more fitting for a European countryside than a suburb of Columbus.

I got off my bike and walked it over the bridge. I stopped halfway across and stared down at the small creek below and the slate stones it ran across.

There was a slight groan beneath me, like wind rushing through a small opening. I knew better though. Only a fool dismissed what their senses told them, especially when they were a spook.

I laid a penny on one of the bridge's sides. The penny was one I'd been carrying for several weeks now, just for this purpose.

It wasn't anything special. Just a 1969 Lincoln penny. Not common, but not rare either. Better yet, I knew it was one my friend under the bridge had been seeking for almost a year now.

Next to the penny I laid a green apple Chupa Chup sucker. He had a sweet tooth and he was limited to what people tossed over the side of the bridge.

My toll paid, I grabbed the bike and wheeled it across, glancing back in time to see a dark green hand the size of my head reach up and gently lift the penny and sucker off the bridge.

"Night, Hector," I called.

"Safe travels, Aileen," a deep rumble responded.

The bridge troll was one of my first clients. They weren't usually violent, unless they felt their bridge was being disrespected or imperiled. Hector was pretty easygoing, but shy until he'd known you awhile. It was almost two years before he let me get my first glimpse of him.

I usually walked my bike over his bridge. He told me once he preferred the days when people walked. Riding over a bridge on wheels was considered disrespectful among his race. Today, most of the traffic he saw was cars and the odd bike. It was a simple act of kindness to walk and it cost me nothing.

My destination wasn't much farther. A small, unkempt building edging up to High Street, the Blue Pepper appeared as if it had never seen a good day, while the bright and festive sign out front looked like it belonged somewhere else.

Despite that, the Blue Pepper had no problem bringing in repeat business. The parking lot was pretty full for a weeknight, which seemed to be the case every time I visited.

I hopped off my bike and wheeled it around back to the bike rack the owner kept there. I was pretty sure I was the only one who ever used it. My bike would be safe despite the fact this area had a lot of petty crime—things like cars being broken into or thefts from front or back yards.

No one stole from the Blue Pepper. The locals all knew better. The owner had a habit of tracking down such foolhardy entrepreneurs and exacting a rather poetic justice on anyone stupid enough to dare her wrath.

The Blue Pepper was the same as always—a local watering hole, pure and simple. They didn't serve food, only drinks, though the owner had an agreement with a local food truck that stopped by most nights.

You were as likely to find an expensive car or SUV sitting side by side with a junker that looked like it might fall apart at any moment.

For the most part, the two types of clientele got along, each leaving the other to drown their sorrows or celebrate with their friends in peace. Every once in a while, an asshole wandered in, then the true entertainment began.

If Dahlia didn't send them packing, one of her more interesting customers did the deed for her. Because the Blue Pepper didn't just cater to humans. Spooks were regular visitors, coming from all over the city to take advantage of a neutral place to drink and socialize.

Her clientele wasn't just spooks capable of passing for human, either. Dahlia had some type of glamour on the place capable of masking a spook's appearance, enabling them to pose as a human while within the bounds of her property.

It was a powerful draw for many in the shadow world. It made the Blue

Pepper a good place to visit, if you were in need of gossip.

Dahlia wasn't the only one to notice me; many of the people inside stared as I approached the bar. There was more than one unfriendly gaze in the crowd, though none knew me personally. More spooks with a bone to pick with a vampire, I noted with a sigh.

While I was within the Blue Pepper, I was safe. Getting home might be a bit tricky, but for now I didn't have to worry about claws in the dark or magic being lobbed at me from the shadows.

They all knew better than to try something here. Not with Dahlia manning the bar. She took such things personally.

Still, a tall, thin man stood, his face wrinkling with hate as I neared.

"Dean, that's enough." There was a steely edge to Dahlia's voice.

Dean hesitated, before taking a seat. His table companion leaned over and patted his shoulder, shooting me a glance over her shoulder.

The humans in the bar glanced around in curiosity, not understanding the sudden animosity floating in the air. They turned back to their drinks without any prompting.

Dahlia watched me approach from her spot behind the bar where she reigned with all the authority of a queen on her throne. She tilted her head to the side, indicating an empty seat at the end of the bar even as she took an order from the human in front of her, giving him a dazzling smile as she flitted back and forth.

He was charmed, handing her a twenty and waving off his change.

Even after knowing her for several years, I still couldn't pinpoint Dahlia's species. She was a tall, lithe woman, with a grace that had always eluded me. She had almond-shaped eyes and straight hair the color of the deepest of shadows that hinted at a middle eastern ancestry. Her skin was a golden tone that made her look sun-kissed even in the deepest parts of winter.

She had the sort of face that belonged on a cover of a magazine or a movie screen. It was the biggest indication she was something other than human. Dahlia possessed the sort of beauty that once might have caused a few wars as men fought to possess her.

She had an otherworldly, mysterious quality that easily ensnared your attention and didn't release it until she looked away again.

She wasn't a succubus—she lacked their raw punch of sexuality—but she shared similar attributes, most notably she could read your deepest desire.

Finished with her customer, Dahlia glided my way, stopping in front of me. She didn't bother asking for my order, her hands already busy in a graceful dance as she prepared my drink.

Her motions paused as her gaze turned inward. She sent me a chiding glance before pouring the pale-yellow liquid into a martini glass.

She held her hand out, palm up. "You should have come as soon as it broke."

I gave her a sheepish smile, reaching up to undo the chain before setting the necklace in her hand. "I got a little busy."

She handed over the lemon drop martini before holding up the small pendant to examine. "This wouldn't have stopped another attack in this state."

I lifted the drink before putting it back on the bar top with a faint grimace. As much as I would love a taste of one of Dahlia's drinks. It didn't seem like a good idea to risk it, not after I'd almost lost the contents of my stomach once this night.

"Can you fix it?" I asked.

She didn't fail to note the drink sitting between us, but made no comment, her attention returning to the pendant.

"The magic that broke this would have been powerful. Most likely lethal," she said.

I'd suspected as much, but it was good to have it confirmed. I gave the pendant a grim look.

Until now, the attacks on me had been annoying but mostly harmless. I might have suffered a few minor injuries but there'd been nothing close to what the woman had thrown at me.

She clasped the pendant in her fist. A small thread of the smoke that always seemed to be present in the Blue Pepper drifted down to wrap around her hand and seep between the crevasses of her fingers.

I found myself fascinated with the process. An intense look of concentration crossed Dahlia's face, her muscles tightening as some hint of other briefly peeked through.

She relaxed and handed the once more fully intact charm back to me. I took it without comment and slid it back over my neck, almost afraid to do so.

This was powerful magic. Not the sort easily performed. There was always a cost to such things. Oftentimes that cost didn't involve money. No, it was exacted through blood and bone.

Unfortunately, I didn't think I could afford to turn it down. Not with half the city gunning for me at this point.

"What do I owe you?" I forced myself to ask.

She shook her head. "One day I'm going to need your help. I hope you'll be there."

I considered her with a serious gaze. "I don't kill innocents." I thought about it. "Or friends."

Her smile was slight. "I'm well aware of your limits, Aileen."

I snorted. Only a spook would consider that a limit.

Her eyes flicked to my right. "Now drink your martini and socialize with your friend. Both will do you good."

She moved away before I could respond.

In confusion, I looked up to find Caroline standing at my shoulder, her face set in a frown.

She glared at the human sitting next to me. "Move."

The man opened his mouth to argue before getting a good look at my friend. Caroline was cute in a way that men often fell over themselves to oblige her. With her blond hair styled into waves around her face and blue eyes that seemed to stare right through you, she looked like the girl next door who'd grown up to be a sexy teacher.

Since being bitten by a werewolf, she'd gone from nice girl, to having a hint of the wild in her movements and expression. To a human, it would be a tempting combination.

This one was no different. He picked up his drink, aiming a flirtatious look her way before stumbling to the other side of the bar.

Caroline settled herself into his seat, flicking her hair over her shoulder and crossing her legs.

"You told me you had work," she said without preamble.

I lifted an eyebrow and gave a meaningful glance at the human she'd just ordered out of his seat. She ignored that to lift a hand at Dahlia, pointing at my drink to request her own.

"I did have work," I said when she gave me an expectant look.

She glanced around the room. "Funny place to run a gas station from."

I shifted uncomfortably. "Liam called in one of his nights."

Her head spun back to me. The way her eyes widened would have been comical on someone else.

"The Liam? The badass enforcer you've been moping over since he left?" She leaned back in her chair. "Now, this should be interesting."

"I haven't been moping," I said in an irritable voice.

Caroline took the martini Dahlia handed her with a smile, taking a sip before making a moue of pleasure.

"This is delicious," she told Dahlia, before drinking some more.

Dahlia's lips quirked in amusement. She picked up a rag and started wiping the bar with it, listening in on our conversation without an ounce of shame. "I find this news fascinating as well."

I glared at the two who'd decided to gang up on me. I focused on Caroline first. "How did you find me and since when do you drink those?"

Caroline set the martini down. "I don't, but I'm going to start. I need a break from all the beer." She gave a delicate shudder. "That's all Brax and his people seem to drink. Beer, beer and more beer."

Somehow that didn't surprise me.

She avoided my gaze, glancing around the bar as she ignored my first question.

I narrowed my eyes at her, recognizing the stall tactic for what it was. "You followed my scent," I accused.

A slight trace of pink tinged her cheeks. I was right. I knew it.

"How?" I asked.

Even if she'd gone to my apartment, there was no way she could have followed my trail here. Nathan had picked me up and driven me halfway across the city. There should have been no scent for her to follow.

She cleared her throat, looking a little uncomfortable. "I live in the area and was out for a run. Your scent is easy to recognize."

A run? I gave her a narrow-eyed once-over. It wasn't that I couldn't picture Caroline running. She played soccer in high school and had been an avid runner. She was the one who'd nagged until I agreed to go, pounding down the trails with her, complaining the whole time.

Yes, I could see her out for a run, but not at eleven p.m. while dressed in a pair of jean shorts and a scalloped edged tank top the color of burgundy.

It made me wonder if she'd been in a two-legged or four-legged form during this supposed run.

I took a sip of my martini as I considered her, the sweet tartness setting my taste buds alive. "Uh huh."

She rolled her eyes at my response but didn't push.

Caroline was like me—so new to the supernatural ranks she was practically in diapers. Only unlike me, she had the full might of the pack behind her. She had the added advantage—or disadvantage depending on how you looked at it—of having a demon taint. It made her more powerful than she should be, a force in her own right. For both those reasons, she enjoyed a rather untouchable status.

I decided to let Caroline be and turned my attention to Dahlia. "You seem busier than usual. Any reason?" I tilted my head at the rest of the bar. The place wasn't just busy for the middle of the week, it was crazy.

More interesting, spooks outnumbered humans. I counted only six humans in the place, and that was being generous, since I wasn't sure if a group in the corner were human or something very adept at pretending to be human.

"It's karaoke night." Dahlia wiped down a glass, twisting it in her hands.

I looked around again, noting the karaoke machine I hadn't paid attention to earlier, along with the small monitor for the lyrics. Several people had already lined up to look at the song selection and the person running it was busy getting everything ready.

"We have it every Wednesday," Dahlia said. "It's one of our biggest draws."

"Oh, we haven't been to one of those in years," Caroline said.

"No," I told her. I wasn't getting up there and singing with half the Columbus population of spooks looking on. They already saw me as a joke. There was no reason to add to that.

"We'll see," she said with a devilish smile before taking another sip of her drink.

I snorted, but didn't comment. I went back to people-watching, letting my gaze skim over the crowd.

Caroline paused in sipping her martini, her eyes narrowing. She looked over the crowd and then back at me. "Oh my God, you're up to something."

I started, my attention swinging back to her. "What are you talking about?"

Caroline set the martini down with a thump. Dahlia ignored a patron trying to flag down her attention, too interested in our conversation.

Caroline pointed a finger at me. "I know that look."

"What look?" I asked defensively.

"The one that says you're trying to plan an angle of attack. The hot vampire you're obsessed with isn't here so I know you're not trying to figure out how to pick someone up. Something either happened that you're not telling me about or you caught wind of something that is making you curious," she said, her voice challenging.

I looked from Caroline to Dahlia whose eyes were alight with amusement. "I don't know what you're talking about."

"Uh huh," Caroline said, picking up her martini again. "I've heard that before."

I tapped my fingers against the bar, considering. It didn't hurt to put out a few feelers.

"You hear anything about a spook trying to fence a scroll?" I asked Dahlia.

She paused in cleaning the glasses and fixed me with a look. "I have not."

I slumped back. I suppose it had been too much to hope the first person I asked would know something.

Dahlia was a good source. Most spooks in the city, especially those on the weaker end of the spectrum, ended up in her bar at some point or another. Of everyone I knew, I figured she'd be the most likely to have heard anything worth hearing.

Not the case, it seemed.

"What type of scroll?" Caroline asked.

Of course, she'd be interested. As a former historian and current bookshop manager, a mysterious scroll would have the same draw that a dead animal would have to her inner wolf. At least she couldn't roll on the scroll.

"No clue," I told her.

She sat back in disappointment, propping her chin on her hand.

"What about Jerry? You hear anything about him?" I asked.

Dahlia fixed me with a look. There was a weight behind it, as if she was considering how much to share.

"It would be best to leave that matter alone," she finally said.

Caroline snorted. "Yeah, that means she definitely won't."

Dahlia dipped her head. "I see your point."

I gave the two of them an insulted look. Caroline's laugh as she took another sip nearly caused her to choke.

"That's not true," I said, defending myself.

Caroline set the drink down when she got control of her coughing. "It is, but it's one of the reasons I love you. You go where other people fear to tread—especially when someone tells you not to."

I couldn't keep my scowl and shrugged. She had a point.

I turned to Dahlia and lifted my eyebrows. "Well?"

She cleaned a glass and set it down before picking up another one. "There is to be a Wild Hunt."

Caroline and I watched her blankly.

"And?"

Dahlia's lips curved just the faintest bit. "And the gallant knight has been pressed into service. Until its end, he must fulfill his role."

I frowned and sat back. That didn't really answer much, and it got me no closer to knowing why he'd closed Hermes.

As if in answer, Dahlia tilted her head in a significant look at the table behind me. I studied the occupants in the mirror, three women. All of them appeared entirely human.

I couldn't quite put my finger on what it was that set my instincts to tingling, telling me these women were more than they seemed. They looked normal enough, dressed for a night out with their friends, dressy-casual but not plain. Their hair and makeup perfectly done. The overall effect said they cared about their appearance but weren't really looking to attract a guy.

They were all older, late thirties to mid-forties. They looked like moms or work friends who'd decided to meet up and leave their husbands and kids behind.

The one nearest me looked uncomfortable, continually fiddling with her drink as the other two watched the room with cool gazes.

That was it. That was what was bothering me. They might look like middle-aged women out for a night on the town, but studied the room with a soldier's focus, noting the exits, the possible threats in the room. Civilians just didn't do that.

The blond looked up just then, catching my gaze in the mirror. I didn't jerk or look away as I sipped on my martini before allowing my attention to wander away.

I ignored the desire to look back, knowing her focus was still on me.

Caroline helped with my deception, leaning over and saying, "Ha, I knew it."

I smiled at her and nodded. "Is she still looking at us?"

Caroline flicked her hair over her shoulder, glancing in the mirror casually and then around the bar. "Yup."

"You've gotten good at that move," I said in approval. "Time was you would have given up the game by staring straight at her."

She gave me a crooked smile. "I've been practicing."

I looked at her and arched my eyebrows. On the tip of my tongue was the question of why that was. I didn't ask it.

Dahlia placed another lemon drop in front of both of us. I blinked at it, surprised I'd already finished the first one.

"What do you think?" Dahlia asked, the barest flick of her eyes toward the women telling me what she was really asking.

"Interesting clientele you have today," I said.

Dahlia leaned on the counter and gave me a small smirk. "Rumor has it that the High Fae are looking to make alliances. They've made known their intention of establishing a presence in the city."

"And the witches can help with that?" I asked.

They weren't Fae. They were too good at pretending to be human for that, and they lacked that extra something that most of the humanoid Fae had— something that compelled you to get closer to them and worship at their feet.

Dahlia lowered her chin in a small nod. "The witches don't have as much raw power as the Fae, but because of their affinity for nature magic their powers are compatible. Together, they might be enough to establish a barrow here. It would be the first one of this modern age."

"And that would be bad?" I made the sentence a question.

The corners of her eyes wrinkled. "The master of the city certainly seems to thinks so."

So that answered why the Fae would want the witches as allies, but what did the witches get out of it besides a chance to stick it to the vampires?

Caroline's eyes moved between the two of us. She leaned forward and stage whispered, "What's a barrow?"

I paused. That was a good question.

We both looked expectantly at Dahlia who rolled her eyes. "The pocket realms the Fae establish are usually called barrows. If they were looking to settle a contingent here, they'd wish to create a place of magic that conformed to their whims. A barrow would give them that ability."

I glanced in the mirror again, making sure my gaze didn't linger on any of them too long. They were huddled together in what looked to be an intense conversation.

The one who'd seemed uncomfortable before, looked up and at me before ducking her head back down.

So, they suspected my interest on some level. They definitely weren't stupid.

"I imagine they'd like to use the Fae for their own purposes." She gave me a darkly significant look before moving down the bar.

I discarded the notion that they could be after me, particularly. I didn't recognize any of the women. That meant it probably had something to do with vampires as a whole.

Thomas's reign in the city was new. It could be some of its inhabitants would like to see him unseated. His policies had made him very unpopular and a lot of people were unhappy. The last vampire lord to control this territory had spent a good bit of his time in Chicago, leaving Columbus' spooks the freedom to do what they want. Thomas had a much bigger presence here and the power to enforce his rules.

Caroline studied me, her forehead wrinkled in thought. "All right, I'm in."

I gave her a sideways look, wondering what brought that on. "There's nothing to be in for."

She snorted. "You say that now, but pretty soon, interesting, dangerous things are going to start happening. You'll need someone to watch your back." Her grin widened as she grabbed my cheek with one hand, ruthlessly pinching it. "You defenseless baby, you."

I batted her hand away, holding the offended cheek as I glared at her. "You're just as much a baby as I am."

Her shrug was rueful as she lifted her drink. "Let's have a little fun tonight, shall we?"

There was a hint of vulnerability on her face, as if she expected me to throw her offer in her face. The thought had occurred to me.

It went against the instincts I'd built up over the last few years. It was almost second nature to refuse at this point. I'd gotten so used to going it alone that the offer of help made me stop and blink.

I sighed and gave in, picking up my glass and tapping it against hers. "Guess I can't argue with that."

Caroline's mouth widened and she took a hasty sip before setting the drink back on the bar. She clapped her hands together and shot out of her chair. "I know just how to celebrate."

"Oh no." I made a grab for her, but she evaded, heading straight for the DJ. "Caroline, I'm not singing karaoke."

A tall, thin man a few seats down the bar gave me a look filled with disdain. "Think you're too good for us?"

I curled my lip, showing a fang. That seemed to shut him up. His mouth snapped closed and he looked away even as his friend shot me an unfriendly look.

Caroline bounced back to me, her energy infectious and spilling everywhere.

"I'm not singing," I told her as soon as she reached me.

"Don't worry. There's at least ten people in front of us. Plenty of time for you to get a few more of these in you for liquid courage." She held up the drink in question.

"You know I can't get drunk on normal liquor, right?"

She nearly choked on the liquid, wiping it away as she gave me wide eyes. "No."

"You probably can't either."

Werewolves had a fast metabolism. Her body would burn through alcohol faster than the drinks would get her drunk. Plus side—she could pretty much eat anything now and not gain a pound.

She stared down at her drink in what looked like sorrow. Her mouth firmed. "Tonight, we're going to test that theory."

CHAPTER FIVE

"It's almost our turn," Caroline said.

I felt no more enthusiastic than when she first suggested it to me. Getting out of it, however, seemed more and more impossible.

For the last hour, Caroline had chair danced to every song, mouthing the lyrics and basically rocking out. She might pull out the demon wolf if I tried to leave without performing one song with her.

We were both on our third drink by then. Surprisingly, I was feeling loose and warm. I remembered this feeling from when I was human. It was that pleasantly buzzed feeling that came from being on that perfect edge between too much and not enough.

From the bright look in Caroline's eyes and the happy smile plastered on her face for the last hour, I was willing to bet she was in a similar state.

I peered closer at my glass.

This should have been impossible. I'd tried on more than one occasion to get drunk since my change. Not just once or twice, but many times. At one point I even paid an Army buddy to bring up some moonshine from Kentucky. Nothing had worked.

Yet now I was experiencing that same lassitude invading my limbs even as my lips tingled, a precursor to going numb.

"Curiouser and curiouser," I told my glass.

It disappeared and another sat in its place. My mouth dropped and I jerked back. Dahlia's face was amused as she watched me.

"You're doing something to our drinks," I accused.

She arched an eyebrow as if to say 'took you long enough' and then moved down the bar to help another customer.

I whacked Caroline on her arm. "We need to be careful. I think she put something in our drinks. Something that can get us drunk."

She giggled into her glass. "It's too late for that."

I looked at her in dismay. "Oh no."

She nodded. "Oh yes."

I shook my head. No. Drunk Caroline and drunk Aileen were an awful combination.

She didn't wait for my protest or my recommendation that we should maybe head home. "We're up next!"

She bounced off her stool, dragging me behind her. Our path was going to pass the women Dahlia had pointed out and I got an idea. One that I probably would have ignored at any other time.

I looked Caroline in the eye. "Sorry about this."

She gave me a startled glance, her mouth opening on a question. I checked her with my hip, timing it perfectly for when she was off-balance and sent her flying into the women's table.

The alcohol and surprise slowed her reaction time. She crashed into the table with a hard *oomph*. The women grabbed onto it reflexively, reaching for their glasses, but not in time. Two of their drinks tipped over.

The thin brunette grimaced in distaste, brushing at her hand, which was now covered in her drink.

"Oh my gosh, I am so, so sorry," Caroline gushed.

I fought to contain my laugh. She sounded like a bubble-headed idiot with more peroxide than sense in her head.

I schooled my expression to sympathy, unsure if I was successful, especially when Caroline started patting at the woman's arm with her hand.

"I'm just such a klutz sometimes," Caroline said, still with that fake voice. "Let me go get you a napkin."

She toddled off even as the woman said, "No, that's not necessary."

The woman's face turned frustrated until she noticed me watching her. I gave her a bright smile. "I hope we didn't ruin anything."

The three shared a glance, visibly withdrawing, unease and suspicion on their faces.

"It's nothing," the brunette said with a strained smile.

I pegged her as the ringleader for these three and gave her another sunny smile in return. Nothing suspicious about this set of circumstances. Just a drunk vampire and werewolf crashing into things.

Dahlia had watched the entire thing go down and had the napkins waiting at the bar when Caroline arrived. She grabbed them and headed back to the four of us.

"What brings you to the Blue Pepper?" I asked. "Are you going to join in karaoke night?"

The woman in charge gave me a hard smile. "No, we're just out to enjoy a few drinks with friends."

Caroline arrived just then. "You should sing. We are. We're performing

Toxic."

I nearly choked. "That's what you chose?"

She gave me a taunting smile. "I thought it appropriate. Next time you shouldn't be so resistant."

I gave her a disgusted look. "I'm going back to the bar."

"Oh no, you aren't. You said you'd sing, so you're singing." She grabbed my arm and hauled me back into place, her strength surprising.

The exchange accomplished one goal, getting the women to relax. Their gazes changed from suspicious to slightly condescending.

Yeah, I bet they thought we were idiots. The baby vampire and her werewolf friend. I was okay with that. I was often underestimated and had learned to use that to my advantage.

"I'm Caroline. This is Aileen," Caroline said, introducing us. I gave them another friendly smile. Just a harmless vampire shanghaied into karaoke night.

The woman who appeared to be in charge gave Caroline a superior smile. "I'm Jennifer. This is Ashley." She pointed at the blonde. "And this is Mary." The overweight brunette shifted in her seat, shredding one of the napkins Caroline had brought over.

"Have you ever been here?" I asked as I tried to think of the best way to get more information out of them.

"First time," Ashley said.

"Mine too," Caroline volunteered. "Their lemon drop martinis are out of this world."

The women shared a conspiring smile. I had to wonder if they knew something we didn't. Like maybe the fact that Dahlia put a little something extra into her drinks.

"We have an acquaintance in common," Mary said abruptly. Her gaze was challenging as it met mine.

"Mary," Jennifer said between gritted teeth.

Mary lifted her chin, ignoring her friend. "You might remember her."

The other two at the table looked unhappy, both shooting Mary looks that said 'shut up'.

I kept a smile on my face. "Maybe. What was her name?"

Mary's eyes narrowed, the cant to her mouth turning nasty. "Angela. My cousin."

That explained the veiled hostility and also confirmed these women were witches.

"How is she doing?" I asked, keeping my reaction off my face. I'd been hoping she was dead. The witch had done her best to kill me. I disliked having potential enemies running around the city.

I took a peek with my left eye, trying to get a glimpse of their magic. It was a mostly useless exercise. The bar was so steeped in power that it was lit up like a neon Christmas tree, making it difficult to see past the bright haze.

I thought I caught a glimpse of yellow and red snakes wrapped around the women's auras but I couldn't be sure.

"She's back after a trip overseas," Jennifer said, interrupting what Mary had been about to say. She gave the other woman a warning look, one that said cross her at her peril.

I wasn't happy to hear the news. It wasn't hard to interpret Angela's punishment was over and she was once again running merrily around the city.

"Is she still working for Miriam?" I asked, keeping a pleasantly inquiring expression on my face. It was a low blow, considering Miriam was probably the reason for any suffering Angela had likely endured.

Mary's face darkened and she stood, her chair scraping back. "You think you're untouchable, but you're not. You'll pay for what you did."

"Mary," Jennifer barked. She spat a word in another language. Whatever she expected didn't happen, judging by the slight surprise on her face.

Mary made an ugly sound. "The wards here prevent that, or did you not listen to anything I told you?"

Jennifer's expression tightened. "It doesn't matter. You will stop talking or I will make you suffer."

Mary's mouth snapped closed even as a defiant look crossed her face.

Dahlia appeared at my side, her expression steely but polite. "I'm afraid I'm going to have to ask you to leave. Personal attacks are forbidden on these premises."

Jennifer lifted her chin defiantly, not seeming at all repentant for being called out on her actions. "You misunderstand. That wasn't a personal attack, merely a corrective measure."

"It would have caused considerable pain and damage." Dahlia's voice had turned to black ice, the smallest thread of power deepening it and sending a shiver down my back.

Jennifer paid no attention to it, remaining unmoved. "It was a little thing. You can forgive it this once."

Arguing with the bartender. Not only rude, but also idiotic.

She should have taken her friends and left without an argument. Now Dahlia was going to have to make an example of her. Foolish move.

I didn't have to look around to know we were part of an ever-widening circle of interest. More and more people were taking notice of the weird little standoff.

A pair of men watched us with avid expressions. They were twins, nearly identical with hair longer than was considered fashionable. There was a weird shimmer over them indicating to me they were wearing some type of glamour. Dahlia's ward prevented me from looking under it.

When they noticed my attention, one flashed me a panty-dropping smile before they both melted back into the crowd.

I sighed and debated the merits of interfering.

Caroline watched the drama unfolding with wide, avid eyes. Somehow, she'd gotten hold of a martini and was sipping on it, looking highly entertained.

I shook my head and waited to catch her eye before mouthing, "Where's mine?"

She pointed to the martini and mouthed back, "This is yours."

I gasped. That bitch. I'd make her pay. I sent her my best 'I will get even with you later' look. She giggled, not appearing intimidated in the least.

We'd see. I had mad revenge skills. I'd figure out her weakness and then strike like a revenge ninja.

I rolled my lips together to suppress a small snicker at the evilness of my plan. It was going to be so epic.

Jennifer's attention jumped to me and she looked coldly furious. I glanced around in confusion wondering what I'd done to deserve such a look. It dawned on me that she thought I was laughing at her.

I shook my head at her to try and tell her she got it all wrong. If anything, it seemed to make things worse as her expression chilled, hate glimmering there.

Dahlia seemed to tire of waiting, her expression hardening slightly, making her seem like an ice princess about to pass judgment on the peasants. She remained remote and unmoving, not saying a word, as several tendrils of the faint black smoke drifted down from the ceiling.

Caroline's eyes widened as they circled the other three.

The women were unaware as they breathed in the smoke, Jennifer and Ashley seeming triumphant at Dahlia's lack of reaction, as if they thought they'd won the confrontation. Mary looked half-afraid, half-combative, as if she wanted to run but also wanted to tear me apart with her bare hands.

She was the first to notice the smoke, going as still as a rabbit glimpsing a snake.

The effects of the smoke were small at first. A coughing fit from Ashley, slightly labored breathing from Mary. Then Jennifer bent forward, gasping, as if she couldn't get enough air. One hand came to her throat as she looked wildly around the room.

Dahlia's face lacked any sympathy. "You were warned."

Mary clutched the back of the seat and lowered herself down, her face turning bright red as she gasped, trying to get enough air in her lungs.

Jennifer collapsed to her knees, making small wheezing sounds.

Dahlia watched them, her expression remote. She really intended to kill them.

I looked around the room. Most seemed enthralled by the drama, their eyes bright with the promise of death. A few, however, looked alarmed. Humans most likely, ones on the verge of calling an ambulance.

I could leave Dahlia to finish giving her lesson. It was a tempting prospect. The witches probably deserved every inch of Dahlia's ire. I had no doubt any kindness given to them would come back to bite me on the ass.

I'd been in this world long enough to know that whatever Jennifer had thrown at her friend hadn't been kind. Worse, she'd done it so Mary wouldn't reveal something, meaning it was related to me in some way.

Had it just been us here, I might have been able to let it go, let Dahlia extract any price she felt necessary, but we weren't alone. Humans were watching, ones with cell phones with the ability to record. I didn't need Dahlia suffering for this, whether from chancing our discovery or the humans spreading the word that this place was dangerous. Not when some of this encounter could be laid at my feet.

I leaned closer to Dahlia and said in a stage whisper. "If you choke them to death, they won't be able to get up and leave on their own."

Dahlia flicked me a glance, the power in her eyes setting my stomach to trembling. This was a being that could easily kill me.

"Just saying. I don't want to carry them out of here or deal with any nasty things their bodies might leave behind. Do you?"

Dahlia's face remained blank and icy. She didn't give any sign that she'd heard my words, much less planned to listen, but black smoke retreated from the women's throats and noses. The smoke curled playfully in on itself as it rejoined its companions on the ceiling.

The three drew deep, gasping breaths, their color returning to normal. They didn't waste any more words on arguing or posturing, grabbing their purses and hightailing it out of the bar, fear on their faces.

Dahlia turned her gaze on me, the look in her eyes indecipherable.

"Do you want us to leave too?" I offered. I would understand if she did. I was the one who'd initiated contact. Some might say that I was the cause of everything that had happened.

Her expression lightened, a small smile curling her lips. "I believe you're next for karaoke. I wouldn't deprive my guests of such an amusement."

I blanched, almost wishing she'd thrown us out.

Caroline whooped and grabbed my arm. "I second this motion."

She didn't give me a chance to protest, shepherding me to the karaoke machine and shoving a microphone into my hand before grabbing her own.

"We're ready," she chirped at the person running it.

He looked between the two of us with wide eyes, as if not quite believing a vampire and werewolf would want to participate in karaoke night. He seemed almost human except for a slight glimmer around him.

Caroline gave him a look that said 'hurry up'.

He busied himself with his computer, lifting his microphone and saying, "For our next song, we have Caroline and Aileen performing Toxic."

Caroline gave me a playful look and took the first part, shaking her hips and performing to the crowd as she got into the song. By the time it was my turn to join in, I'd forgotten my reservations and just enjoyed playing my part.

Caroline grinned at me as I sang the first notes, putting her back to mine as we hit the chorus.

After that, we strutted our stuff, riling up the crowd before sashaying past each other. We finished to thunderous applause.

Caroline bowed and waved as we handed our microphones back to the DJ who looked impressed.

We headed back to our seats to find two shots already on the bar. Caroline grabbed hers and downed it before I could stop her.

She picked mine up and handed it to me. "You're drinking. I've been stuck cataloging at the bookstore and I'm ready to live it up. We haven't had a night like this in ages."

I gave her a sideways look. It'd been a long time since I had a drunken night of revelry. Already, I was tipsier than I'd been in years.

Seeing my hesitation, she threw her arm out to indicate the rest of the bar. "You don't even have to worry about losing control here. Dahlia will keep an eye on things, won't you?"

Dahlia gave my friend an amused look. "You are correct."

Caroline's face turned mushy. "Aw, I love this woman. Lena, you have such awesome friends."

I threw back the shot before I could think better of it. Caroline cheered and slapped the bar. "Another."

It turned out the shot was just the beginning in a long line of drinks that got wilder as the night deepened. The bar turned into a giant rave as we progressed from shots, back to martinis, then to a delicious fruity concoction that reminded me of rainbows.

Dahlia didn't bother taking our requests, serving us whatever took her fancy at any given moment. She had a new drink waiting every time we finished the last.

I bypassed tipsy and headed straight to Inebriationville, letting Caroline convince me to perform two more songs with her, the last one of which we sang from the top of the bar as our adoring crowd gathered before us.

Caroline bopped next to me, her body gliding to the music and managing some semblance of grace despite the amount of alcohol she'd had.

We were on the last chorus, the crowd singing with us, when I looked down and spotted Liam frowning up at me from beside the bar, his face slightly incredulous.

I gave him a lopsided smile and a happy wave. His lips parted in a smile so slight I might have imagined it.

Brax stood next to him, arms folded across his chest as he watched Caroline with a dark look. He looked less than pleased to find one of his wolves dancing on top of a bar with half the spook population of Columbus egging her on.

The alpha was a tall, imposing man, with a harsh masculine face and a body that would have made a gym rat jealous. I wondered idly if running around on all fours helped build all those muscles.

He looked ex-military with his hair cut close to his head and a rigid, upright posture. It was apparent he had experience with martial arts, his stance perfectly balanced, weight distributed so he could move to avoid an unexpected attack.

Even relaxed like he was, he projected the sort of presence that demanded obedience from those mortals around him.

The two were a matched pair, a circle widening around them as the crowd unconsciously gave them space.

I nudged Caroline and jutted my chin at the two. "Busted. Looks like Sir Crankypants and Mr. Grumpsalot don't approve."

I snickered at my joke.

Caroline's expression was curious as she looked where I indicated. A comical look of dismay crossed her face. She missed a step in her dance and toppled off the bar. I tried to grab her but missed.

One of our erstwhile fans caught her in his arms, his face creasing into a pleased smile. "Woah there. You don't want to crack your head."

He set her down gently, even as he grinned at her flirtatiously.

Caroline gave him a drunken smile that changed to a grimace as Brax loomed over his shoulder, a dark glare aimed at the man.

The man noticed and let go of Caroline, holding his hands up and backing away. "I'll just go then."

"You do that," Brax said.

The man beat a hasty retreat, leaving a morose Caroline in his wake.

I suddenly noticed I was standing alone on the bar, holding a microphone in my hand as the last notes of the song played.

I bent a goofy grin on Liam. "Sing with me?"

His gaze was faintly amused. "I don't think so."

I gave him a mocking frown. "Come, Sir Crankypants, a little bit of fun won't kill you."

A choked laugh from Liam's side drew my attention.

"Nathan, you tattled again. No one likes a tattletale," I said, shaking my finger at him.

The motion upset my balance and I wavered before righting myself. I gave the two of them a proud smile at the feat.

Nathan snickered as Liam reached up and grabbed my hand, using it to drag me down off the bar.

"I think you've had enough fun for the night," Liam told me.

"Poppycock," I said, waving his words away. "We're just getting started."

The crowd around us booed at the delay in entertainment, before edging away from the dark scowl he aimed at them.

"I'll take that, Aileen," the DJ said.

"I'm trusting you'll bestow this on only the most worthiest of individuals," I said, handing over the mic with an expression of grave seriousness.

He gave me a small bow. "As my lady commands."

I beamed at him, then frowned as Liam shot the minor Fae a look that invited his absence.

The frown popped and fizzled as Liam tugged me against him, muttering. "How did you get into this state?"

I didn't answer, too absorbed with getting lost in the deep blue of his eyes. The depths beckoned, calling to the most secret parts of me.

"You have pretty eyes," I sighed.

"And you are very drunk," he stated. His face looked torn between being amused by that fact and upset.

I raised one hand and squished those features together.

A song started playing and Caroline appeared over my shoulder. "It's our song."

I bounced in place. "We should dance!"

"You're not dancing," Brax told Caroline.

"Watch me. You're not the boss of me," she said, lifting her chin stubbornly.

"Hate to break it to you, sweetheart, but I am," Brax said in a sardonic voice.

Caroline got a stubborn look on her face as she shook her head emphatically. "Nope. The bookstore's shopkeeper is my boss. You're just a bully with fur."

Brax's expression turned scandalized at Caroline's denial. I chortled, unable to contain my amusement at the sight of Caroline giving the alpha hell.

She stalked off before he could stop her, heading for the dance floor.

Brax's furious eyes came to rest on me. "I blame you for corrupting my wolf."

I snorted. "That happened way before you came into the picture."

Brax didn't respond, stalking off without another word.

"I've never seen the alpha look so out of sorts," Nathan drawled next to us. "If you're not careful, he may decide to keep you two separated in the future."

"He can try," I said, twisting out of Liam's arms. The action upset my precarious balance, sending me staggering into the bar. I draped myself over it, resting my hot cheek on its cool surface.

"I think I need water," I groaned. That was still a thing, wasn't it? I vaguely recalled it being necessary from the nights of drunken revelry back when I was still human.

As if by magic, a glass of water appeared next to my head. I lifted my face off the bar and gave the bartender a hazy smile.

This man was a stranger. Dahlia was at the other end of the bar taking care of customers.

"Thanks," I told him, grabbing the water and trying to wrap my lips around the straw. It kept evading me, taking several attempts to capture.

Liam gently tugged me away from the bar. "That's not what you need."

"How did you even find me?" I asked, my path slightly meandering.

I was drunk. So very, very drunk.

I didn't even remember the last time I was this drunk. I was definitely going to regret this tomorrow night. Meh. That was tomorrow Aileen's problem. Tonight's Aileen was going to embrace the madness and suck all the fun out of the night that she could.

"Nathan couldn't have followed me." A thought occurred to me and I jerked out of his grip. I held my arm up between us, outrage on my face. "Are you using your microchip again?"

A while back, Liam had lain his mark on me—unasked for, by the way. An oak tree that was slowly filling in with leaves, roots beginning to appear at the bottom, tangible evidence of the link between us.

I knew he could use it to track me, but I thought it was difficult and something he did rarely.

"You assume I'm here for you," he said, bending a censorious look on me that turned devilish. "This is just a happy coincidence."

I stared at him, my eyes narrowed as I sifted through the different possibilities, trying to decipher the level of truth in that statement. The amount of liquor in my system didn't make that task an easy one.

"Is this part of the reason you asked me to look at you earlier?" I asked.

He gave a small huff. "Ask me again in the morning."

"Okay, I will," I said, giving him a small nod for emphasis. Detecting doubt on his face, I widened my eyes. "I will."

Another song came on, one that made my body sing and begged for me to dance.

"I love this song," I declared, jerking out of his hold and zigzagging through the bar to where a small dance floor had appeared.

Caroline was already there, dancing with wild abandon, her hair flying and her hips keeping rhythm with the pulsing beat.

It had been years since I danced in public. Occasionally, I turned the music up and danced alone in my apartment.

This was different. So much better in every way. You could feel the electricity in the air, taste the vitality as the crowd came alive, carried by the wave of sound and energy.

I put my hands above my head, rolling my hips in a provocative glide as I joined Caroline, the two of us dancing together as the magic in the air invaded, lending each movement a tantalizing promise.

This was what I'd been missing in my life. I felt alive in a way I hadn't felt in a long time, the pulse of the crowd around me buoying me up and pulling me in its wake.

I caught sight of Liam watching me, a dark light of promise in his eyes, the shadows wrapping around him in a loving embrace.

Brax joined him, the two of them using lethal glares to scare anyone foolish enough to attempt to join Caroline and me as we danced.

Unconsciously, my dance turned seductive, beckoning him to join me. I needed him, wanted him with a sudden ferocity that stole my breath.

I turned as he glided forward. His hands settled at my hips, pulling them against him as he caught my rhythm, rolling his hips against mine.

"You're playing a dangerous game," he whispered in rough voice against my ear.

The sensation sent delicious tingles down my back. Desire rose in delicate waves as I turned against him, letting my chest brush his as I gave him a sultry smile, my fangs peeking out.

"Those are the best kind," I said, my gaze locked on his lips.

I glanced up at him in invitation, drifting closer, pulled in by his magnetism.

His chest expanded with a deep breath as his eyes turned nearly black with suppressed passion.

Suddenly, I wished we weren't surround by people, that we were somewhere private and I could indulge in all the thoughts currently running through my head.,

My eyes caught and lingered on the vein in his neck, my fangs tingling. I'd noticed passion for vampires often involved blood in some way. I knew from prior experience just how good he would taste too. The faintest bit of pressure, and the decadent taste of his blood would send me to dizzying heights.

It was a drug I desperately wanted another taste of, even as a voice in the back of my mind warned me of all the reasons I shouldn't.

I shut the voice off. Tonight was my night. Worry and regret could wait until tomorrow.

I swayed closer, brushing my nose along the side of his neck.

His hand tightened at my waist, squeezing and massaging as he groaned. "I think that's just about enough of that."

I ignored him, leaning closer, breathing in the scent of his skin, warm and male and oh so very Liam.

I was up in the air in a dizzying second, his shoulder under my stomach in an instant. I let out a small squawk of surprise.

"We're leaving," he said, sounding more composed than I would have guessed he could in that moment.

He took a step and then stopped. "Move."

I craned my head to see what was happening, but didn't make it far given the steel band of Liam's arms wrapped securely around my thighs.

"All here are under my protection. You may not take them unless they wish it," Dahlia's voice sounded as cold as winter as it wrapped around us.

"What did you give her?" Liam asked, ignoring the inherent threat in Dahlia's words.

"Nothing that would cause harm," Dahlia responded.

"That doesn't answer my question," Liam snapped.

"Some fairy tears mixed with blood." Dahlia's voice remained calm.

Liam grunted, evidently finding the explanation satisfactory.

He advanced forward again and came to another stop. Again, I tried to see what was happening but settled down when Liam wrapped a warm hand around my upper thigh.

"Careful, djinn, you're here at our sufferance. Your presence in this place can be revoked," Liam warned, responding to something I couldn't see.

Djinn? I lifted myself up and peered at the ever-present haze of smoke in the room. That made a strange sort of sense.

"Your threats do not change the facts." Dahlia sounded coolly amused.

"She's one of mine," he said.

"Does she know that?" Dahlia asked archly.

Liam didn't like that response, letting out a soft growl.

With alarm, I saw the black smoke shifting and slithering as it sank down from the ceiling. Visions of what happened to the witches stole through my head.

Before I could think better of it, I lifted my hand bringing it down on Liam's ass with a loud crack.

The bar went silent, conversation screeching to a halt as I became the focus of several disbelieving pairs of eyes.

Liam went still, his muscles pulling tight under me until they felt like a tightly corded piece of steel.

"Did you just slap my ass?" Liam asked in a deceptively calm voice.

It occurred to me even in my slightly inebriated state that I'd just tap danced onto dangerous ground without concern for my safety or an exit strategy.

I hung there debating the merits of answering.

"Ah, yup," I finally said in a falsely confident voice.

"I thought so," he responded. To Dahlia, he said, "We're done here."

Then we were moving. As he strode for the door, I lifted my head and gave Dahlia a small wave. Her eyes danced with amusement as she bit her lip to contain her smile.

Glad someone was finding my situation hilarious.

I felt a little more sober as Liam stepped out of the bar, the darkness wrapping around us with cool arms. Now that the full repercussions of my actions were at hand, I was beginning to rethink this whole night.

CHAPTER SIX

The air was cool on my face as I dangled over Liam's back, my thoughts quiet for the moment. I enjoyed the ride, the steady sway as Liam carried me through the parking lot, Nathan cackling as he trailed us.

I hummed, just enjoying the warm glow I was currently experiencing.

Sound poured outside as the door to the bar opened then slammed shut. Caroline appeared, Brax behind her.

Liam reached one of the ubiquitous black Escalade's his people always seemed to drive around in. He lowered me to the ground and leaned me against the side.

"Why are all your cars black?" I asked, frowning at the car. "It wouldn't kill you to add a pop of color every now and then."

I blinked as Brax and Caroline joined us.

"Did you want a ride?" Liam asked.

"Please," Brax said.

"Or gray," I said suddenly. "Gray would be different. Well, most people have gray or silver, but for you lot it would be practically rebellious."

Liam opened the door and helped me inside.

"I always wanted a car that was candy apple red," Caroline said.

I nodded at her. "I could totally see you in something like that. I always thought I'd get a car that was burnt orange. Something stylish but fast."

"You have a car," Liam said as he slid in beside me.

Nathan got in the driver's seat. Brax joined him up front.

I blew a raspberry at the vampire by my side. "That's not a car; it's a leash with wheels. Besides, it's pretty much useless when you can't afford to fill it with gas."

Liam gave me a thoughtful look, grabbing me when I lunged forward with the intent to turn on the music.

"Stop that," he ordered.

"It's boring driving in silence. At least turn on the music," I whined.

"Yeah," Caroline echoed.

Nathan's shoulders shook as Liam gave a long-suffering sigh.

Brax reached forward and flipped the radio on, turning it to a pop rock station. Caroline and I let out twin cheers, dancing along with the music as Nathan turned down a side street, winding his way in the same direction I'd come earlier in the night.

I bounced to the music, watching the neighborhood outside Liam's window as I wondered why we'd taken this way. We reached a part of the song that I loved and I forgot about my question, belting out the lyrics with Caroline matching me word for word.

We'd just hit the final chorus when there was a whoosh of sound. Glass shattered and the Escalade flipped.

Caroline screamed, a short burst of sound as we went weightless for a stomach-churning moment. Then we hit, the side of the Escalade crunching. We went airborne again, landing on the roof.

Liam grabbed me, his arms hard bands around my chest and waist as he tried to keep me from careening all over the car.

My arm flew up, hitting the roof. Something snapped in the wrist, a brief spot of pain that stole my voice.

Several seconds of terror and confusion later, the Escalade slid to a stop on its roof, the metal screeching in protest.

I lay there stunned, thanking my lucky stars I was a vampire and that Liam was there to keep me from breaking my neck. Had I been human, the crash might have been the end of me.

Caroline flipped herself upright, her eyes flashing amber as her wolf pressed close to the surface. I stilled, remembering when Caroline's wolf had tried to kill me.

She had a lot more control over her other side now, but while hurt and in pain, there was no telling what the wolf might do.

Caroline reached out and touched my hand, the wolf receding as concern appeared. "Aileen, are you okay?"

"Think so," I said, wiggling in Liam's arms. "Liam? You still breathing?"

His eyes flashed open, power giving them a slight glow as he looked me over. For a moment, I froze, painfully aware I was in the presence of an apex predator, one that was as deadly as it was unpredictable.

We remained still, locked together as I waited. He blinked, one hand coming up to run along my back as if to reassure himself I was still in one piece.

"I'm fine thanks to you." I patted him on the arm even as I winced. I hadn't lied. He'd protected me from a lot, but I still had several bumps and bruises that were just now making themselves felt.

68

"What the hell happened?" I asked, pushing out of Liam's hold. He didn't relinquish his grip immediately, his hands tightening before sliding away reluctantly.

"I would like to know as well," he said.

We hadn't been going that fast, and the way we'd rolled, it hadn't felt like Nathan had hit a curb.

No, we'd been hit by something. The glass had shattered before we'd started our roll. Whatever it was, I doubted it'd been another car. At least I didn't think so. There'd been no headlights, no sound to indicate an oncoming car.

"Brax," Caroline exclaimed, she crawled forward under the seats.

I finally noticed what I should have before. Blood, the scent of it cloying in the small space. The alpha made a high whining sound of pain.

His side of the car was crumpled and bowled inward, like a giant fist had tried punching through the metal.

His head was bloodied and I suspected he also had some kind of laceration on his side or lower body.

"Brax, can you hear me?" Caroline asked, her voice slightly panicked.

"Yes," he said, his voice tight with pain.

"We need to get out of the car," Liam said.

I nodded. I had a sneaking suspicion that whatever had done this might figure out they hadn't completed the job and return while we were vulnerable.

The car groaned and then spun as something rammed it again. A groan of pain came from Brax as his door peeled back. The fingers of a mud-covered hand speared through the metal.

An animalistic growl came from Brax as he swiped a hand turned furry at the fingers.

"Out, out now," Liam ordered.

Nathan yanked Brax's seatbelt apart, releasing him from the restriction. Brax's upper body thunked onto the roof of the car, his leg still caught in the twisted metal under the dash.

Nathan leaned forward, punching the metal several times before reaching in and grabbing a piece, twisting it out of the way. It gave under his hand with a screech. Brax's leg came free. Nathan grabbed him by the shoulder and hauled him out through the driver's side door as Caroline and I crawled out after Liam.

I spilled onto the asphalt on my hands and knees, skating back as a giant hand the size of an SUV sprouted up from the ground to reach under the car and toss it into the air.

Liam grabbed me by the back of my shirt and hauled me up, dragging me away as the car crashed down. Caroline scrambled after us.

Guess that answered the question of what caused the crash.

We'd crashed near one of the small, hidden ravines that riddled this part of the city. They were an unexpected gem for those who lived here, a remnant of a time when the river hadn't been quite so stationary, water carving into the rock and leaving a small slice of nature in the middle of Columbus.

Something or someone had taken advantage of that fact, creating whatever this was. It smelled of Earth with the tangy bite of magic. Made from dirt and leaves and twigs, the hand looked like something that belonged in the deepest parts of a forest, one steeped in heavy magic and prone to giving life to odd dirt creatures.

"What is that?" Caroline asked, a touch of horror in her voice.

"It's a magical construct," Liam said, his voice distracted as he examined the thing, analyzing it for weaknesses.

"Guess we know for sure the witches are involved," Nathan said in a sour voice.

Liam made a small sound of agreement.

We were arranged defensively facing the hand, watching to see if it would try anything else since its first attempt had failed. It was odd to be so afraid of an appendage, less so when it was nearly the size of a house. It looked like a giant's hand, if that giant was submerged under the ground and was trying to claw its way out.

There was a stillness to the night, the insects silent as if they too recognized how unnatural this thing was.

The power animating the hand felt dark and ominous. Its presence skating along the nerves as it whispered of death.

A countless number of green lines the color of plants ran from the hand into the dark surrounding it. They wound around and through it, like a puppet master's string, controlling each flex of the fingers and swipe of the palm.

"Someone's controlling it," I noted.

Liam nodded. "I know."

Which meant our true enemies hadn't even revealed themselves yet.

Bright flares of that same green, wound with small strings the rich dark brown of freshly turned dirt, appeared in the ground surrounding the hand.

I backed away, tugging Caroline and Brax with me. "Multiple hostiles incoming."

Seconds later, blobs appeared from the ground, dirt falling away to reveal skeletal forms made of rock and wood, their "tissue" that of mud and leaves.

Around them a whip of green flame searched across the ground, its movements sinuous and questing as if hunting for prey.

I edged further back, not wanting that thing to touch me. It gave off a sense of wrongness. I sensed it wouldn't mean good things if it caught hold of any of us.

"Golems," Liam spat.

Many of them. I counted at least fifteen.

"Damn it, I hate those things," Nathan complained.

"Can they be killed?" I asked, even knowing it was a pointless question.

"Anything with form can be destroyed," Liam said grimly.

True, but not always easily or efficiently.

"The problem isn't killing them; it's keeping the golem from re-assembling," Nathan explained.

The golems rushed forward, their hunched forms remaining on all fours in a loping gait as they surged out of the ravine.

"Run," Liam barked.

I didn't wait to be told twice, half carrying Brax with me as I raced away. A dry rattling sound followed us, like dead sticks being slammed together.

I didn't turn around.

Liam and Nathan brought up the rear, guarding our backs as we moved.

Even as I strained for every scrap of speed in me, Caroline doing the same at my side, I knew it wasn't going to be enough.

The golems were too fast, their odd skittering movements eating up the ground, and we were too slow. Even if Brax had been able to run on his own, I doubted we would have been fast enough.

They were playing with us, veering close and then falling away.

Liam punched through the chest of one as it leapt for the three of us. His hand emerged on the other side. The huge hole in its middle didn't seem to bother it as it writhed and wiggled, trying to tug itself closer.

Liam grabbed its torso with his other hand, ripping it in two. It crumbled into so much dirt, the flame at its center winking out.

Nathan was similarly occupied on the other side of us, this time with two golems that had started to merge into one, like some weird variation on a Siamese twin. Only the head of one had disappeared, leaving the main torso with too many arms and legs in an awkward amalgam of the two.

"I need to change," Caroline said, fear in her voice.

Any effects from the alcohol and fairy tears were gone, leaving both of us stone-cold sober.

"No time," Brax grunted beside me. "They'll be on you before you complete your shift. They'll rip you apart while you're vulnerable."

Frustration was evident in his voice as he kept up a staggering run beside us, using his injured leg in a way that would have caused permanent damage in a human. It should have been impossible, but I knew firsthand the stubborn persistence even humans could draw out of themselves when they felt their life was in danger. I'd seen soldiers on the battlefield force themselves to walk to safety after being wounded, so their battle buddies didn't have place their lives in danger to rescue them.

For Brax, it would be worse, with his wolf demanding to shift so it could heal him and defend them from threats.

That he remained relatively human, fur dotting his arms and his eyes the ice blue of his wolf, was a miracle and a testament to his iron will.

"We're not far from Lou's Bar. If we can make it, my wolves can help," he grunted.

Close was a relative term. I'd been to Lou's several times before, sometimes welcomed, sometimes to stir the pot.

Nathan had turned toward the bar's neighborhood after we'd left the Blue Pickle. As the crow flies, we were maybe just under a mile away. Not too far for a vampire and werewolf. But it would mean going back the way we'd come through the golem creatures. Something I doubted any of us wanted to do.

I looked back as Liam shouted something in Gaelic, his face creased in a slight smile as he tossed one golem like a bowling ball at its brethren. Nathan tore the head off his own golem before using it to bludgeon another.

"They look like they're having fun," I remarked, tightening my grip on Brax.

"I may be a wolf in truth, but Liam was once known as the Black Wolf of the Galway," Brax said as we moved. "He was a war leader, fierce and said to have once eaten the heart of a wolf to consume its power, strength and cunning. The civilized man he presents is just a mask. At his core, he's a killer."

I could see that. He seemed perfectly at home disassembling the golems as they tried to swarm past him, breaking them with sharp blows before tossing them away like broken dolls.

Still, he and Nathan were only two people. Each time they took apart one golem, two more rose in its place.

We needed to limit the avenue of attack until help could reach us. I knew just the spot.

"I have an idea," I said, before leading Brax and Caroline in the opposite direction of his bar.

The three of us limped across a yard and onto another street, Nathan and Liam battling at our rear.

The sound of pebbles skating down a roof next to us drew my attention.

A golem perched there, crouching to leap. He sailed through the air. With a nasty snarl, Caroline leapt to meet him.

She grabbed him by the throat, the tips of her fingernails hardening into claws. She raked them down his face, snarling the entire time.

The golem kept coming, the little flame of power flickering merrily.

"His chest, Caroline," I called. "Destroy his chest."

She listened, plunging her arm in up to her elbow and yanking her fist out. The golem crumpled into dirt in her hand.

She met my gaze with wide eyes, holding her fist out to me. She opened it to reveal a pea sized stone, one that lit up my othersight with the same flame I'd seen in the golem.

That's how they were animating these things.

"Don't let it touch the dirt," I warned.

She nodded and pocketed it, not arguing with me.

"We're not far now," I told her, adjusting Brax's arm over my shoulder.

Liam and Nathan had nearly caught up to us by this point, some of the golems keeping them occupied as the rest spilled around them and headed for us.

"Aileen," Caroline warned.

"I see them. We're almost there."

We cut through the yard, emerging onto the next street. Hector's bridge was a dull shadow in the distance. There were no streetlights on this street or next to the small ravine. The only light was what was provided by the houses.

I pulled Brax along with me, heading for the bridge. We stumbled onto it and I lowered Brax down, setting him against the stone side.

"This is your plan," Caroline asked, gesturing at the bridge. "Aileen, we're surrounded by dirt."

I ignored her, running to the bridge's side and peering down into the darkness. "Hector, look alive, buddy. You've got company."

Liam and Nathan pelted out of the dark, their skin almost glowing white as they streaked toward us. They slid to a stop on the bridge, Liam's gaze appraising as he took it in.

"A bridge. You're hoping a troll is under it," he said in realization.

"I know there's a troll under it," I told him.

He inclined his head. "If you're right, they're notoriously protective of those who use their bridge and even more difficult to kill."

Just what I was thinking too.

He gave me a seductive smile. "Very smart."

"I have my moments," I told him.

The golems appeared at the end of the bridge, their makeshift forms shedding dirt and forest debris. It fell off them in clumps. Whatever magic had kept them animated was fading, but not fast enough.

"Caroline, howl," I ordered, not taking my eyes off the golems or the snaking lines stretching out behind them.

The golems' creator wasn't far, I'd wager. They thought they sensed the end to the hunt, that we were tired and weak, defeated and ready for the kill.

A haunting sound lifted to the sky as Caroline tipped her head back. It was the call of the wild, a cry for help from one who was pack. If any of Brax's people heard it, they'd come.

The golems inched onto the bridge, their eyeless faces turned toward us as if they could see. One jumped up onto the railing and skittered across it towards us.

"Any time now," Nathan said, his body going tense as the golems advanced.

They were twenty feet away, now ten.

"Where is the troll?" Liam asked, his voice tight.

I shook my head. The golems were on the bridge by now. Hector should have reacted. I ran to the side of the bridge and looked down. Come on, big guy. Where are you?

"We're going to have to run," Liam ordered. "Aileen, take Brax and Caroline. Nathan and I will try to hold them off."

I didn't listen, too busy staring down into the dark. The flash of white fur and antlers caught my eye just as the stag moved out of sight. There was a low snort from under the bridge.

This was the second time the stag had made himself known to me in one night. It meant something. I just had to figure out what.

"I'll be right back," I called to Liam. I didn't wait for a response, ignoring his order to stop as I threw my leg over the railing and jumped.

I landed with a grunt. The bridge wasn't high off the ground and I made jumps higher than that every day, but the abuse my body had taken earlier was making itself known.

I turned to look under the bridge and froze.

I'd been right. The stag had wanted my attention. He stood on Hector's chest, dwarfed by my friend's considerable size. Hector's large body was curled into a ball, his head nearly bumping against the supports of the bridge above him. I'd never seen all of him before. Just an occasional hand or part of his head. He was even bigger than I'd imagined.

I didn't know how he could live under this small bridge. He must be more than ten feet tall and was almost as wide as he was tall.

That wasn't what surprised me, however. The stag stomped his foot and snorted, tossing his head at a cocoon the color of moonlight, shimmering with an opalescent sheen. A large butterfly, the size of a small child, with insubstantial wings of white fluttered on Hector's face.

I realized with a start that its mouth was in the shape of a long tube and it was feeding on Hector. With every flutter of its wings, Hector's breath grew more and more shallow while the rock-grey color of his skin got paler until it was close to a chalky greyish-white.

The unmistakable sounds of fighting came from above me. The

distinctive growl of Caroline's wolf told me she'd found time to transform.

There were several thumps behind me as golems dropped off the bridge. I'd hoped Liam and the rest would keep them occupied for a while. No such luck.

More and more golems fell, like muddy rain from the sky. How were there so many? There hadn't been that many before.

When I looked back, the stag was gone but his message was clear. I needed to get the butterfly creature away from Hector if I wanted my friend's help.

I didn't waste time thinking, darting toward Hector. I could consider how the damn golems had multiplied later. For now, I needed to get my friend upright and lucid.

First order of business was that butterfly. I had a feeling it was the biggest reason for Hector's apparent coma.

I grabbed a rock and tossed it at the butterfly, watching in disbelief as it sailed through the insect's form as if the butterfly was as substantial as air.

Shit. Not good.

If it wasn't really there, my job had just gotten a lot more difficult. I had about three seconds to figure out how to free Hector from the creature's influence before the golems permanently solved all my problems for me.

I grabbed onto a piece of Hector's trousers, using it to leverage myself onto his reclining body. I scrambled up his massive leg and onto his chest as the golems rushed forward.

I did my best to avoid any of the white strands of the cocoon as I climbed higher. I wasn't sure if they would affect me, but I wasn't taking any chances. The last thing I wanted was to become immobilized while the golems tore me apart.

Panic gripped me as one of the golems leapt, catching hold of a foot. I kicked back with the other foot, knocking it away. He slipped off, taking one of my shoes with him.

More and more of them spilled over the edge of the bridge.

There wasn't a lot of time.

The golems milled in front of Hector, seeming unsure what to do. I didn't know why the rest hadn't followed me up here, but I was grateful for the reprieve and space to think.

I reached down and grabbed some of the strands, swearing as they slipped through my hands.

Except one. That one lifted from Hector, snapping out to wrap around my wrist. I fell to my knees, my eyes suddenly heavier than they'd ever been. Even the sun had never made me feel like this, as if staying awake a single moment longer would kill me.

Still, I resisted, knowing if I collapsed now, I was done for. Worse, my friends above would be left to deal with the fallout from my brilliant plan.

I propped myself up with my other hand, my head bowing as I struggled to stay awake.

I touched the strands softly. They shimmered in my othersight. The disconnect between what I felt and what I saw was disconcerting. Just when I thought I'd gotten used to the oddness of seeing a world that no one else could, things like this happened.

I concentrated on feeling the strands. Carefully I plucked at them, willing them to shift, just a bit.

I looked deeper into their soft glow. Ah, there. In the deepest part of them was a small spark, one that I could feel as well as see. I gently grasped it, pulling with my mind as well as my body.

It was like watching a skein of wool caught on the smallest of splinters. Snag it and pull on it enough and eventually it'll ruin the whole pattern you're trying to make, turning it into a snarled, fuzzy mess.

That was what I concentrated on doing. Pulling on it until it barely resembled the pattern of before.

A few golems had gotten over whatever fear had kept them from following me, creeping onto Hector with small, awkward leaps.

More. Just a little more.

One of the golems landed beside me, its twig-like hands reaching for me.

I wrenched hard, feeling my mind protest. The skein fell apart, the butterfly dissolving into nothingness and taking its cocoon with it.

Out of the deep abyss, a small spark raced, gathering speed and mass. I fought to get away, knowing when it hit it would feel like a freight train. The light of its magic was searing in its intensity, burning the shape of the stag into my eyeballs.

Hector rolled, unseating me and freeing me from the spell's clutches. I tumbled onto his lap as a groan rumbled from his chest.

A large hand came up, slapping the golem to him and turning it into a brown stain. Hector's head lifted and he looked down at me with groggy eyes.

"Aileen, what are you doing here?" he rumbled.

I gave him a loopy smile. "Thought you could use a wake-up from your nap."

He glanced around with a furrowed brow. On a bridge troll, a frown was the stuff of nightmares. It was an expression that said you were about to be pounded as flat as a fly on a windshield.

His mouth dropped open at the sight of the golems that were trying to climb up his leg.

"I could use a little help," I told him, falling sideways, suddenly too exhausted to support my own weight. My wrist throbbed sharply, reminding me that I hadn't come through the car crash entirely unharmed.

One of his big paws caught me, preventing me from rolling off him. He set me behind him, as if the golems attacking were no more than irritating bugs to him.

"Stay there," he told me.

I gave him a thumbs-up with my good hand, keeping the injured wrist tucked in close. Staying put wasn't going to be a problem.

I watched, as ducking under the supports of the bridge, Hector focused on the golems.

He lifted one foot, stomping hard and crushing several of the creatures. He reached down, sweeping several of them up before tossing them towards the small creek that ran under the bridge.

After that, Hector kicked and stomped his way through the golems, never once flinching as they tried to attack him en masse. His large rocky body eclipsed the bridge as he swung with abandon, seemingly happy, if the chortles coming from him were anything to judge by.

Furry streaks poured from the road above—Brax's wolves finally joining the fight. They attacked those golems who tried to scurry around Hector's feet, dispatching them with violent pounces and vicious shakes of the head.

Hector grabbed one golem in a meaty paw before body-slamming it into the ground, leaving nothing behind but a wet, muddy smear. I'd like to see the thing regenerate from that.

Liam and Nathan waited until the remaining golems were dispatched and Hector had moved away before dropping from above then moving toward me with powerful strides. I remained where I was, exhausted, in pain, and still slightly drunk.

This was not how I pictured my evening ending.

CHAPTER SEVEN

My head felt like a marching band was performing on it. I curled up into a ball, pulling a cover over my head as I tried to reclaim the slumber that had been mine until just a few seconds ago.

My mouth tasted like a cross between sawdust and a football player's gym bag.

Everything ached. My body, my teeth, my eyes. Even my hair.

I just wanted the world to go away and come back later. A ringing under my bed told me that wasn't going to happen.

I groaned and burrowed deeper under my blanket. Hangovers. The bane of my existence. I could strangle yesterday's Aileen for the poor life decisions she'd made.

Never again, I told myself, just as I'd done many times when I'd been human. Never again was I going to let myself get into this state.

The phone stopped ringing and I relaxed once again into the comfortable bed. Perhaps I could go back to sleep and not think on this until I felt halfway normal again.

The phone started ringing again.

With a muffled curse, I flopped to the side of the bed, feeling like a beached whale as I felt around under it for my phone. My hands touched a pair of pants. One eye cracked open. My pants.

I pulled them up onto the bed and under the covers with me, searching through the pockets for the ringing box of destruction.

I hit the answer button without checking to see who was calling. "Hello."

At least that's what I meant to mutter, instead what came out was a garbled bit of nonsense.

"Where are you?" Caroline asked.

My eyes were still closed and I made a grunting sound. "I'm at home. Where any good vampire belongs after last night."

"No, you're not. I'm standing in your apartment and you're not here. Are you aware that you have no stairs?"

I lifted my head, my eyes finally opening all the way as I processed that statement.

"Yes, and what are you doing in my apartment?" I asked.

I tugged back the covers and took a look around the room. It was not mine. Not the room, or this bed, or these sheets. I should have known. My pillow was nowhere near this comfortable, and my sheets were nice, but they weren't this kind of nice—the kind of nice indicating you had more money than you knew what to do with, so you bought Egyptian cotton sheets.

"I wanted to check on you after last night. Your roommates let me in," Caroline said.

I blinked, not knowing how to interpret that statement.

"Now, where are you?" she asked.

I looked around at the nice room, one I knew I'd never been in before. "I'm not entirely sure."

Except for my pants, I was still fully clothed. A fact I was grateful for.

"What can you tell me about the end of the night?" I asked.

My memory of things got kind of blurry after Hector woke up. I wasn't entirely sure what had happened after that, or how I'd come to end up here—wherever I was.

"The bridge troll helped dispatch most of the golems and then the pack arrived to take care of the rest." Caroline was silent a moment. "Liam and Nathan grabbed you. They didn't stick around to answer questions. Just hopped in a black Escalade when it pulled up."

Ah, that probably explained my location.

We weren't in the Gargoyle, the vampire master's mansion in downtown Columbus that acted as the hub for Liam's enforcers and Thomas's main advisers. It was both their home and workplace.

This had to be Liam's house, the one he'd bought.

I swung my feet to the ground and stood with all the confidence of a hundred-year-old woman. I shivered and shook as I made my way across the room, heading for the bathroom. Why did I feel this bad? It was worse than any hangover I'd ever experienced. Considering I shouldn't even be able to get hangovers any more, I wasn't happy about this.

Note to self—never drink Dahlia's concoctions without first asking what it was in them.

"How are you so damn chipper after last night?" I asked, still groggy.

"My alcohol tolerance has always been better than yours." Caroline's voice was filled with a ridiculous amount of cheeriness.

This was true. Mine had always been hideously low. Two or three drinks was enough to make me feel like the world was an awful place the next day. Five or six, and it left me wishing the world would end in fiery destruction.

Being a vampire obviously hadn't changed things any.

A thought occurred to me. "How's Brax?"

I sensed rather than saw Caroline's shrug. "He'll survive, though I'm sure I'll get an earful when he catches up to me again."

That reminded me of my own troublesome male.

"Can you do me a favor and start researching the Wild Hunt for me?" I asked.

"That shouldn't be too hard," she said.

"Oh, and find me everything you can about golems," I told her. I knew a little but my memory was spotty.

"On it," she said.

"Good, I'll check in with you later. For now, I've got to go."

"Wait! What about—"

I hung up before Caroline could finish her sentence. Now that I was awake, truly awake, in a way that meant I wasn't going back to bed anytime soon, it meant I had to figure a few things out.

I grimaced in distaste at the sight of muddy streaks on my legs and arms. The smell of golem clung to me, offending me on a deep level.

Whatever surprises this night held for me, I would face them after I was clean.

One long, hot shower later and clad in clothes I'd found in a dresser by the door, I headed downstairs. I felt semi-normal again, except for the pounding headache, and the overall lethargy and lack of energy that usually characterized my old nights out.

My suspicion earlier turned out to be correct. This was Liam's house. That was the same entryway I'd lingered in and the sitting room Liam had shown me to.

The house had a warm and welcoming charm that invited you to linger. It encouraged you to curl up on one of the window seats with a good book as you watched the weather outside. It wasn't what I expect from the head vamp enforcer.

Seeing no one around, I headed toward the back of the house, slowing at the sight of Liam. He looked pensive, sitting in an armchair gazing out the window of his study with a frown of concentration.

I didn't know what was bothering him, but a small part of me wanted to smooth the deep furrow on his forehead.

I resisted, and instead leaned my shoulder against the doorframe and waited.

He didn't immediately acknowledge me. Not that he didn't know I was there. It would have been impossible to sneak up on him. No, he was just playing vamp dominance games.

I decided to indulge him. I kind of owed it to him for last night.

Together we stared out the window for several minutes, neither of us speaking.

"How are you feeling this evening?" Liam finally asked, not turning from the window. There was no indication of his thoughts.

"Like death warmed over," I said, not bothering to hide the extent of how awful I felt. I'm sure I looked even worse.

His lips quirked and he finally looked over at me. "Fairy tears can do that to you."

I shifted, the faintest bit uncomfortable. I cleared my throat. "Guess I owe you a pretty big apology, huh?"

He lifted one eyebrow, faintly amused, an evil glint taking up residence in his eyes. "For what? Trying to seduce me on the dance floor or slapping me on the ass?"

Blood rushed to my face and I knew without looking I was blushing. Silently, I willed my body to stop. At the very least I didn't need to be wasting blood on such pointless things as blushing.

"Both. All of it," I said. If I could summon some magical vortex to whisk me away by route of the fires of hell, I would do it in a heartbeat.

I'd been an idiot from start to finish last night. Embarrassing myself in so many different ways. I hadn't often gotten drunk as a human—and never that drunk—not liking the loss of control and the way it often felt like someone else had taken over and thrown caution to the wind.

He flicked his fingers in dismissal of my apology. "Don't be. Had it been any other time, I might have joined you."

It was an easier absolution than I'd expected. I thought there would be lectures and rules and ultimatums. That there were none, threw me off-balance.

"I had Nathan retrieve your bike and return it to your apartment," Liam said when silence stretched between us.

I nodded my thanks. With everything that had gone on, I'd forgotten the bike.

"Were they after you or me?" I asked.

His face turned dour, the amusement of before draining away and leaving the hunter in its place. "I thought it was me, but given the way they followed you under the bridge, I can't be sure."

I let out a heavy sigh. More people trying to kill me. That was just great.

"What could have created those things?" I asked.

He shook his head. "Constructing golems of that caliber isn't hard. It would be easier to give you a list of who couldn't do that."

I shoved away from the doorframe and stepped into the room, taking a seat on the couch against one of the walls.

"You're friends with a bridge troll."

It wasn't quite a question. Liam stared at me in expectation.

I lifted one shoulder. "Of a sort. As much as you can be with a guy who never leaves his bridge."

"Bridge trolls are rather rare in this country," Liam said. "The American obsession with cars and metal make most bridges too full of iron and noise. How many other 'friends' do you have around the city?"

"Enough."

"Not so alone after all," he said with a tiny tilt to his lips.

"Guess not."

We fell back into a companionable silence.

Last night could have gone very differently for me if Liam and Nathan hadn't been there—if they hadn't bought us time to reach Hector and then kept some of the golems off me while I woke him.

I missed being part of a team, of knowing there were others out there to watch my back. I might have friends scattered around the city, some like Dahlia surprisingly powerful, but it was unlikely any of them would fight by my side.

"I'd like to take that job you were offering me, if it's still available," I finally said.

If I was the target, I'd need Liam's help to keep myself alive. That was clear. If it was something he was involved in, I still wanted to be part of this, if only because the bastards had nearly killed me yesterday. Either way, working together could only benefit me.

I found myself holding my breath as I waited for his response.

I was very aware that he might tell me to pack sand; that after my last refusal, he'd changed his mind and decided my help was unnecessary. Or that the attack last night might have shifted things.

Still, I'd rather try. So many times, people gave up before they got to the starting point, defeating themselves before they'd even begun.

His expression remained calm as arrogance settled on his face. "What brought on this change of heart? Not that I'm complaining."

I kept my snort to myself. Yeah, right. He'd probably use this opportunity to twist the knife if he could.

"Let's just say I take it rather personally when people try to kill me." I thought about it. "And I can use the money."

He tapped one finger on the arm of his chair, his thoughts hidden behind a calm expression as he considered me. "You'd have to stay here during the course of your employment."

I couldn't help my tiny flinch at that. I preferred to be surrounded by my own things, to retreat to my haven of safety every morning. It felt like I'd just gotten back into my place and now I was leaving it again.

"Fine." I gave him a strained smile.

"And you'd have to agree that I'm your boss," he said.

I nearly choked at that.

This was amusing him. The bastard.

"You'd have to obey all my orders." He gave me a smug smile and arched an eyebrow, knowing exactly what I would think of that.

I bit back my instinctive response and choked out, "Fine. Sounds good."

His laugh was husky. "Oh, this is going to be such fun."

My smile turned into more of a baring of teeth. Glad one of us thought so.

"When do we start?" I asked, forcing myself to a modicum of professionalism. After being in the military for nearly four years I'd dealt with officers who didn't know their ass from their head and NCOs on a power trip. I could deal with Liam ordering me around, even if he did make me want to ram my fist into his throat on occasion.

"Right now." He slid out of his seat, moving across the room in a lethal glide.

I levered myself out of the chair, following him.

"Nathan tells me your fighting skills have improved," he said in a silky voice. "I'd like to verify that fact for myself."

"Now?" I looked down at myself. I was wearing jeans and a simple shirt. Not exactly attire suitable for sparring.

"No time like the present."

I came to a stop, giving his back a look of extreme dislike. This was going to hurt me a lot more than it hurt him, I realized in resignation.

*

I concentrated on the man across from me, wanting to punch his pretty face so bad it was an itch beneath my skin.

He cocked an arrogant eyebrow at me, as if inviting me to try.

That urge shifted from an itch to a heated fire in my belly. Punching him in the face became my new life goal.

Not that I was likely to achieve it anytime soon.

Five minutes of sparring with him felt like an eternity. My breath heaved in and out as sweat dripped off me.

Even worse, in that five minutes I hadn't managed to touch him once. The same couldn't be said of him.

No, he'd danced across the grass, delivering blows with a careless precision when he wasn't using opportunities to sneak touches. A hand to my back. A touch to my shoulder or cheek. It was humiliating to be so outclassed he didn't even pretend to be working up a sweat.

Nathan and Eric watched from the sidelines.

"Is that all you've got?" Liam asked, his voice taunting.

I took a moment to catch my breath, knowing anger would just make me careless and lead to further humiliation.

"Just getting started," I told him.

Fighting, despite what many might think, was just as much about brains and strategy as it was strength and speed.

My opponent was ridiculously fast and frighteningly powerful. Sparring with him wasn't like sparring with Nathan, who while also faster and stronger than me, had nothing on Liam. Taking one of Liam's punches was like being hit with a sledgehammer. It made you want to curl up into a ball and slink away in defeat.

Liam gave me a dangerous smile. It was all the warning I got before he was right in front of me. I ducked away, sidestepping his arm, and throwing a feint, not putting my weight behind it as I followed it up with a blow from my other arm.

He caught my arm and yanked me past him, a touch gliding across the back of my neck. I kicked out behind me, not looking.

My foot glanced off his stomach and I heard a grunt. At least that was something.

I whirled, already putting my arms up to protect me from reprisal.

Liam moved with precision, no movements wasted. His muscles flexed as he sparred with me. It was a graceful dance on his part and a staggering embarrassment on mine as we swept across the grass.

His blows came faster and faster until it was all I could do to keep up with him, my breath sawing in and out of my lungs as I defended myself and evaded when I could, all the while watching for my chance.

There, a slight opening. I moved, realizing too late it was a trap.

Liam slid to the side, grabbing my outstretched arm and tugging it behind me, fitting his chest to my back.

"Your form has much improved since I last saw you," he said into my ear. "Though you are still holding back."

I sent my elbow hard into his stomach. A slight puff of air on my neck was the only sign that it had affected him.

He released me, his hands sliding away with the smallest of caresses.

I turned to face him and raised an eyebrow. "So, did I pass?"

He observed me with an inscrutable expression. "For now."

Well, that was something at least.

"Nathan, let's see what you've got," Liam said, looking away from me to where his enforcers watched.

Nathan grinned, his expression turning anticipatory.

I headed towards the side where Eric stood, meeting Nathan on my way. He patted me on the head. "Not a bad effort."

I snorted. "I don't know what fight you were watching."

He gave me a crooked smile. "Not many can touch Liam. He's one of the council's best enforcers for a reason. You did better than most vampires a century your senior."

I guess that was some comfort. Though not much. My inner competitor didn't like being beaten for any reason.

"Now step back and let a pro show you how it's done," Nathan said, the look in his eyes wild and happy. The prospect of fighting Liam excited him, his eyes taking on that slight glow all vampires got when they were excited.

"Are you going to talk all night or are you going to fight?" Liam asked, folding his arms across his chest and giving the two of us a smug smile.

That smile brought back the need to see him punched in the face.

"Kick his ass," I told Nathan, slapping him on the back before heading over to Eric.

I folded my arms and settled in to watch the sparring match.

Both men were preternaturally still, the only sound in the night that of insects and the wind rustling in the trees.

Nathan moved first, his body blurring as he darted across the grass. Liam's grin was bloodthirsty, exposing his fangs.

He held still until Nathan was almost on him, then he stepped to the side and moved. Several blows were exchanged, almost faster than I could process, neither man giving an inch.

The sharp slap of flesh on flesh filled the air and I winced, knowing how hard each man could hit.

Liam let out a laugh, right before Nathan sailed through the air, hitting the ground and rolling.

Liam sprinted toward him, his eyes avid as he drew his leg back to stomp the other enforcer into the ground. Nathan rolled out of the way, gaining his feet in a graceful move.

Liam showed no mercy, on him in the next second, a flurry of blows raining down, his face focused and intent.

It was a startling contrast to my fight. Neither man was holding back, both going full-out. It was a sobering display, showing just how weak I was in terms of physical strength and speed when compared to them.

"Both are in good form," Eric said, his voice soft.

I glanced at the other enforcer.

"Though, Liam will win within the next few seconds," he said almost as an afterthought.

Sure enough, Liam grabbed Nathan's arm and used it to throw him. Nathan hit the ground with a grunt, Liam's knee coming down on this throat in the next second. Nathan slapped the ground to tap out.

Liam stood and helped his friend to his feet.

"You were a little enthusiastic there at the end, don't you think?"

Nathan said, rubbing his throat.

"You've gotten lazy," Liam said. "Perhaps you shouldn't hold back quite so much when training Aileen."

I blinked and stiffened at the mention of my name.

Nathan paused, his expression turning thoughtful.

Liam moved away, meeting my irate gaze with a hint of smugness. I rolled my eyes. Yes, yes, he was very strong and manly. Unmatched in a fight. I got the point.

"Come, you haven't had anything to eat tonight. We can take care of that while we discuss what I need from you," he said, his feet whispering across the grass.

I followed reluctantly, already beginning to regret our agreement. Vampires. Their sneaky machinations knew no bounds.

The kitchen was surprisingly updated, given the fact Liam had no need of one. Most vampires, I'd learned, didn't eat food despite the ability. I was one of the few who still clung to its comfort.

He headed for the fridge, opening it and grabbing a wine bottle.

I lingered by the doorway of the kitchen, mentally bracing myself. I didn't want to embarrass myself by throwing up the blood Liam gave me. I already knew that if I tried to avoid drinking blood, he'd force the issue.

I resigned myself to the upset stomach and cramps I knew were in my immediate future as he poured blood into a glass.

"You're not drinking?" I asked.

"I already met my needs for the night," he told me, his piercing blue eyes coming up to meet mine in a challenging stare.

I firmly squelched the spark of jealousy that threatened to upset my mood. There was nothing between Liam and myself aside from a few kisses resulting from an overpowering blood lust on my part. That's it.

He could find sustenance from whoever he wanted. Both Nathan and he had assured me feeding didn't require passion— it could be no more personal than a visit to the doctor's office to have blood drawn. Still, I knew from my stay in the mansion that some vampires preferred a little sex with their blood.

I'd never been able to bring myself to ask whether Liam was one of those.

"How nice for you," I said, grabbing the glass and lifting it to my mouth. The stench of rotted meat wafted up to me.

I tilted the glass up, draining it in seconds. As soon as it hit my tongue and coated my throat, I had to fight the urge to choke, forcing it down through sheer stubbornness.

The glass empty, I scrubbed my hand across my mouth, wishing I could scrub my tongue at the same time.

"Mm, mm, delicious," I said. I breathed through my nose, hoping doing so would help keep it down.

"Is that so?" he asked, arching an eyebrow, a watchful look on his face.

I gave him a fierce smile even as my stomach turned fretfully. "Yup."

He poured another glass and slid it toward me. "In that case, you wouldn't mind drinking another."

I stared at the glass, feeling something like horror slide through me. There was no way I could drink that, not without losing the battle with my stomach.

"Not necessary," I forced myself to reply calmly. "This should be more than enough."

Nathan and Eric entered the kitchen behind us, their voices quieting once they got a look at the standoff taking place between the two of us.

"I disagree," Liam said, his voice equally calm even as a storm gathered in his eyes. "You need to replace your reserves from last night."

This asshole knew, I realized. He knew how blood was beginning to affect me; knew it and was forcing me into a situation where I'd have to admit it.

My head spun toward Nathan. Had he been the one to tattle? The slight confusion in his expression told me he didn't quite understand what was going on.

Nope, not happening.

I pushed the glass back toward him. "I'm full. Maybe later."

His fangs glinted in his sharp smile as he pushed the glass back toward me. "I insist, and as your boss, you have to listen. Or did you forget the agreement we made earlier tonight."

Son of a—he wouldn't. His deadly smile said he would. He'd take pleasure in snatching this job away from me, and knowing him, he'd stick me in the mansion and have Thomas sit on me until they'd dealt with whatever this was.

"Fine," I snapped, grabbing the glass.

I could do this. Mind over matter. One little glass of blood wasn't going to bring me down. I'd done much harder stuff than this in my life.

I only made it half-way through the glass before I choked, setting the glass down hard on the marble countertop. My mouth filled with salty saliva and my stomach began to cramp as I held myself still, praying this would pass.

It heaved. Nope, it wasn't going to pass.

I lunged past Liam for the sink. Everything I'd just downed came right back up, my stomach twisting and knotting as it forced the blood out.

Cool hands touched the sides of my face, lifting my hair away. Liam rubbed a soothing pattern on my back.

There were exclamations behind me over the sound of my throwing up.

"I didn't know," Nathan said, sounding horrified. "I've seen her drink before. I knew she was having trouble but not to this extent."

"We'll discuss this later," Liam told him. His voice held an undercurrent of steel, an indication he wasn't happy with his enforcer.

When my heaves had abated, but my stomach was still a twisting mass of pain, Liam handed me a wet napkin.

"You have got to be one of the most stubborn women I've ever met," he said. It did not sound like a compliment.

I wiped my mouth, then gratefully took the glass of water he gave me, swishing it around in my mouth before spitting it out.

A toothbrush with toothpaste already on it appeared in front of me. Seemed like he had thought of everything.

By the time I finished brushing my teeth, I was shaking, my muscles acting like they'd run a ten-mile race rather than just three feet to the sink.

I slid down, not even bothering to pretend I had strength.

"How did you know?" I asked, resting my hot cheek on the cool floor.

He crouched beside me, before sitting and gently drawing my head into his lap. I wasn't in any shape to resist, his strokes along my hairline and neck lulling me into complacency.

"There are only a few reasons to lose as much weight as you have," he said.

I shut my eyes. Of course.

"I've also been expecting it."

I turned to look up at him. He gazed down at me, his face cruelly beautiful. In another time and place, I would have been happy to stare at him forever.

"There is a vital nutrient that is nearly impossible to get, except from a live donor," he told me. "You made it longer than most, but this is inevitable. You're fighting against biology. The odds aren't in your favor."

"The catalyst was your blood," I told him.

He inclined his chin. "I suspect it was. You were able to exist on the bagged stuff as long as you did because you had no access to a master's blood. It meant there was nothing keeping your transformation going. Tasting my blood and then Thomas's jump-started the process again."

"So, this is your fault," I said, closing my eyes.

His touch hesitated. "In a way. You would have arrived at this point sooner or later, regardless."

A particularly nasty cramp had me curling onto my side. Liam's hands steadied me.

When it had passed, I panted and said, "I take it this means you're going to make me drink from a human."

"We're past that point," Liam responded. "You need a master's blood now."

Alarm distracted me momentarily from my pain. Not his. "I'll try

Nathan or Eric."

Not Liam.

Together, we were too combustible.

He gave me a look that was seductive and arrogant even when viewed from upside down. "You can try, but neither of them possesses the nutrients you need."

I snorted. Arrogant man.

His smile widened. "You're welcome to test it out, sweetheart. Of course, when it doesn't work I'll have to send you to Thomas so he can keep you out of harm's way while the rest of us work this case."

My eyes widened as my mouth fell open.

"I need people who are in top shape," he told me. "My blood is the most potent here. Maybe if you hadn't just downed two glasses of blood, you might have been able to get by on theirs. As it stands, mine is the only one that will help." He gave me a wink. "Don't worry, I'll be a perfect gentleman. I promise not to ravish you while you're drinking."

"Son of a bitch, you planned this," I breathed.

He dropped a kiss on my lips and moved me off his lap. "Don't dawdle now, I have a lot to accomplish tonight."

CHAPTER EIGHT

He sauntered out of the room, leaving me sitting on the floor fuming at my situation and his ultimatum.

I clambered to my feet, still slightly unsteady and followed him. There weren't a lot of options. His threat wasn't an idle one. I knew if I refused, he'd do exactly as he'd warned and deliver me to Thomas. My reasons for taking the job hadn't changed, even if I hated how circumstances had evolved.

I tracked Liam down to a bedroom on the upper floor.

"Why couldn't we have done this in the kitchen?" I asked. Or anywhere other than a bedroom.

I didn't trust myself. That was the sad truth. Liam's blood was like catnip to me. It stripped away any inhibitions and reduced me to my base desires. In my head, I might know all the reasons it was bad to get involved with Liam, but throw blood into the mix and I forgot myself.

"Because, I'd like to be comfortable for this and sitting on a hard floor is counterintuitive to that," he said in a dry voice.

I frowned at him, even as I knew his words made sense.

He reclined on the bed and held one autocratic hand out to me. "Come, let's get this over with. I promise not to bite."

Because I'd be the one doing the biting.

With reluctance I advanced to the bed and stood beside it, staring down, not really sure what to do with myself.

Liam lifted his chin, baring his throat.

"Nice try, but if we're going to do this, I'll be taking blood from the wrist," I told him.

"Have it your way," he told me.

I narrowed my eyes at him. He was enjoying this. A lot.

He held out his wrist to me. I took it and then hesitated. Biting from this angle would be awkward. It would be better to sit beside him on the bed with my back towards him.

He watched me with half-lidded eyes as I moved around. "You're stalling."

"I'm getting comfortable," I muttered.

"You're—"

I bit down before he could finish that thought. A muffled groan was my reward. Stalling, my ass, I thought.

The blood hit my tongue and all my sense of gloating fell away. Decadence with a hint of chocolate swept me up. Energy filled me almost to bursting.

There was no comparison between this and what I'd drunk in the kitchen. This was life, pure and sparkling, snapping and crackling on my tongue as I gulped it down.

It was fire and lightning. Wicked heat that ignited every nerve in my body.

Liam wasn't the only one moaning now. It was hard to remember anything with this stuff coursing through my body. I wanted it all. I wanted to climb inside him and never come out.

He curled his arm, pulling me back against his chest, crooning in a different language as I fed from his wrist.

Distantly, I felt the unmistakable sign of his desire against my ass. I wiggled against him, gratified when he hissed out an oath.

Need rose up, potent and almost all-consuming. I resisted the urge to turn in his arms and lose myself to this desire.

My mouth popped free and I sucked down breaths as I shivered, the feel of his blood and the raw desire for his body almost too much to bear.

Liam's arms were wrapped around me, his body pressed tight against my back, one leg pressed between mine. We were on our sides in the bed.

I started to move and his arms tightened.

"Not yet. Give me a moment," he rasped.

I settled back, secretly enjoying the weight of him against me, his cool heat against my back.

"You're going to be the death of me, *acushla*," he said.

His arms slackened. Even then it was an effort to force myself up and out of the bed. My legs didn't want to support my weight and the rest of me wanted to crawl back in bed and find a better use for my night.

Liam sighed behind me. "One day, *acushla*."

"Not in this lifetime, Liam," I said with a bravado I didn't necessarily feel.

He chuckled, not sounding the least bit disturbed by my rejection. "Then it is good we have many lifetimes."

"How many of these feedings do I have to go through?" I asked, turning my attention to other matters.

He snuggled back into the bed, his arms clasped behind his head, showing off their well-defined muscles. "Many."

I paused and narrowed my eyes on him. He wouldn't draw this out just to make me feel uncomfortable, would he?

"I assume any master vampire would do," I said slowly, prodding him.

His eyes flashed and he gave me a wicked grin. "I'm sure."

My shoulders relaxed.

"You could always go to Thomas for blood."

I stiffened. "There are other masters in the city."

His nod was slow. "There are, and you would have to join their clan before they'd open a vein for you."

His expression said checkmate. He had me and he knew it. Thomas wasn't an option for so many reasons. Similarly, I was unlikely to agree to joining a clan, which left me with Liam. Damn it.

He jackknifed out of the bed, brushing past me, his hand coming to my waist briefly.

"So, how many feedings will I need to endure?" I asked, following him out of the bedroom.

"As many as I deem necessary."

I stopped before chasing after him. That could mean a lot of things and I didn't trust him not to take advantage of the situation by stretching these feedings out.

"What if I refuse?" I asked.

Liam stopped, his broad back stiff before he spun, aggressively stepping into my space. I held firm, though it was difficult considering the furious expression on his face.

"Your body will continue to cannibalize itself until you lose who you once were and become a danger to everyone and everything around you. At which point they will call me to put you down like a rabid dog." Curling his lip, he snarled as he backed me into the wall. "I will not allow you to put me in such a position."

I nodded. "Got it."

He remained still, examining me, searching for any hint of subterfuge. For once, there wasn't any. Not just because of the grim picture he'd painted, but because he'd given me a glimpse of his emotions. There were feelings there.

Strong ones, if his reaction to my question was any indicator.

He straightened and continued down the hall as if the moment had never happened.

I let him have that, willing to pretend none of this was happening. That my life hadn't careened wildly out of control. Again.

"There were at least two, probably three or four people responsible for last night," I said.

"Why do you say that?"

I thought about it. Telling him it was just a feeling probably wouldn't instill a lot of confidence in my skills.

"The colors were all tangled," I finally said, struggling to put into words something I just knew on an instinctual level. "From what I know of animating and controlling several constructs, it would be extremely difficult to direct that many golems unless the person was packing some serious juice."

And we would have known if there was anyone like that in town.

Three golems, maybe five, but nearly thirty? I doubted there was anyone local capable of such a feat.

"Also, Hector wasn't just sleeping. He was kept in a state of stasis while some type of white butterfly fed from him. It was totally different from whatever created the golems." Whoever had done that to Hector was seriously powerful. As Fae, Hector would have had his own innate defenses against such magic. The fact they had overpowered him, signified we were dealing with a major power.

"I agree," Liam said simply.

I stopped, frowning at his back. If he agreed, why did I have to explain all that?

"You have good instincts, but you also need to know why something feels the way it does," he said in explanation. "Magic is tricky. It's half-instinct, half-experience. You need to be able to distinguish between the two in order to use your ability to its full potential."

He didn't wait for my response, striding into the living room where Nathan sat on the couch flicking through TV channels and Eric stood with his back to us, staring out into the dark.

"Any news?" Liam asked.

Nathan straightened. "Thomas called, the High Fae arrived last night."

"I'd hoped to have more time to prepare, but this isn't entirely unexpected," Liam said.

"Why is it important that they've arrived?" I asked, looking between the three.

Dahlia had implied last night that the vampires weren't happy about the High Fae's visit, but I couldn't see why. Thomas had never shown any particular desire to ban any of the spooks from the city, much less an entire species.

There were Fae all over the city. Granted, they were the minor Fae, most not powers in their own right.

"The High Fae can be difficult." Liam chose his words carefully.

Nathan scoffed. "That's one way to put it. They're xenophobic assholes."

"This world tends to be hard on them," Eric said, his voice a quiet rumble. "The amount of iron and human technology messes with their magic."

"Then why are they coming here?" I asked.

"We don't know," Liam answered, his face grim.

They were worried, I realized. All of them. Whoever these High Fae were, they were dangerous enough to make even the vampires concerned. That, more than anything, told me how much I didn't want them in my city.

I frowned thoughtfully. "Dahlia seemed to think they might be trying to establish a barrow here."

The three of them traded looks at the news.

"How good is her information?" Eric asked.

"She's my go-to person for gossip," I said. "A lot of information runs through her bar and she hears all of it."

If she said they were trying to establish a barrow, I was inclined to believe her.

"What's the game plan, boss?" Nathan asked.

Liam was quiet, his forehead creased in thought. I remained on the edge of the group, watching and waiting.

"I want you and Eric to head back to the Gargoyle and watch over Thomas," Liam said. "They'll eventually need to meet with him to formally declare their intent."

"What about you?" Nathan asked.

"Aileen and I are going to visit a friend of hers," Liam said.

Nathan cocked his head. He looked like he wanted to protest as he shot me a glance devoid of his normal friendliness.

"You can't go alone," Nathan said. "You need one of us at your back."

I tried to keep from feeling insulted. I wasn't a big fat zero. I might not be as powerful as the others, but I'd shown on more than one occasion I could hold my own.

"I'll be fine. I need both of you with Thomas. Keep your eyes peeled." The tone of Liam's voice dissuaded any further discussion.

Irritation flickered on Nathan's face. There, and gone in an instant. I probably wouldn't have noticed if not for the amount of time I'd been spending with him lately. Whatever emotion it was, it was quickly masked, and I couldn't be sure of what I'd seen.

His expression changing like quicksilver, Nathan resumed his easygoing smile, replacing the faint awkwardness of moments before.

He sat back, his arms coming up to rest against the couch back. "Since you've stuck us with the unpleasant task, what will you two lovebirds be up to?"

There was a bit of insinuation there I didn't like. I narrowed my eyes at him and frowned. He wasn't acting like the Nathan I knew.

"We have business to take care of from last night." Liam's voice was crisp, the dismissal clear.

Eric stirred at the window. "We'll keep you updated on our progress."

Nathan betrayed only the faintest bit of reluctance as he stood and strode from the room, not looking at either of us.

Liam waited until both men had left the house, and their car had started before he turned to me. "Is there something you'd like to tell me about the relationship between you and my enforcer?"

I blinked dumbly at him, not understanding the question for a long moment. When I did, rage boiled up.

Surely, he couldn't be that stupid.

"Because if that's the case, I need to know so I can make the appropriate decisions," he said, not giving me a chance to answer.

Yes, yes, evidently, he really could be that stupid.

"Yes, our training sessions have mostly been us getting naked and sweaty," I said in a completely serious voice.

That seemed to set him back. Thunderclouds gathered on his face.

I turned and stalked out of the room.

I didn't know where that had come from, and quite frankly I didn't care. If I hadn't already accepted this job, I'd be heading out the door toward home right about now.

Liam's footsteps were angry as he followed me. "Aileen."

I held up a hand. "We're not talking about my personal life."

"I have the right to know."

I spun to face him, ready and raring to go for this fight. "No, you don't. You're not my boyfriend, my lover or anything else."

The words didn't make him back down. If anything, they seemed to spur him on. "And if I wanted to be?"

I scoffed. "You don't want that. You want a convenient body that's there when you've got an itch."

His face darkened. "Don't presume to know what I want, sweetheart."

I lifted an eyebrow, abruptly willing to follow this wherever it might lead. "Okay, answer me this—where were you for the past three months?"

I waited. A mask slammed down on his face, and suddenly he was the Liam I'd first met. A statue impersonating a person. Cold and impersonal, no hint of his true thoughts.

"Yeah, that's what I thought," I said. I'd expected his response, but somehow it still stung. "I'm not your toy. I won't be waiting for you whenever you deign to return. I suggest you go elsewhere if that's what you're looking for."

"And what would you have of me?" he asked, wielding his words like a whip. "You treat anything to do with vampires like it's the plague. I can't share because I can't trust what you'll do with the information."

The words hurt, even if they were partially true. I did avoid all things vampire. However, if he thought I would use knowledge he'd given me to hurt him, he didn't know me at all.

Some of that must have been written on my face, because his expression thawed slightly.

"I guess we each know where we stand," I said, my voice flat. I turned toward the door. "I believe you said you wanted to see one of my friends. Which friend?"

He remained still for a long moment, long enough that I thought he was going to ignore my question before he started after me.

"You still have connections with the witches?" he asked.

I nodded. "They're tentative. I can't guarantee she'll talk to us."

In fact, I wasn't sure she wouldn't try to hex us at first sight. She wasn't exactly my biggest fan.

"That'll have to do," he said.

"What's the interest in the witches?" I asked.

"I suspect some of them were part of the group that came after us last night," he replied, moving past me to a car, one that was sleek and sporty and looked wicked fast. It was a burnt umber color, a treat for the eyes.

I paused at the sight of it, recalling the conversation we'd had last night. For a moment, I thought he might have gotten this because of what I'd said. I shook off the thought in the next second. There was no way he would have had time to get this car between now and then. This was coincidence, nothing else.

"You coming?" he asked, pausing on the driver's side.

I nodded and joined him. Whether this was because of me or not, I heartily approved of the ride.

*

Elements was much the same as I remembered. Liam hadn't had any trouble finding parking near it. He seemed to possess some uncanny knack to arrive at the exact moment someone was vacating a spot, a feat I never seemed to manage. Whenever I came to the Short North, I usually ended up parking a mile away from my destination.

Named for its location just north of downtown Columbus, the Short North was on one of the busiest streets in the city. Once upon a time, it had been considered little more than a dying neighborhood. When I was growing up, people avoided this place after dark and sometimes before it. Since then it had undergone a revitalization and was now home to some of the funkiest and coolest shops and restaurants in the city. Ostensibly it was known as the arts district, but it was so much more than that.

At ten on a Wednesday night, it was still hopping, the bar and club scene just beginning to pick up.

Columbus wasn't a big city, therefore many of the districts were left to butt up against each other. The start of the Arena district was just one street over, and marked the beginning of many vampire owned bars. The witches had claimed the Short North— a decision that allowed them to take advantage of the attractions drawing tourists and sightseers who didn't mind the new age mysticism permeating everything.

Somehow the two groups made it work despite the thin line of separation. At least, that's what I had always figured.

Given the dissatisfaction on Liam's face as we parked and got out, I was forced to question my assumption. He didn't seem happy at the prospect of visiting Miriam's store.

"Perhaps you should allow me to speak when we get in there," I said, following him from of the car.

"I'm perfectly capable of speaking for myself," Liam declared, stalking along the sidewalk.

Maybe so, but he was also perfectly capable of destroying any goodwill by doing so. Liam tended to use force to get what he wanted. That worked sometimes, but in cases like these, I'd found battering the truth out of someone rarely yielded the sort of results you wanted.

The store's sign was flipped to "closed." Not surprising, given most shops on the street shut down around nine.

Liam grabbed the doorknob and wrenched. The door shivered under his hand, but remained closed.

"That's not a good idea," I said.

"When I want your input, I'll ask for it," Liam said, jerking the door again.

My othersight caught a small pulse within the door—the ward readying itself. Before I could warn Liam, it flashed, reaching out and wrapping around his hand.

His face showed the slightest flinch of pain as he remained still, letting the ward creep up his arm. The smell of burnt flesh reached me, but other than that first small glimpse of pain, Liam's expression remained neutral.

"Ready for my help now?" I asked, folding my arms across my chest.

"No need." He bared his teeth at me, and with muscles bulging, he ripped the ward to pieces until all that remained visible in my othersight were small, barely glowing fragments.

"Very mature," I told him.

"It worked," he responded. This time when he yanked on the door, it opened with a screech.

I shook my head as he sauntered inside. What exactly was that supposed to have accomplished? All it likely did, was antagonize Miriam and ensure she didn't talk to us.

"Why is it that every time you show up, the company you keep gets worse and worse?" Miriam asked from behind me.

"I don't even know," I said exasperated.

I turned to find Miriam looking over the remains of her ward with an irritated expression. She wasn't what you'd expect when you heard the word "witch." She didn't wear soft, wispy clothes or embrace the fashion choices of the granola loving crowd. Nor was she dressed all in black, wearing pentagons or other witchy symbols.

She looked young—younger even than I. I'd been turned when I was twenty-six, which would be the age I appeared until my true death.

Miriam, on the other hand, looked barely twenty. Furthermore, she was dressed like she was off to rush a sorority with her blond hair pulled back into a high pony tail while wearing a bright pink and glitter shirt over a pair of loose cotton pajama bottoms. She came across as dangerous as a powder puff. Despite that, she was a powerful witch. As tricky as the day was long.

Liam gave the witch a fang-filled smile, one meant to be threatening. "Witch. I've got questions for you."

Miriam failed to be intimidated, her gaze flicking to me as if to ask if I was serious. I shrugged at her. Liam was doing his own thing at the moment.

"I see you've failed to keep your freedom," Miriam observed.

"Not quite," I said, surprised when Liam didn't have something snarky to add. He seemed content to let me lead, staying quiet as the two of us talked. Given his demonstration from moments ago when he'd broken into the shop, it was unexpected. "I'm still clanless."

"But not unclaimed," she said, indicating my forearm and the oak tree that was Liam's brand. "It seems he's a tad possessive, too."

My attention shot to Liam, who gave me an innocent shrug of his shoulders and lifted his eyebrows as if to ask if I really wanted to discuss this in front of the witch.

Ass. I left the matter of the mark for later.

"What brings you to my shop?" Miriam asked, moving past me and into the darkened room.

When Liam still didn't answer, letting the silence deepen as he moved through the store looking over the contents, I stepped forward. "We were attacked last night."

She looked over incredulously. "And your first thought upon waking was to come here?"

I shrugged. "I don't know many witches."

I let her process that. There was a sly twist to her lips that suggested she thought she had the advantage.

"And I ran into a witch beforehand who mentioned Angela."

That wiped the smile from her face. Her expression turned blank.

Thought that might do the trick.

"Whatever happened to her?" I asked idly.

Angela had tried to kill me and been partially responsible for several other deaths in the city.

"She cannot hurt anyone again. That's all you need to know," Miriam said firmly.

Hm. I didn't know how to interpret that.

"Are you aware the High Fae are in town?" Liam asked, picking up one of the items on the counter, a small glass ball the color of a cat's eyes.

Miriam frowned at him. "That's not exactly news. Several of the minor Fae have made themselves scarce since their arrival."

Liam let the glass ball fall. It shattered against the floor.

Miriam and I watched the destruction with similar looks of dismay. Her face turned angry as Liam moved to another display case.

"Put that down," Miriam snapped as he picked up a vial of neon blue liquid.

I gave Liam a look of warning.

He shrugged at me and threw the vial into the corner. I watched it hit the wall and shatter, its liquid contents sizzling as a light blue smoke rose from them.

I dropped my face into my hands as Miriam sputtered next to me.

Liam gave us a charming smile as if he wasn't acting like a bull in a china shop.

"Get that vampire under control," Miriam hissed at me.

I shook my head at her. "Sorry. He doesn't answer to me."

"I heard a rumor the witches had planned an alliance with them," Liam said, turning and fixing Miriam with a cold stare.

"I don't concern myself with rumors," she said.

"That's an unusual statement for a witch to make," Liam said, his voice full of menace. "Even more so, since you are the crone's apprentice. You're both known for acting rather decisively when rumor of one of your witches' rebellion reaches your ears."

Miriam regarded him through narrowed eyes, then shifted her focus to me. "Is this what you've come for? To throw accusations and innuendo around?"

"I just had a few questions about some witches," I said.

Her mouth twisted down in a frown. "Maybe you did, but I'm sure the vampire over there has a different agenda."

Liam seemed amused at the accusation but didn't bother denying it.

Yes, I could see that now. I watched him with a resigned look.

"Last night I ran into three witches. One of them said she was Angela's cousin," I said, trying to steer us back onto steady ground.

"Mary?" Miriam seemed startled. Her expression turned cagey as she moved around the room.

"Yes. Could she have had something to do with the attack on us?" I asked, following her.

"Without knowing the manner of attack, I couldn't say," Miriam said, her eyes on her hands.

I paused. That wasn't a no, which meant there was some anger among the witches at me. Interesting that they'd lain the blame for Angela's earlier actions at my feet. I wondered if they were more angry about her being caught, than at what she'd done.

"They used golems," I said, watching Miriam carefully. I didn't trust that she'd be entirely truthful. Until now, I'd never have said she would deliberately mislead me, but these were her people we were talking about. I doubted she'd reveal their secrets to an outsider.

"How many?" she asked.

"Thirty. Maybe more," I said.

She was quiet. She looked up at me, her expression reverting to its normal mysteriousness. "I doubt Mary had anything to do with it. She lacks the power."

"And if she worked with others?" I pressed.

Miriam shrugged, the gesture flippant. "Still doubtful. Her circle is just as inept as her. The witches with power steer clear of her sort."

I tapped the counter in thought, frowning at Miriam. There was something she wasn't telling me. Her denial was too quick.

Liam stirred, seeming to think so too. He gave her a menacing smile. "You know what I love about witches?"

Miriam didn't answer, watching him with wariness as magic gathered at her fingertips. I didn't have to use my othersight to realize she had something nasty brewing.

"Miriam, don't be foolish," I cautioned as the spark became a blaze.

Liam moved, his hand shooting out to grab hers, crushing her fingers as he twisted. He raised their hands between them in a grip that put tension on her wrist, ensuring she couldn't move without causing herself extreme pain.

"They have a low pain tolerance," Liam said, satisfaction in his voice.

"Liam, let Miriam go," I warned.

Neither one of them paid any attention to me.

Miriam seemed not to have learned from her thwarted first attempt, magic sparking in her other hand as she turned it to face Liam. He barked out a laugh and used his free hand to grab hers, then pushed it away from him.

The magic flew, crashing into, and pulverizing several shelves. I jumped before looking back to witness Liam maneuvering her hand into another twisted grip, making it impossible for her to cast any further spells.

I let loose a frustrated sigh. Spooks and their stupid dominance games.

"Tell me what you know of the Fae and the crone's plans for them," Liam said, bringing his face close to Miriam's.

She struggled, attempting to turn away with little success. He let go of one hand, grabbing her chin and yanking it towards his.

Her face went slack as his eyes caught hers. He repeated his question of before.

"She hopes to strengthen our position," Miriam said, sounding calm and blissful. Not at all like the confident woman I'd come to know.

I hated the vampire's ability to hypnotize. It subsumed a human's will and turned them into mindless drones.

It usually didn't work quite as well on spooks, but then, Liam wasn't exactly an average vampire. He had centuries of experience with the power to back it up.

Miriam answered his questions with little hesitation.

He let her go and stepped back.

"Happy now?" I snapped. We'd learned nothing of note from that exchange.

"For now," he said, turning toward the door.

Miriam slumped against the counter, every line of her body speaking of exhaustion.

"I hope the Fae turn you into their pets," Miriam said. The words sounded like a curse. "Although, from what I hear, it wouldn't be the first time."

Liam froze in place, giving me the brief impression of stone. His face was cold and furious, while power shone in his eyes like a beacon in the darkest part of night.

I grabbed his arm and towed him toward the door. "Nope, I think you've had enough fun for now."

If I didn't get him out of here, I feared for Miriam's life.

"Aileen, don't come back," Miriam said, her voice quiet but clear nonetheless.

I hesitated at the door. With reluctance, I nodded. I could see why she might not want to see me again. Not after what Liam had just done.

Gazing back at the destruction in her shop and the bone-deep weariness on her face, I couldn't help but be sad at what I had wrought, even if that had not been my intention in coming here. It made me feel like a curse in truth.

"This wasn't what I planned," I said. Miriam still didn't look at me.

I sighed.

"Blessed be upon your house and future endeavors," I said, giving her the witches' blessing. It was a small thing, but it was all I had for the moment.

She flicked her fingers at me, a spell wrapped around them. I ducked out before it could land.

The cool night air embraced me as I headed toward where Liam waited by the car. He leaned against it, his face arrogant as he watched me approach.

I stopped inches from him, anger burning through me. "What the hell was that?"

The question was out before I could think of a better way of phrasing it.

"That was me getting answers," he coldly responded.

My eyes widened. "That was you burning a bridge. What do we do if we need to go back? She won't talk to us again. We'll be lucky if we can get within three feet of her shop after this."

Liam watched me, my anger having no effect on him, as if my worries had no bearing. It ramped my rage up another notch and I fought not to rearrange his pretty face.

"We were getting nowhere doing it your way," he said. "I expedited matters."

Expedited matters right off the edge of a cliff.

He opened the car door, not waiting for me to argue any further. "Let's go. There are others I'd like to visit before the night is through."

I remained locked in place. "Oh no, you're on your own for that."

"It was not a request. Get in the car," he ordered.

I folded my arms. "You're not going to alienate any of my other contacts."

He gritted his teeth, obviously losing patience with me. "Quit with the hysterics. I haven't the time today."

Hysterics. Nice. I narrowed my eyes at him, baring my teeth at him.

He responded brusquely, "You accepted this job. Quitting now would only have nasty consequences for yourself."

Was he actually threatening me?

He lifted an eyebrow. "You can either come along and keep me from killing anyone, or you can stay here, leaving me to run wild. Your choice."

I snarled at him. That was no choice and he knew it. "You're an unfeeling jackass."

His lips twisted in a victorious smile as he held my door open for me.

"Thought you might see it my way," he murmured.

I seated myself as he walked around the car. He'd just slid inside when a crash came from Miriam's shop.

CHAPTER NINE

"What was that?" I asked.

It had sounded like glass breaking. A woman screamed seconds later.

"That's coming from Miriam's shop," I said, already reaching for the door.

Liam hit the locks, twisting the key in the ignition as the car rumbled to a start.

"You're not going to help her?" I asked.

"You expected different from an unfeeling jackass?" he mocked.

"Forget it," I said. I put my shoulder into the door, the metal squealing in protest as I slowly forced it open.

Liam swore and hit the button, unlocking the door.

Knew he'd see it my way, I thought smugly as I shoved it open and got out.

"Aileen, don't be stupid. This is the witch's problem," he argued, not getting out.

I leaned down and looked through the open door. "Guess that's the difference between you and me. You can watch as someone is hurt because they're not one of yours, while I never could."

I slammed the door on whatever response he might have made, jogging back toward the shop. It would have been nice to have a weapon, not that my gun would do me much good if I faced golems.

To my relief, Miriam hadn't gotten around to locking the front door behind me. I slipped in, grabbing the bell on top of the door to stop it from announcing my presence.

The front of the shop was still empty, shadows making the counters and collection of items seem more ominous than they would have normally. There were a lot of good places for an enemy to hide in here.

I moved forward, my feet whispering across the tile. An ornate umbrella, one of those paper ones that would melt in the rain, caught my eye. As a weapon it was lacking, but it was better than nothing.

I plucked it from its place and crept forward. A woman chanted in an unfamiliar language. I'd only heard it a few times, but I recognized it. It was the witches' unique language of power, used to channel their magic in ways that had never been properly explained to me.

She shouted one last word, the spell's trigger. There was a burst of air, like someone had punctured a balloon and all the air rushed out. Then the tiny shop shook, the glass rattling before settling.

I dashed into the other room, not letting the logic-bending sight break my focus. I'd been in here before so I knew what to expect.

Miriam's back room had a stone floor and glass walls and roof, with an antique table in the middle of a mass of greenery. Every plant you could imagine took up room on every available surface. It was a gardener's paradise, a greenroom where there shouldn't have been one, the smell of dirt and growing things permeating the air.

Miriam stood in the midst of it all, her back against a wall, several of her plants knocked over at her feet.

Across from her stood another woman, her face wrinkled in rage as she faced down Miriam. Her skin was sallow and cracked, her hair lank around her face. She looked sick. And oddly familiar.

Between the two women, Miriam's oasis had been turned into a nightmare scene—golems in the midst of pulling themselves out of pots. These golems were different from the ones of last night. For one thing, they were thinner, almost reedy-looking and a lot shorter.

For another, there were green leaves growing from the dirt of their skin. Some had flowers sprouting from their arms. They looked less menacing this time and more like the jolly green giant if he'd been hit with a flower stick.

Miriam spat another word, a ball of magic the color of midnight hitting a golem in the chest and sending it staggering back a few steps. It shook itself, advancing on Miriam again with slow ponderous steps as she backed along the wall, trying to avoid any more of her pots.

I drove my umbrella into the back of one golem. It sunk into the creature's chest with a wet glugging sound. I tugged on it, but the umbrella didn't budge.

The back of the golem's head melted, a face forming.

I jerked back. Not fast enough, as ropes of mud shot up from the umbrella to wrap around my arm up to my elbow.

Oh, that wasn't good.

The other witch cackled. "Bet you wish you'd sold me the diet coke and candy bars now."

The gas station. That's why she seemed familiar. She'd looked a lot better then, nothing like this pale, sickly creature in front of me, lips cracked and dry and the skin under her eyes sunken and dark.

I didn't waste time arguing with her as I tugged harder. My arm didn't budge.

The mud crawled higher, reaching my bicep. I didn't dare touch it with my other hand, too afraid the mud would latch onto that hand as well and I'd be stuck defenseless, both hands trapped.

There was a thump as the enemy witch slumped to the ground, Liam standing over her with an amused look on his face as he watched me struggle.

I waited, expecting the golems to fold in on themselves. When the mud inched higher, I let out a sound of frustration.

"Are you just going to stand there?" I asked.

He tilted his head and smiled. It wasn't a particularly nice smile, more like one a wolf gives its struggling prey. "Yes."

I growled at him as the mud crept higher. It was almost at my shoulder now.

Liam's smile turned seductive. "Say please."

"What?"

"Say 'please Mr. Jackass, save me from my pride." His eyes twinkled at me.

He was having fun. I was so glad.

I turned back to the golem and gave another vicious tug. There was no way I was begging him for a rescue like some damsel in distress. This damsel was perfectly capable of saving herself. She just needed to calm down and figure out how.

I forced myself to take stock of the situation, to ignore the mud creeping past my shoulder and analyze what I saw.

By this point, Miriam had given up on destroying the golems. She'd locked herself in a bubble of magic that shone with the ferocity of a star.

A faint flicker of magic in the center of the golem called my attention. These were simple constructs. Break the magic it housed and the rest should fall.

That was the theory anyway.

Instead of fighting the onslaught of the mud, I gave into it, plunging both hands deeper. I took a last deep breath, noting distantly that Liam had jolted forward. I was too occupied with my battle to care.

I reached with everything in me for that tiny spark, throwing both my physical and metaphysical self at it. I strained until it was nearly within my grasp, crushing it with my mind and extinguishing its small light even as my physical hands reached the lodestone at its center and yanked it out.

The golem crumbled into dirt. One by one the rest of the golems followed it.

"Guess I didn't need your help after all," I told Liam.

He gave me a slow clap.

Miriam's protective shields slowly dissolved. She looked around at the disaster of her back room with displeasure.

I propped one muddy arm on my hip. "So, Miriam, who's trying to kill you?"

"I told you she was holding something back," Liam murmured, coming to stand at my side.

I ignored him. We didn't know that for sure. Someone had tried to kill us and we were still no more knowledgeable than we were last night.

Miriam's expression was furious as she took in the greenhouse, her plants in disarray, the roots ragged, her pots cracked and on their sides. I didn't blame her. The place really was a wreck.

She didn't answer my question, shooting black lightning at me faster than I could dodge. Pain crackled along my nerve endings, my aborted scream cut off as my lungs seized. Black raced along the edges of my vision, consuming everything.

*

"I'm going to kill that witch," I groaned, bringing my hand to my head. It pounded with the fury of a thousand drums.

I shouldn't have dropped my guard. There was no one to blame for my predicament but myself. Stupid mistake, Aileen.

"Consider it done," a voice rumbled from next to me.

I stilled. It hadn't occurred to me that I wasn't alone. It should have.

I squinted over at Liam. His eyes snapped with blue fire. To someone who didn't know him he looked haughty and remote, but his eyes blazed at me, hinting of anger and worry, and a depth of feeling I would have said was impossible if I hadn't seen it for myself.

He didn't move a muscle, just sat there staring at me. Abruptly, I became aware of my hand cradled in his, his thumb stroking slowly over my skin.

"You didn't actually kill her, did you?" I asked suspiciously.

His face lightened, just slightly, enough for a hint of a smile to come out. "Not yet. Though I cannot say her condition is entirely as it was. The other witch wasn't so lucky."

I snorted at the small display of humor. I tried to sit up, groaning, and abandoning the endeavor halfway.

"For once, I'm not going to get angry about your tendency of solving all problems with extreme violence," I said, wincing.

My entire body ached. Even my teeth hurt. It felt like someone had poured an entire city block worth of electricity into my body. It was not a comfortable feeling.

"Your forbearance is appreciated," Liam murmured. He watched me closely, his body tight.

"This feels worse than anything the sorcerer ever did to me," I said.

"It should. She was trying to kill you," Liam said, his voice grim and his expression turning frightening as his inner monster peaked out.

Everyone had one. A monster they kept buried deep inside, forgetting it even existed until some situation or stimuli triggered its return. Most humans liked to pretend they didn't have one, and for the most part that worked. We lived in an era where people could lie to themselves and pretend they were civilized—that violence didn't live in them.

Vampires didn't have that luxury. Our monsters were close to the surface—just waiting for the slightest spark to set off a killing spree, complete with requisite bloodbath.

His words gave me pause. Miriam wasn't my biggest fan, but it was hard to wrap my brain around her wanting me dead. Especially considering I'd just helped save her ass.

It would also help to know why Dahlia's pendant hadn't worked. I patted my chest for the item in question.

Liam watched me. "Looking for this?"

He held out the small pendant.

"Where did you find it?"

"On the floorboard of my car."

I examined it, noticing the clasp was broken. That would explain why it had done nothing to repel Miriam's attack.

Liam's face was carefully guarded as he watched me. "That is a dangerous toy. I'm surprised the djinn injected so much of her essence into it."

I gave him a quizzical glance before looking back at the pendant.

"You must be closer to her than I realized," he said.

He had an odd look on his face as if he didn't know whether to be happy about that fact or not.

"Should I not wear it?" I asked.

He folded my fingers over it. "Keep it. At least until whatever is going on has run its course."

I nodded.

"Where is she?" I asked, forcing myself upright.

Liam's hand tightened before he reached around to steady me.

"Whew, that was a lot harder than it should have been," I said, finally sitting without assistance.

"We have her in a secure place," Liam said.

"I'd like to talk to her," I told him. My body felt shaky and weak.

"No."

"No?" I ignored my weakness to fix him with a death stare.

He didn't look phased by it, but that might have been because I looked and felt like a stiff breeze might blow me over at any moment.

He lifted an eyebrow as if daring me to argue.

I shut my mouth and studied him. He looked intractable, an unmovable mountain that would just get more stubborn the more you argued.

I left the matter for now. We'd come back to it when I didn't feel quite so weak.

"Where are we?" I asked in a shift of topic.

The bed I'd woken up on was nice, masculine, in a room that matched it.

"The Gargoyle," he said, his gaze telling me he was anticipating my reaction.

I nodded. The base of operations for the vampire in charge of the surrounding territory.

"Is there a reason you brought me here?" I asked calmly.

"Because I told him to," a voice said from the doorway.

I twitched but didn't react, my gaze fixed on Liam's. Maybe if I ignored the source of the voice, he would go away.

The action seemed to amuse Liam, and he lifted an eyebrow at me as if to ask how long I could pretend the giant prick in the room wasn't there.

"You couldn't have brought me anywhere else?" I asked him.

He relaxed back into his chair. "I thought this place had a certain charm."

I just bet he did.

"Pretending I'm not here won't make me go away," Thomas said, his voice patient. Despite that, I thought I detected a note of frustration in his voice.

That was something at least.

"Will it make you fix my damn stairs?" I asked, finally looking over at him.

He gave a long-suffering sigh. "There was a delay in construction. The human company I employed is suffering from personnel problems."

Another excuse in a long line of them. I believed it as much as I had the last one. If he wanted, he could have the problem solved in less time than it took me to get dressed in the morning. All he had to do was work his vampire mojo and the humans would be falling all over themselves to fulfill his desires.

My expression must have said as much because he gave me a charming smile, though its affect was completely lost on me. I'd never fall for that smile again.

"You are welcome to call the foreman and find out for yourself," he told me.

Like that would help. The human would probably just end up parroting whatever Thomas wanted.

Such was the case whenever humans brushed up against the spooks. Most times they came out the losers. And Liam wondered why I refused to give my alliance to the vampires.

I chose to ignore Thomas and the tangle of problems he represented. "I'm awake now, so we can go on about our business."

Liam didn't move, his gaze sardonic. "Our presence is required here for the remainder of the night."

His words stalled me right as I was contemplating the chances of me remaining on my feet if I tried to stand.

"You're joking," I said.

That seemed to amuse him. "I'm not. You will be required to portray the part of Thomas' yearling."

"You must know that's not happening," I said flatly.

He gave me a victorious smile that said checkmate as clearly as if the words were spoken out loud. "But it is."

Rebellion skated across my face.

He leaned closer, pressing one fist on the bed at my side as he said, "Just earlier tonight you accepted employment from me. Do you remember the terms?"

My scowl should have lit paper on fire. I didn't speak, anger strangling my vocal chords. I got a sinking feeling I knew exactly where this was going.

He drew back, his smile widening at my expression. "You agreed to follow my orders."

Yup. I'd been right.

I narrowed my eyes at him. No. Just no.

"Checkmate, darling," he whispered.

The urge to go for his throat tingled through my body. I might have tried it too, if I didn't ache so fiercely moving would send me crashing to the ground.

Liam straightened as I remained silent, fuming, so angry I couldn't even formulate a response. "I need to get ready. Thomas will brief you on what is expected and find you clothes."

He walked out of the room, leaving Thomas and me alone.

I bent my head and sighed. Point to Liam. He'd out-maneuvered me. I'd compliment him if I didn't want to slap that smug look off his face.

I lifted my head and sent a dour glance in Thomas's direction.

My sire was the handsome sort. It enabled him to lure his prey to him, lulling them into a coma of lust pheromones so he could royally fuck up their life while they were still none the wiser. His jaw was strong and hinted at a personality nearly as stubborn as mine.

"Many think Liam is the more reasonable between the two of us, but

I've always found his games to be rougher and more vicious. They sneak up and hit you in the face while you're not looking," Thomas observed. If I didn't know better, I thought I detected a hint of sympathy in his voice.

"You would think it'd be the other way around," I said.

Thomas inclined his head. "You would. Yet, I tend to prefer blunt force to achieve my desires whereas Liam goes after what he wants in a decidedly sideways manner."

It was odd to agree with my sire, but there we were.

"Now, let's see about getting you dressed in something appropriate," he said.

*

After an hour of poking and prodding, of people pulling me one way and then another, and Thomas critiquing dress after dress, I was ready.

I had to admit he had good taste. The dress he'd chosen was silver, setting off my grayish blue eyes to perfection and turning them stormy. One of the humans, a male, grabbed my shoulder-length brown hair and pulled it back, braiding pieces of it so its reddish tint caught the light and shone.

In very little time, I stood there, makeup perfect, hair styled back in an elegant swoop. I had to admire their work. I would never have been able to pull this look off had it just been me.

I looked elegant, infused with danger, the type of person you'd treat with respect even while trying to figure out how you could get closer to their orbit.

To my eternal surprise, Thomas hadn't abandoned me when the stylists arrived. Instead he'd tutored me on his expectations of me for the evening. It seemed a yearling vampire's duties were much the same as children from an earlier time in humanity's history—to be seen and not heard. I was expected to be a pretty ornament, gracing my master's side until he decided otherwise.

In a weird sort of way, it made sense. Vampire society had many things in common with a feudal one. You wouldn't want a page possibly offending important visitors. No, the page or apprentice was there to learn and observe so when they went off on their own, they would know what to do. In this instance, a yearling might see how vampire dealings were conducted so if and when they rose to a position of power, they could conduct themselves in an acceptable manner.

Only one problem. I had no plans to take my place in vampire society. There were no positions of power in my future; no circumstances where I would want something similar to what Thomas had.

It made me question why they'd gone to all the trouble of securing my presence at this shindig. It wasn't like they needed me as a guard. Liam and his enforcers would be plenty of protection for Thomas.

I had no expertise to offer, no skills they needed. It was not a good place to be, when knowing your footing was paramount to surviving the shark-infested waters the vampires liked to swim in.

Not knowing where else to go, I ended up standing in the main entrance foyer. The one thing Thomas had forgotten to brief me on before leaving to get himself ready, was where exactly this event was supposed to take place.

I was all dressed up with no clue where to go. It left me wandering aimlessly, hoping to find someone who could point me in the right direction.

"Thought I might find you here," a voice said from above me.

I turned to see Rick bound down the stairs toward me. Stairs I'd just come down, and I hadn't seen anyone in the corridor. It left me questioning how he'd managed to arrive unseen and unheard.

The enthusiastic vampire reached the bottom of the stairs and gave me a courtly bow with all of the mannerisms of a born courtier. It was a gesture suited to his current attire. Like me, he was dressed to impress in a full tuxedo, his auburn hair styled and his curls tamed.

I still wasn't sure where he fell in the territorial vampire hierarchy. He seemed to be on good terms with Liam's enforcers, but I'd seen him act as an advisor to Thomas before as well.

His face was open and welcoming as he straightened, grinning. As a redhead who hadn't seen a lot of sun since his turning, Rick had a smooth, pale creaminess to his skin I would have envied when I was younger. His bright green eyes stood out with his pale coloring, reminding me of a cat's eyes.

Or the Fae, I thought, as those same eyes went unfocused and soft, as if they were looking at a scene only he could see.

I waited quietly to see if he'd return to the present. This had happened once before during the drama with Caroline. He'd given me a warning afterwards, one I hadn't been able to make sense of until much, much later. At the time I'd simply thought him a little wacky.

He shook off whatever he was seeing to give me an even brighter smile than before.

He held out his arm. "Shall we?"

"What? No dire warnings this time?"

"Can't make it easy for you every time," he murmured gently.

I barked out a laugh. "I'm all dressed up. It would be a shame to waste all this work."

"For the rest of us, as well," he said roguishly, looping his arm through mine.

His arm was surprisingly sturdy under my hand, given he wasn't muscular like the other enforcers I was used to hanging out with.

Rick was a warm presence at my side as we made our way through the mansion. The Gargoyle appeared big from the outside, but once inside, its layout threatened to send the mind into a tailspin. The interior was a maze of corridors, each neatly folding in on themselves. You needed a map just to find the kitchen.

I slid him a sideways glance, wondering how much information I could get out of him before he realized what I was doing. As part of the Gargoyle's household and someone who probably interacted with my sire on a regular basis, he might know something that could prove valuable down the line.

"Have you met the visitors yet?" I asked, keeping my voice idle. I didn't want to scare him off by seeming too interested.

His cheeks creased with a smile. "Indeed."

"What are they like?" I asked. "Are they different from the rest of the Fae in the city?"

Liam had referred to them as High Fae but I wasn't entirely sure what that meant. I'd never met one before, despite meeting many of the Fae who'd called the city home.

"Very," Rick said.

I struggled with impatience. One-word answers weren't feeding my need to know more.

"How?" Two can play the one-word game.

"They're more."

Two words this time. That was an improvement at least, though it still didn't tell me what I wanted to know.

"You're more like us than you think," Rick said. Seeing my confusion, he went on, "Vampires learn from the start that staying one step ahead of everyone else is the only way to ensure survival. Our kind like to play at diplomacy. We walk the fine line of power. We're rarely satisfied, always grasping for more. If we're not careful, it's easy to fall to the wolves below."

His voice became that of a mentor lecturing a student.

"Huh. I've never been one to pursue power," I observed. It was nothing but the truth. Even as a human, I'd gone out of my way to avoid leadership roles. I was promoted to sergeant despite my best efforts.

"Don't you?" he asked. "There are different kinds of power. You may not desire a leadership role, but you crave control of your own life and your own little piece of this world. You just have a different way of going about it."

We walked through several more corridors in silence as I digested that. I wasn't sure if I agreed with him, but I was willing to consider the point.

I dropped the facade. "You didn't answer my questions. Not really."

His smile turned wicked, rivaling Liam's for deviousness. "I didn't, did I?"

He seemed pleased by my claim. I didn't know what to make of that.

He patted my hand. "The Fae are never what they seem. Our unwelcome guests even more so. The High Fae have assumed the mantle of leaders of all they consider theirs."

I frowned. "Even in another's territory?"

"And therein lies the problem," Rick said in a soft voice.

We stopped near doors I recognized. The ballroom. I'd been here once, during the selection of the territory Master. This place didn't hold a lot of pleasant memories for me.

"Ask your friend these questions," Rick said, lifting my hand from his. "He among us all is uniquely suited to provide answers about our new guests."

I looked where he indicated. Liam stood at the end of the hall, brutally handsome in his formal wear. It was a kick to the chest seeing him like that. Most of the time I forgot just how breathtaking he was, lost in the irritation he engendered simply by breathing.

But dressed like this, his hair styled away from his face to reveal his fierce bone structure, eyes blazing at me as Rick leaned in to kiss me on the cheek, I couldn't help but see and wonder. He was like a beautiful painting come to life so it could plague and tempt me.

His face tightened as if he saw something he disliked, abruptly turning unhappy.

"Good luck," Rick whispered near my ear before striding away, sending a jaunty wave Liam's way.

Liam's face grew even more taut at Rick's statement, his eyes snapping back to mine. The expression on his face said he thought I was an idiot.

I gave him a narrowed-eyed glare telling him he was the dumbass who forced idiot me into this situation.

He *huffed* a little, impatience in the sound. He stepped forward, capturing my arm and hauling me after him.

"What are you doing?" I hissed as he propelled me into an alcove off the hall, using his larger body to block the view of us from anyone who might pass.

"What are you doing?" he returned. "Rick might seem harmless and fun, but he's every bit as dangerous as the rest of us. Probably more so, because no one suspects what waits beneath his mask."

I rolled my eyes at him. "I was pumping him for information, not offering to do the horizontal tango with him."

Liam propped a hand on the wall behind me, caging me in as he loomed over me. Suddenly, the intimacy of the situation struck me, awareness coursing through me.

"You might think you're in control, but Rick has a way of turning things to his advantage," Liam said, destroying the moment.

I blinked at him, then blinked again. "Yes, because I am a helpless woman who doesn't know her own mind. I will just fall prey to his lascivious urges. I can't help it. Really."

Liam glowered at me in displeasure, not appreciating my humor in the slightest.

I sighed and shook my head. "Is there a reason you pulled me into this dark alcove?"

He straightened. "Yes, but I'm not entirely sure I should share it with you anymore. Your choice in companion shows a distinct lack in judgment."

I gave him my death glare. He remained unmoved. Hm, it seemed my death glare could use a little work.

I shrugged, affecting a nonchalance I didn't feel. Curiosity about what he'd planned to tell me burned in me. "Suit yourself. I'll just go find some of that Fae wine Nathan told me about and make even more poor judgment calls."

The way he took up the small space meant making a grand exit was out, so I settled for gazing up at him expectantly.

He sighed and reached into his jacket. "You're a pain in the ass."

"The Judge," I gasped, snatching the gun from his hand.

I hadn't seen my old friend since Nathan confiscated it during my last visit to the Gargoyle.

I'd missed it. Of all my guns, this was the one I most preferred. It was a revolver, a .45 caliber long Colt. Its stopping power would put most things in the ground, especially when you took into account my homemade ammunition incorporated silver nitrate into the mix.

"Where'd the ammo go that was in here?" I hissed when I noticed the rounds had been switched out.

"These are iron, much more appropriate for the current situation," Liam murmured.

I lifted my head, slightly surprised. "This wasn't all just an elaborate excuse to get me all dressed up, then?"

His gaze turned amused as he tweaked a piece of hair that had slipped free to curl against my cheek. "No, that's just a happy bonus."

I leaned back against the wall. Iron for our Fae guests. They were said to have a weakness for it. The Judge was the perfect weapon, effective on our potential enemies and next to useless against a vampire.

This indicated trust from Liam—but only to a point.

It didn't make me any less surprised to have my friend back. Vampires didn't like when guests went armed in their homes. I'd almost kissed any thought of getting the Judge back goodbye.

"You'll need this," Liam said, handing over a thigh holster.

I made a face. Those never fit as well as they should. Not to mention they were crazy uncomfortable. Still, the thigh was the only place I had a hope of disguising a revolver.

Liam loomed between me and the rest of the hall, giving me privacy to slip my dress up and attach the holster to my leg.

His eyes gleamed appreciatively at the long expanse of bare skin.

"You could be a gentleman," I told him.

His grin was roguish. "I was never that. A lord's airs don't suit me."

My fingers paused on the fastenings. This was a rare, tantalizing hint to who he might have been before his transition to vampire.

I wanted more. The knowing look on Liam's face said he guessed as much and was waiting for inevitable questions.

For that reason, I kept my silence and straightened, testing out the holster's ability to stay put. It would hold, I concluded after several experimental movements.

I looked to where Liam still waited, watching me with the kind of look a man gives a woman he intends to get naked. I let confidence infuse my movements as I sauntered over to him, placing my hand on his chest.

I was gratified and emboldened when his breath caught. I shifted onto my tiptoes, my lips hovering near his, not quite touching. "It's too bad. The gentleman would have received a kiss in thanks."

I dropped back to my heels and smiled up at him, enjoying the slightly frustrated expression. That should teach him to taunt me.

I swished past him out of the alcove, my shoulder brushing the front of his tuxedo as I began to slip by him.

His hand shot out, cupping the back of my neck as he pulled me slightly into him.

"Aileen." He waited until I turned to look at him. "Only use it if absolutely necessary."

I nodded, understanding the warning as his hand slid away.

I stepped fully out of the alcove, never suspecting my promise would be tested so quickly as I staggered to a stop.

CHAPTER TEN

I nearly choked on my spit as a being straight out of my worst nightmare blocked my path. He was tall, his head only a foot below the ceiling, a red substance that looked like blood dripping from the red helmet atop his head. It made him seem even bigger than he was, and he already looked like a small giant.

But the red stuff couldn't be blood. Civilized beings didn't walk around with blood dripping from their heads. I didn't care if they were Fae or not.

His arms were the size of tree trunks. He wasn't quite as big as a bridge troll but he wasn't far off.

His face was a stony mask as he surveyed his surroundings, his gaze passing over me as if I was no more a threat than a fly. I was okay with that. Really.

Liam's hand touched my back. "Steady."

I nodded, despite the strong urge to pull the Judge.

"The red cap is a guard. He won't hurt you unless provoked," Liam continued in a murmur meant only for my ears.

I nodded again. That didn't really make me feel much better. I had a terrible habit of being provoking.

"How can he wander around the city without people losing their minds?" I asked in a near hiss. It was a legitimate question. Social media alone should have blown up if anybody caught a snap of the big guy.

Liam paused. "You're probably seeing him in his natural form."

"What do you see?" I asked. For once, my ability to see under illusions was not one I cherished. I could have gone a lifetime not knowing what lay under the Red Cap's glamour and been perfectly happy.

"A man. Slightly taller than me, wearing armor that would be better suited to a period three hundred years in our past," he murmured.

"I wish I saw that."

"I can imagine," Liam said, his voice grim.

I finally noticed what I should have before. A woman standing slightly to the right of the guard, her covetous gaze fastened on Liam.

She was beautiful, probably more so than any other woman I'd ever seen, which was saying something, since vampires tended to pick their companions with an eye to their looks. Her face possessed a flawless perfection almost painful to look at.

If the sun had been molded into the shape of a human, she was the form it would have taken. Her hair nearly shimmered, a golden-white blond that fell in soft waves down her back. She was clad in a dress appearing both delicate and impossible as it clung to what few curves she had before falling to the ground in a graceful arc.

She should have been untouchable, with the sort of beauty only found in paintings created by long dead masters. Instead, all I could see was lust coupled with greed stamped on her features as she looked at Liam. It drained some of the light, revealing dark shadows beneath her pretty surface.

"My pet, it has been ages," the woman said, her gaze never leaving Liam who had gone stock-still at my side.

I didn't have to look at his face to read how unwelcome the sight of this woman was.

"Niamh." He spoke her name in a low voice, more for my benefit than hers.

She glided toward us, her advance silent as she seemed to float over the wooden floor. I might have been invisible for all the attention she paid me. The red cap lumbered by her side.

Behind them, two Fae men paused, taking note of the unfolding scene. The two were nearly identical; obviously twins. Tall and thin with an athletic build, their faces held a hint of cruelty. Their hair was the color of autumn leaves and their eyes the amber of tree sap.

They were the men I saw last night in the bar. I think.

One whispered something to the other, causing his twin to smirk. When they noticed me watching, they gave me a long stare before slyness replaced the amusement.

"I heard you passed through our fair lands and was hurt when you didn't stop to pay me a visit." Her voice held the tinkle of bells, light and delicate.

Her words made Liam tense even further, his body like granite at my side.

She raised her hand, the gesture that of a queen expecting a subject to pay obeisance.

Liam didn't move as he radiated an otherworldly stillness seemingly unique to vampires.

There was a history between these two, and it was not a good one. I could see a banked rage in Liam's gaze, as if violence was only a breath away.

I had a feeling that would not be a good thing. Before I could think better of it, I moved between the two, smiling brightly. I grasped the woman's hand and shook it.

"Hi, I'm Aileen. You're awful pretty," I chirped. Airy yearling intent on ingratiating herself with the beautiful Fae woman. That was me. "I love your dress. I wish I could wear that color."

The woman's lilac gaze shifted to me for the first time. She blinked as if only just noticing my presence. The twins behind her dropped their air of sardonic amusement, appearing genuinely interested for the first time. I wasn't sure I liked that, since they still didn't seem as if they saw me as a thinking person, but instead a pet who had just performed a particularly clever trick.

Niamh studied me, her face beautiful and still. Nonetheless, I had to fight to keep from backing away. The way she looked at me made me think she was calculating how many bites it would take to gulp me down.

Not a lovely thought given the red cap by her side.

Without warning, power began to roll off her. She looked just an ounce more beautiful, her eyes transcendent. For a brief moment, I experienced an urge to bow at her feet and worship her, to make a sacrifice in her name.

I bit down on my lip and looked away, shaken at how easily she could have rolled me.

Liam stepped up to my side, his face cool and composed as he took my arm, neatly removing my hand from Niamh's. "You'll excuse us. We're late."

He didn't wait for her response, dragging me in his wake toward the double doors that led into the ballroom. The twins watched us go with fascination before sharing a conspiring look. I felt whatever had just happened, it had put me on the radar of some very bad and very powerful people.

"What was that?" he asked through gritted teeth.

"I didn't want to risk blood staining this dress," I told him.

"Why am I not surprised?" he asked, not giving me time to look around the room as he hurried me to the dais where Thomas sat on an ornate chair, like a king surveying his subjects.

It was a surprising sight. Thomas expected a certain respect from those under his command, but he hadn't struck me as the type to go this feudal. He watched us with an interested gaze, noting the tension in both our faces.

"Usually one tries not to bring themselves to the attention of the biggest predator in the room," Liam said.

"You're welcome," I told him.

"For what?"

"For interfering before you could do something you'd regret."

"I had myself perfectly under control."

I gave him a sideways look. "Uh huh."

A small growl slipped from him as he propelled me up onto the dais, positioning me at Thomas's side, just behind his chair before taking his place next to me on Thomas's other side.

"Problem?" Thomas asked.

"No," came Liam's abrupt response.

Thomas looked at me.

I shrugged. "He's sensitive."

Thomas's lips twitched.

"Your yearling shook Niamh's hand and introduced herself," Liam said through gritted teeth. "The twins seem very taken with her as well."

Thomas choked.

"Only because you looked like you were going to snap her neck," I returned.

Thomas's shoulders shook as Liam let out a sound very similar to a growl. "She does have a point, *dearthair*. You do get a certain look about you whenever that creature's name is mentioned."

I shot Liam a look that said "see, I'm not the only one."

He ignored us both and signaled to his men near the door. Thomas and I turned our attention back to the matter at hand.

I took in the room, noting several vampires lined up at the foot of the dais. Aiden, a clan Patriarch I'd run into more than once and who'd proven an ally on occasion, caught my eye and winked at me before turning to face our visitors. His presence gave me the hint I needed. These men and women were the Patriarchs and Matriarchs of their clans. Powerful in their own right, and if I kept to my normal way of operating, to be avoided at all costs.

Everyone in the room was dressed to the hilt. The women wore designer gowns and the men wore high end formal wear.

Against the wall I spotted Liam's enforcers, for the first time noticing the similarity in their dress. Their clothes were just as formal as the rest, but managed to make it appear they were wearing a uniform of dark pants and a dark jacket, the cut of which indicated all of them carried weapons.

I realized abruptly there were no humans in the room. Just vampires. Powerful ones, if what I was sensing was correct.

A woman stepped forward as Anton, one of Liam's enforcers, opened the door. "The Fair Folk of the Silver Hills."

Through the door stepped several Fae, each as beautiful as the last. The twins were among the first to step through, their faces coolly amused as they paced into the room, their stride that of confident hunters. By their side marched the red caps, forming a line between the Fae and the vampires.

Niamh was the last to enter, a Fae man prowled by her side with a lazy stride. He looked bored as he surveyed the room. He was just as beautiful as the rest but there was a hardness to him. This was no creature of light and laughter.

"Here we go," Thomas said in a soft voice.

"I do not like the fact that they brought the red caps," Liam murmured. "They're bred for war."

"Let's hope it doesn't come to that," Thomas said softly.

The Fae glided across the floor, the magic that was a part of them seeming to spill out over us, shining a light on their small group.

There were only a handful of them, but it felt like we were facing an army.

I went still at the sight of a familiar pair of eyes the shade of the land after several weeks of soft rain. Delicate features that should have seemed feminine except for the cold look on his face. Ash blond hair fell across his forehead.

Niall. My downstairs neighbor and evidently one of the High Fae.

Now that I'd spotted him, it was easy to find Cadell, his copper hair drawing my focus as he kept pace with the red caps. His attire was much different than the last time I'd seen him in jeans and a t-shirt. Now he looked like a hunter fresh from the woods, wearing a loose green tunic over buckskin pants.

He met my gaze, a clear warning in his.

I settled back. Fine, but the two of them were going to explain themselves as soon as the time presented itself. I wanted to know what a pair of important, powerful Fae were doing as my downstairs neighbors.

Aiden stepped forward. "The master of these territories greets our friends from the summer lands. We give warm welcome and a warning. Offer no violence to ours and you shall receive none in return."

A man stepped forward from amidst our guests. His size alone should have meant I noticed him before now.

I'd always thought Jerry was huge. Standing next to the High Faes' guards he seemed almost inconsequential, half their size, but still taller than any of the Fae beside him.

His gaze flicked to mine and held. His expression was grim and stoic as he gave the slightest shake of his head before bending in a half-bow toward Thomas.

"Esteemed lord, my mistress and masters have given me leave to speak for them," he said. "They are most happy to accept guesting rights and give you a token of their gratitude in return."

He turned and gestured, from the midst of the Fae a small boy walked. He appeared human, his frame thin and slight, dark hair on his head and eyes the deep color of mud that seemed to take in everything and nothing at the same time.

The men beside me went stock still.

I didn't know enough about the Fae to be able to read the situation. I did know that nobody on the dais was happy.

Aiden looked back, obviously unsure of how to handle the situation.

"The days of trading humans has long since passed," Thomas said, raising his hand and waving Aiden back.

Niamh moved forward, her lips curled in a feline smile. "You'll have to pardon us. It's just so hard to keep track of human convention. They die off so quickly."

Thomas didn't answer, just regarded the woman steadily.

It didn't take a genius to know the offering was an insult, meant to goad a reaction from the vampires.

From the little knowledge I possessed, I knew the Fae had a nasty habit of stealing children away from their parents, concealing them in their hidden lands, only to release them much later when everyone they knew was old or long dead.

I didn't know how long this boy had been gone from this world. For all I knew he could be centuries older than me.

She shrugged slim shoulders. "If you do not wish to accept, I can always get rid of the boy."

She raised a hand. One of the red caps unsheathed a sword and advanced on the child.

Only years of standing in formation, expressionless as someone yelled in my face kept me from reacting. That, and the knowledge of the gun strapped to my thigh. If need be, I'd act, but not yet. Not until I saw how Thomas handled this situation.

From my position behind him, I could see the way his hands tightened on the arm of his chair. He was no happier about this than me.

The red cap neared the boy, his lips curling as he raised the blade.

"Your hosting gift is accepted." Thomas's cool voice rang out in the silence.

The red cap hesitated, the promise of a fresh kill tempting him. Only Niamh waving him off with an impatient gesture compelled him to sheath the blade and return to his place in line.

"Excellent," she said, clapping her hands together. "We look forward to our stay." Her gaze wandered to Liam, the expression on her face turning hungry. "Our appetites are many. Providing us with something to pass the time would help keep us out of trouble."

Thomas showed no evidence of the suggestion being abhorrent, not even a muscle twitch betrayed him. "I'm afraid that is not possible. The enforcer has important business that would not leave him time to entertain."

Niamh gaze turned toward me. "Her, then."

I didn't twitch. If Thomas tried to give me over to this woman as a plaything, I was shooting her with the cold iron at my side. Consequences be damned. I had a feeling the world would be a much better place without her in it.

"My yearling would not survive the attentions of one such as you," Thomas said in an amused voice. "She is not far removed from her human beginnings and still rather breakable."

Niamh made a moue of disappointment even as she eyed me like she was the cat to my mouse. "Pity. I could think of many things to do with one such as her."

"Control yourself, Niamh. This is not the time for such transient pleasures," a man drawled.

It was the man who had accompanied her into the room. As with all the High Fae, he possessed an otherworldly beauty that made my teeth ache. It was spoiled by the haughty twist of his lips and the way he looked around the ballroom like it was little more than a dirt hut.

His hair was the color of freshly turned earth and longer than most modern men kept theirs. It didn't make him seem effeminate, more like someone who belonged in an older era, one that lacked the distractions and noise of today's world.

His eyes were tilted at the corners, almost almond-shaped and the color of amber. His skin looked like the sun had lovingly kissed it. He probably never had to worry about sunburn a day in his life.

His gaze moved past me as if I wasn't even there as he focused on Thomas again.

Niamh didn't seem entirely pleased with her companion's interruption, but she bowed her head and stepped back, ceding the floor to him.

"You will have to forgive my wife. She grows bored when so far from home," the man said.

As if boredom could excuse using a child as a token to trade.

"I am Arlan, Lord in the Autumn Lands." He dipped his head the smallest bit.

Liam's dislike and unease at this information buffeted me, his emotions easy to sense despite no outward sign of them. Something about the man's presence disturbed him.

"Welcome Arlan, Lord in the Autumn Lands, also known as a Lord of the Wild Hunt," Thomas said in a dry tone.

Recognition jumped through me as Thomas gave him his second name.

Dahlia had brought that up last night.

Arlan's smile widened. "I am one of many Lords of the Wild Hunt as the dog at your side might tell you."

Thomas didn't react to that, just stared the man down with a superior expression. "And may I inquire as to what brings you so far from the Shining Lands?"

"There is to be a Wild Hunt." He paused as the rest of the vampires stirred, his words having the effect of a bomb.

Some of the vampires seemed uneasy at the news, while others exhibited avid anticipation.

Arlan spread his hands. "Of course, you and yours are welcome to participate. I caution you, however, the hunt is fickle. Those who join are as likely to end as prey versus hunters."

Thomas remained motionless even as his vampires stirred, hushed whispers traveling through the room. Some of the clan leaders appeared to be considering the invitation. Aiden and a few others exchanged grim looks.

"We will consider your invitation," Thomas said after a drawn-out silence.

Liam tensed, his eyes a blaze of fire under a mask of haughty disdain.

Thomas rose from his seat. "Come, let me show you our home so we might get to know each other."

I lingered where I was, watching the High Fae mingle without actually mingling. They remained as apart from the vampires as if they had stayed standing by the door.

"Is this as bad as I think it is?" I asked as Liam came to stand beside me.

"Worse," he said.

I nodded. That's kind of what I thought.

"The Wild Hunt is an old tradition. It uses ancient magic that can't be controlled."

"And Arlan is its lord?" I asked.

His smile was grim. "One of them. There is no true lord of the hunt. The most powerful on that night becomes its Lord until the hunt is done. The magic chooses who among those present will be the hunters or the prey. Usually the weak and criminals are chosen as prey, but not always."

I looked back at where the Fae had begun to move through the room. For the most part they remained in a group, only a few of them drifting off on their own, Niall and Cadell among those.

The twins remained with the group but seemed more interested in watching Liam and me.

"And Niamh? How does she factor into all this?" I asked

"She's the high king's youngest daughter," Liam said.

"Somehow, that doesn't surprise me," I murmured watching the newcomers carefully. She had the spoiled entitlement down pat.

"I'm surprised to hear she married, and to Arlan of all people," he said.

"Jealous?" I asked, giving him a quick look.

"No, just surprised. Her unfortunate appetites are well known among their people. Even for one of them, she is considered cruel," he said softly.

"How is she tied to the hunt?" I asked.

"Blood and death are her two preferred pastimes. Hunting others down for sport is her favorite activity. She has participated in more hunts than any other Fae I know of."

"She's a lady of the hunt then?" I asked.

Liam's small laugh held little humor. "She is far too weak for that. At least she was when I knew her. Now? It's hard to say."

I sensed a story there, but I didn't push, knowing how the past could tangle and tear a person up inside. If he wanted to share, he would do so in his own time.

"This doesn't seem like a good thing," I said. "Can't Thomas just forbid the hunt?"

Liam shook his head. "It's not that easy. The Wild Hunt goes where it will. That's the nature of old magic. Even if that wasn't the case, he still couldn't forbid it in his borders. We have a treaty with the Fae, and to forbid it would make him seem weak in front of potential allies."

That was just great. A Wild Hunt where anyone could be victim or perpetrator. Even worse, I seemed to have friends caught up in the middle of things.

"All we can do is try to control who participates and attempt to keep it out of the city," Liam said.

His words didn't fill me with confidence.

"I've heard stories about the Fae," I said.

And had experienced more than one encounter with the minor Fae, who could be considered capricious and mischievous on a good day. Everything I'd learned about the High Fae pointed to them being worse.

"Everything you've heard is true," Liam warned. "They have turned lying through truth into an art form. Be very careful with them, Aileen. They will seek to trick you just because they can."

I nodded.

"Is that where you were when you were gone?" I asked, in a soft voice.

By the way Liam went still, I could tell it wasn't a topic he welcomed.

"Briefly," he said, his voice husky.

Not too brief, considering he was gone for nearly three months. Of course, given rumors the Fae lands experienced time differently from us, perhaps his brief visit had translated into months here.

Seeing Niamh approaching, he stepped away as he said, "Keep an eye on yourself and try to stay out of trouble for the night. Find me if you see anything amiss."

I let him go, not wanting to attract the attention of the Fae woman or any of her companions. I moved through the crowd, giving the rest of the Fae delegation a wide berth.

Niall and Cadell remained on the outskirts of the gathering, not socializing with their own kind or any vampires. They watched the scene with bored eyes as they sipped their wine.

Cadell caught my gaze and gave a slight shake of his head, warning me off. I hesitated, my desire to know why they were here, participating in this Wild Hunt, warring with the knowledge it might be better to wait for a more opportune time when we weren't so closely watched.

I sighed and turned away, the act enough to let them know I understood. I wasn't going to wait forever, but I could give them this. If they didn't find me and explain before too long, I'd get the information I wanted another way, their machinations be damned.

I drifted in Jerry's direction, taking a circuitous route to where he stood against the wall. He was one of the few not watched by the red caps, either trusted or considered so unimportant a guard wasn't necessary.

"Not exactly your scene," I told him. I lifted the wine glass I'd plucked from a server's tray to my lips and feigned taking a sip as I looked over the crowd, making a concerted effort not to pay any attention to the giant next to me.

"Aileen, you're wading in dangerous waters," he said, not looking at me.

Jerry was a tall man and before I'd met the red caps I would have said he had some troll in him. Compared to them, however, he looked like a foothill standing next to a mountain.

Still, that didn't mean he was the type of person you'd like to meet in an alley at night. The permanently grumpy lines of his face alone were enough to send you screaming. Add in the mammoth build and the fact even his muscles had muscles, and the impression you took away was that of a bruiser capable of crushing your skull.

"I think mine are a little less dangerous than yours at the moment," I told him.

He made a gruff sound that could have been taken as agreement—or he had something stuck in his throat. With Jerry, it was always hard to tell.

"What are you doing here?"

Especially since I knew for a fact that he hated vampires. He'd suffered my presence because of a favor he owed my former captain.

"It is an honor for one so humble as I to be called on to serve our lord and lady." The words were said in Jerry's deep rumble, but the emotionless way they were recited and his closed-off expression said they might as well have come from someone else.

"Well, I never would have called you humble," I told him.

Imposing. Intimidating. Gruff. I could come up with twenty words to describe Jerry, but humble wouldn't have been among them.

"It is my honor to serve, as it is for every being with a drop of Fae blood," he continued. He certainly didn't look like it was an honor. No, he looked like he would chew through iron to express his displeasure about his situation.

"Did they give you a script to recite?" I hissed. All this babble would make so much more sense if that was the case.

He snorted, but didn't respond.

"What's this I hear that Hermes isn't currently carrying messages?" I asked.

I'd written the sphinx's declaration off as exaggeration, a fanciful turn designed to influence me to help. In fact, I never gave the claim an ounce of credibility, but standing here next to Jerry with him acting like a puppet, maybe I should have.

"Everything I have serves the lord and lady's agenda," Jerry said, turning his attention to me for the first time since I'd arrived. His words had a certain weight to them, the significance of which wasn't lost on me.

My eyes widened, even as I fought to keep my reaction under control.

That, more than anything I'd heard or seen tonight, unsettled me. I nodded to show my understanding of the message.

"Aileen, lass, you have a good heart, but listen to me this time. Steer clear of this," he warned. "You're digging on unsteady ground. Throttle your normal reckless impulses and keep your head down."

Jerry didn't wait for a response, plodding away, his broad shoulders cutting through the crowd with little effort on his part.

I watched him go as I took a sip of the fairy wine. The taste of it burst on my tongue, tantalizing and sweet, the endless possibility of spring coupled with the refreshing bite of the season's first snowmelt.

A person could get addicted to this stuff if they let themselves.

I set the almost full glass of wine on a passing server's tray as I considered what Jerry had told me. I was afraid it would be impossible to follow his advice.

Even if I wasn't hopelessly entangled, I would have become invested once I'd learned about Jerry's presence and the likely fact that all his couriers had been enslaved to the High Fae's service.

The thing I hated about loyalty was that it wasn't so easily discarded. You couldn't shrug it off like you could a pair of dirty clothes. It was there, an undercurrent to every action. Whether you wished it to be or not.

Jerry had received my loyalty when he gave me a job at a time when I was lost. He'd earned it when he kept me on despite the considerable trouble I brought to his door.

I didn't know what he'd gotten himself caught up in, but I wasn't going to sit back and watch him and the rest drown. Not if it was in my power to throw him a lifeline.

How, was the question.

CHAPTER ELEVEN

During my perusal of the room, I slowly became aware there was almost as much attention being directed toward me by the vampires, as there was to the Fae.

I watched them, even as they watched me. I supposed it made sense, given my reputation. I was the rebellious baby vamp who'd made it possible for their master to claim his current lofty position, even as I rejected everything to do with their society.

I'd probably be curious too if I was in their position.

"How very understanding of you," a voice murmured from a few feet away.

I didn't jerk, having spied Aiden's approach. I hoped he'd bypass me, but it seemed the younger vampires before me weren't the only ones who were curious.

"How rude," he said.

Aiden took a sip of his wine as he joined me. His hands weren't the overly manicured ones of many in my generation. They were rough and calloused. It was obvious at one point in his life he'd worked in some type of manual labor. A trait he must have continued for his hands to be as rough as they were.

Aiden always reminded me of a young boxer, with his slightly crooked nose that had been broken and not set when he'd been human, and strong, square jaw that practically dared someone to come at him.

"I thought my mental defenses prevented you from reading my mind," I said.

He gave me a slight smirk. "They do. Except when you think very loudly."

I hadn't been thinking loudly. Protecting my mental space was a technique I'd had to develop as a courier, since a few of the people I served were skilled empaths and telepaths. Letting them pluck secrets from my head would have meant a much shorter career and possible death for breaking my contract with Hermes.

Those telepaths had been on par with Aiden. Or so I'd thought. Either he had downplayed his strength or something had changed since our last encounter.

"Of course, your face is also very easy to read," he said with a teasing glint in his eyes.

I wasn't sure if I believed that. Perhaps that was his intention.

He propped himself against the wall with me. Together we watched the rest of the crowd.

"Have you come to tempt me to join your clan again?" I asked.

"No, I'm afraid that is no longer an option," Aiden said, his voice idle.

I glanced up at him and frowned.

"You're the master's now," he explained. "Any clan you join would be his."

I settled back. That was an interesting little tidbit. So, when Liam and the rest pressured me about a clan, they were in effect pushing me towards Thomas. Good to know.

"What do you think of your guests?" I asked.

"You mean 'our.'"

"Right, that's what I meant."

Aiden's gaze was watchful as he turned his attention to the party. Musicians had begun playing and there were several people gliding about the dance floor elegantly. Nothing like what Caroline and I had been doing last night. These were stately movements in a graceful pattern that almost made me wish I hadn't quit those dance lessons as a kid.

Before Aiden could answer my question, he let out a small curse and took a gulp of his wine. I looked to see what had caught his attention and nearly cursed myself.

I was familiar with the woman striding purposefully toward us. Kat, formerly of the Davinish clan, was one of the first vampires I'd ever met, aside from my sire and Liam.

Needless to say, she hadn't left a good impression. She'd done a thorough job of souring me on my fellow vampires when I didn't need the extra help.

She was an unrepentant social climber, determined to rise to the top of their society by any means necessary. It seemed to be working for her too, because she'd somehow inveigled a way into a position as one of Thomas's aides.

Her skirt whipped around her legs, a clear sign of her agitation as she approached. She looked at Aiden like he was scum on the bottom of her shoe. The expression didn't suit her model-perfect face.

He sighed. "You do know I still outrank you?"

She scowled at him.

"I see your rise in circumstances hasn't made you any better at guarding your thoughts," he observed.

There was a banked rage in her gaze as she turned to me, obviously intent on ignoring the patriarch. Always a mistake. You never put a predator at your back unless you were sure you could survive them.

"Your master desires you make yourself useful," she said.

"Oh?"

It was interesting how he had passed along that message when he hadn't gotten within ten feet of Kat all night. I knew because I'd been watching.

She arched an eyebrow.

I didn't twitch, meeting her gaze with a calm that seemed to irritate her. Petty of me, I know, but in the case of this vampire, I was okay with resorting to such tactics.

"What are you waiting for?" she snapped.

Aiden didn't bother concealing his amusement at her expense, his expression slightly taunting. "Perhaps she is waiting to be told what exactly it is you expect her to do."

I snorted, not even bothering to pretend a respect I didn't feel. The vampire before me was a bully, one who liked to use her status to get others to dance to her wishes. I didn't plan to be one of them.

"You're needed in the parking lot." Her very red lips curved upward. "To park cars."

When I still didn't move, her gaze turned angry. "Now what's the hold up?"

I favored her with a bland smile. "I have my orders and they don't come from Thomas."

She rolled her eyes. "Thomas's orders trump everyone else's."

"If they had come from Thomas, perhaps," I said, pleasantly. Even then I probably wouldn't have obeyed. To do so would be to admit his hold over me was real.

"I outrank you," she spat, insult on her face.

I shrugged. "I don't care."

She huffed and stalked off.

"That woman is either going to end up ruling us all or dead when her maneuvering finally backfires," Aiden observed.

"Someone like her is too smart to take the wrong side of any battle," I said tiredly. "She's like a virus that just won't go away."

Aiden's laugh was surprised. I noted a vampire in the crowd near us turn his head slightly, intelligent eyes meeting mine before he bent his head to his companion. Neither vampire had moved in the entire time Aiden had been standing near me, as if they were hoping to listen in on something interesting. Or act as guard and protector, I thought, noticing as they shifted to block Aiden from view as one of the Fae circled in our direction.

They must be part of Aiden's clan. Enforcers by the look of them, their presence unobtrusive but with the obvious intent of protecting their patriarch.

It was similar to those revolving around Thomas as he mingled with his visitors.

"She doesn't outrank you. In case you were wondering," Aiden said, pulling me from my thoughts.

I hadn't been. What I told Kat was true. I truly didn't care if she outranked me or not. She was playing a game when I wasn't even on the board and had no intention of ever being on it.

Aiden seemed to follow the line of my thoughts or at least had learned to accurately read my body language. "Fascinating. I think I will enjoy watching you find your place."

"I already know my place," I told him, turning back to the crowd.

He took a sip of his wine. "Do you? Please, enlighten me."

I didn't answer.

"Because from my eyes, you're lost and alone yet you yearn for purpose."

I didn't react, even when his words seemed to channel thoughts that plagued me during the deepest part of night when the world was still and I was on my own.

He was wrong, but he was also right.

I wasn't lost; I knew exactly where I was. It just wasn't necessarily where I wanted to be. I missed being part of something. I missed the sense of purpose that came from doing what you loved, or at least doing what was important.

In that sense, I was lost, but I also knew joining the vampires and toeing their line wasn't going to give me what I wanted. It wouldn't fill that void inside me, despite what vampires like Aiden and Thomas might believe.

"You never did answer my question earlier," I said, not reacting to his words.

He tilted his head as I looked up at him.

"About your thoughts on our guests," I said, expanding.

"Didn't I?" He took a sip of his drink.

"I would remember."

"Hm."

"There you are," a velvety voice said.

A woman approached, her eyes alive with laughter, dancing to a joke only she knew. She glided across the floor, the movement seduction itself.

"Sofia Davinish, you are breathtaking," he said, appreciation in his voice.

He took the hand she offered and brought it to his lips.

Interest filtered through me at her name. This was the Davinish matriarch. I'd been to her clubs, met some of her vampires but had never met the woman herself.

She held herself regally, her head up as she flirted with Aiden—surprising given the depth of dislike Kat had always shown the patriarch. I'd always assumed that Aiden's clan and the Davinish clan didn't get along.

From the byplay between the two now, I saw I might have to revise that assumption.

"From the look on my protégé's face, I can assume you've been tweaking her tail again," Sofia said, amused.

"Your protégé is a shark given legs," Aiden said, his voice light and airy as if he hadn't just insulted someone from the woman's clan.

Her laugh was throaty and husky as she threw her head back.

"One of the reasons I chose her. Even as a human she possessed few scruples."

"Be careful her ambitions don't turn in your direction," he cautioned.

I glanced at the man and woman who had trailed behind Sofia. Unlike Aiden's guards, these two made no attempt at blending into the crowd. They were dressed alike, their clothes dark and tight, while still managing to not seem entirely out of place in this glittering room.

The man matched Sofia's coloring—they both looked like they were of Italian descent, or full-blooded Italian. His dark eyes surveyed the room, cataloging. The woman at his side was shorter than him by only an inch, her hair cut short and pulled back from her face. She had high cheekbones and plump lips, with skin the color of night. She was striking, and not just because of her bone structure. She looked like a sharpened blade, meant to cut through everything.

She met my gaze briefly, interest and curiosity there, before returning to watching the room.

Both of Sofia's guards were powerful. Not as powerful as the two flirting beside me, but enough so that a small headache was forming.

"Is this Thomas's wayward charge I've been hearing so much about?" Sofia asked, her eyes bright and curious.

Aw, how nice. Being discussed as if I wasn't standing right there, a thinking, feeling being.

I held my peace even as irritation bit at me. However, Thomas had been clear—seen and not heard.

It was a phrase I had to repeat to myself as Sofia drifted closer, reaching out and touching the lock of hair that curled against my cheek.

"Very pretty," she said as if looking at a piece of art. The art being me. "And more obedient than I'd been given to expect."

I didn't react, just met her eyes with a bland expression that said I couldn't be bothered with responding to such ridiculousness. It was the avid interest in her eyes that told me she was testing me, poking and prodding to get my measure.

She'd have to work harder than that.

I turned to find Aiden staring at me. He knew what I was up to.

For whatever reason, he decided to take pity on me.

"Shall we dance?" he asked Sofia, holding out one hand.

She took it with a coy smile. "I thought you would leave me in suspense for a little longer."

"Never," he told her.

The two left me to hold up the wall, waltzing toward the dance floor, a string quartet playing as people slowly rotated before them.

Sofia's guard hesitated, giving me a small nod before she and the man slowly trailed after their matriarch.

"I'll never understand the draw between those two," a slightly accented voice said by my side. Anton stared after the two clan leaders, a considering expression on his face.

I felt a small flicker of surprise that he was addressing me. Another of Liam's enforcers, Anton had made no secret of the fact that he wasn't my biggest fan—even going so far as exiting any room I happened to enter, or turning on his heel and heading in the other direction if he happened to approach me in the hall.

That he was addressing me now, had even made a point of tracking me down to talk to me, left me feeling like the world might be in imminent danger of ending.

His dislike of all things me was understandable—up to a point. It was my presence and stubbornness about joining a clan that had, in a roundabout way led to the death of his human companion. Granted, she'd been plotting against me and had gone so far as to attempt to place the blame for several werewolf killings at Caroline's feet. In addition to that, she'd had several vile things planned for my eventual demise.

"Then again, Liam's obsession with you doesn't make sense to me either," he said as an aside.

My lips twitched at the statement. So, we had progressed from him ignoring me to thinly veiled hostility. I suppose that was progress. At least he wasn't pretending I didn't exist anymore.

The formal uniform Anton was dressed in seemed ill-suited for the man. He wore it poorly, like he itched to tear it off. He would have been more at home on some battlefield swinging a sword, a warrior from some long-ago era.

His skin was permanently tan. The crow's feet at the corners of his eyes and the faint lines on his face said he'd been turned later than me, after a lifetime spent living to the fullest and laughing at every opportunity.

"Speechless. This is a first." His words were dry and cutting, his dislike coming through very clearly. "I hadn't thought you capable of such restraint."

"Tell me—are you mad I exposed your companion for what she was or because you didn't see it?" I asked, finally turning to look at him fully.

I'd had time to think since everything had gone down. Granted, his obvious problem with me didn't take up a lot of headspace given all the other problems in my life, but I had given him some consideration.

My bet was on the latter reason. I'd seen him with his companion before she died, and while there'd been affection there, it had seemed almost patronizing—that of an older man with a woman he thought cute but ultimately slightly stupid. Not to mention, Anton had a bit of a reputation as a player.

His expression turned frosty, implying I'd guessed correctly. It seemed finding her killer and delivering him for Anton's revenge hadn't been enough to alter his attitude toward me.

I didn't let it bother me. I had never aspired to be liked by everyone. His sour outlook, while slightly irritating, had little impact on me in the long run. One of the perks of not being very involved in Thomas's affairs.

A waiter appeared before us, a woman whose gaze was bright and her smile cheery as she offered a tray of drinks.

"Can I interest you in a refreshment?" she asked, tilting the tray our way to entice us. She was a bright spot in the somber room where the laughter seemed more playacting than reality.

"Run along, the adults are speaking," Anton said in dismissal.

The woman's smile wilted and for a moment she looked like a kicked puppy.

I smiled at her, noting the small fangs denting her lower lip and the faintest trace of power. She was older than me by at least a century but not much more than that.

"I'll have one," I told her, grabbing a glass of what looked like white wine.

She beamed at me.

Anton made a small scoffing sound, waiting until she had left. "Kindness won't get you far in our world."

I shrugged. Maybe, maybe not.

I sniffed the liquid. It smelled lighter and sweeter than any wine I'd ever had. Given the fairy wine circulating, I decided it might be best to hold off on tasting the drink.

"What is it you want?" I asked, still considering the liquid. It was obvious he wanted something, or he wouldn't have deigned to visit me in my little corner.

He handed me a pair of opera gloves. "He said you forgot part of your outfit."

There was only one person he could be referencing. I turned, spotting Liam in the crowd, his gaze on mine.

As I watched, Niamh laid one hand lightly on his chest. A flash of jealousy at the other woman's proprietary gesture took me by surprise.

It didn't help that Liam made no effort to evade her touch, standing there stoically, his expression unchanging as her hand moved up to his shoulder.

"She wants him back," Anton observed unhappily.

Back implied they'd been together before.

"Who is she to him?" I asked, curiosity prodding me.

"An old flame," Anton said, a twist to his lips.

The words did nothing to stem the jealousy that was winding its way through me. The two seemed like they'd stepped straight from a painting, from some bucolic scene. The Fae princess with her prince. How sweet. Not.

"I have a hard time seeing the two of them together," I said. She was vicious and petty. Liam gave every indication of wanting to be as far away from her as possible.

"What? From your limited time spent with Liam, you think you know him?" Anton asked. He thought about it before conceding. "Maybe you'd be right about the current Liam, but once upon a time the two made quite the name for themselves, each trying to outdo the other for pure viciousness."

I held up the gloves. "What are these for?"

"Just put them on," he said impatiently.

I held his gaze with my own, not changing expression and not making any move to don the gloves.

"It escapes me why you were the first person he visited when he returned," Anton muttered, reaching for my arm and turning it up.

First person? I looked back at Liam again, remembering his recent visit, seeing it in a new light with this news.

"It's best not to advertise your marks to the world," Anton explained with a forced patience, grabbing one glove and pulling it up my arm as I watched Liam.

He glanced up at that moment, his gaze connecting with mine. It was like being hit with a fist of electricity, an inescapable awareness, as potent now as the first time it had happened.

He took in the two of us as Anton shoved on my other glove. The smallest warmth entered his expression and he cocked his head, the gesture an unmistakable summons.

I gave him a look that said ask nicely.

In response, he glanced at Anton and jerked his head.

"We've been summoned," Anton muttered, grabbing my arm and hauling me after him. He took the glass from me and set it on a waiter's tray as we passed.

Liam looked at me and smirked, obviously feeling pretty pleased he'd gotten his way. I gave him a challenging smile. We'd see how long that lasted.

"Are you my keeper for the evening?" I asked Anton, shifting my attention from the small group we were approaching.

"Something like that."

I gave him a considering look as he avoided my eyes. That was not the response I'd been expecting.

A shoulder bumped me and a pair of familiar eyes met mine. Cadell looked at my companion and then touched my shoulder. For a brief moment, his hand was warm, almost hot against me.

"You should watch where you're going," he said. The words were at odds with the slightly wary look in his eyes, one I understood when a piece of paper was slipped into my hand.

He turned and walked away before I could say anything, weaving around the floor as he headed back to Niall, who very carefully wasn't watching us.

I looked around, finding no one seemed to have noticed the exchange, or if they had, they'd written it off as the baby vampire making a fool of herself.

"What was that about?" Anton asked, his gaze suspicious as if he knew something had just happened, but not what.

I gave him a bright smile, clasping my hands and hiding the paper. "Nothing. Let's find Liam before he has a coronary over you not doing what you're supposed to."

I stepped past him before he could say anything, reaching up casually to tuck the folded piece of paper into the top of my glove.

Before Anton could ask any further questions, we reached Liam. He slipped smoothly away from Niamh, evading her as he reached me.

"Aileen, good. You saved me that dance you promised," Liam said smoothly. "Come, dance with me." It wasn't really a request.

I took the hand he offered, somewhat reluctantly. My dancing skills were average at best.

I was very aware of Niamh glaring at us as we walked away.

A new song started up as he set one hand against my waist and took my hand in his other.

"This brings back memories of the last time we danced," Liam said, his body brushing against mine as he turned us and set us to gliding across the dance floor.

"Hopefully, this evening has a better ending than that one," I said. Last time we'd ended the night with a body on the ground.

Liam was a masterful dancer, making it seem like I halfway knew what I was doing. He led me through the steps, the slight pressure of his hands guiding me.

"What did the Fae slip you?" Liam whispered in my ear.

I leaned back, catching a glimpse of Liam's face as he swept me across the floor. He looked like he was making idle chatter about the weather.

"What makes you think he slipped me anything?" I asked, stalling. I didn't know what Cadell had given me, but from the way he and Niall were acting it must be important.

"Anton wasn't in a position to see, but I was," Liam said, never raising his voice or losing that slightly patronizing look on his face. "It was a skilled pass."

I remained quiet, unsure what would be the best response. Liam was technically my employer. Yet my previous relationship with the two Fae complicated things, especially since I felt like I owed them a debt.

"I have to commend you on your lack of reaction. If I didn't know you so well, I would never have spotted anything amiss," he murmured, his expression loving.

To the ballroom's occupants, it would seem like we were having a moment between lovers. An impression that didn't seem to go over Niamh's head, her expression turning vindictive as she glared at us.

If I didn't know better, I would think Liam was doing it on purpose.

"How do you know the two of them?" he asked.

His question answered one thing. He didn't know they were my downstairs neighbors, something I found surprising given how he seemed to know everything else in my life.

I sighed. "We should really leave this conversation until we're not surrounded by potential enemies."

My forced smile was loving, adulation shining from every pore.

"A secret," Liam murmured. "You know how I feel about those."

Yes. It seemed most vampires couldn't resist a secret, going to excessive lengths to ferret them out. Secrets might as well have been the lifeblood of my new species. That, and actual blood.

"I will find out what you're hiding," he warned in a deep voice as if he relished the thought.

"Yes, but perhaps not here," I told him.

"Challenge accepted."

I fought against rolling my eyes.

The music ended and we both clapped politely before Liam escorted me off the dance floor to where Anton stood watching. He'd drifted to the opposite side of the room from Niamh and the other Fae, something that was no doubt on purpose.

"Anything interesting to report?" Liam asked Anton when we reached him. He kept one firm hand on my waist, keeping the side of my body pressed against the length of his.

Anton shook his head. "It's been quiet, so far."

I subtly watched the gathering through my othersight, noting the thin streams of magic that drifted through the air. They seemed aimless, harmless as they ducked and swooped near the ceiling.

"What is it you think will happen?" I asked.

"If I knew, I wouldn't be stuck waiting," Liam said. "I'd already have taken care of the problem."

There was frustration in his face and voice. I could tell he didn't like sitting back and waiting for his enemies to strike. No one did.

Waiting was the worse feeling in the world. Knowing there were people out there who wanted to kill you or at least fuck up your world, but not being able to do a damn thing about it because you didn't know how or when they would strike.

A server circled our way. I shook my head when the tray of wine was offered to me, noting Liam and Anton did the same.

As they resumed their hushed conversation, I watched the magic, fascinated. It was rare to see so much of the stuff in an ambient form, just swimming through the room as if it was a giant aquarium. I idly wondered whether the ribbons of magic had been created or if they were a natural phenomenon.

Columbus was supposedly on several ley lines, one of the reasons it had such a strong supernatural population. Ley lines were great wells of magic that could be tapped to amplify a person's strengths. Not to mention, their presence was capable of sustaining those spooks whose very lives were dependent on its presence.

I was so consumed with the hypnotic beauty above that I momentarily forgot about watching the people around me.

A server drifted past, jostling me and distracting me from my thoughts. I stared at her, not knowing why a sense of danger and impending doom skated along my nerves, wondering why the woman had snagged my attention in the first place.

It was the one from earlier, the one who had interrupted me and Anton.

I couldn't quite put my finger on what exactly it was about her that struck me as "off". Soldiers understood instinct and gut urges. Sometimes a soldier could look at someone and know they had an IED or weapon on them. Later they wouldn't be able to explain how or why they knew, they just did. It had something to do with experience and intuition converging to warn them. Of course, sometimes they got it wrong.

For that reason, I remained in place, watching for a clue that would tell me how to act. I didn't want to start something without knowing for a fact I wasn't simply being jumpy.

She seemed normal enough, the tray in her hands oddly full despite the crowd she moved through. I saw why, as she ignored a vampire who tried to signal for a glass of wine.

She was moving too fast through the crowd, not using that slow meandering walk most of the servers used while enticing people to take another glass. Her path was too direct, her mission pre-determined.

Then I realized what had bothered me all along. It was her expression, eyes vacant, face blank, as if she was a doll someone else had wound up and sent on her way.

I moved before I could think, cutting through the crowd at an angle from her.

"Aileen," Liam snapped.

I barely paid attention, conscious of the server as she momentarily moved out of view when a red cap lumbered past.

Liam's hand caught my arm and pulled me to a stop. "What are you doing?"

"Something is wrong," I said, already twisting to locate the woman.

"What?" he asked.

I grimaced. "Not sure."

"Try to explain," he said with forced patience.

I considered. It couldn't hurt.

I nodded to the woman. "You see her."

He frowned and nodded.

"She's not in her area," I said, finally articulating one of the things that had been bothering me.

It wasn't obvious at first glance, but the servers had cut the room into quadrants and tended to stick to their space unless summoned. This woman, however, was ignoring all that, moving in a way counter to the rest of the servers.

Liam picked up on the significance of that.

"Anton, find out who she is and her master's name," Liam ordered.

Anton looked between the two of us but didn't argue, already moving to follow orders.

"Do you see anything else?" Liam asked, a weight to his question that told me what he really wanted to know.

I shook my head. "There might be something, but I'm not sure. There are too many power players to get an accurate read."

He touched me on the hip. "Then we'll get her to a place where you can get that reading. Stay here."

I was more than willing to oblige as he signaled one of his enforcers before moving away. The crowd parted for the dangerous shark in their midst as he cut through them.

Even as young as this vampire was, she could probably wipe the floor with me. She had to have decades on my three years. Vampires were like fine wine, they grew more powerful and dangerous with age. Something I wouldn't have for many, many years to come.

Liam appeared in front of the server, a genial smile on his face. She stepped back and drew up short as another enforcer appeared behind her. The one I called Viking. He was large and intimidating as he scowled down at her.

The tension I'd been carrying in my shoulders dissipated as they corralled her. Whatever her intent, whatever had been planned was contained now.

A sharp scream ripped from her. She crumpled in the Viking's hands, falling to the ground as she jerked and shook. A space widened around the three as those in the vicinity drew back to watch the drama in their midst.

Liam and the Viking tried to protect her from injuring herself, their efforts only mildly successful as she convulsed, her eyes rolling up in her head as white froth spilled out of her mouth. Blood leaked out of her ears and mouth.

A halo surrounded her in my othersight, getting stronger and more vivid with every scream. Whatever was happening to her, it sounded like she was being slaughtered as we watched helplessly.

I glanced away, looking in the direction she'd been heading. Distantly, I noted Thomas surrounded by his guests, Niall and Cadell among them. They all watched dispassionately as the woman's cries suddenly ceased.

That was nearly scarier than her screams, the silence unbearably loud in the full ballroom.

Thomas frowned with curiosity as he looked between where I stood, and Liam and the woman on the ground, something building in his gaze.

A movement to his right caught my attention. A vampire, vaguely familiar, turned toward Thomas's group. His face displayed the same vacantness as the woman.

His lips moved as he muttered.

I moved before I could think better of it, discarding the possibility of using the Judge. There was too much of a chance of hitting civilians.

Fifteen feet from Thomas. Ten.

I wasn't going to be fast enough. The man raised his hand, something warping the air in front of it.

I sprinted for them.

Thomas's eyes widened at the sight of me pelting in his direction, his gaze rotating as he sought what had caused my panic.

The vampire threw the ball of writhing air. I arrived, yanking Thomas out of the way. Not fast enough. The protection Dahlia had given me shredded with a crack that ripped through the air.

The ball hit me—excruciating pain consuming me. Arlan and the twins watched with fascination as they sipped on their drinks. Then nothingness.

CHAPTER TWELVE

"When were you going to tell me about this?" Thomas asked. His voice sounded overly loud to my pounding head.

Not my favorite way to wake up. I didn't bother opening my eyes, not ready to leave the cool darkness quite yet. You never know when someone might let something interesting slip, and with vampires, it paid to overhear as much as you could.

Liam remained stubbornly silent. I could almost imagine his cold gaze in my mind.

"Perhaps if you looked beyond your own concerns every once in a while, I wouldn't have had to," Liam said.

Thomas scoffed. "Bullshit. You were hoping to capitalize on her ability without my interference."

"I have no need to go to such lengths when your yearling hates you." Liam sounded coldly amused.

The smallest growl escaped Thomas. "She's mine, Liam. Not yours. Her secrets, her life, are mine to protect or use as I see fit."

And he couldn't understand why I didn't trust him or want anything to do with him. It was statements like that which reminded me why I'd remained stubbornly independent despite the cost.

"She is yours in name only," Liam said. "Everything else belongs to me."

And on that note.

I sat up, not wanting to listen to any more of this.

I glared at both vampires, neither of whom acted the least bit ashamed at being caught talking about me like I was a piece of meat.

If anything, Liam seemed amused.

"How long was I out?" I asked, ignoring all the things that were wrong in the conversation I'd just overheard.

"Not long, only a few minutes," Liam responded.

I nodded but didn't make any move to stand. Sitting up seemed to be the extent of my ability right now. Already my head pounded and dizziness threatened to put me on my back again.

"You should be dead," Thomas said.

I lifted my head as I gave him an incredulous look. Was that a threat?

"He's right," Liam said, sounding grimmer than I'd ever heard him.

Not a threat then.

"I returned your weapon to you for a reason," Liam said heavily.

"You also said only use it in an emergency," I said, feeling a small twinge of shame.

I'd reacted rather than acted. There was a fine difference between the two. One led to stupid actions, the other to victory. Tonight, I saw the threat and instead of pulling my gun, I'd thrown myself in front of it. What a foolish mistake. I couldn't believe I'd been that dumb.

"This situation qualified," he said. "He would have survived several rounds as long as you didn't hit his head or heart."

"I'm interested to know how you survived something designed to kill a vampire master," Thomas said in an idle voice.

At least this I had an answer for. I drew out the small pendant Dahlia had given me and winced. The pretty stone looked like it had been shattered and then glued back together, the number of fine cracks in it almost infinite.

Thomas reached out and studied the pendant. "That is an interesting bauble you have there. Where'd you get it?"

I shrugged. If he didn't know, I had no plans to tell him. Liam knew. If he wanted, he could inform Thomas.

He set it down very gently, squatting so he could study me carefully. He reached for my hand and paused, his mouth tightening when I drew back the faintest bit.

"Your necklace absorbed a good portion of the attack but not all. I need to assess the extent of the damage," he said with a forced patience.

"Have Liam do it," I told him, more to see his reaction than anything else.

"It's in your best interests that I do this," Thomas said, giving me a sharp smile as he grabbed my hand and held it in an unbreakable grip. "This is better suited to my skill set than his."

Liam stood behind him, unmoving. I took that to mean Thomas wasn't lying.

I forced myself to remain still as Thomas's power swept through me, brushing against my insides. It wasn't a bad feeling, more uncomfortable than anything. Like someone shoving a needle into the nerves just under the skin, a thousand pinpricks that made me want to rub my hands down my body to dispel the sensation.

Instead, I sat uncomfortably as Thomas's gaze turned inward.

Liam loomed over his shoulder, his face just the slightest bit pensive as he watched. The faint worry in the lines around his mouth told me how important this was. As if I didn't already know.

I'd missed it upon first waking, too distracted by the awful way I felt to notice it, but now, with Thomas's power calling my attention to it, it was impossible to miss—a piece of magic, wriggling as it burrowed into my shoulder. It felt alien and wrong there. Almost physical as it hunkered down.

I briefly considered finding a scalpel and trying to cut the offensive piece of detritus out, like it was a tumor I could get rid of.

I doubted it'd be that simple. Spook-related things rarely were.

"What happened to the woman?" I asked in an effort to distract myself.

"Dead." The words were grim.

A soft sigh of regret escaped me. I hadn't known the woman, hadn't wanted to either, if I was being honest with myself. I wanted no further ties binding me to the vampires and would have resisted any overtures of friendship from her, would have hardened my heart and erected my barriers so high she never would have had a chance to scale them.

Still, it was sad to think her open gaze and happy smile had been erased from this world. She would have left people behind, people who no doubt cared for her and would miss her now she was truly gone.

Wrapped in all of these thoughts was the belief her death lay at my feet in some way. If I'd been faster, handled things differently, maybe she wouldn't now be dead.

"She wouldn't have survived even if you hadn't brought her to Liam's attention," Thomas said, his eyes closed, his power still questing.

I didn't know if I believed that.

His power began to withdraw and he looked at me, his silver-gray eyes startlingly clear. "Think it through. She was killed as soon as it became apparent she wouldn't complete her mission. If she had managed to do as ordered, she would have faced the same fate."

I was quiet as I processed that statement. "Is that what happened to the other vampire?"

He inclined his head, his gaze steady. "His strings were cut as soon as it was clear he was no longer of use."

I blew out a breath. The thought of being responsible for a person's death lifted just slightly. I hadn't realized how heavy that burden had been until it was gone.

Thomas stood. "The person controlling him took care of the task for us. Had he survived, my enforcers would have ended him shortly afterward."

"It wasn't his fault. They were being controlled." My gaze went between the two of them.

It was the only explanation that made sense. I'd seen that blank, vague look before in other victims of compulsion.

"Right?" I asked Liam.

He hesitated before nodding. "I had Makoto look into both of them. Neither one displayed any indications of disloyalty."

Thomas didn't look affected by the words. "It doesn't matter. We can't afford to let people know vampires can be so easily compelled and the public nature of the attacks would have forced my hand."

I didn't like that answer, but I understood it in a way.

Thomas had taken over the city not too long ago. He couldn't afford to appear weak, and having his own people try to assassinate him did not send the right kind of message to his enemies.

"Beyond that, it is difficult to lift a compulsion. Unless we found the person responsible and killed them, we would never be able to trust them again," Thomas said, appearing unaffected at the thought of killing his own people.

"How did she die? I thought we were nearly indestructible," I asked. Beyond severing our heads or burning us alive, it was very difficult to kill most vampires. The older one was, the more difficult.

"We don't know," Liam said, folding his arms over his chest. "I have Joseph going over the bodies to see what he can find."

Joseph was a doctor and understood more about supernatural physiology than anyone else I knew. A benefit to being nearly immortal—it gave you a lot more time to study the topics that interested you.

Thomas stood and circled to my back. I edged forward in my seat, preparing to stand.

A hand on my shoulder pressed me back. A fact I was grateful for when the edges of my vision darkened, dizziness threatening to send me back to unconsciousness.

He pulled aside the strap of my gown and cursed. "Liam, look at this."

Liam stood and moved around me. His fury hit my back in the next second, the tension from it making me edge forward again.

"She's been marked by the hunt," Thomas said.

My stomach dropped. "The hunt? You mean the Wild Hunt?"

The two shared a look over my head. The silence was filled with the heavy weight of unsaid things.

"Liam?" I couldn't help the tremulous quality of my voice.

"Yes, the Wild Hunt."

The hunt the vampires were so worried about? The one that had the

Fae of the city in a tizzy?

"How can I be marked?" I asked, groping for calm and logic.

"That is a good question," Thomas said.

Liam stepped around me, his face hard and his eyes glittering. "I have a way of finding out."

"Stop," Thomas's voice rang out, filling the room with power. My breath stuttered in my chest, the compulsion in his words unmistakable.

That didn't affect Liam as he continued to the door.

Thomas hissed, the sound edging toward a catlike growl. "You will not threaten our position."

Liam turned on him, his fangs dropping down as he snarled. "They have gone too far this time."

"We have no way to prove it's them," Thomas snapped.

"It's them alright. We both know it. Someone in the hunt would have needed to mark her, and you know as well as I do that Niamh has most of the lords caught in her thrall," Liam said, his voice hard.

"It's not a full mark. Her role isn't set yet. They can claim this is the effect of the hunt's magic. They'll say the hunt chooses its prey," Thomas argued.

"The lords mark potential prey. They open their victims up to the magic, making them more susceptible for being chosen by the magic," Liam argued.

"That's supposition. You said yourself no one truly understands how the hunt works. You cannot go and accuse them based upon guesswork and feelings," Thomas said.

Frustration and anger were written in every line of Liam's body. I sat quietly, feeling like a bone two predators were fighting over. It didn't help to know fear had invaded, sending my stomach rioting.

Liam paced in front of me, his power crackling through the air. Whatever reins he kept on himself had snapped. This was the real Liam—raw, dangerous, savage.

"Then we get her out of here. We hide her," he said.

I nodded. I was all for this plan. I'd already spent one night being hunted through the woods. Sometimes I still woke, gasping for air, feeling like I was back there being chased and terrified I wouldn't see the dawn. I had no desire to add another version to that nightmare.

"You, of all people, know how impossible that is," Thomas said.

Liam's flinch was barely there, unnoticeable to those who didn't know him well.

"The hunt will just follow. You've seen this." Thomas's face was sympathetic.

Liam ran a hand over his face. This was the most discombobulated I'd ever seen him. It brought home how much danger I was currently in.

"Can we get them to take their hunt elsewhere? Or tell them not to hold it?" I asked.

"It's doubtful that will work," Thomas said. "They've made clear their intentions to start a barrow here. The treaty we have in place with them does not allow for our interference."

"How does a Wild Hunt lead to establishing a barrow?" I asked, thinking aloud.

Liam stirred. "Fae magic is old magic. Primal. Its roots are deep in the earth. Once upon a time, they were easily able to establish little boltholes close to this world, entire realms they could rule while still touching the magic of this plane. That is no longer the case."

So, Dahlia had been right in the information she shared last night.

"Another reason I can't stop the hunt," Thomas said, almost seeming regretful. "The council is interested in knowing whether they can succeed. Better for it to done under our watchful eye than somewhere our presence isn't as strong."

Liam was quiet, his eyes coming to rest on me. I stared back. It was tempting to let him try to protect me from this, to hide me somewhere the hunt would never find me—if such a thing was even possible.

But I had friends here who needed me whether they knew it or not. Jerry, for one. There was also the question of how I got the mark. Leave now, and I might never know and whoever had done this to me could just wait until all this passed to try again. Only next time they might succeed.

Forewarned is forearmed. At least now I knew what I was up against.

Liam read all this on my face. His sigh held a note of frustration and he looked like he wanted to keep arguing.

"We'll figure this out," he told me.

I nodded. We would. There was no other choice.

"For now, I say we figure out what happened to your vampires," I told him.

It would keep my mind busy and away from thoughts of what might happen a few nights from now. There was also the fact that the two matters were connected. It was clear Niamh had a hand in both. Figure out one thing and you were halfway to figuring out the next.

He nodded, reluctantly, still frowning darkly at me.

I prepared to stand. "We should see what we can find out about the bodies."

"You need blood," Thomas said, his voice implacable. "You're weak and can barely stand."

I grunted, not needing the reminder. Much as I hated to admit it, Thomas was right. I wasn't going anywhere. Whatever strength I'd managed to gain from Liam's blood, it was gone now. Wiped away as if it had never been.

I hadn't felt this weak since waking up from my change. I was as unsteady and exhausted as a newborn.

The magic on my shoulder flexed, reminding me of another reason I needed to find strength. Right now, it seemed dormant, content to remain where it was. That probably wouldn't last. When it acted, I needed to be at my best, not my worst.

I settled back and nodded.

Thomas seemed slightly surprised by my capitulation, even as he turned away to summon refreshments.

I sighed. Sometimes I hated being as weak as I was.

Before any of us said anything, a soft knock came at the door.

"Enter," Thomas called.

Deborah slipped in, her gaze lowered submissively. A companion of one of Thomas's vampires, Deborah was human and regularly donated blood to her chosen vampire.

I held myself stiff as I watched the three people in the room. Thomas knew my rules. I didn't feed from humans.

"How may I be of help, master?" Deborah kept her voice diffident and her eyes lowered. It was a complete difference from the strong, assertive woman I'd met before.

I had to wonder if this was the appearance she gave to all vampires or just something reserved for Thomas.

"My yearling is in need of your services," Thomas said. He watched me much as a cat watched a mouse, waiting for the inevitable explosion.

His request startled her, enough that she dropped the facade, her head jerking up as her gaze met mine. There was anger there, loathing too. She didn't want to be my walking meal for the night. That much was clear.

She lowered her head and said, "Of course, master."

I snorted. He would have respected her more if she was honest.

All companions wanted to join the ranks of the undead. It was why they let the vampires feed from them. It was why they accepted a status of being second class, little more than indentured servants, from what I could see. It was true some vampires treated their companions with love and affection, but a human would never be the dominant in any relationship. Not even an equal, if what I'd seen was anything to go by.

If Deborah thought this little display would be more conducive to obtaining her lofty goal of the kiss, she should think again. Vampires respected strength and stubbornness. They had to. Too many of them succumbed to death during the transition. Only the strongest survived.

"No, thank you," I said politely.

Deborah didn't like that. She might not want to be my donor, but she also couldn't fail to notice the insult being rejected would bring. Not that I meant it as a rejection.

I turned my attention to Thomas. He stared back at me expectantly.

"You know I don't drink from humans. Bring bottled blood if you have it, and if not, I'll wait until I get home," I told him firmly.

It was the only way to be with this vampire. If I gave him even a little bit of space, he'd push for more. He did it time and again.

"You're being stubborn," he said. The slight smile on his face said he didn't truly object.

Before I could respond, he leaned closer, his eyes hypnotic in their intensity. They were liquid silver as they became all I could see, so focused on them the rest of the world faded around us.

Power arced between us, warmth spilling through me.

"You're so thirsty," Thomas said, his voice a thrumming purr. "You want to drink and her blood would taste so good."

He looked at the woman, my gaze turning with his until my vision spun down to Deborah's slim neck. Her pulse pounded at the base, calling me, tempting me.

My gums ached as my fangs descended, my gaze never wavering from that pulse. It was a siren call, a demand, one that overrode the small voice at the back of my mind telling me I didn't want to do this—that following this urge to its conclusion would cost me more than I could understand.

Just a small taste wouldn't be so bad. I'd been so good for so long. Feeding from her wasn't so different from feeding from Liam. It wouldn't make me less human; It just made me what I was. Vampire. Top of the food chain. The only predator that mattered.

The world popped and I was standing before Deborah, the fear pouring off her potent as it called to me, whispering to my most base instincts.

I grabbed her shoulders, yanking her to me.

"Easy," Thomas crooned in my ear. "You don't want to hurt her."

No, I didn't. I needed the blood in her veins. Hurting her might cost me that.

I bent lower, my fangs piercing the delicate flesh. The first taste of blood brought me back to myself, the warm copper coating my tongue restoring my sanity.

A strong hand on the back of my head kept me from jerking back.

"Not yet. You need more," Thomas said.

His grip was implacable, impossible to budge. My defenses teetered as blood filled my mouth.

"Swallow, my dear," Thomas urged.

I couldn't. Blood dribbled out the side of my mouth.

"Aileen, swallow." His voice turned dark with power, impossible to resist.

The first mouthful overrode my willpower. After that, I drank without thought, pressing the woman against me as I fed from her throat, that which made me Aileen, washed away on a sea of decadent life. It was like biting into a lightning bolt, powerful and bold, but instead of being singed, it restored the pieces of me that I didn't even know were missing.

"That's enough. Let go now," Thomas said. A pressure on my neck forced me to unlatch.

I made a wordless sound of protest. The urge to drink the source dry was almost undeniable. I struggled for a long second, trying to fight my way back to the nectar of life. He held me easily, with no more effort than he might use to subdue a week-old puppy.

"Shh, enough of that," Thomas murmured, his hands strong as he turned me away.

I came back to myself with a start, a sick feeling in the pit of my stomach and the taste of blood in my mouth. The wound I'd made at her neck had already closed, the anticoagulant in my saliva and something about my bite working to make sure she didn't bleed out. Within the next few minutes, the wound would be fully-healed and it would be as if this had never happened.

Abruptly my walking meal bag became a person again. Someone with thoughts and dreams of their own. Someone I had just turned into my dinner and if I hadn't been stopped, would have gladly murdered so I could gorge myself on her blood.

Deborah wavered and staggered to a chair, lowering herself with shaky hands. Her skin was pale, and she appeared frail, as if a stiff wind might blow her away.

I stared at her, stricken, my entire being frozen, the warmth of her blood still in my mouth. Despite having just fed, I wanted more. I wanted to do it again and again. I couldn't wait until the next time.

My line had been crossed. The last line I'd held onto with a fanatic's zeal—gone. Erased so easily. As if it had never been.

"You may leave," Thomas told Deborah kindly. Despite the soft words, it wasn't a request, the steely undercurrent in them making it clear there was only one correct action.

Deborah understood and nodded, her gaze skating to my horrified, sick expression before she lifted herself out of her chair. She snuck one last glance at me as I stared at her feeling more lost and alone than I had felt since day one of this new life. Her path to the door was wobbly and unsure. I'd done that. I'd taken enough that walking was difficult.

She needed a cookie. Orange juice. Something with sugar, I noted distantly. An urge to laugh struck me followed immediately by an urge to cry. I was treating this like she'd just given blood to the Red Cross, not like I'd buried my fangs in her throat and sucked her down like she was an ice cream sundae.

No one spoke until we were alone in the room.

"I feel sick," I said, bending over as my stomach rebelled and I made a small retching sound. Thomas grabbed my chin and held my mouth closed, his fingers bands of steel around my jaw.

"Oh no, you're not going to dishonor your donor by throwing up her life's blood," he said.

I breathed through my nose, fast pants that did nothing to quell the nausea. A prickling sensation teased the bridge of my nose as tears threatened. I held them back through sheer force of will, unwilling to let this man know just how much this little experience had devastated me.

"Calm *a stór*. Calm. Things are not so bad. You are still you. There is no need for this carrying-on," Thomas crooned, his hard hold turning soothing. His thumb caressed the skin just below my jaw.

I jerked out of his grip as soon as I was able, unable to help the half-sob that tried to well up. I would have crawled across broken glass if it would have meant escaping him.

My actions seemed to amuse him rather than deliver insult, and he watched me go with a small twist of his lips, his expression calm and unaffected.

He remained crouched for a long moment before standing, adjusting the lapels of his coat and tugging his cuffs down.

"You can thank me later, *dearthár*, for doing what you could not." Thomas's gaze was unsympathetic as he looked to where I huddled in on myself, trying to contain all the broken pieces of me, the ones that had been ripped open again with one simple act— parts I'd stitched together with impossible wishes and broken dreams and held together with sheer willpower and a staunch need to deny the truth.

It felt like I'd been stripped bare, sanded down until all the wounds that had only partially healed were visible again, the air stinging their half-formed scar tissue.

"Why did you do this?" I asked, my voice barely sounding like mine. It was raw and bewildered.

"You like to lie to yourself," Thomas said. "Tell yourself pretty stories about how human you are, but you're not; pretending otherwise will only hurt you in the long run. I made you face the truth. One day you will thank me for this."

"No, I won't." Pure conviction sounded in my voice. There was no way I'd be thanking him for this. Never. Not in a million years.

I was beginning to regret stepping in the way of that spell. I should have let it have him.

"There were better ways," Liam said, his voice quiet in the silence.

Thomas's snort was elegant, as was everything else about the man. It made me want to rend and tear, leave him maimed and feeling like his world had just been yanked from him. "You know there wasn't. Not when her blood had already gone toxic."

The words were delivered like a blow.

Liam went stiller than I'd ever seen, his chest not moving with breath. He was like a painting, life size but just as remote. Slowly, his gaze swung to me a question in his eyes.

I looked away, hugging myself tighter. I might not have realized how bad things had gotten but I couldn't deny something was drastically wrong, even to myself.

Realization and something like a soft regret filled his expression.

It made me want to withdraw even further into myself, as if I'd disappointed him in some way.

"She had already begun rejecting blood. Had I let it continue she might have entered devolution." Thomas's gaze was brooding as he looked down at me. "She needed human blood. Your blood would not have been enough."

I remained still, afraid that if I moved, if I shifted even a little bit, the things that made me Aileen Travers would shatter and what would emerge would no longer be me. That thought was scarier than any monster I'd ever faced.

"You're going to hate me for this," Thomas told me. "Rail at me, despise me, tell yourself all the pretty lies, but in your heart, you know I did you a favor. Know this my *a stór,* I will always do what I feel is best for you. Your conscience is clear. I made you take this step. Just like I'll make you take the next."

He sauntered out of the room without waiting for another response.

I stayed where I was. This all felt like a dream, a horrible nightmare.

Liam's sigh was heavy as he reached for my shoulder. I flinched away from his touch.

"Don't touch me. Never touch me again," I said, my tone steely, determined. It sounded like someone else talking, someone more put together than me, not this hot mess who was barely holding herself together.

"Aileen."

Just that. Just my name.

I moved to the door, my back bowed, my steps as tentative as a century-old grandma. "We have a pair of bodies to look over."

I didn't wait for an answer, leaving the room where I'd lost the last remnants of my human self without a backward glance.

Liam would follow or he wouldn't. If he didn't, I'd head home and forget. Or maybe I'd head for Dahlia's for a little help in forgetting. It didn't really matter to me.

CHAPTER THIRTEEN

I stood in the corner, arms folded across my chest and shoulders a little more bowed than usual as Joseph referred to his notes.

A tall man with skin the color of coffee and eyes a very light hazel, Joseph had a face that invited sin and a presence that always reminded me of a caged tiger. Beautiful but deadly, if you got close enough to touch.

He didn't remark on the tension my presence had caused or the clear awkwardness between Liam and me. We stood on opposite sides of the room. If I could have found a spot farther away, I would have. Right now, I didn't want to be in the same space as him—or any of the vampires really. Right or wrong, they'd all been painted with the same brush. As dangerous for my continued health and wellbeing as the master of the city.

The last thing I wanted to do was be standing in a room with them, but there was a job to do. Until it was done, I'd suck it up and work with them, but as soon as it was done, I planned to never cross a vampire's path again. I didn't care what it took or even if I had to move to the sunniest spot on earth to accomplish my goal. One way or another our association was at an end.

The rest of Liam's enforcers had gathered, at least the ones I knew. There might be more, but I had yet to meet them.

The only one missing was Nathan. Away on some mission only he and Liam knew about, no doubt.

A few of the enforcers glanced in my direction, picking up on the tension between Liam and me. They were subtle about it, until they weren't, staring outright when neither one of us made any move to address the problem.

Men. They were as bad about gossip as any group of ladies I knew.

153

I stared at the bodies on the table, ignoring their side-looks.

Even Joseph seemed to be aware something was going on, his gaze curious and considering.

"Something I should know?" he asked.

"It doesn't concern you," Liam replied, not looking up from the bodies. "Makoto, what do we know about these two?"

Makoto busied himself on the tablet in his hands, quickly sifting through information as he bopped his head to a beat only he could hear, numerous earrings glinting along the upper rim of his ear.

He had shaved his head on both sides, leaving the hair on top slightly longer. Today it was green, a bright spot of edginess in the otherwise formal room.

Joseph's study looked about as far as you could get from a morgue. The furnishings were all antiques with a mixture of textures and clean lines. Masculine and formal at the same time.

"Alright, the woman was Joanna Saska, from clan Raelle. Her sire was Angelique. She was practically a baby. Only a few years out of her hundred years of service," he recited, eyes focused on his tablet.

"Shame, that," Anton drawled.

Daniel grunted and folded his arms across his chest, his pretty hazel eyes fixed on me. He wore a beard, something rare in most of the vampires I'd met. It made him seem even gruffer than he already was. I didn't normally care for beards but on him it worked, adding to the impression that he was just off a battlefield, ready and willing to pillage the surrounding land. He was tall and fair-haired. A Viking through and through.

For once there was no hostility radiating from him, just a calm consideration as if he saw something the others had missed.

That was hard for me to believe. Of Liam's enforcers, Daniel knew me the least. He should have been the least likely to stare at me as if he guessed at exactly what I was going through.

"The man's current name was Frederick Mayer. Formerly of clan Davinish, now of clan Glaise."

"Aiden's clan?" Liam lifted his head.

Makoto frowned as he stared at the tablet. "Seems so."

"Two clans, neither likely to assassinate the master of the city," Anton said.

"Perhaps Thomas wasn't their target," I said.

All eyes turned to me. I didn't move, even as I found myself under the regard of several predators capable of turning me into mincemeat.

"Why do you say that?" Liam asked.

"We assumed Thomas was the target because he was the destination of the attack," I said, working through a theory that had been tickling at the back of my mind. "But he wasn't the only one there."

"That's ridiculous. We know the Fae are responsible," Anton said. "It only makes sense that they were after Thomas."

"What would have happened if one of the Fae had been hit in the crossfire?" I asked.

I thought the fact that they used vampire puppets a very telling one.

"They would have expected a weregild to honor their dead—we would have been required to pay some form of recompense. The master would have had no choice but to give into their demands," Daniel rumbled.

"What would be the purpose of that?" Anton asked. "They don't view gold or wealth in the same way we do, and we have nothing of magical value to them."

Liam seemed contemplative. "Either way, we can't discount any theory."

Anton grimaced.

"What can you tell us about how they died?" Liam asked.

Joseph stirred and bent closer to the bodies. I pushed my personal issues to the back burner and stepped forward. There was a job to be done, and as tempting as it was to find a deep dark hole and burrow down for the foreseeable future, that wasn't who I was. Who I was trying to be.

I was stronger than that. At least, that's what I kept telling myself.

"Are you sure they're dead?" I asked, joining Liam beside the bodies. I didn't spare him any attention, treating his presence like a piece of furniture as I concentrated on what Joseph was doing.

Vampires technically didn't need a heartbeat. Not really. We could go for long periods without one.

The first time I'd woken to discover my heart not functioning, or just so slowly my heartbeat was practically nonexistent, I'd panicked. It had taken me a while to get used to the lack. After time, I found it usually only stopped when I went too long between feedings.

It was the same with breathing. I could hold my breath for an indefinite amount of time. If I wanted to, I could probably sit on the bottom of the ocean for a year without moving.

"Pretty sure," Joseph said, not displaying any impatience at my question.

I lifted my eyebrows. Pretty sure wasn't a "yes".

"Their essence has fled, leaving their bodies inert," he explained.

I noticed he didn't use the word soul. Before my undeath, I'd never concerned myself about the state of my soul, but now I had to wonder. Did I have one? Was a single act, one that wasn't even my choice, enough to cost me the intangible, yet essential part needed to keep me human?

"I still don't understand how they died," Anton complained. "We're not human, something like a few convulsions shouldn't have been enough to do this."

"Normally you would be right," Joseph said, his expression holding a peculiar light as if he relished the mystery. "In this instance, that convulsion effectively snuffed out the source of their magic. It killed them."

"What could do something like that?" Liam asked, his gaze intense.

Joseph shook his head, one hand going up to pinch the bridge of his nose. "You've got me. I've never seen anything like this. Whatever was done to them would have been excruciatingly painful. Like their soul was being ripped from its shell."

"I hate magic," Makoto said, his voice grim.

"We all do," Anton responded, for once no trace of teasing in his tone.

"How did this happen?" Eric asked. "I thought our wards were supposed to protect us from their magic."

I looked up with interest. This was the first time I'd heard that.

"I don't know," Liam said, his gaze still on the bodies. He seemed pensive, almost regretful, as if the sight of these dead vampires pained him, reminded him of his failure.

I ignored it, unwilling to let my anger go, even if he was showing a trace, a very tiny bit, of humanity.

"You should bring Miriam in," I said. "She could probably tell us more."

He narrowed his eyes at me.

"I'm sure she'd be happy to leave whatever hole you dropped her in." My words held more of a bite than I intended.

"Would you rather I left her to wander loose after nearly killing you?" he asked, a forced politeness in his voice as he responded to the faint judgment.

"I wouldn't dream of it." There was a snap to my words even as I gave him my sweetest smile. "We both know you wouldn't want to disappoint the person holding your leash."

His eyes burned, the blue twin flames that threatened to sear. No one spoke, holding their breath as the moment pressed down on us. I refused to back down, stubbornly holding Liam's gaze.

I let him see inside me, let him see that whatever we thought we'd been building up to with the flirting and the games, it was over now. The sides were very clear, and he wasn't on mine.

"Fine," he bit out. "We'll ask the witch. Makoto and Anton, bring her."

The two enforcers excused themselves as the rest of us waited silently, the room full of strained tension.

Miriam walked in, flanked by the enforcers. There was a bruise along her chin and her skin looked pale, lines of pain around her mouth and dark circles under her eyes. Around her wrists were a pair of handcuffs that seemed to eat the magic she emitted naturally.

Gone was the facade of the perky coed, in its place was an exhausted, irritable woman.

Miriam's glare could have lit the room on fire had her handcuffs given her even a little access to her natural magic. As it was, she had nothing but a frown to strike fear into our hearts.

"I see you survived," Miriam said in a dour voice when she saw me in the corner. "Pity."

"You have a very interesting way of thanking someone when they save your neck," I told her.

She scoffed, the sound full of derision. "Save me? They would never have come after me if not for you."

"Who?" Liam asked before I could speak.

Miriam spared him a brief glance. Her lip curled in disdain. "What's this? More pointless questions? I've already told you I don't know anything."

Liam bared his teeth at her, his expression chilling. This was a man who'd gladly end her existence. Tear it from her and not spare a thought or ounce of regret for his actions later.

I was tempted to let him, but we'd be right back where we started.

"I'll make it easy for you, Miriam. We already know your coven has made a deal with the Fae," I told her.

She watched me with a guarded expression.

I gave her a humorless smile. "They've just shown they don't consider you one of them, which in a way is good for you since it means these guys will be less likely to kill you."

As if on cue Daniel and Anton glowered at her, their expressions menacing.

"All you need to do is fill in a couple blanks for us."

I waited as she studied us.

"Bullshit, he nearly killed me last night," she said, tilting her head at Liam.

He stepped forward, aggression in every line of his body.

I caught his arm and pulled him back. "You did try to kill me. I can't really blame him for retaliating."

Despite the turmoil of earlier and how fragile I still felt, I managed to come off sounding strong and confident.

Miriam reached up to flick her hair over her shoulde. "I may have overreacted to the situation."

Anton gave a small snort. "That's one way to put it."

Sensing I'd gotten somewhere with her and not wanting to lose the small glimmer of cooperation, I pointed at the bodies. "Tell me what you know about these."

Miriam took a step closer, careful not to get too close to Joseph who watched her with fascination.

"They're dead," she said.

"We know that. How?" Liam asked.

She shrugged, the motion careless.

"You're not even trying to lie well," Anton said silkily.

Insult flashed before she controlled the emotion.

"Do you know what we can do to a witch like you?" he asked, circling her. "We'll drink you down to nothing."

"Try, and my power will burn you from the inside out," she snapped.

His smile was full of dark promise. This wasn't the charming rogue; this was a predator pure and simple.

From the unease on Miriam's face, a part of her understood that.

"We're not like the rest of our kind, pequeña. We're the council's enforcers. We've drunk down much more powerful beings than you."

"You lie." Miriam's protest lacked oomph. Some part of her believed Anton.

Hell, I believed Anton.

He tapped her on the nose. "Keep being difficult and you'll find out."

He stepped back and gave her a self-satisfied smirk.

She watched him like a mouse watches a snake, no longer convinced of her invincibility. Still, a touch of stubbornness remained. This wasn't someone used to being at the bottom of the food chain. She might refuse simply out of misplaced pride.

"Miriam, just help us. Your coven has already turned from you. They've proven they want you dead," I said.

Her eyes narrowed. "Not all of them. Just Sarah's disciples."

Now we were getting somewhere.

"Why try to kill you?" I asked.

Her smile was bitter. "Because I'm the only one with the power to stand up to that bitch." A trace of uncomfortableness crossed her face. "And because Angela was her grandniece. She blames me for what happened to her. Almost as much as she blames you."

I digested that.

"And them?" Liam indicated the two on the table.

"Unfortunate casualties in Sarah's war," Miriam said.

There were sounds of anger from the men around me.

"Sarah got the Fae here with promises of information on you," Miriam said, a sly look on her face.

I blinked at her in surprise. "I find that hard to believe."

Her smile turned taunting. "It's true. The Fae have always been interested in those who can see through their glamours. When Sarah whispered in their ear the possibility of such a one being here, they came as soon as they could."

I went still at that, not blinking as she held my stare.

"Why would Sarah think I had such an ability?" I probed.

Miriam's expression told me my casualness wasn't fooling her. "Because you never had a reaction to the tea."

Tea? What tea? It took several seconds before I remembered. The first time I'd met Sarah she served me tea. Both she and Miriam had looked expectant and then shocked after I drank it without experiencing any effects.

But that had been before the sorcerer's spell gave me the ability to see magic. It shouldn't have indicated existence of any abilities because I didn't have them yet.

Unless this was another situation where that magic Joseph swore crouched deep inside me had reached out to turn everything wonky, just like when it interfered after Thomas's bite transforming me into a vampire despite all odds.

"What was in the tea?" I asked.

She shrugged. "Just a little bit of this and that."

"Anton, she's all yours," I said.

Anton didn't budge—perhaps because I wasn't the one holding his leash. It didn't matter. Miriam believed my threat.

"It was a spell. It was supposed to make you amenable to our suggestions and denote how powerful you would become."

There were angry sounds from the vampires around me.

Miriam hurried to continue. "It failed in its purpose. You had no reaction to it. There are only a few reasons for that. Sarah decided it was enough to convince the Fae you could see through a glamour, and if you couldn't, she could always claim your lack of power messed with her reading."

I digested that statement, feeling cold inside. Miriam had no idea how close that spell put her to the truth.

"She probably just messed up the spell anyway. Her magic has been slipping," Miriam muttered. "Either way, their Fae lady was especially interested to hear of the hold you have over your enforcer. She seemed to have something special planned for the two of you."

The sound that came from Liam tore from the deepest parts of him. He advanced on Miriam, his expression ferocious and enraged. She backed away from him, fear suddenly present as he grabbed her.

"Liam, no!"

He hesitated, his fangs poised above her throat as he looked over at me. There was only a small spark of intelligence there.

"We still need her," I tried. Reason and logic were hard when fear and terror coated my insides. His loss of control reminded me of my own tenuous hold not long before. "She might have information that can be useful."

Reason re-exerted itself and Liam relaxed, the harsh lines of his face turning cruel. "You're right. There are many ways she can be assist us."

He released his brutal hold on her and stepped back. "Anton."

"With pleasure," the other vampire said with a predatory smile.

Miriam tried to back up as he advanced, resisting his hold. She struggled as he turned her back to him, grabbing her hair and pushing it aside to bare her neck.

With sick horror, I realized what he was doing. "Liam."

"It's this or death," Liam said.

"You're not going to accomplish anything. She's too powerful a witch for Anton to influence," I said.

"We'll see."

I started forward, to do what I wasn't entirely sure.

"Daniel," Liam said, command in his voice.

"Yes, my lord." Daniel dipped his head and caught me by the arm, pulling me out of the room and away from what I'd caused.

*

I sat with my back against the wall, waiting. Daniel had made it clear when I tried to leave that I wasn't going anywhere.

I pulled out the note Cadell had given me during the party. All it said was *"Meet us at the apartment. Come alone."*

That wasn't vague or anything. I balled up the paper and slipped it into the dress. Cadell could have been slightly helpful and at least given me something to go on.

I'd already decided to track them down. The note was just a risk without a lot of payoff.

It didn't take long for Anton to finish his feeding. I watched as he helped Miriam out of the room, supporting her weight as he guided her down the hall.

Liam stepped out next, his thoughts veiled.

"What will happen to her now?" I asked.

"She will remain with us while Anton completes the bond," he said.

"And if it doesn't take?"

"I'll order her death."

I shook my head, anger and sorrow tangling inside me, leaving me with the bitter taste of defeat.

Things had seemed so easy earlier tonight. Help Liam figure out who was trying to kill us and make them pay. Now, I was party to my worst nightmare.

I stood. "I'm going home."

I needed space and time to process. Not to mention there were a couple of High Fae waiting on me.

"You're not." The words were a whip.

"Oh? Did you become my keeper while I wasn't looking?" I asked, acid in my voice. "Dawn will be soon. I plan to spend it in my bed."

"Think again, *macushla*. You're not leaving my sight until this is over." There was no softness in his expression. He meant that. He had no intention of giving me space.

A strangled sound left me. "I have an errand to run."

He remained unmoved. "Then we'll run it together."

He didn't give me time to argue, glancing at Daniel. "Watch her. I have something to take care of."

Daniel nodded, moving closer as if his presence alone could keep me there.

Liam stalked away.

"That was mean," Joseph remarked from the doorway.

"I don't care," I snapped.

Daniel stepped into my way when I would have walked past, his hazel eyes holding mine, calm in their depths.

"For my first feeding, my sire bade me drain my ten-year-old sister. It was punishment for leading a raid on her lands," Daniel said without preamble.

I blinked at him, horrified and lost for words.

"She then slaughtered the rest of my family and had me lick the blood from her body," he continued.

A dull horror moved through me at the picture he painted.

"Why are you telling me this?" I asked, my voice hushed.

"Your first feeding could have been worse," he stated plainly.

He was right, the words shaking me out of the pity party I'd been falling into. Things could have been much worse.

What Thomas had done wasn't right. Subsuming my will in favor of his—forcing me to commit an act that I was by no means ready for, was wrong on so many levels—but the world wasn't over. I was still me. I still had control. I wasn't a ravening monster roaming the streets.

"I'm sorry for what was done to you," I said in a quiet voice. I meant it, too. Daniel might not like me, nor I him, but no person should have to go through that. It spoke of an almost unfathomable level of cruelty.

"It happened a long time ago," he said.

"That doesn't make it any less painful," I said.

He tilted his head slightly and gave a small nod. "You are right in that."

"If you two are done communing over your crappy histories, maybe I can show you something, Aileen," Joseph said caustically.

Daniel didn't react, obviously used to the other man's abrupt manner.

Joseph didn't wait for my response, going back into his office. I trailed after him as he headed for his desk. He flipped his laptop open and hit a few keys, bringing up a video.

"Watch this," he said, before stepping back.

I moved closer as the video started. The content gave me pause. There was a man in a cage, his back to the camera. I glanced at Joseph, wondering what he hoped I'd get out of this. So far, I just had serious concerns about whether he'd gone mad scientist on us and kidnapped some poor sap off the street to conduct experiments on.

The man threw himself at the bars of his cage, snarling like a wild animal, appearing out of his mind with rage.

The camera caught a glimpse of his face. Flesh fell off it in ribbons, like he'd raked his fingernails down it, exposing the tendons and muscles underneath the surface. The whites of his eyes had morphed to red and the iris was a coppery color, probably from burst blood vessels.

His expression was bestial, his eyes empty and glazed, no sign of sanity present. He opened his mouth and roared. This was a vampire, his fangs oversized as he bit at the air.

"What is this?" I asked, slightly horrified.

Joseph stuck one hand in his pocket and leaned a hip against the desk next to me, his tiger eyes watching me with a sick fascination. Neither Daniel or I could turn from the screen and the enraged vampire on it, too consumed with the horror of it.

"Devolution isn't a pretty process. Your body begins to rot as the toxicity of your blood climbs. It starts in your extremities as your body falls apart around you. The last to go is the brain. Once the devolution reaches the brain, there is no saving you," he said, his voice that of a teacher lecturing a student who wasn't particularly bright.

He cocked his head, a sardonic expression on his face. "Just thought you should see what you were up against before you judged Thomas or Liam too harshly."

I forced myself not to react, not to shoot straight to denial. It was different hearing what you could become and then seeing it. One was theoretical, real but in a very removed sort of way. Seeing the facts for myself, watching a vampire throw himself mindlessly against silver bars with no care for the pain he might be experiencing was different.

"Is this common knowledge?" I asked.

Joseph studied me, his eyes slightly narrowed. "Common enough."

"And does devolution happen often?"

"No, it does not," he said. "It's almost unheard of nowadays. Those in their first century are most vulnerable."

I nodded slowly, ice invading my center. "And is it only caused by abstaining from taking blood from humans?"

Joseph looked thoughtful. "There needs to be a perfect storm of circumstances. There are properties within human blood that can't be replicated any other way. It feeds the vampiric virus—for lack of a better word—that sustains us. Take away that nutrient source, and it'll start attacking your system. There have been cases where vampires subsisted on bagged blood for decades. We're not quite sure why some devolve while others simply weaken."

"Most spooks are aware of devolution but not the cause," Daniel said.

"What about only feeding on vampire blood?" I asked.

The two traded a look.

"That comes with its own set of risks," Joseph said after a pause. "Our blood might stop the onset of toxicity but it won't treat it once it's started."

I didn't respond, too locked in my own thoughts. Several things that I thought I knew about my past were being rewritten. It seemed people I thought I could trust, people I would have sworn had my back had lied to me, turned me onto a path that could have very well led me to devolution. That, or they were just seriously ignorant.

I didn't know which was worse.

The captain should have known about this, yet he'd steered me away from the vampires deliberately, told me to avoid them at all costs.

I turned away from the video and started. Liam stood behind me, his thoughts hidden by a wall.

I hesitated, not knowing what to say after watching that video.

His gaze was cool as he noted my hesitation. "We'll head out on your errands. You were right. There isn't much more time before sunrise."

He moved to the side and gestured for me to precede him out of the room. To my surprise, Daniel followed, bringing up the rear.

"Where do we need to go?" Liam asked once he reached the car. It was the same one he'd used the night after Caroline and my drunken revelry, its burnt umber color mocking me.

"My apartment."

His head jerked towards me. He sat back and fixed me with an intent stare.

"The car won't start itself," I noted, glancing at the push start.

"I told you you're not staying there until this is over," he said with forced patience.

Daniel was a silent presence in the back seat, watching the two of us like we were a particularly volatile tennis match.

"As much fun as it would be to show just how much you're not the boss of me, I have other reasons for going there," I said through gritted teeth.

Cadell and Niall had made it clear they wanted to meet with me. Call me curious, but I wanted to see what they had to say.

As furious as I was with Thomas and Liam, I still couldn't forget Jerry was caught up in all this. He had earned my respect and loyalty. I still wasn't sure if he needed my help but I wasn't going to walk away until I had an answer.

Not to mention the woman and man lying dead in the Gargoyle through no fault of their own. They'd just been in the wrong place at the wrong time. Call me crazy, but I found that offensive. I wanted to find the bastards responsible.

None of that touched on the fact that these people had come after me and would probably do so again, if they weren't stopped. So, yeah, it was tempting to stick it to Liam, to go off on my own, but I wasn't stupid or crazy. I needed him and his power to deal with this threat. That meant playing nice for the time being.

Liam gave me a scathing smile. "I thought I was the boss of you. Wasn't it you who begged to be part of this?"

I gritted my teeth. He was tap dancing on my last nerve. "Careful, before I forget all the reasons I need to work with you."

"Would you two like some room?" Daniel leaned forward, his voice serious. "I can get out and wait."

I turned and gave him a polite smile. "No need. There's nothing he and I need to discuss."

Liam flicked his fingers. It must have been some type of signal because Daniel got out, the door shutting quietly behind him.

The car filled with tension, the air fairly crackling with it.

"Go on, get it all out," Liam said, giving me a come-hither motion.

I lifted an eyebrow but didn't speak.

"Come on, tell me about how much of an asshole I am, about how you hate me and never want to see me again," Liam said. "Let's hear it."

"Is that what you think this is about?" I asked. Liam was an asshole, no doubt about that, but that wasn't why I was so upset. I wasn't angry, or at least not entirely angry. I was upset, hurt in a way I didn't realize I could be.

"I didn't know he was going to do that," Liam shouted.

"But you stood there and let it happen," I screamed. "You didn't say anything. You didn't try to stop it. You just let it happen." The last sentence was almost whispered, the emotion running out of me.

Liam closed his eyes and bent his head, not looking at me as the silence deepened. I sat there, feeling numb all over again.

"He took everything from me," I said quietly. "My present, my future. Now he's taken this, too."

There was sorrow on Liam's face. Understanding too. I turned away from him, not wanting to see.

"Tell me the truth, would you have drunk from a human?" Liam asked.

"Guess we'll never know now," I said.

The sound he made wasn't happy. "Don't lie to yourself. As much as you might hate what he did, and my part for standing by, he saved you from a fate worse than death. I'm glad for what he did, and if I'd known how far gone you were, I'd have done it myself."

That shut me up.

Daniel climbed back into the car as Liam started it. The drive passed in silence.

*

"We're here," Liam said. "Now what?"

I undid my seat belt and shouldered open the car. "You stay in the car while I get some things."

There was a slam of a door, then Liam was beside me in the next moment, his eyes snapping blue fire at me. "That's not how this works."

"Liam, don't be ridiculous. I just need to grab a few things," I said.

He leaned closer, caging me against the car. I had no way to escape, not with the car at my back. I noted distantly Daniel had elected to remain inside. Smart man.

"You don't trust me, that's fine," he said, lips curved in a decadent smile that should have scalded me. "I don't trust you either. Now, I can either come with you or we can go back to the mansion. Your choice."

It was no choice, really. Given everything that was happening, we needed an inside look at the other camp. This was our best shot.

Seeing the answer written on my face, Liam straightened. "Thought you might take that option."

He didn't wait for my response, leaning down and telling Daniel. "Drive around until I call for you."

Daniel must have agreed because Liam started for my apartment. I trailed behind him, fuming.

Liam had already climbed up to my apartment and unlocked my door by the time I reached the half formed stairs. I couldn't even find it in me to be surprised he had a key. Of course, he did. Thomas was my landlord after all.

Liam prowled around my apartment while I stood in the living room. Inara fluttered into sight while I was still debating my next step and jerked her head toward the bathroom.

I followed.

"Where are you going?" Liam asked, not looking up from where he was examining my bookshelves. They were full of books and little items from all the places I'd visited and adventures I'd had. There should have been more of them, but becoming a vampire had put a serious crimp in my travels.

"The bathroom. I need toiletries," I said.

Liam grunted but didn't say anything else, secure in the knowledge there was no way to escape. It was a logical assumption, given there were no windows in the bathroom and its door could be seen from where he stood.

I stepped inside, Lowen and Inara darting in after me. They landed on the sink as I opened the medicine cabinet and grabbed a few toiletries to give credence to my fib.

"What's with the fanger?" Inara asked, jerking her thumb toward the living room where Liam waited.

"Don't ask," I said, slamming another item down. The act didn't make my anger lessen any.

She rolled her eyes. "Doesn't matter anyway. Close your eyes."

"Wha—?"

Before I could finish my question, the world spun around me in a dizzying hurricane of kaleidoscopes.

I landed on my ass with a thump, my head still spinning and a headache beginning right behind my eyes.

"Inara, what the hell?" I asked, groggily, feeling like I'd just gone on a three-week bender and then been thrown into a wood chipper.

The door to the bathroom yanked open. Cadell peered down at me with an inscrutable expression. "Good, you brought her."

CHAPTER FOURTEEN

I sat up from my sprawl on the floor and looked around. Their bathroom's layout was similar to mine. Whereas mine had spots of bright colors in the towels and photos I'd hung on my wall, theirs was sparse of any decoration—except for a surprisingly healthy plant on a shelf over the toilet.

"Come," Cadell said before disappearing into the apartment.

I aimed a glare at Inara and Lowen as I picked myself off the floor. They ignored me, fluttering into the apartment with a flick of their wings.

I grumbled about annoying house guests as I followed. It would have been nice to have had a little warning before Inara shifted me through time and space once again, but at least this dealt with one problem—getting me a meeting with Niall and Cadell without Liam's knowledge or interference.

After the whole debacle with Miriam, I was hesitant to introduce another set of contacts to him.

I walked into the living room to see that unlike me, Niall and Cadell had found the time to change since the party, looking almost human in jeans and t-shirts, instead of like Fae lords about to jaunt off into the woods.

I felt slightly self-conscious in my rumpled dress, which was looking worse for wear. I scrubbed at a spot of blood that had dried on the beautiful fabric. I wondered vaguely if vampires had dry cleaners who specialized in blood removal. It would make sense, given what they liked to eat.

"Aileen, I want to express my appreciation to you for coming," Niall said in a cordial voice.

"Your lackey over there didn't give me much of a choice," I said, turning my stare on Inara.

She flicked her hair over her shoulder and met my glare with a haughty look, not repentant in the least.

I turned to the other two. "I can't stay long. Liam is going to notice I'm missing."

If he hadn't already. Vampires didn't have need of toilets. He wasn't going to believe the excuse of "I just had to use the bathroom".

"You want to tell me what a bunch of fairy princes are doing living in a place like this?" I glanced around. Their apartment was nicer than mine. A lot nicer, but it wasn't exactly what I pictured them calling home.

A guffaw escaped Cadell.

Niall's face was slightly startled at the sight of his friend bent nearly double, lost in laughter.

"Our people don't really have princes as you understand it," Niall said.

"And if we did, we would not be among their number," Cadell chimed in.

"Our fairy tales beg to differ," I said.

"Because they're so reliable," Cadell said, his amusement fading slightly. "How's the state of your soul? Have you turned into a ravening monster yet?"

Point taken. Many of the myths about vampires weren't true either.

"Jury's still out," I murmured, my thoughts turning to earlier in the evening.

"The proper term would be lord or lady," Niall said. "But it's not so straightforward as your human inheritances."

"Anybody who is powerful enough can earn the title, regardless of lineage," Cadell said. "Niall is one such person."

"But you're not?" I asked, just to be sure.

Cadell smirked, letting that be his answer. No, I was betting he served as Niall's guard. He moved with the sort of purpose and confidence acquired through extensive training in the deadly arts.

While the lesson in Fae hierarchy was interesting and all, it didn't answer my question.

"We're in hiding," Niall said.

I snorted. "You sure could have fooled me."

I wouldn't exactly call it "hiding" when you show up at a vampire get together with the same people you're supposedly avoiding. That was the exact opposite of hiding.

Cadell looked at his friend. "I have to agree with the vampire."

"I told you we had no choice," Niall said. "Niamh felt us the moment she crossed over. Running or hiding would have brought unwelcome suspicion."

"And so, the very people we're trying to avoid now know exactly where we are," Cadell said flatly.

"But not why," Niall returned.

It seemed like this was a familiar argument between the two.

"How dangerous is this Wild Hunt?" I asked, watching them. I knew what the vampires thought of it but wanted their take as well.

"They've called a hunt?" Inara asked, sounding alarmed.

"Yes," Niall confirmed.

Her wings beat rapidly. Lowen watched her with a concerned expression.

To me, Niall said, "And very, if you're the prey. There are only a few who can survive a hunt."

They all studiously ignored the small pixie queen as her wings gave away her tumultuous emotions.

"I feel bad for whatever poor bastard Niamh decides to hunt," Cadell muttered.

"I thought the magic of the hunt decides the prey." At least that was what Liam had led me to believe.

Inara's laugh was ugly. "Perhaps once, but not now that she has gotten her claws into half of the lords of the hunt."

Niall and Cadell's faces were grim. They agreed with her.

"How is that possible? I thought wild magic couldn't be tamed or controlled," I said.

A faint agitation showed in their faces. Niall was the one to answer. "That isn't entirely true. There are those among us who are closer to the wild magic than others. People like Arlan. I don't know if I'd call what they're able to do "control" so much as influence."

And because Niamh held influence over them her will bled down into the hunt.

"Tell me about the hunt's mark," I said.

Niall went very still. "How do you know about that?"

How much to tell them?

"Because I have one on my back," I said.

The words that came from Inara would have put a sailor to shame. They were jarring coming from the small pixie queen.

"Show me," Niall said, sitting forward.

I turned and moved the back of the dress from the mark.

There was an indrawn breath and then warm fingers touching me lightly. "You're lucky. It's only half a mark," Cadell said from behind me.

I let the dress fall into place and turned to face him. His gaze was intense and his thoughts hidden.

"What does that mean?" I asked.

"You've been marked by the hunt, but you are not yet its prey," Niall said.

Okay, that fit with what Liam and Thomas had said.

"A lord of the hunt would have needed to physically place that mark on her," Inara said, fury radiating from every small line of her body. Her glare could have scorched flesh as she aimed it at the two Fae.

The revelation was jarring. "Neither Arlan nor Niamh got close enough to lay a hand on me."

I tried to think back if I crossed paths with any of the other Fae in their party. I didn't remember any run ins, certainly not the type where they could lay a mark on my back.

The only Fae who'd gotten close to me all night was Cadell when he passed me the note.

I'd looked at the mark in the mirror earlier. It was simple, something any tattoo artist could do, a drawn bow with arrow nocked in it.

"That may be, but someone got close to you," Cadell said.

The statement was disquieting in more ways than one. I turned my attention to matters I could still control.

"You said it's only half a mark. What would turn it into a full mark?"

Niall's expression was sympathetic. "I don't know."

I rubbed my forehead. That wasn't the answer I wanted. Not even by a little.

The situation was starting to spiral out of my control. I was marked for a hunt I wanted no part of, with no way of knowing how to keep myself from turning into its prey. Half the city wanted me dead and I could no longer trust Liam or the other vampires, not after what happened tonight.

Nor could I trust the people in front of me. They had an agenda, the same as everyone else. They might appear to be on my side for now, but they were working from a plan I couldn't yet see.

Being out on my own in the cold was a lonely and scary place. It was a position I'd promised myself I'd never be in again.

"The attack tonight. Was that aimed at you or Thomas?" Dwelling on my problems wouldn't solve them.

"I'm not sure," Niall said.

"Why would they want to kill you or Thomas?" I asked.

"We don't know if that was their goal," Niall said carefully.

"They weren't throwing marshmallows around," I said. "That spell I intercepted wasn't the sort of thing that would have made you sing arias and see sparkling unicorns. It was a nasty piece of work. They intended their target to die a horrible, horrible death."

"Yet you survived." Niall contemplated me as if he knew a secret I didn't.

I shrugged, affecting nonchalance. "I got lucky. A friend gave me a charm to ward off attacks."

"Your friend is very powerful then." Cadell said. His tone made it clear he wasn't entirely convinced with my explanation.

I didn't respond to that. Too many people already knew my secrets. There was no need to add four more to the mix.

"Why here? Why now?" I asked.

Niall seemed slightly uncomfortable. "That's hard to explain."

"I'll try to keep up," I said with a hard smile. My patience with these games was wearing thin. I was tired and my bones ached, to say nothing of the mental and emotional fallout from this evening I still hadn't worked through. I was done with all the tap dancing.

"The Wild Hunt is important, but it's just one piece of a larger puzzle," Niall explained.

I got that, but I still didn't know why.

Irritation crossed Cadell's face. "Stop dancing around it. The Wild Hunt is pure, untamed magic, wild and primal. When the prey is killed, it acts as a sacrifice to the old gods. For a very brief moment in time, its potential is nearly limitless."

"The barrow," I said.

He nodded. "Every inch of the Summer Lands is spoken for. The only way to move up is to kill those above you. A new barrow—especially one with such strong ties to the human world and its magic—would open up new possibilities."

"Our politics tend to be drenched in blood and death. A change of power is rare but when it happens it usually results in a high body count. There are many who would welcome the creation of a new barrow," Niall said in a soft voice.

And Thomas had been asked by the vampire council to let it happen. It made me wonder what benefits such a barrow would have for them. Because there would be a benefit. Vampire politics were no less deadly and bloody than the Fae's. They never did anything without a reason. It was finding the reason before you were dead, that was the tricky part.

"How do the witches fit into all this?" I asked.

"Niamh is using them. When they fulfill their purpose, they'll be discarded like all the rest," Lowen said in a low voice.

Inara looked startled at his interjection, then realization dawned on her face. Outrage filled her as she rose several inches above the shelf she'd grabbed as a perch.

"You went spying for Niall?" she asked.

He ducked his head. "We needed to know what Niamh and Arlan were up to."

"She could have killed you," Inara screeched. "You know how dangerous she is. Was her destroying our court not clue enough?"

Grief and devastation were obvious in Inara's face as she stared at her consort. Watching the two of them felt awkward, as if we were spying on a private fight between lovers.

"That's why I had to do it," he said, lifting his head and meeting her gaze. Inara was the more dominant of the two, a tempest waiting to blow. Lowen had always been calmer and less inclined towards anger. He had a steadiness that made one listen. "You know her. She's already spun her web on half the Fae in the city."

He turned to me. "Your old boss is caught by one of her glamours. He has no choice but to help her."

I figured as much. There weren't a lot of reasons Jerry would abandon all he'd built over the years.

"How do you know that?" I asked.

"That's how she caught our old court. She uses geases and glamour to entrap people. Once trapped by such vows, they have no choice but to obey."

That would explain why Jerry had been acting so weird, why he'd looked like he'd wanted to be anywhere but there, and why he had brushed me off.

"Shit," I said. A thought occurred to me. It was insidious and I didn't want to give it credence.

"Can she use the hold she has on him on the rest of his couriers?" I asked. I know Jerry had his Fae employees swear different vows. I wasn't sure, but I'd heard one of them was a vow of loyalty and fealty.

The resigned looks on the others faces told me all I needed to know.

"He's established a court here through his couriers. The first of its kind. It's likely she'll have control over any Fae who swore fealty to him. We're not sure about the rest," Niall said reluctantly.

Damn it, that was not good.

"Good thing you were fired," Inara said.

Yeah, except it didn't feel like that right now. I wasn't super-close with any of the other couriers, our schedules kept us too busy, but I'd had a few friends among them—work friends I said hey to every now and then. I couldn't just leave them in that woman's control.

"Who else did she bring with her?" Inara asked.

"The twins, Breandan and Baran," Cadell responded.

Inara let out a filthy curse, the word surprising originating from such a small creature. "Those two are hunters. They'll be dangerous."

"You seem to know a lot about these people," I observed. Understandable, if Niamh had really killed the rest of their court.

Inara lifted her chin. "One of the reasons they chose this place is probably because of me."

I arched an eyebrow. "Oh?"

It seemed like a lot of trouble to go to murder one small pixie, queen or not. My roommate was annoying, tediously so, and she could be more prickly than a mama porcupine, but I couldn't see holding an entire city hostage just to kill her.

"We have a history. I stole something of hers," Inara said, her chin lifted, and her voice proud.

I waited.

"What did you steal?" I asked, when it became clear she'd said all she was going to say.

"You don't need to know that yet," she said, her chin lifted in challenge.

I stared at her for a long moment. I didn't need to know? This crazy Fae was going around the city and enslaving people to her will, including my friends. She'd already tried to kill me once—which did not make sense—and I'd upset her plans earlier that night. But I didn't need to know Inara's secret.

"What she means to say is that we can't tell you quite yet," Niall said, stepping into the breach, his tone placating.

"Why did you pull me down here?" I asked abruptly.

Niall's forehead wrinkled, his expression a perfect impression of confusion. I wasn't buying it.

"We thought you deserved a warning," he said.

"No." I shook my head. That's not what this was about. "You wanted me to keep your presence here a secret. I'm willing to bet your 'friend' doesn't know you've been here longer than a couple of nights."

There was a slight flinch from Niall. Cadell went stiff, his body tensed and poised as if he was expecting an attack.

I was right. This wasn't about helping me. It was about covering their own asses.

Fine, I could play that game too.

"We need you to make sure Cadell and Niall aren't chosen to be prey," Inara said, not letting my anger affect her. She met my gaze with a steely resolve.

"How do you expect me to do that when I can't even figure out how to keep myself from being chosen?" I hissed.

None of them answered me.

We sat in angry silence for several long moments.

"I'll return you to your apartment," Inara said, lifting off the shelf.

"Would killing her work?" I asked, holding my ground.

Niall and Cadell traded looks. I narrowed my eyes, not able to decipher what message they sent each other.

"It should," Niall admitted. "But she has powerful allies. Drawing their ire would be inadvisable."

"Nor would it be as easy as you seem to think," Cadell said. "Niamh has many enemies and they've all tried to wipe her from this world. You are barely into your eternity. What makes you think you will fare any better?"

I didn't answer, following Inara out of the room. Most of what they'd told me had been things I'd known or guessed, but I'd learned enough to have a hundred new questions.

Inara fluttered into the bathroom, waiting for me to join her. This time Lowen stayed behind, the quiet murmur of men's voices following me.

I was ready as the magic rose, using my othersight to watch as hundreds of glittering lights surrounded us. They reminded me of fireflies buzzing around us as the magic built.

Even watching, I couldn't tell how she did it, or pinpoint the exact moment when she broke the laws of physics as humans knew them.

With a pop, the world jerked sideways in a sickening lurch and I once again ended up on my ass. This time in my own bathroom.

I picked myself up off the ground with a groan.

"I will never get used to that," I informed Inara as she settled on my upraised knee.

I started to push my way to my feet and froze at the sight of the open door. Liam leaned against the doorframe, his body perfectly relaxed as he watched me.

"Oh shit," I gulped.

Inara froze, her small eyes growing comically wide as she noticed Liam.

The three of us stared at each other, Liam contemplative, Inara and I in horrified shock.

"I guess you're wondering what's going on," I tried.

Liam didn't respond, just turned and disappeared into the apartment. We heard the front door open and shut moments later.

That wasn't good.

"Stop him, you fool," Inara screeched, pinching my ear.

I flinched at the pain before batting her away as I scrambled to my feet and darted after Liam.

He had a decent head start. He was already out of the apartment and had reached Niall and Cadell's door by the time I landed somewhat ungracefully on the ground.

"Liam," I warned.

He raised his hand and knocked.

Before I could say anything—not that I could think of anything to say—the door swung open, Cadell's eyes narrowing as he tensed.

Liam pounced. A light shimmered around the door. Liam bounced off it and flew past me.

He rolled to his feet, his fangs down and his eyes a sea of blue. He shook himself. Then he crouched, took a deep breath and sprinted for the door.

Cadell had relaxed when Liam was repelled but now he tensed again.

Liam hit the door with a crash, the light sparking. There was a boom as Liam sailed past me again.

"Liam, that's enough," I said when he climbed to his feet.

He gave no sign he heard me, sprinting for the doorway. Another boom, this one louder than the last.

"Are you done?" I asked when he got to his feet again. A snarl was my only answer.

I rolled my eyes and walked away. Stupid man. If he wanted to throw himself against the equivalent of an unmovable wall, he could be my guest. I wasn't sticking around to watch.

I stalked back to my apartment, repeating the laborious climb up.

"Did you distract him?" Inara asked as soon as I reached the door.

"Does it sound like I distracted him?" I asked just as there was another loud crack.

We both looked down at where Liam was picking himself off the ground, giving no sign that he was tiring. I was actually surprised his antics hadn't attracted any onlookers. It was the early morning hours, but the noise should have drawn some attention.

Inara sighed. "What does he think he's going to accomplish?"

I shook my head. Her guess was as good as mine. Vampires couldn't enter a home unless they were invited. It was one of the very weird myths that turned out to be true. Not to mention, I strongly suspected that Niall and Cadell had their place warded to hell and back to prevent any uninvited guests.

"Where are you going?" Inara called after me as I left the door and headed further into the apartment.

"As amusing as this is to watch, I have better things to do," I said.

Before I made it more than a few steps, I heard a sound beneath my door. I backtracked and watched the edge, poised to attack if a golem or anything Fae appeared.

A hand landed on the threshold and Caroline pulled herself up, panting. "You really need to do something about those stairs."

"What are you doing here?" I asked her, rushing forward to help pull her into the apartment.

She stood and dusted her hands off. "Thought I'd update you on my progress." She jerked a thumb at the door. "You know tall, dark and handsome is throwing himself against your neighbor's door, right?"

I rolled my eyes. "Yeah, he's not exactly rational at the moment."

"You do have a way of driving people out of their minds," Caroline said, looking around.

"Thanks, friend. It's always so good to hear what you think of me," I said, heading back toward my room. Caroline followed me, throwing herself onto the bed as I rummaged through my dresser.

"Do you want to hear what I found?" she asked.

It took me a moment to remember what she was speaking of. It felt like months had passed since I asked her to look into the golems and the Wild Hunt.

"Regale me with your knowledge, oh smart one," I said in a dead pan voice.

Her smile was quick and sly before it faded. "A whole bunch of nothing."

I paused and looked over at her. She could have called and told me that.

She chuckled at my expression and sat up. "I'm not lying. Golems are mostly associated with early Judaism. You can even find a couple of references of them in the Bible. Most versions I found said they have a written Hebrew word inscribed on their heads, which when removed destroys the golem."

"That doesn't describe what came after us," I said. None of those had writing on their foreheads. I would have noticed.

She nodded. "You could say they've been improved upon since the first golem's creation. Nowadays, anyone with enough juice can make one. All they need is a focus to which they affix their magic and then you've got an army of inanimate mud at your beck and call."

"The pebbles," I said.

"Yup, I took a look at the one I had. There are small symbols inscribed on it. Runes similar to the language of the witches," she said.

That wasn't exactly nothing. Unfortunately, it didn't tell me much that was new.

The periodic booms from outside told me Liam was still preoccupied with trying to get at Niall and Cadell.

To my not so surprise, I found what I was looking for in a drawer of my dresser. I picked up the book that now had the title *Dangerous Waters Ahead - Turn Back, Stupid.*

"I see you managed to make it back," I told it. Not that I'd really been worried. This book had a tendency to roam. I still hadn't figured out how or why it had chosen to follow me around like a lost puppy.

"What's that?" Caroline asked, leaning forward with interest.

"A pain in the ass," I told her.

I'd tried many ways to get rid of my not-so-welcome guide to all things supernatural—including losing it accidentally on purpose, tossing it from a bridge, putting it in the trash can on trash day and even giving it to a random stranger. Nothing worked. It always returned, usually with a sarcastic title designed to insult me. The only thing I hadn't attempted was setting it on fire.

"It looks interesting," she said.

That was one way of putting it.

"I'm less interested in the golems now than I am in the Wild Hunt," I said.

"You and everyone else. Brax has forbidden the wolves from taking part in it. He said anyone caught in those woods during or after the hunt would be punished severely."

I frowned. "I would have thought the hunt would appeal to your natures."

It involved donning their fur and chasing creatures through the woods with the end resulting in a fresh kill. It seemed right up their alley.

"Probably, but I think he's more worried one of us will end up as the prey," she said.

"I thought only the weak became prey."

She shook her head. "Common misconception, according to my research. It depends on who calls the hunt. The more powerful the hunter, the more powerful the prey. From what I can tell, the more difficult and challenging the hunt, the more magic generated from it."

"I was told the kill acts as a sacrifice," I said.

She tilted her head thoughtfully. "Perhaps, though from what I can find it's the hunt itself that really gives the magic the boost. Either way, if you sacrifice something that's weak, you get weak magic out of it. That's what the book keeper said anyway."

Ideally, they'd want someone strong enough to give the hunt a good chase but weak enough to be caught.

"What about the mark of the hunt?"

She lifted herself half off the bed. "Why the interest?"

I fiddled with the book, unable to look her in the eye. I thought about keeping the reason to myself. Just as fast as the thought occurred, I discarded it. Hiding and keeping secrets was what had nearly destroyed our friendship in the first place.

"I have one on my back."

Caroline was off the bed and in front of me, moving with a preternatural speed. "Show me."

Reluctantly, I did.

"Okay, we're going to figure out a way around this," she said, sounding calm. "I'll talk to Brax, get him to let me attend the hunt."

"No, Caroline, that's a bad idea."

"I'm doing it," she snapped. "You'd do it for me."

She was right. I would.

Still, throwing a demon wolf into the mix would probably make matters worse.

"For now, figure out all you can about this. I'm told it's only half a mark right now. There's a set of criteria I need to meet before the hunt

T.A. WHITE

chooses me as prey. Find out what they are and how I can avoid them," I said, trying to use logic to keep her from an unwise course of action. "We can create a plan after that."

She nodded. "Alright, I can do that."

I held up the book. "I'm hoping this might help."

I set it down on the bed and flipped through it. Caroline crowded closer, curiosity in her face even as she held her silence.

"Oddly enough I picked it up from the book keeper," I said, referencing her boss and the book store for spooks where she worked. "Sometimes it's more helpful than others."

She made an interested sound as she bent closer.

"What stellar advice do you have for me today?" I asked it.

Something on how to break Niamh's hold on half the Fae in the city or how to keep me from being part of the Wild Hunt would be good. Hell, any advantage would help.

I doubted it would be that simple however. The book seemed to take a perverse pleasure in tap dancing around an answer. It liked to give me just a hint, a small tease, but refrained from ever being truly helpful. You had to read between the lines with anything it shared. Its advice was often subtle and not apparent until the moment when you needed it most, when it was oftentimes too late.

Those were just a few of the reasons I could never truly trust it. Not to mention the odd way it had come to me and the mystery surrounding it.

I flipped it open, randomly selecting a page. My intent was to look for an entry on the Fae, hoping to glean some small tidbit that might help me.

It opened on a blank page.

"Not helpful," I told it.

I flipped to another page. A picture of a forest looked back at me. Another page, another part of the forest. This time with the remains of train tracks partially covered by overgrowth. Again, and again, each time showing me a different part of the same forest.

"Is it supposed to do that?" Caroline asked.

I slammed it shut and threw it on my bed. That was even less helpful than normal.

"Perhaps I should give more thought to the fire idea," I said to where it lay on the bed.

There was a soft sound and then abruptly the book was on fire.

"Oh my God," Caroline shouted at the same time I yelled, "No."

We both leapt into action. I grabbed a towel from my closet, while she picked up a pillow. Together, we beat frantically at the fire, trying to smother it.

After several heart-pounding moments, it went out.

I lifted the towel, cringing at the sight of my blackened bedspread, small holes in it from where the fire had touched. The stark markers of soot were very noticeable on the soft blue. There was no way to salvage it.

Caroline stared back at me with wide eyes, saying without words 'what the hell just happened'.

In the middle of it all, lay the book, untouched, not a mark on it. Nothing to show it had been on fire moments before.

I glared at it, wanting more than anything at that moment to put it in a shredder but not daring to voice that thought. Who knew what it would do if it knew what I was thinking? Nothing good.

"Did the bed offend you?" Liam asked from the doorway, his gaze on my ruin of a bed.

Caroline jumped, while I sighed, depressed all over again. It would take money I didn't have to replace the bedspread and possibly the sheets. I just hoped it hadn't burned all the way through to the mattress.

Liam's gaze moved to Caroline. "Leave, wolf."

She looked back at me, a question in her eyes. I nodded and indicated she should go.

"Alright, I'll call you later," she said. She edged past Liam before shooting me a significant look with raised eyebrows as she disappeared down the hall.

"What did the wolf want?" he asked, ice in his voice.

"She was just helping me with something."

His gaze turned back to my scorched bedspread. "So, I see."

We were quiet for several seconds as we observed the destruction.

"If you wanted to come home with me, you only needed to ask," he said.

I snorted. "You can hold your breath about that ever happening."

"Why? Because Thomas showed you a few unwelcome truths?"

I hesitated in the act of tossing the book to the floor, eying the wood there. On one hand, Thomas owned the apartment. He was the one who would have to deal with the aggravation of fixing it when I moved out. On the other, I didn't trust that he wouldn't figure out a way to take the damages out of me, whether monetarily or by binding me ever tighter to him.

Yeah, it wasn't worth chancing the book having another spontaneous combustion episode.

Liam ignored my preoccupation as I looked around the room for a better place to stash my current pain in the ass. He prowled along the perimeter, fiddling with the things I'd collected through the years, picking one up before placing it down and picking up another. He held up a glass ocean buoy I'd found when I was a kid on a trip to the ocean.

"We both know it's only a matter of time," he said, putting the buoy back down.

"Maybe before. Not anymore."

With a sigh, I placed the book on an end table. It was the cheapest piece of furniture in the room. Replacing it would hurt, but not as much as if the book did permanent damage to my floors.

Liam brushed past me, his smell, the scent of a spring thunderstorm, wrapping around me as it danced along my senses.

I moved away from him. I didn't need distractions and Liam was the biggest of them all.

"Believe me, *a chuisle*, you'll be mine in the end. Fight it all you want," Liam said, giving me a smile that invited sin and decadence. It was the type of smile meant to con a woman out of her underwear. The kind of look that said he'd give you a night you would never forget, a night you'd spend the rest of your life measuring other men against.

Despite what I knew of him, the anger I still had, his smile got to me. Just a little. Just enough that warmth filled me even as I brushed it off.

I arched my eyebrows and smirked. "You have an inflated sense of your irresistibility."

His smile widened, a hint of fang peeking out, his eyes heavy-lidded. "There's nothing inflated about me."

I rolled my eyes at him. Sure, there wasn't.

"What's that?" Liam asked, his gaze going to the book on the table behind me.

"What's what?" I asked, looking around the room.

"The book you just had in your hand."

I glanced at the nightstand.

"Nothing. Have you finally tired of throwing yourself against my downstairs neighbor's door?" I asked, stepping between Liam and the book, not fully recognizing what I was doing. There was this need, urgent and all-consuming, to prevent him getting a look at my book. To keep him from knowing, just what, I wasn't sure.

Liam's gaze sharpened. I fidgeted.

He relaxed. "I'm glad you mentioned that. When did you plan to tell me a deposed Fae lord and the captain of his guard had taken up residence in the apartments below you?"

I snorted. "Why ask questions you already know the answer to?"

He didn't seem to appreciate that answer, his eyes darkening as he prowled closer, stopping just far enough away I couldn't object to having my personal space violated as he examined the burn marks on my bed.

"I remember Niall of old. He is dangerous and always liked to play with his food before he ate it."

And I suppose in that analogy, I was the food.

"Everyone is dangerous," I told him. It was true. Compared to me, everyone was. Even Inara and Lowen could be deadly if they put their mind to it. Their magic, for one, was way out of my league.

"Are you sleeping with him?"

The question came out of nowhere leaving me to blink dumbly at Liam. Anger erupted in the next second, heating my blood and setting my pulse pounding.

I threw my hands up. "Yes. That's it. You've got me. I was down there for a secret assignation."

His gaze went stony. That was all the notice I got before he made his move, skirting past me and grabbing the book from the end table. I yelped and lunged after him.

He hissed and dropped it, cradling his hand as he glared down at the offending piece of leather and paper.

I crouched and grabbed it.

"How did you get an object of power?" Liam asked, staring at me like he'd never seen me before.

I straightened and held the book in front of me. "What are you talking about?"

"That," Liam said pointing. He seemed disturbed by the fact that I was holding the book against me. "Where did you get it?"

"It just came to me," I said. In a way it had. And now it refused to leave.

"Those things don't just come to people," he said. "You need to get rid of it."

"Can't," I said.

His stare said that wasn't answer enough.

I sighed. "I've tried. It just keeps coming back."

He grimaced. "Yes, I've heard of some being able to do that. It usually means they're very powerful with a mind of their own."

"You know what this thing is then?" I asked.

Because the last time I'd asked a witch, the response I got in return was that it was powerful but didn't mean me direct harm. Not exactly a comforting thought.

"Enough to know this is one of the higher objects of power. It was probably created by a Fae; they've always been amused by such things. I'm surprised to find it here," he said. "Has it done anything for you?"

"Depends on your definition. Mostly it gives me little hints when problems arise in my life."

Setting it back down, I moved into the living room, looking for my phone. Liam followed after another dark glance at the book.

The phone was in my fridge. Definitely not where I left it, but given who I had for roommates, it could have ended up in a much worse place— like the toilet. It had taken me a week to dry the phone off enough to work the last time that had happened.

I flipped it on and paused. There were fifteen missed calls and five messages from my sister starting around ten p.m.

I hit play on one of the voicemails and lifted the phone to my ear. Only seconds later, my face paled as I listened.

"Aileen, where are you? Please, pick up. I need my sister." My sister's soft sobs filtered through the phone. "Linda's in the hospital and they don't know what's wrong. She keeps throwing up blood."

CHAPTER FIFTEEN

Liam straightened from the counter, the irritation and sharp playfulness disappearing from his face as the blood rushed from my head.

My hand with the cell phone fell to my side.

Liam didn't ask what was wrong. With our superior senses, he already knew. Sympathy crossed his face and a tense watchfulness as he slipped the phone from my hand.

I let him do it.

Fifteen missed calls. Jenna must have been going out of her mind.

"I need to get to the hospital," I said through numb lips.

Liam nodded. "I'll have Daniel drive us."

I didn't move. I couldn't. I was stuck. The sound of the barely controlled hysteria in Jenna's voice played in my head over and over again.

"Sun's coming up soon," I said, softly.

It was a little after six. Already, I could feel it lurking just below the horizon. The threat of its presence burned a hole in my chest.

"What am I going to do if I pass out?" I asked.

"I'll be there. I won't let you go alone," he assured me, his voice quiet and steady.

I nodded.

He paused, watching me carefully. "But it might be wise to take some of my blood. It can help you resist the sun."

I shut my eyes, already resigned. I knew that.

He correctly read that as my agreement, lifting his wrist to my mouth. I bit down, the warmth of his blood hitting me, the power zinging through my veins. The usual lust was still there, but this time its urgency was overridden by my need to get to the hospital and check on my niece.

He pulled me away shortly after I started drinking, murmuring small words in his native language.

After that, the trip passed in a haze. He gave Daniel the hospital name, having paid more attention than me to the end of Jenna's message. I spent the drive staring out the window, trying to remember the last time I'd seen Jenna and my niece.

It had been months. Months of silence because I'd shut everyone out. Months of lost time because I couldn't figure out a way to fit in with my family anymore.

Daniel parked near the entrance as Liam and I got out. He used his whammy to get Linda's location out of the first desk we stopped at, then it was an endless maze as we traipsed throughout the hospital looking for the right floor.

Technically, it wasn't visiting hours anymore, but whenever someone stopped us to challenge our presence, Liam pulled out his abilities and sent them on their way.

My normal dislike of manipulating humans was a distant memory, the overwhelming need to find Jenna and my family showing my true self. It's easy to hold to your principles when times are easy. It's much more difficult to do so when you're tested. That's when you find out which of your values are important. Turns out the vampire's ability to mesmerize wasn't nearly so objectionable when it was being put to use for me.

I rounded the corner and stopped, catching sight of my mother slumped in a chair, her face pale as she blankly stared into the distance.

My dad sat next to her. The man who'd raised me always seemed larger than life, but at that moment he seemed a shadow of his normal self. He looked older than his years. They both did.

My mother's blank gaze drifted my way as if sensing she was being watched. "Aileen, what are you doing here?"

I stepped forward, her words getting my feet moving again, when I would have remained frozen in place. "I came as soon as I heard."

They both took me in, still in the dress from the evening, my hair a tangled mess down my back. I never had gotten the chance to change.

A shutter slammed down on my mother's face. "You shouldn't have bothered."

I felt the words like a physical blow.

"Elise," my dad said, sounding shocked and chastising.

My mom's face tightened. "Have you gone back to get help?"

My silence was answer enough.

"Then I don't want you here." She stood.

Liam moved at my side. I grabbed his arm, holding him back.

I lifted my chin. "I don't care. Jenna asked me to be here. She can ask me to leave."

"We've been here for hours. You're just now getting here. Where have you been?" my mom asked, her eyes hard.

I stared at her, wondering how we had gotten to this point. This wasn't my mother.

"I was at an event. I didn't have my phone on me," I said, trying to stay calm.

Emotions were high. There was no need to make things worse than they already were.

She made an ugly sound. It was half- laugh, half-scoff.

I didn't respond, just stared her down.

Liam's hand moved to the small of my back, a silent message he was there, that I wasn't alone.

The movement attracted her notice and she narrowed her eyes at him. "You're her doctor, aren't you?"

We both went stiff. I hadn't thought she would remember his face. He'd whammied her pretty good the one and only time he'd met her. Humans under that much influence often had trouble remembering what the vampire looked like, a natural defense mechanism to the way we tended to hunt.

"I'm her boyfriend," Liam said easily, flashing my mother a charming smile and ignoring the way I stiffened.

My mother didn't look placated, if anything his statement made her more suspicious as her attention swung back to me. "Is that how you got out of the hospital? By fucking your doctor?"

I sucked in a breath, shocked.

My mother rarely cursed, and never so casually—in a way designed to hurt and flay the flesh from your bones.

"Elise!" my father barked, horrified.

"Mom, that's enough," Jenna said, her voice strong. She stood in the hallway, her gaze fastened on my mother, the door slightly ajar behind her.

Liam had gone preternaturally still at my side and was now eying my mother in a way that made me think of a predator assessing the vulnerable points of their prey.

My mother stooped, grabbing her purse and straightening. "I'll be in the cafeteria."

She walked away without a word, leaving the rest of us staring at her.

My dad stood with a sigh. "I'd better go after her. Make sure she doesn't get lost."

He crossed to us and squeezed my arm. "Don't hold it against her, Lena. This thing with Jenna has her out of sorts."

I gave him a strained smile, not saying anything. There was nothing to say. Hurt had stolen my voice. Anything I said now wouldn't be very nice, even if it was true.

There was a slight limp in his step as he headed down the hall after my mom.

Jenna watched me, the look in her eyes guarded.

"I'm sorry I wasn't here earlier," I said, not moving toward her for the hug every part of me begged for, too afraid of her rejection to attempt it.

Her shoulders slumped and she sighed, one hand coming up to scrub at her face. "I heard what you told mom. You can't help that you didn't have your phone on you."

She took in our ruined and rumpled clothing. "Looks like you two had quite the night."

I looked at the two of us, realizing for the first time how we must appear. The dress had seen better days and looked like I had grabbed it off the floor after a long night. Liam was in a similar state.

I sighed, at least there were only a few spots of blood. That wouldn't be too hard to explain.

Jenna offered me a small smile. It wasn't much, there and gone in moments, barely touching her eyes. "Thanks for coming, Lena. It means a lot."

Finally, I stepped forward, wrapping her in my arms. "Of course. I'd do anything for you, little sis."

She felt frail and insubstantial in my arms, the events of the night taking their toll. I couldn't even imagine what she was going through. I was a wreck, barely holding it together. For Jenna, it had to be a hundred times worse.

We let each other go, neither commenting on how the other was discretely swiping tears out of their eyes.

"Can I see her?" I asked, hesitantly. There was every chance Jenna wouldn't want me around Linda, even after the apparent welcome she'd given me. It would hurt but I was prepared to accept whatever decision she made.

"Of course," Jenna said, stepping to the side. "The doctor said only two at a time. Really, he wanted mom and dad to leave hours ago, but they refused, so we've been taking turns."

Liam touched my arm. "I'll wait here."

I clasped his hand gratefully, letting him see my gratitude. I was on borrowed time. It had taken half an hour to get here and then another twenty minutes just to find Jenna and Linda. The sun was already edging its way above the horizon. If it hadn't been for his blood, I would be minutes away from collapsing.

"I won't be long," I told him.

He nodded, his face unconcerned, his gaze soft.

I followed Jenna into the room, the smell of the hospital making me slightly queasy. Why was it that every hospital I'd ever visited smelled the same? Like puke and antiseptic, sickness and death. I didn't care what cleaning products they used, it was always the same.

I hated that Linda was here. Hated she had to smell this air, that it would linger long after she was out of here.

Her room was private at least, with a window overlooking the parking garage and a chair in the corner. A book on the table told me that was where Jenna had been before my confrontation with our mother had pulled her out of here.

The bed was the last object I took in, reluctant to see my niece so small and frail, hooked up to monitors that beeped incessantly.

This wasn't the first hospital room I'd ever visited. I had more friends than I cared to think about who'd had stints in places like this. Most had survived, some had not.

Somehow this time, it hurt worse.

My feet took me over to Linda, but still, I hesitated to touch her. Her skin was pale with bruises around her eyes, her hair limp around her face.

"What happened?" I asked, reaching out to touch the top of Linda's hand.

She didn't stir, remaining locked in slumber, for which I was grateful. She didn't need to see the fear on our faces or hear the desperation we were feeling. She deserved all things sunny and beautiful, not this sterile place that smelled like death.

Jenna shook her head, her arms folded in front of her as if holding herself tightly might keep her from falling apart. "The doctors don't know. They said she'll need all sorts of tests before they can tell us anything."

Her gaze darted to Linda and back before she blurted, "I don't know how I'm going to pay for everything. My insurance isn't going to cover all this."

"I thought your job had good benefits," I said.

Jenna worked at a law firm. It had been one of the many things my mom had thrown in my face when she'd been harping on my lack of direction.

Jenna shook her head. "I don't work there anymore. I took a new position with a startup. It has great pay and vacation, but the medical and retirement benefits are nowhere near as good as my last job."

I hadn't known she'd changed jobs. Just another way I had lost touch.

"We'll figure it out," I told her.

I didn't have a lot of money, but what I had, I'd give her. This job with Liam would help.

Jenna nodded, though she didn't look particularly convinced. It was hard to blame her. She knew I didn't make much.

"There was no sign that she was sick?" I asked.

"Not that I saw," Jenna said, her voice rising. For the first time anger threading through it. "I would have taken her to the doctor if there was."

"I know you would have," I said soothingly.

Jenna was a good mom. If Linda had so much as a sniffle it was off to the clinic or an urgent care. Before this, I would have said she was a little too neurotic about it. Now, Jenna would no doubt be kicking herself over supposed missed signs.

I'd had to ask though.

"What time did she start throwing up?" I asked.

"A little before ten, I think."

That was before I foiled the assassination plot.

I didn't know if I was hoping for a link between the two events or not. Children got sick. Sometimes they got very sick, the type of illness that would impact the rest of their lives if they were lucky enough to survive.

If this was something done to her as a result of my actions, it would kill me to know I'd caused it, but at least the solution would be much more straightforward. There would be a solution, I knew that much. Even if I had to kill every High Fae in the city.

"I get it now," Jenna said, her voice still raw from choking back tears.

The words yanked me from my dark thoughts and I looked up. "You get what?"

"Why you were so angry every time we tried to interfere. Why you pulled back every time we pushed."

The words were so unexpected I went silent, watching her with a careful gaze. Of all the things I'd expected from her tonight, this was not among them.

"We shouldn't have done some of the stuff we did," she confessed. "If you'd come into my house unannounced or rearranged my stuff, I would have lost my mind."

While I appreciated she finally understood where they had crossed the line, I didn't know where this was coming from.

She caught the baffled look and gave me a sad smile. There was a hint of shame on her face. "You know when I first got pregnant, you were the only one who never judged me. You just took my hand and told me we'd get through this. I never did thank you for that."

"I wasn't the only one. Mom was there for you too."

Jenna shook her head. "Mom didn't talk to me for the entire pregnancy. She didn't let up until after Linda was born."

That wasn't true. It couldn't be.

"The baby shower she threw you."

"Dad made her. If you recall, she didn't invite any of her friends or most of our family. She didn't even talk to me during it. She spent the whole time cleaning and setting up," Jenna said, seeming resigned.

I sat down on the chair next to the bed. I did remember that. I thought it was just our mom's usual neurotic antics before a party. She had to have everything perfect. She always had. Mom loved to entertain, but she was a pain during the preparation and decoration phases. It might be one of the reasons I hated parties or any entertaining that was more complicated than popping open a beer and a bag of chips.

"How did I not see this?" I asked myself.

"Because you were always the strong one," Jenna said. "You never tolerated her silent treatment. Whenever she tried, you just went your own way and never even noticed, or you just pestered her until she reacted."

Still, I wasn't an unobservant person, you would have thought I'd remember.

"She tried to get me to put Linda up for adoption," Jenna confessed.

Shock held me immobile. I hadn't known that. I knew Mom hadn't been exactly thrilled to learn her daughter was pregnant by a married man—especially given how young she'd been—but I hadn't thought she'd go that far to correct Jenna's mistake.

"Then after Linda was born, she was always there with her tips and opinions," Jenna said.

Yes, and Jenna had always taken them, but perhaps not for the reason I'd always assumed.

"I was so happy she was talking to me again that it was just easier to do things her way," Jenna said.

"Why are you telling me this?" I asked.

Jenna sniffed. "Because you were there for me. You never wavered even when I was being a bitch. I wish I could have done the same for you."

I stood rooted to the spot, not knowing how to respond. It was true. My family had been difficult when I got back. They'd sensed something was wrong, and I couldn't tell them what that something was. Not without risking their safety.

Instead, they had jumped to conclusions. They thought everyone who came back from serving there had PTSD and other issues. They assumed I had a drinking problem.

PTSD is a real and very present issue with service members. I had friends who suffered from it.

Most who came home were affected by the war in some way. It didn't have to be PTSD, though that is where civilians' thoughts always seemed to go.

Simply put, war affects you. It changes you. It should.

It's hard to put into words for people who've never experience it, but being over there was like having every nerve in your body stripped raw and then wound tight. So tight that just the smallest pressure could send you to angry town.

Time and distance helped with recovery. Pressure from the people who should accept you and their relentless pushing for you to be just as you were, didn't.

Tears welled in Jenna's eyes, "I'm sorry, Lena. Can you forgive me?"

I crossed to my sister and pulled her into a hug. "There's nothing to forgive."

We held each other for several long minutes. I felt the sun rise, that burning ball of fire reminding me why I'd had to pull back, had to let them keep their misconceptions.

I drew away and gave Jenna a shaky smile. "How about you go find mom and dad and get something to eat? You'll need your strength for today. I can sit with Linda until you get back."

She hesitated, the struggle between staying with her daughter and finding something to eat visible.

She nodded, crossing to Linda and bending down to place a kiss on her forehead, her pain obvious to anyone watching.

She squeezed my arm as she went by.

I waited until she was out the door before going to Linda's bed and taking a seat beside her. I reached for her hand. "You're going to be okay, little girl. I know this might seem scary right now, but your Aunt Aileen is going to figure this out."

Even if she had to kill a lot of people to do it. My niece was not going to lay bedridden a minute longer than she had to.

Liam entered seconds after Jenna left, his thoughtful gaze taking in the two of us.

"Could your old girlfriend have done this?" I asked, not wasting any time.

I needed to know.

Liam moved closer, his path silent. His hand went to Linda's forehead, the touch surprisingly gentle for the deadly enforcer.

"The Fae have many ways to hurt the young," he said, his voice serious. "Some consider children to be the most delicious of delicacies."

My hands tightened into fists at that news. My fangs slid down and I let out a small, enraged sound. Liam noted the action but didn't comment on it.

I closed my eyes and repeated to myself. Linda was safe. We didn't know yet if the Fae even had anything to do with this. It could be some crazy coincidence.

"What else?" I asked after I'd calmed sufficiently.

"There are those who place changelings in the child's place so the parents don't miss them," Liam said softly.

"Changelings." My voice was flat.

"Sometimes they're lesser Fae who stay for a time. Other times it's a piece of wood. Always the child sickens and dies after a while," Liam said.

We both looked at where Linda lay on the bed. The only sign of life the lift of her chest and the persistent beep of the machines.

"You think she's a changeling," I said, the question a statement.

"I don't know. It is a practice that has fallen out of favor, though there are occasionally instances where it is still done," Liam said, choosing his words carefully. "Do you see anything to suggest that might be the case?"

I got up, pacing away. "Nothing. There's nothing there. Not even a shadow. She looks just like my niece, feels just like her."

She looked perfectly normal in my othersight. There was no trace of magic.

Liam watched me, his expression sad. "Then you must consider the possibility that this is a human ailment. Not everything has a magical explanation."

That was not what I wanted to hear. I wanted this to be something I could fix. I wanted to take that look of fear from my sister's eyes.

"But it could be?" I asked.

He hesitated, before reluctantly nodding.

That's all I needed to know. I might not be able to prove it, but I knew that Fae bitch had something to do with it. I would make her pay for messing with my family.

After that we sat in silence, the sun becoming more present in the sky, turning the window outside the room into a painting that still, after all this time, managed to take my breath away and remind me humans were just a small part of the greater whole.

I'd seen many sunrises in the military, some beautiful, some lackluster, some bashful and shy. I'd missed them when I became a vampire. Now I counted each one I saw as the blessing they were.

It was while I was staring out the window, my hand on Linda's that Jenna stepped into the room, lingering in the doorway as her gaze slid from Liam back to me.

He ignored her hint, staying by my side as she finally moved into the room after a long pause. He'd gone still, his expression cooling considerably as she approached.

I glanced at him in confusion, noting my mother peering through the window in the door. The abrupt reversal in his manner suddenly made sense.

I didn't pay much attention to his coldness or the way his gaze had turned unfriendly, grateful for Jenna's return.

As much as I hated to admit it, I wasn't going to hold out for much longer. The sun was beginning to win out over my will. I could still function, but exhaustion lurked just under the surface. If I thought too hard about how tired I was, I knew I wouldn't make it out of this chair, let alone the hospital.

"Aileen, can we have a minute?" Jenna asked.

The question made me blink dumbly, the fatigue slowing my thoughts.

I looked up at Liam.

His answer was simple. "No."

I frowned at him. He gazed down at me, the unhappiness there surprising me, especially considering the moment we'd just shared.

It woke me up a little, alerted me to the fact something wasn't quite right. I straightened in the chair and looked at my sister, finally tuning into the look on her face. One that was part shame and part stubbornness. It was an expression completely at odds with the Jenna who had just left here.

I couldn't help but brace myself. Liam's caution invaded me and I wasn't so sure I wanted to spend any time alone with her.

"Just say what you need to say," I said, my voice hardening just slightly. I forgot my promise to myself, that I was going to make more of an effort to understand where they were coming from, that I wasn't going to treat them as potential hostiles anymore.

Jenna's lips firmed and she stepped forward. "Alright, I wanted to ask if you'd be willing to donate blood. I checked Linda's blood type and it matches yours."

I stared at her, processing her words. They didn't make sense. I was familiar with blood donation practices, everyone in the military is, given what we do. You want to know the extent we'll go to for each other, have someone call out over the base's speaker for people with a certain blood type to report to donate for a wounded soldier, and you'll see everyone with that blood type drop everything to run and volunteer. So many, the medics had to turn people away.

I'd even donated quite a few times both for military purposes and civilian ones. The United States had a large pool of donated blood. The only time they asked family members to donate was if there was a rare blood type or antigen in the mix.

I was A positive. That wasn't exactly rare. There should have been plenty available unless the city had suffered a rash of incidents all involving people with that blood type.

I didn't answer Jenna, standing and making my way to the door.

"Aileen," Jenna protested.

I stopped and turned to her, the expression on my face hard.

Jenna's expression turned pleading. "Just donate the blood. Please."

I turned and walked out of the room.

My mother waited in the hallway, her arms folded over her chest and an expression on her face that said I'd reacted just the way she thought I would.

"Why did you do that?" I asked, perfectly calm.

"Because she needed to know the truth," my mother said, her face serene.

I nodded. The truth. Right.

"And what truth is that, Mom?"

My mom lifted her chin. "That there's a reason you won't give her daughter, your niece, your blood."

"And what reason did you give her?" I asked, not letting myself feel. I felt detached from myself, like this wasn't happening to me, but a different Aileen.

I was curious in spite of myself.

My dad stared at her like he'd never seen her before, meeting my gaze with a worried one of his own.

"You won't give blood because you're hopped up on some illegal substance or alcohol," she said, her face hard, her expression bitter and angry. It turned her into a stranger I didn't recognize.

I nodded slowly. She wanted truth. My lips twisted. "Well, you're right about that. I can't give blood."

Her expression turned triumphant.

"I'm sick," I told her, watching that victory freeze before turning to horror. There was a gasp from Linda's room. "Something I picked up while in Afghanistan. I can't give blood without getting that little girl sick too."

In a way it was the truth. Vampirism might not be so easily caught, but it was a magical virus all the same.

"What are you sick with?" my mom challenged.

She was a bloodhound on a scent. I had to give her that.

I shook my head sadly. "No, you don't get to know that anymore."

I looked over my shoulder at my sister. "You know why she cut me off?"

Jenna just stared at me, her eyes wide and shocked.

I turned to face my mom. Once, the fury on her face would have stopped me. It would have sent me scurrying for cover or apologizing for disappointing her even as I begged her forgiveness. Those days were over. She'd seen to that.

"Because she let something slip. Something that made me question whether Dad was my real father." My gaze lifted to him. He stared at me with sad eyes, the understanding there confirming what I suspected. It hurt worse than a knife to the chest.

"You're lying," my mom said, her voice ugly with repressed emotion.

"Don't be ridiculous, Lena," Jenna said. "I have photos of him holding me when I was born."

"Yes, you do. Funny how all my photos have disappeared," I said, looking at the two people who'd raised me, the man who had kissed my skinned elbows and knees and then put me back onto my bike to try again.

"There was a fire," my mom said.

Jenna looked like she might buy into the lie, even as I read the small signs that shouted the deception for what it was. The increased respiration, the sped-up heartbeat and the small changes to her pupil.

My first time being able to sense a lie and it came at the worst possible time. I almost wished I still believed in my fairy tale, that my dad was my dad and we were one big happy family.

"It's true," my dad said, his voice hoarse, his gaze never leaving mine.

"Patrick," my mom said, sounding betrayed.

"You should go," he told me.

I didn't respond, his words feeling like a wound. I'd known it in my head. Having him confirm it was just that much worse.

"Aileen," Jenna said, her voice thin and reedy, an apology already in her eyes.

I held up a hand. "No, not this time. You gave me a pretty song and dance in there, then the first time she whispered in your ear, it was the same old thing. Stay away from me until you learn how to separate her opinions from your own."

I didn't wait for a response, walking slowly down the hall. I had no idea if I was going the right way. I just needed to leave, to not be around the people who shared my blood, who were supposed to love me unconditionally and have my back against the world.

I guess those things only applied when you weren't a vampire.

Liam didn't say anything as we made our way out of the hospital, letting me lean on him when I got too tired to stand straight, eventually taking me into his arms when it became clear I wasn't going to make it out of there under my own steam.

His handsome face above me was the last thing I saw before I let my exhaustion and grief carry me off.

CHAPTER SIXTEEN

I woke facedown in a strange bed, my legs pinned and a warm weight against my back.

Awareness returned in spurts. Gradual, as I drifted out of slumber-land only to fall back into it again. Eventually I forced myself awake, the unfamiliar feeling of another person wrapped around me tugging me from sleep.

A leg pushed between mine from behind as I became aware the firm shape under my head wasn't a pillow but was in fact a nicely muscled arm. One I recognized.

I lifted myself up, or tried to anyway. The arm around my waist tightened, flattening me down again.

Unable to escape, I twisted my head and stared blearily at a sleeping Liam.

His face was relaxed, peaceful even. It was the first time I'd seen him so unguarded. I wouldn't go so far to call him innocent or childlike, there was too much masculinity, too much potential for sin even when sleeping, but he looked softer.

I allowed myself to stare, my eyes running over him as I lay my head back down. Like this, his beauty was even more evident. For once, I didn't immediately want to punch him in the throat.

The events of last night came back to me. The trip to the hospital had changed things between us, but I still couldn't determine the extent.

He'd been an unwavering support at my back, doing what even my family seemed incapable of. I still didn't know if I trusted him, not entirely, but in certain things, I knew he wouldn't let me down.

It was enough. For now.

His eyes blinked open. He stared at me, desire in his gaze, his arms tightening.

Intent was there. Passion too. He looked like a man who was about to take what he wanted. He dragged me over him and hesitated, giving me a chance to say no for one endless slice of time.

The denial hovered on my lips. This was a bad idea on so many levels. We argued as easily as we breathed. He had secrets wrapped in secrets. I doubted I'd ever know the real Liam. This would likely be a brief interlude that flamed out as fast as it burned.

Somehow, I couldn't voice the word that would end all this as he put slight pressure on my neck, his eyes never leaving mine.

For the first time in a long time, I felt like I was right where I was supposed to be. Warm and safe. I couldn't explain it, and I didn't want to question it. The normally banked fire that flared to life anytime we got within feet of each other turned into an inferno.

For just one night, I wanted to forget the differences between us. I wanted to forget we were on two sides of a divide, forget all of the reasons this wouldn't work.

Instead, I wanted to feel, to throw myself over the edge and not come up until I had sated myself.

It was a purely selfish desire. I was okay with that if it meant getting what I wanted.

He seemed to sense the change in me, one hand coming up to tuck a strand of hair behind my ear, his eyes questioning.

We didn't speak, each of us afraid to break the moment for fear of it disappearing, of it turning as ephemeral and fleeting as a ghost light.

His hand tightened on the back of my neck as he drew me down, his eyes never leaving mine.

Our lips touched and thought disappeared. The desire we'd been denying rose up, swamping any remaining semblance of thought.

We became two creatures intent on glutting ourselves on the other. It was raw and violent, as if we didn't consume the other right this second, we would die from the lack.

He was a cool spring lake, stealing my breath and stopping my heart.

I gasped as his fangs sank into my breast, piercing the flesh around my nipple. My hands clutched his back as fire raced from the bite.

I returned the favor seconds later, my eyes fluttering at the first sweet taste of his blood, my head dizzy as we fought for dominance, turning the bed into a tangled nest of blankets.

His skin slid against mine, hard and warm as one hand glided up the inside of my leg, blazing a trail of ice and fire that sank deep.

A husky laugh reached me as I writhed, unable to keep still as he teased and played. "I've been waiting to do this since the first time I saw you, *a chuisle.*"

"Then stop messing around, or I'll find someone more willing to get things done," I hissed, my fangs fully extended and my vampire nature engaged.

I regarded him with an obsessive possessiveness, one matched by the dark need in his eyes. It should have scared me, should have sent me running, but somehow it fed the deepest parts of me, ramping up my desire until I felt like I'd do considerable violence if I didn't get what I wanted right the fuck now.

His smile turned wicked as he read the need in me. It was all the warning I got before he pinned me in bed, his face hovering over mine. "Oh no, *macushla.* I've waited long enough. We're doing this my way."

His lips descended as his hands played along my side. Soon my moans filled the air as he left bites along my body, each one sending me higher and higher until I felt like I might spontaneously combust from the feelings running rampant in me.

I arched up, rubbing myself against him, my lips skating over his neck and collarbone as my fangs left another mark. The decadence of his blood made me wild.

His hands found my hips, his fingers tightening and then he was sinking home, filling me up as my neck arched and I lost myself in him.

His eyes shut and he murmured in his native language, words I didn't understand even as I caught the meaning behind them.

Together, we ignited, each touch sending us higher as he moved within me. His pace quickened, every muscle in my body drawing tight in anticipation, pleasure biting deep. My climax swamped me, sending wave after wave of sensation quaking through me. Liam gave a guttural groan as he followed seconds later.

It was a long time later when we came back to ourselves. I was plastered against his side, he on his back, one hand drawing random patterns on my skin. Shivers skated down my back at each touch as my body rested, resplendent and replete, against his in the aftermath.

I didn't know if it was because we were both vampires or if it was us, but the intensity of what we'd just experienced was almost scary. It made me want to do it again and again while at the same time I wanted to run fast and far, for fear of losing myself.

I sighed and rolled onto my back. Liam moved beside me, coming to hover over me, his weight supported on one elbow as his hand moved, caressing my side and playing with my hair.

His eyes were wondering, his focus intent, as if he was committing this moment to memory so he might never forget.

"Is it true my apartment was your first stop upon returning?" I asked, feeling vulnerable all of a sudden.

What we'd just done felt momentous. At least for me. For him, who knew? Given his lifespan, he'd probably had lots of lovers. The perfect-looking Niamh being one of them.

I remembered his face the night he'd returned. Expectant and anticipatory, like a starved man seeing food for the first time. He'd hummed with energy, almost desperate, when we kissed.

He made a small sound and dropped a kiss on my collarbone. "Yes, though I'd hoped for a better welcome than the one I got."

I snorted. "You're lucky I didn't shoot you. Again."

"*A chuisle*, you're so violent." His smile deepened. The look in his eyes grew wicked as he nipped my chin. "I find I like it."

"That's good. Because I'm not likely to change."

He lifted his head, his expression turning serious. "Nor would I want you to. I am fascinated by your stubbornness."

I gave him a flat look. Fascinated. Right. That's why he sometimes looked like he wanted to murder me when I challenged him.

His smile turned playful. "It makes me want to break it down and turn it to better uses."

That sounded more realistic.

"How is it that I awoke before you?" I asked. He was centuries older than me. He should have been awake hours before me.

"My day was more active than yours," Liam said, his gaze steady on mine, his hands tightening just slightly. "And the sun isn't quite down yet."

I nodded. Now that he'd said something, I could feel the sun in my chest, its presence waning but still very much there. No wonder my waking had been so slow and disjointed, similar to the way a human would wake.

This was the point where I normally drew back, put distance between the two of us. Somehow, I couldn't bring myself to do that just yet.

He rolled onto his back, pulling me with him and arranging me on his chest. I let my chin rest on him.

"Why did you leave?" I asked, almost wincing at the vulnerability the question hinted at.

It wasn't like I was some insecure teenager unable to cope with someone I was interested in being gone, but for some reason the manner of his leaving bugged me. Much as I hated to admit it, it had hurt he could head out without even a word.

Over three months without communication. It was hard to let that go. Especially given the direction we'd been heading in.

"I got word that someone I've been searching for a very long time had been spotted. I didn't think I had time to delay."

I rested my chin on his chest as I considered him. "And did you find this friend?"

He stared up at the ceiling, his face pensive. "Yes and no."

I lifted myself up so I could see his face better. "It's a pretty straightforward question."

His eyes turned me. "I found this person, but he is trapped. I'm not even sure he recognizes me. I don't know how to free him. Yet."

"This person is why you left?"

It was something I could understand. I had people I would drop everything to find if they ever went missing. From the way he spoke, whoever this person was, they were extremely important to him. I could hear the yearning in his voice when he spoke of them, sense his frustration that he didn't know how to help them.

He made a wordless sound of assent. "It was supposed to be a quick mission, there and back. Unfortunately, complications delayed my return," he said.

"Complications that followed you back here?"

The look on his face was all the answer I needed.

An irrational surge of jealousy rose. I already knew Niamh and he had had a relationship, now I had to consider whether that relationship was a little more recent than I'd previously thought.

"I've lived a long life, not all of it good. There are things in my past that I'm not proud of. I would prefer those things not touch you," he said, his voice serious.

He wasn't the sort of man who explained. You took him as he was or you walked away. There would be no changing Liam, no softening him or using feminine wiles to civilize him. The fact that he'd bent to explain that much said he took this thing between us seriously.

I didn't react for a long moment, letting his words sink in. It was enough that I didn't get up and walk away, though it was tempting. He had heartache written all over him.

"Niamh is one such thing?" I asked, giving in.

His nod was small. "Yes."

"She wants you back," I said. Liam was a fine specimen of manhood. The way she'd looked at him had been possessive, not the sort of look a woman gave an ex-lover.

"She is a collector," he said. "She sees me as a challenge, someone who got away, something that she can possess. However, she will not let that desire interfere with their purpose here."

I drummed my fingers on his chest. "You had me look over you and Eric to see if either of you were under her influence."

"Yes."

"And if I'd found her fingerprints all over you two?" I asked, lifting up, alarm finally taking hold.

"I would have had to take drastic action," Liam said in a calm voice.

I didn't have to ask what kind of drastic action that would be. I remembered the screams of the woman when the geas had taken hold.

If I'd found evidence of influence, Liam could very well have gone the same way.

The knowledge I might have come close to losing him struck deep. In all our back and forth, I had never considered a world without him in it. It was a much-needed reminder that despite the fact we were both immortal, life was still short. You had to grab it while you could or else be left standing battered and beaten in its wake.

His hands stroked my back, the touch drugging. I put my head back on his chest. The faintest trace of a heartbeat fluttered against my ear as he went back to playing with my hair, picking it up and letting it fall with a fascinated expression on his face.

"Speaking of our Fae friends, what did they get up to today?" I asked, needing a change of subject. I assumed he knew since he'd evidently been up most of the day.

His hand stroked along my back as he shifted under me, trying to get comfortable.

"They met with the witch's hag," he said.

Not good. I couldn't think of a worse partnership than Niamh and Sarah. The two apart were forces in their own right, both as tricky and devious as the other. Together they would be a nightmare to deal with.

"I'm still surprised Sarah agreed to an alliance with them," I said. "She doesn't strike me as the type to work well with others."

"She's not," Liam said. "But she hates Thomas. She'd do anything to bring him down."

That was a depth of hatred I just couldn't understand. Whatever had caused the enmity between them had happened centuries ago. To still be plotting and scheming to get back at Thomas, took a dangerous amount of persistence.

I sighed as the sun sank fully below the horizon, the tight feeling in my chest loosening for the first time since I'd awoken.

Liam's knowing gaze was on me when I looked back up. "It'll get better with time."

I sure hoped so. Being this conscious of the sun's movements was disconcerting.

"There's still one thing that's bugging me," I said.

His chest moved under me as he chuckled. He ran his fingers through my hair, smoothing it out. "Just one?"

"That first attack, how did the person know I would head for the troll?" I said thinking out loud.

His fingers paused as he gave consideration to my observation. "You assume the troll's sleep was because of you."

"You don't?"

"I had the enforcers check on a few other of the known Fae in the city, especially the powerful ones. Two others were in a deep slumber like your friend," he said.

Which meant Hector and the butterfly might have been a coincidence. I could almost see that.

"I don't think the attack on us was on purpose," I said, thinking out loud.

He shifted his head so he could see me better. "What makes you say that?"

"It was sloppy, and it doesn't fit with everything else going on. I think whoever did it saw an opportunity and took it."

It would explain a lot. My bet was the witches at the bar. Whether it was revenge for getting them kicked out or because of my connection with Angela, they made the most sense.

Once you took Hector out of the equation, the attack pointed directly at the witches.

"We should get going," I said. "I'm sure whatever Niamh and her companions are after won't wait much longer."

I still had to get to the bottom of Niamh's role in my niece's sickness, and Liam probably had to make a plan of action with his people.

Liam's face was regretful as he stood, stretching that long expanse of fine skin over glorious muscles. He pointed to a door to my left. "You can take a shower in there."

I nodded, getting a good look around the bedroom for the first time since I'd woken. It was surprisingly sparse, just a big wooden bed with a dark coverlet and strong, dark pieces interspersed throughout the room.

"Where are we?" I asked.

The room lacked the easy charm of his house, leading me to believe he'd taken us somewhere else.

"The Gargoyle," he said. "The sun was already up by the time we left the hospital. This was closer and it was safer to wait out the day here."

I couldn't argue with that.

"I selected some clothes from your room last night. They're on the chair," he said, pulling his pants up as he grabbed his cell from the end table.

I didn't waste any time grabbing them and heading for the bathroom, the thought of a shower a welcome one.

It wasn't long before I was clean and dressed and ready to tackle the day. Liam was already gone when I re-entered the bedroom, so I left as well, sparing the rumpled bed a last, lingering look.

I stepped into the hallway, closing the door softly behind me. I didn't want to advertise where I'd spent the last night. While I didn't plan to hide what Liam and I had done, I saw no reason to announce it to the world.

Seconds later Makoto rounded the corner, his head down as he studied the tablet in his hand. I froze just as he looked up.

His eyes went from me to the door, his smile widening. "You dirty girl, you."

I gave him a quelling glance. "Stop."

"No, no, it's cool," he said, pretending to wipe the smile off his face. "I'll just ignore the fact that you came out of Liam's room and are wearing that just-been-fucked glow."

"You mean the just got out of the shower look," I returned.

He gave me a grin that told me I hadn't fooled him. "Don't deny it. I can practically sense it on you."

I gave him a dark look. Sometimes living around creatures with senses even more finely tuned than my own sucked.

"Besides, Liam made an announcement earlier this evening. Your status has been upgraded to his most special person. Anyone caught trespassing on his territory will be dealt with harshly. That usually only means one thing," Makoto said, tossing the information out like it was unimportant and not the type of thing capable of making my head explode.

I stopped in the middle of the hallway, staring at nothing as anger welled deep inside. He probably hadn't used those exact words, but the sentiment would be the same.

"Where is he?" I snapped.

"Uh oh," Makoto said.

Uh oh was right. When I got done with Liam he was going to think twice about sharing personal business with his underlings.

"Where?" I asked.

"The war room," Makoto said.

Of course, he was. One of the few parts of the mansion off-limits to me.

"He said to bring you there when you got out of the shower," Makoto continued.

"Lead on," I told him with a pointy smile that didn't quite disguise the fury crackling through me. Makoto looked like he'd prefer to be anywhere else right then.

The mansion was surprisingly full tonight. For once, vampires were in the halls, a few of them sliding me unsure glances as they passed.

"What's going on?" I asked.

"Everyone's on edge because of what happened last night," Makoto said, sending them a dismissive look. "No one wants to admit it, but they're afraid. Most of the civilians don't face death on a regular basis. It's got them rattled."

"But not you?" I asked.

He shrugged. "This is just another day, another situation. Vampire

202

politics are no less bloody. Every one of the people here would probably kill if it would advance their station. They're running scared because they don't understand what happened and they don't like facing the idea there are creatures out there more powerful than them."

After that he fell silent until we came to a halt in front of the war room. He headed inside, going directly to a spot in front of a laptop, setting his tablet beside it.

I stepped in, my gaze immediately drawn to Liam. His eyes met mine as his mouth quirked. I sent him a look that said we were going to have words later. His smile turned smug, his eyes communicating he was looking forward to it.

We'd see about that.

After the exchange I found a spot along the wall, noticing most of his enforcers were in attendance. Thomas entered moments after me, guards flanking him. He was dressed in a suit, looking incredibly formal, as did his guards. My jeans and nice top didn't compare.

He took note of me where I stood along the wall, before turning his attention to Liam. Looked like we were about to get started.

The situation felt oddly familiar. I'd sat in pre-mission briefings before, and that was what this was. No doubt about it. Everyone listened with attentiveness. A single overlooked detail now could mean the difference between life and death later.

These people moved and spoke with an ease and purpose that came from doing similar briefings time and time again. It was odd how comfortable I felt falling into this role.

Granted, the mission briefings I'd sat through in the military usually didn't have the same level of high-tech equipment. It looked like the sort of briefing room you might find in a movie about spies or something. There were more monitors than I cared to think about, and so many technological gadgets even I couldn't recognize all of them.

Vampires might be known for being old-fashioned, but you wouldn't know it from looking at this place. My old commander would have sold his own mother to get his hands on a few of these toys.

"Our guests have informed us the hunt will likely start tomorrow night," Liam started.

The others stirred, the news unsettling them.

"Do we have any idea who the hunt has chosen as prey?" Daniel asked.

Liam's eyes met mine before he turned his attention away. "Not yet. They've assured us those who participate do so voluntarily and will be compensated appropriately should they survive the Wild Hunt," Liam said, not seeming happy about that fact.

The news didn't resonate well with those around me either, if their somber and irritated expressions were anything to judge by.

"If I were the designated prey, I would find a deep, dark hole to crawl into until this hunt is over," Anton muttered, not bothering to keep his voice quiet.

"Be that as it may, this is happening," Liam said. "Our job is to make sure there are no incidents."

Liam nodded at Makoto, who hit a few keys on his laptop.

A map popped up on the large-screen TV next to Liam. It zoomed in on a section just north of the city.

"The hunt will begin near the Alum Creek Reservoir," Liam said, pointing to a place that was right next to the dam.

"So close to the city?" Anton asked. "What if it moves into the populated sections? It's not exactly known for obeying borders or rules."

"It's the best we could do," Liam said. "Arlan and Niamh are holding a party tonight to celebrate their gods and the return of the hunt. Then tomorrow, starting at sundown, the hunt will begin. Daniel and Anton, you'll be with Thomas tomorrow. Nathan is already on-site preparing for our arrival. For tonight, I want everyone on the lookout for anything unusual. Our guests will probably try something. It's our job not to let them. Any questions?"

Anton raised his hand. Liam looked resigned and gestured for him to speak.

"What's the yearling's role in all this?" Anton asked, jerking his thumb at me.

All eyes swung my way. I returned their gazes with a placid expression, outwardly calm at being the focus of several top predators.

"You don't need to know that," Liam said in a voice that meant business. It did not invite questions.

Anton didn't seem satisfied. A feeling that seemed to be reflected in several of the enforcers' faces.

Still, they respected Liam, and kept their doubts to themselves despite their reservations.

"Alright, let's survive the night," Liam said in clear dismissal.

His enforcers filed out while Thomas and I lingered. I didn't move from my spot, hoping Thomas would finish his business so I could have a moment with Liam.

To my surprise, Thomas turned to me, propping his hip on a desk. "Liam tells me your niece is sick."

I didn't answer, my gaze going to the man in question where he had busied himself tidying up several papers. I didn't like that he'd shared that news. I liked it even less, that he'd done it without giving me a heads-up.

"She'll be fine," I said. She would. I'd make sure of that.

"There are ways to help her," he said, his words meaningful.

"She doesn't need help. I know how to fix her," I told him. I wasn't accepting anything else from Thomas. Not after the stunt he'd pulled with Deborah. He was the enemy pure and simple.

His expression grew confused as he looked between Liam and me. "Is there something I don't know?"

I didn't answer, holding my stony silence. The less he knew about anything, the better.

Liam put down his papers and sighed. "She thinks Niamh or one of her people might have something to do with her niece's condition."

Thomas's face turned alert. "Is that a real possibility?"

"Yes."

"Unlikely," Liam said at the same time, giving me a warning look. "And we're not going to make any accusations unless we're sure."

I lifted my chin but didn't answer.

"Aileen, I need you to promise. These aren't the type of beings you take on at a whim," he said, his voice serious.

I jerked a shoulder up. "I'll be smart."

I had to be.

Thomas made a small sound of amusement. He looked like a cat infinitely entertained by the two fools performing for him. He glanced at Liam. "She's your responsibility tonight. Make sure she doesn't get herself killed."

Liam grunted as Thomas straightened and glided out of the room, leaving the two of us alone.

I fidgeted, finally giving in to the urge to move as I explored the room. These types of conversations weren't my forte. Throw in the fact that I had intimate knowledge of his body now and couldn't help but remember a few of the things we'd done not that long ago, and it was a recipe for awkwardness.

Liam watched me, his gaze enigmatic as he leaned against the side of the table, arms folded across his chest. The flexed muscles reminded me unnervingly of how strong he'd been earlier. How effortlessly he'd held himself up.

I blinked and shook my head. None of that now. I needed to concentrate.

"Makoto tells me you've been making announcements. Something about how I'm yours," I said, my voice eerily calm.

Liam's smile flashed; he knew what he'd done and was amused by it. Great.

"I simply relayed the facts as I saw them," he said.

He waited expectantly. I didn't fail to disappoint.

"Is there a reason you felt the need to share our personal business?" I asked tightly.

He lifted a shoulder, the picture of unconcerned relaxation. "I felt it best to head off any misunderstandings now."

"Misunderstandings?"

He nodded. "I've found clear communication is always best."

"Clear communication." Great. Now I sounded like a damn parrot. I took a deep breath, trying for patience.

"Were you aware this isn't the middle ages?"

Liam cocked his head. "It's not?" Fake surprise was in his voice.

I narrowed my eyes at him as his lips tilted up in a wicked smile. He thought he was winning this little battle.

"No. And in this time period, people aren't owned," I said through gritted teeth.

"Are you sure? Because I'm pretty sure you're mine," he said, purposely missing the point.

My smile bared teeth in an expression an animal would have recognized as a threat. "Only in your dreams, pretty boy."

He leaned forward. "Only every day and every time I shut my eyes. Over and over again."

I folded my arms. Okay, that hadn't gone the way I'd thought. Time for a new approach.

"What was the purpose of telling everyone what we'd done?" I asked, point-blank.

I didn't enjoy having my personal business bandied around the water cooler. It wasn't the end of the world that others knew, but I wanted to understand the tricky vampire. He never did anything without a reason. Understanding was the best way to tilt the odds in my favor.

"Don't tell me you're ashamed of me," he said with a teasing glint. His confidence was such that I knew the question was more to pull at my tail than anything else. He exuded sexuality. There weren't many women dead or alive who wouldn't have taken him up on what he was offering.

"If you needed compliments to stroke your male ego, you only needed to ask," I said in a saccharine voice.

His laugh was short as he gave me a glance from under his eyelids. It was packed with all the seduction in his repertoire. I'd be lying if I said the look was ineffective; it stroked across my senses as I flashed to what we'd been doing earlier.

I leveled a look on him that meant business. I wanted answers.

He sobered slightly, some of the teasing playfulness falling from his expression. "Vampires are territorial by nature. By making it clear that you and I are involved, I've simply made it so no one will see you as a viable bed buddy. It keeps them safe since they know the state of things."

I went still, processing that statement. I didn't know which part of it to address first.

"You assume that we're going to be doing that again."

His gaze turned provocative. "Oh, I can promise you we will."

I folded my arms across my chest and snorted. "I think you're going to need my full cooperation for that sort of thing. Somehow, I just don't see that being possible after this little conversation."

He moved closer, looming over me so I had to tilt my head to look at him. His personal scent reached out, wrapping around me and making me slightly light-headed. The man was heady and dangerous. No doubt about that.

"I like my chances of convincing you to change your mind," he rumbled, looking me over in a way that told me he was remembering what I'd looked like rising over him in bed.

The sound he made then was half-purr, half-growl. I fought to keep it from getting to me, knowing that way lay danger.

Liam was too used to getting his way. If I let him, he'd grind me up and spit me out, leaving behind nothing but a heartbroken mess.

"I think it's best if I work next to someone else for the remainder of this job," I said, my eyes never leaving his. "To cut down on distractions and all that."

He lifted an eyebrow. "I didn't know your willpower was so weak. I'll be sure to limit my allure when you're around, if that makes you feel better."

My smile turned brittle. "It's not my willpower I'm worried about. After all, I'm not the one going around metaphorically pissing all over me."

Having said my piece, I headed for the door.

He stopped me with a hand on my hip. "I'm looking forward to this dance, *a chuisle*. Run all you want. In the end, you'll still end up back in my bed. Mine, as I'm yours."

I stepped free. "I think you're confused. I'm not part of the hunt."

The door was closing behind me when his words floated out. "No, you're the prize."

CHAPTER SEVENTEEN

The clearing fairly thrummed with energy, beings of all types throwing themselves into the madness. Music, amplified by magic and science, filled the air. A band played their hearts out on a small stage on the far side of the clearing, their movements almost frantic as they poured their entire beings into the music.

"Humans," Thomas said grimly. Liam and he exchanged a significant glance before he shook his head.

I glanced at him, not quite understanding.

Liam touched my waist and murmured in my ear. "The Fae can be rather hard on their human companions. They both rejoice in a human's ability to create, and hate it, jealousy turning their love to darker things."

"What do you mean?" I asked softly.

"In the country of my birth, they used to tell tales of humans who got caught in a fairy circle, made to dance or play until they dropped dead from exhaustion."

My gaze went back to the humans playing with frenetic energy. I'd thought they were simply caught up in the moment. After Liam's words, I had to wonder if there was more to it.

"But they wouldn't do that here, right?"

We weren't in Fairy. They wouldn't be so bold as to kill humans through compulsion here, would they?

Neither Liam nor Thomas looked particularly hopeful.

"Shouldn't we do something?" I asked.

Liam shook his head. "There's not much we can do. Tonight belongs to the Fae."

I didn't like that answer, and I was tempted to try something. Liam took my hand and drew me after him, tucking me in close as he shadowed Thomas.

We were all dressed similarly, the men in dark pants and leather jackets. It was the most I'd seen them embrace the vampire stereotype. All of them were armed under those jackets. I'd seen more than one enforcer add a few blades to their arsenal, and even a gun or two.

My room in the mansion had evidently come equipped with clothes that fit right in. Pants that had to cost hundreds of dollars, given the nice things they did for my ass, and a jacket with leather soft as butter. It was the real deal and probably cost more than the pants and silk dress shirt under it.

Once upon a time, I'd had a thing for leather jackets in all shapes, sizes and colors, so I knew a thing or two about how much something like this ran. This was nicer than anything I'd ever dreamed of back in those days.

The best thing about the outfit was the lack of high heels. This time, I was in motorcycle boots that were infinitely more comfortable. I don't care what anybody said, walking in heels was a perishable skill. I'd take the boots over those any day.

Liam prowled next to me. He surveyed the spooks around us, watching for any signs of danger.

His enforcers had spread into the crowd, but the two of us were stuck looking after Thomas for the next hour.

The spooks around us writhed and raged in time to the music, its beat picking them up and carrying them off. I felt the notes humming through my blood. Magic was in the air, potent and powerful and difficult to ignore.

There was an almost wild look in the men's faces, the magic setting their instincts firing. It seemed the Fae weren't the only ones affected.

We stood on the edge of the crowd observing, for which I was grateful. Already the magic had raised hairs on the backs of my arms and set my blood pumping. It was like standing on a precipice, the anticipation coursing through your blood, and the knowledge that you were just seconds away from death making you feel more alive than you had any right to be.

"Remind me again why we're here. What if they try another attack?" I asked through gritted teeth.

"As the master of the region, Thomas has no choice. To not attend would imply insult and make him look weak," Liam murmured.

"And me?"

"You're here for appearances. As the master's yearling, you affect his image. For the same reason he couldn't miss it, neither can you. I had your witch friend increase the wards against their magic. It should be safe."

Should, maybe, could. I didn't have a lot of faith in such words, especially when dealing with the Fae.

A Fae man stumbled into our path. He leered at me as he struggled to focus. "It's the dancing vampire. Sing for us, pretty vampire."

I was going to kill Caroline when I next saw her.

"Move along or else you'll be the one singing," Liam said, the threat in his voice clear.

The Fae held up his hands. "Alright, jeez. I just wanted to hear her sing again."

I narrowed my eyes at him as he slid back into the crowd.

There was a choked sound beside me and I swung my glare to Liam as he fought to keep his expression neutral.

"Don't start," I warned.

"As my lady wishes," he said, in an admirably neutral voice.

I stalked forward as he murmured, "Though if she wished to dance, I would not object."

I stiffened but didn't turn, not wanting to dignify his ridiculousness with a reaction. After that, the Fae didn't bother us, content to turn their attention to those there to celebrate.

We were only a third of the way through the gathering when several women stepped into the clearing, surveying the area with cunning eyes. They weren't Fae—they lacked that sparkling aura and otherworldly beauty. They were human with only the slightest of glimmers around them.

"When you increased the wards, did you think to protect against witch magic as well?" I asked, watching as the gaggle approached.

There were at least five of them, their hair glossy and bouncy. They wore dresses that were short and more suited to a night in a club than a forest. Every one of them had smooth skin and seemed young. It was like watching a swarm of co-eds approach, only their eyes showed they weren't quite the lambs they appeared. More like deadly tigers waiting in the brush to ambush their prey.

The curse Liam muttered was in a different language. "What are they doing here?"

"Looks like we weren't the only ones the Fae invited tonight," I said, watching the women greet one of the twins. Baran, I thought.

They giggled, twiddling their hair as they tittered. The look of superiority on Baran's face said he was used to this behavior and tolerated it because he had nothing better to do.

"Sarah," Thomas said, appearing by our sides. He looked almost stricken as he watched the group.

I looked the women over, not spotting the witches' crone. It should have been easy, given all that nubile young flesh.

But then a woman looked over at us, her smile turning cruel as she caught sight of Thomas. She was obviously the ringleader of the group.

She wasn't just beautiful in a gold-colored dress, her luxurious hair in soft waves around her face. She was stunning—the type of woman who could walk into a room and command the attention of everyone there. It wasn't just appearance either, she possessed a charisma that made it hard to look away.

The structure of her face was familiar. I'd seen her before. I squinted at her, mentally adding wrinkles and age spots.

I wasn't sure, but it could be Sarah, only a few centuries younger. Which was impossible, unless she had discovered the fountain of youth or had access to powerful magic. Maybe magic like the Fae were said to be capable of?

"I guess that answers the question of why they're working with the Fae," I murmured, looking over the other women.

I had a feeling Sarah wasn't the only one who'd benefited from their little alliance.

"Sarah wouldn't align herself with a dangerous ally like the Fae for such a superficial reason," Thomas hissed.

I wasn't convinced. "Are you sure about that? Because it sure seems like it to me."

As we spoke, Sarah took Baran's arm and let him lead her into the crowd as she sent a triumphant smile to Thomas.

Neither man responded, watching the women as they followed their crone. More than one gave us a sideways look, flicking their hair like they were a group of mean girls in truth. I was interested to note I was the target of several of those hostile looks.

"Just how bad was your breakup with that woman?" I asked.

A woman scorned was dangerous, but to hold onto a grudge for a few centuries? That was next level stuff.

Niamh glided out from the trees just then, wearing little to disguise what was underneath. The thin scrap of material she wore was nearly seethrough, with the torches set up throughout the clearing highlighting her figure beneath, giving those present a glimpse of everything in the cookie jar. In the ballroom the other night she'd been beautiful. Here, surrounded by nature, she was otherworldly.

I could see why humans through the ages have been obsessed with her kind. It would be so easy to get caught in her trap, to think beauty equated with good and righteousness instead of a facade meant to trick and tempt.

It was Liam's turn to become stiff and unyielding as she glided past. I couldn't help a spurt of amusement at the entire situation.

I slapped him on the back. "Look, both your and Thomas' old flames are here. Tonight should be super fun!"

There was a choked sound of amusement from Anton a few feet away. Neither Liam or Thomas seemed to appreciate my humor as they turned serious faces on me.

Thomas shook his head at Liam as if to say "you deal with her," before moving away.

I gave Liam an innocent look. "Is it something I said?"

His answering frown was long-suffering as he followed Thomas. I lingered behind, checking my phone messages.

A text from Caroline in answer to the one I'd sent earlier that night asking if she'd found anything.

Nothing useful.

I could almost sense her frustration over the phone.

Keep checking, I typed back.

Will do. Let me know if you need me. My car can be used as a getaway vehicle and to run any would-be hunters down. It's a twofer special, she typed back.

I huffed out a laugh before sliding my phone back into my pocket. I looked over the crowd, surprised to see most of them had thrown off their glamour.

I'd never seen so many Fae in one place. All types, some I recognized, many I did not.

The definition of what was Fae fascinated me. It didn't seem to matter what species or type of Fae they were as long as a spook fit into their pantheon somewhere. The characteristics of what made someone Fae seemed to be loosely defined.

I spotted harpies in the trees, not a creature I'd ever associated with the Fae, but who knows, maybe they were just here to play. It was the sort of out of control party that seemed to attract them.

Dryads frolicked through the clearing, their leafy hair and bark-like skin distinctive.

"Someone should have told me Wild Hunt was code for a rager," I muttered, following slowly after Liam.

I'd dropped back a few paces which was why I was in a better position to notice the gnome, Tom, a man who had proven himself an enemy, as he ran through the crowd, deftly avoiding the High Fae present.

I don't know what made me follow, but I turned on my heel and chased after him. I waited until we'd neared the edge of the crowd, grabbing the back of his jacket and using it to propel him into the trees.

"Hey Tom, fancy meeting you here," I said.

He tried to jerk out of my hold. He almost succeeded, too. Gnomes were known for their strength, and Tom had the additional benefit of being wily as hell.

I managed to retain my grip, my newfound strength making it possible, where the old me would have failed.

"Let me go, you worthless fanger," he snapped.

I did just that by shoving him forward. He crashed into a tree and bounced off it before aiming a baleful glare my way.

"Now is that any way to treat the woman who holds your fate in her hands?" I asked, crossing my arms over my chest. "The vampires are still pretty pissed about your interference in their selection. Just imagine what they'd do if I called one of them over here."

Tom jerked his shirt into place, straightening it before aiming a fierce frown my way.

"Go on, do it. I know you're just dying to see me torn apart," he snarled.

"Don't tempt me."

The little bastard would deserve it if I did. He'd nearly gotten me killed the last time I saw him, not to mention his actions had resulted in Caroline being turned into a wolf.

It would be so satisfying to turn him over to Thomas. Unfortunately, there were several things preventing me from doing just that.

The first, was that I knew Tom wouldn't be here unless he had a very good reason. He had several things in common with a cockroach. He liked to scurry around the edges and he had the enviable ability to survive pretty much anything.

The second was that despite what he thought of me, I was not a stone-cold killer. I had no wish to see the vampires exact their revenge on him for something that had turned out in their favor.

Tom's grumpy face got even grumpier as I made a gesture for him to hurry it up.

A thought occurred to me and I cocked my head. "Is this about Jerry?"

His expression turned defensive. "What if it is?"

"I just didn't think you had any loyalty in you, is all."

The gnome had made a habit of being as snappish and difficult as possible the few times I'd seen him. He'd also made no secret how much he disliked vampires in general, and me in particular. Evidently, he blamed me for getting the courier job he felt should have gone to his nephew.

"You don't know anything about me," he snapped.

"I could claim the same about me."

His frown was grudging, as if he might concede that point if he'd been a different, less difficult man. "I don't have to justify myself to you, but if you had even a little bit of loyalty to Jerry or any of Hermes, you'd let me go."

I cocked my head. "Is this about the fact that Niamh has enslaved him to her will?"

Shock crossed his face. "How do you know about that?"

I gave a small snort.

He turned suspicious. "She's got her hooks in you too."

I couldn't help the guffaw that escaped.

He didn't look appeased, his eyes narrowed as he tensed as if in preparation for flight.

My laughter wound down. "No more games. Tell me why you're here."

"I'm interested to hear that myself," Liam said in a silky voice full of threat as he stepped out of the trees.

Tom blanched, the presence of the other vampire doing what all my threats could not. His bravado drained away, leaving behind exhaustion and defeat.

"I was just trying to help Jerry," he whined.

"How?" I asked.

His shoulders slumped. "It's the hunt. Who do you think she's going to use as prey?"

I considered. Maybe I wasn't the only one who'd received the half mark. That didn't make me much happier than the thought of me being prey.

"I know you don't like me much," he said, misreading my silence. "But Jerry gave you a home. He and the others don't deserve to be hunted down like animals for their amusement."

There was a world of loathing when he referred to the High Fae. Hate showed on his face, the type that went right into the very heart of a person. It was the sort of emotion that could rot you from the inside out if you let it, festering and growing until it consumed you and led you down some very dark paths.

"How were you going to do that?" I asked.

He shrugged. "I thought if I knocked him unconscious and carried him away it would remove him from the hunt."

I stared at the being who stood no higher than my hips. Jerry was even taller than I was. How exactly had Tom planned to knock out a man when he could barely reach above the man's knee?

My skepticism must have shown on my face because he bristled. "I could do it."

"Uh huh." My voice didn't sound very certain.

"It wouldn't work," Liam said crisply. "The hunt would have just eliminated him first before going after the rest of the marked prey."

"How do you know that?" Tom asked, giving Liam a sideways look.

Liam arched an eyebrow and gave him an unamused smile. "Because I used to run with the hunt."

Both of us jerked toward Liam, surprise on my face, a sick horror on Tom's.

He scrambled away from us. I lunged after him and grabbed his pants.

"I've heard of him. He's her vampire lover! The master of the hunt. Everyone knows it." I dodged a kick he aimed at me as I dragged him back. He snarled at me. "I knew I couldn't trust you, you damn fanger."

"Settle down, Tom," I said through gritted teeth.

He fought harder, thrashing in my grip. His pants came loose and he wriggled out of them, darting away, only a small pair of boxers and his shirt preserving any modesty he might have.

"He sure is fast for such a little guy," Liam remarked, watching as Tom moved through the trees.

He moved faster than I'd ever seen him, disappearing before either of us could stop him.

"Great, I had more questions for him," I said, standing.

Liam's shrug was unconcerned. He didn't seem to care that the gnome had escaped.

He held a hand out to me. "Come, let's go."

"What did he mean when he said you were the lord of the hunt?" I asked.

Liam sighed. "It's been a long time since I was called that."

I waited as he stared into the darkened forest, a pensive look on his face.

It was hard enough dating a human man with a mortal lifespan, given all the baggage people tended to accumulate over a few decades. I couldn't imagine how much more baggage someone with centuries behind them might have.

It made me wonder if I knew Liam at all.

"It's not a time in my history that I'm proud of," he said, his words surprising me. Liam had always been reserved, keeping a large part of him a mystery. "For a time in my youth I was known as the lord of the Wild Hunt. One of them anyways."

"I thought only the Fae could participate in the hunt. How could a vampire become its lord?" I said, watching him.

He shook his head. "Anybody can be called to the hunt, whether it be hunter or prey. It helps to have Fae blood in you, but it isn't necessary. Fairy magic is strange. It doesn't always obey rules. It deemed me powerful enough and so I became the hunt's lord."

"Why did you leave it?" I asked.

He looked away. "In the hunt, little else matters except the kill. It was a different age and I was a different person. I'm not that person anymore."

There was a hint of vulnerability in his expression, as if he expected me to reject him because of this. I couldn't exactly blame him. Until now, our entire relationship had been a matter of him pushing and me running away.

We moved through the trees together, heading back to the clearing and the revelry that was waiting there.

As we prepared to step out into the clearing, I noticed a slight glimmer on the bark of several trees. I looked further, noting that all the trees rimming the clearing had something similar.

I grabbed Liam's arm. "Wait. I see something."

He went still, his head lifted as his eyes turned alert. "What is it?"

"There's something on the trees. Some kind of symbol."

His arm relaxed. "We warded the clearing to prevent Niamh pulling any of her little tricks again."

I frowned at him, looking past him to where the Fae gyrated to the music. Pockets of the clearing had descended into an orgy, the occupants coupling with mad abandon.

I blinked as a satyr mounted a dryad. They certainly weren't shy.

Niamh's laugh rang out, the sound of tinkling bells lifting above the music. She hung onto Arlan's arm, her face turned toward his.

This was the woman who had once held a large piece of Liam's heart. He'd given up his humanity, embraced his baser nature for her. What did it say about me that jealousy still managed to bite at me? A simple thing like her laugh made me want cringe. I doubted I'd ever be able to listen to bells without flinching again.

Her gaze slid our way, turning vindictive and cruel for a split second before smoothing into the same too-beautiful lines.

Oh yes, that she-demon definitely had something planned for the evening.

I glanced around. Thomas had Eric and Makoto with him as he stood in the middle of the clearing, watching Sarah and her witches as they cavorted with the rest of the Fae, some of the women already half-naked as they danced.

I couldn't read the look on his face. It could have been desire or hatred as he watched his former lover.

Movement in the crowd drew my attention. Nathan headed toward us, cutting through the party goers as if they weren't even there, stepping over bodies writhing on the ground or knocking people out of his way.

I started to raise my hand to wave, a smile already on my face.

My hand paused midway and the smile fell away.

There was a small shimmer to the air around him, just barely there. It was kind of like staring at asphalt on a hot summer day. A small mirage, barely noticeable or distinguishable from the rest of the party goers.

"Liam, I think we have a problem," I said as calmly as I could.

He glanced in the direction I was looking, reading the look on my face correctly. "Impossible. He was there when you checked the rest of us for any sign of compulsion. You would have seen then."

I shook my head, trying to think as I ran through the sequence of events. Nathan had ducked out moments before I examined the rest. I never checked him.

"He wasn't there." I said with dawning horror. "He wasn't in the room when I looked over the enforcers. You'd already sent him ahead to look over the clearing, remember? He wasn't in the room with you and Eric that first night either."

Liam cursed and started to intercept Nathan.

I grabbed his arm and dragged him back. "You can't. If he causes a scene here and Thomas finds out, he might kill him."

I stood glued in place, not knowing what to do. This was different than last night. Those had been strangers. This was my friend. The person who had helped train me while Liam had been away, someone who made kickass shakes in an effort to help me drink blood.

And he was a ticking time bomb that our enemy planned to use against us.

"We need to get him away from the rest," I said softly.

Somewhere we could contain him. If we kept him clear of Thomas and any possible triggers, maybe we could keep the compulsion from completing itself.

If we didn't, he was as good as dead. Thomas had been very clear on the measures he'd take to preserve his position and reputation. Given enough time, we could figure out a way to lift the geas from Nathan and figure out a way to keep him alive, but not if he attacked the master of this territory.

"Wait, Aileen," Liam said, grabbing my arm and pulling me to a stop.

Nathan's smile waned as he looked between the two of us, confusion on his face. He knew there was something going on, but not what. Not yet.

I gave him a wooden smile. Nothing wrong here. Just a lover's tiff. No reason to be alarmed.

He didn't look any more reassured.

"Take him away from the clearing but be careful," Liam said. "I'll find the other enforcers and meet you."

I nodded and stepped away as Liam walked past me, speaking into the mic attached to his collar.

Nathan glanced between the two of us as I gave him a radiant smile. "What's going on?"

"Nothing," I lied.

Nathan's frown deepened as his eyes narrowed. "You know I can sense lies, right?"

I blinked. I did know that.

I came unstuck and gestured for him to follow me. "Yup, my bad. Habit and all that."

Nathan didn't follow me as I'd expected, turning in the direction where Liam had headed.

I darted in front of him. "What are you doing?"

He stepped around me, impatience stamped on his features. "I don't have time for your neurosis. I need to speak with Liam."

I stepped in front of him, my eyes wide and my smile as bright as I could muster. "He said he had to speak with one of the enforcers. How about you talk to me for a second? I haven't seen you in the past few days."

Nathan gave me a look like he thought I was acting like a crazy person. That was okay. I kind of was.

"I've been busy," he said. He tried to move past me again. We did an awkward two step as I fought to stay in front of him.

"Really? With what?"

There was none of the usual sly humor in his eyes. Now that I got a good look at him, he looked tired and wane.

Impatience crossed his face. "Aileen, I don't have time for these games. I need to find Liam. If you're bored, why don't you run along and pick another fight with Thomas so you can remind yourself of all the reasons you hate vampires?"

I didn't let myself react to his words, hurtful though they were intended to be. It was just more evidence that Nathan wasn't quite feeling himself.

I needed to figure out a way to get him out of here without anybody getting hurt. The way he was staring at me, like a man willing to bulldoze any obstacle in his way, made it clear getting him away from the gathering wasn't going to be as easy as saying 'follow me.'

"I think I may know where he's going," I said, making shit up as I went along.

Nathan scrubbed tiredly at his face, biting out irritably, "Don't keep me in suspense."

"If you'll follow me," I said turning.

"No, tell me where he's going and I'll find him myself," Nathan snapped.

I blinked at him. I could do that, but then I'd lose control of the situation.

"Don't be an ass, Nathan. I need to talk to him too," I said, trying to keep from tipping my hand.

He made an angry sound but followed after me. My shoulders relaxed. That was one problem down, at least.

Niall and Cadell caught my eye as we walked away from the party. They looked questioning. I shook my head at both of them. The last thing I wanted was their interference. Despite the heart to heart last night, I didn't trust either of them.

They remained in place as I stepped into the trees, breathing a sigh of relief. Nathan's expression was still irritated, but at least he was listening. That was something at least.

His eyes were bloodshot, his skin the palest I'd ever seen it. For a moment I wondered when the last time he ate was.

He reached up and rubbed his head, not quite hiding a wince.

"Headache?" I asked.

"Vampires don't get headaches," he snapped.

Not true. We just usually had a very good reason for getting them, like maybe a compulsion we were fighting against and losing.

I studied him, doubt wiggling its way in. Maybe I was wrong in my assumption that he was under a compulsion. It wasn't like I'd had a lot of practice with this. I was feeling my way through blind, hoping and praying I got things right.

Part of me hoped I was wrong. I would be so happy if it turned out I'd misinterpreted that small shimmer.

I checked again. It was barely visible now.

I didn't know what that meant or if it was even important. Once again, I cursed the limited knowledge at my fingertips.

We were far enough from the clearing now, the music from the band faint, a light background buzz. The Fae lights merely a distant memory as the dark pressed in all around us.

"I don't see Liam," Nathan complained.

"I'm sure he's here," I said over my shoulder. "Somewhere."

He'd better be, and he'd better have brought back-up. I did not want to take on a pissed-off Nathan by myself. I'd trained with the man; I was intimately acquainted with how good a fighter he was. He'd kicked my ass on a regular basis. Sometimes with one hand literally behind his back. Nothing made you realize how weak you actually were than a grinning vampire who ties his own hand behind his back and then kicks your ass anyway.

I glanced around, searching the shadows. No evidence that anyone but Nathan and I were out here.

"Enough," Nathan barked, coming to a stop.

I glanced back, my eyes wide, fear jumping into my throat.

He didn't move toward me, just glanced at the looming trees around us with a deep suspicion in his face. "What is this, Aileen?"

"What do you mean?" I made myself ask, even as I fought the urge to back away. Running would be useless and an admission of guilt. Nathan could outpace me in moments, anyway.

"You're stalling." His posture became threatening and he advanced on me, his expression tight. "Why have you lured me here?"

I backed away, the danger I was in suddenly very real. I resisted the impulse to go for one of the blades on me, silver all of them. The Fae had insisted no iron be brought to the celebration, and like the good little hosts we were we'd listened.

"Nathan, I need you to stay calm," I said, reaching for that calmness myself.

He cocked his head, breathing hard through his nose. "You know, I'm beginning to think that some of the enforcers might be compromised. I didn't think you'd be the same."

I went still. "It's not me that I'm worried about."

He jerked, his forehead wrinkling, the thought that he might be under a compulsion never having occurred to him. "You're spouting nonsense."

I stepped to the side, away from the tree at my back, giving myself room to run if I needed to.

"Am I? Think. Why did you want to see Liam?" I asked, putting a little more distance between us.

Thought flew behind his eyes. "I need to talk to him."

"About what? Do you even know?" My voice was soft.

He stared into the distance, his expression haunted.

"Nathan, were you ever alone with Niamh?"

He rubbed his forehead again, shaking his head back and forth. "I'm an enforcer. It's not strange to want to speak to my commander."

I nodded. He was right. It wasn't, but the severity of the need, the shaking in his hands when he was denied that opportunity, was.

For a split second, it looked like I'd gotten through to him, that I might have broken through the bonds the compulsion laid on him. He lifted his head, a monster looking out of his eyes—the element that made him Nathan, absent.

His expression turned feral. "He's not coming, is he?"

He didn't wait for an answer, his lips drawing back as his fangs dropped down.

I palmed a silver blade, holding it in front of me. "Don't make me use this."

"I'm right here, Nathan," Liam said, stepping out of the trees.

Nathan's advance halted, his head swinging toward Liam.

The thought that had been niggling at the back of my mind since I first intercepted Nathan crystalized. All this time Nathan had been focused on Liam. Not Thomas. If the geas was driving him to kill Thomas or even Niall, then why was he so focused on finding Liam.

Unless the other two weren't the targets.

"Liam, wait," I shouted.

I was too late.

Nathan charged, a roar filling the air as he flew at the other man. I raced after him, my speed no match for his.

Liam looked startled for a brief moment, before he crouched to meet him. The two men clashed, the sound of battle ferocious and violent as they moved almost too fast to see.

Thomas arrived in the next second, Anton and Daniel behind him.

"Sweet Jesu. I didn't believe it," Anton said, his voice hushed as he watched the two fight.

All three men were grim-faced and disbelieving as they watched Liam and Nathan tear into each other.

"Help him," I said.

Daniel waded into the fight, grabbing Nathan from behind and throwing him to the ground. Anton was there in the next second, helping hold Nathan down as Daniel fished out a pair of silver handcuffs from his pocket.

Together, the two of them subdued Nathan, forcing him on his knees, his hands bound behind him.

Nathan looked around, betrayal written on his face as Liam walked over to where Thomas and I stood.

There was blood on his shirt from a bite and several bruises on his face that were already healing. Nathan had a swollen eye and several cuts and bruises in a similar state of healing.

"What are you doing?" Nathan asked.

"Settle down, brother," Daniel said. "This is for your own good."

Both Anton and Daniel looked sickened by the whole matter.

Liam touched my hand when he reached me, a silent acknowledgment he was fine.

"Explain this," Thomas said, his voice quiet.

"Nathan is under a compulsion," Liam turned and looked at the man who was considered his second. "His actions are not his own."

"Bullshit," Nathan said. "I'm fine."

"Then you just felt the sudden need to rip Liam's head from his body?" I asked, a bite in my voice.

Nathan looked away, his expression slightly lost. He didn't try to explain it. He couldn't, and we all knew it.

Defeat shone in his gaze as he stared down at the ground.

My heart tightened, seeing the dejection in the slump of his shoulders. I couldn't imagine what he must be going through at the moment, to know that he wasn't quite in control of his actions, that he might betray his friends for reasons he didn't know or understand.

"Why go after you?" Thomas asked Liam.

I looked up to find a considering look on Liam's face. He crossed his arms and looked contemplative.

"None of this makes sense," I said. "First the attack by the bridge, then the attacks last night. Now this. It doesn't fit."

It was like our enemy had split personalities and couldn't decide on what objective they wanted. It made it difficult to see the big picture, let alone stop it.

"Perhaps that's the point," Liam said. "Fae plots tend to be convoluted, at best."

Thomas shook his head and speared Liam with a look. "It doesn't matter. You know what you need to do."

Liam's nod was slow, grief on his face. He stepped forward, going to a knee in front of Nathan.

For a moment I didn't understand. Not until I saw an answering pain in both Anton and Daniel's expression, the resignation on Nathan's.

"Wait. You can't," I asked.

"Aileen, go back to the clearing," Liam ordered. He'd taken a knee in front of Nathan, placing one hand on the back of the other's man's neck.

I stepped toward him. "He's your friend."

"That's why I have to do this." His voice was a quiet hum. He'd already accepted this as his only course.

"It's okay, A. It's for the best this way," Nathan said, trying to comfort me.

Bullshit. This was not happening. I wasn't letting it.

"We stopped it in time. There's no reason to kill him," I said, looking around at the others.

Thomas was unmoved. He'd retreated behind a mask, watching the events unfold with a closed expression, his bearing as unruffled as ever.

"This is a mercy," Liam said, his voice raw. "Now leave."

I refused. There was another way. I just needed to find it.

"Thomas," Liam said.

Thomas sighed, turning toward me. I dropped my gaze, knowing he'd try to compel me to go back to the clearing. Not this time. Not with Nathan's life hanging in the balance.

"Don't do this. We can find another way," I said, desperate.

I didn't want to stand over another grave. I didn't want to have questions about whether I could have made a difference if I'd just been a little faster, a little smarter.

Thomas grabbed my chin, exerting pressure on it as he slowly forced me to face him.

"Liam, I can break it," I said, resisting. It was like trying to resist gravity—impossible.

My chin lifted and I slammed my eyes closed.

"Wait," Liam said.

To my surprise, Thomas did. I opened my eyes, slowly, tentatively, not trusting the easy capitulation.

"Let her go," Liam said.

Thomas and he locked gazes, a wealth of unspoken words exchanged between the two. Thomas turned back to me, studying me as if I was some rare creature.

He released me and stepped away.

I turned to Liam, taking in the other enforcers at a glance. There was hope on Anton's face, while Daniel looked guarded, not quite trusting. Nathan's expression was resigned. He'd already given up hope.

"Can you really break the compulsion?" Liam asked.

I jerked my shoulders. "I don't know, but that doesn't mean I shouldn't try."

The woods were quiet as Liam stared at me. I waited, anticipation drawing my nerves tight as I tried to will him to have faith in me, to take a chance even though every instinct he had told him it was pointless.

"Okay," he said. "We'll try."

Relief made my knees weak. I didn't think he'd change his mind.

I stepped toward Nathan. Liam stopped me.

"Not here. The magic is rising. The hunt will begin soon," he said.

"I thought the hunt wasn't supposed to start until tomorrow," I said.

Liam's face turned grim. "It seems we were misled. This area won't be safe once it starts. We'll break the compulsion back at the mansion." To the other two, he said, "Get him up. We're going back to the car."

Anton and Daniel lifted Nathan to his feet. He didn't resist, going with them easily.

Liam, Thomas and I waited until they passed.

"Are you sure about this?" Thomas asked.

Liam looked infinitely weary in that moment. "No, but I don't have it in me to not let Aileen try."

Thomas nodded, his face grave.

I couldn't help but be surprised when he didn't argue with Liam. I thought he'd insist on Nathan's death. I'd been prepared for a fight.

"This will leave you with only Makoto and Eric," Liam warned.

Thomas flapped his hand. "You forget who I am. I'm perfectly capable of protecting myself."

His gaze caught on me and he studied me with a slight smile. "Besides, if she's successful, it'll make for a powerful weapon in my arsenal."

I glared at him. That wasn't the point and he knew it.

Thomas chuckled as he followed after the others.

CHAPTER EIGHTEEN

The trek back to the clearing went quickly. None of us were in the mood to linger. No one wanted to be out here with the magic rising like a tidal wave intent on sweeping up everything in its path. I could practically feel the call of the hunt as the forest loomed over us, silent and mysterious. Sinister as it watched our retreat.

We had to pass through the gathering to get to the cars. Things were quiet. The music had died down during our confrontation.

The magic felt suffocating in the night, heady and electrifying, building the anticipation in the air and fanning its flames.

"There are our guests of honor," a tinkling voice said as we stepped through the trees. Niamh approached, her eyes glittering as she took in our small group.

Bit by bit, the people in the clearing fell silent, obeying some unspoken signal as they turned to face us.

I caught sight of Jerry and several of his couriers. Shame and fear were on some of my former coworkers faces. Harry had his arm around Ruth, both doing their best not to see me, while Catriona lifted her chin in defiance and anger.

The faces of the High Fae were guarded as we came to a stop. Tension rose in the air, curling around the magic. The clearing felt like a powder keg.

I shifted uneasily. I recognized this. Oh, not the hunt or the Fae in particular. Both of those were new. But that feeling you get when something is about to happen, something big and momentous and potentially life-ending.

I'd felt this before. Another time, another country where mountains stabbed the sky's belly and it sometimes felt like the people had never made it all the way to this century.

That same feeling was here, like the universe was holding its breath while you teetered on a precipice. Just waiting to meet the bullet with your name on it.

Niall and Cadell stood in the crowd along with several other Fae I knew. I saw the flicker of purple wings in the trees above. Inara and Lowen were probably somewhere out there, waiting, watching.

Liam's enforcers stirred uneasily. The hostility in the air was impossible to ignore. It warned of danger long before the first blow was ever struck. How I wished we could listen for it.

Thomas stepped forward, his expression calm, congenial. He gave no indication of uneasiness or fear, which was impressive, given my stomach was trying to crawl its way out of my throat.

I felt hyper-aware, cognizant of every stray brush of the wind, the slightest shift of movement in those facing us.

I wasn't the only one. Liam was tense behind me, prepared to act should violence erupt. The same for Anton and Daniel, both had a hand on the weapons at their waist as they observed those around us with a soldier's heightened awareness.

"My lady, how kind of you to wait, but it wasn't necessary," Thomas said, stepping forward.

Niamh's attention remained centered on us. "Are you intending to leave? So soon?"

Thomas gave her a small smile. "One of our number is overcome from the magic. You understand."

She cocked her head, her expression turning coy. "Yes, not everyone can withstand the hunt. Those who are weak will forever fall prey to it."

Arlan stepped from the crowd with the same arrogant expression from the previous night. He looked over our small group with little interest. He didn't seem to care about our presence one way or another, directing his attention towards Niamh.

"The hunt draws near. All those who wish to cast their fate to its whim must prepare," he announced.

Niamh's lips curled up. "You must stay. All of you. The Wild Hunt is not an experience to be missed."

It wasn't a request. She expected to be obeyed. Getting out of here was going to be difficult.

"They cannot," Thomas said, his voice implacable. The glib diplomat was gone, leaving behind the autocratic master vampire. "Liam, get her to the car."

Liam didn't delay, grabbing my arm and hustling me away. All the while, the magic continued to build, the pressure threatening to crack my head.

"What about the others?" I asked as he tugged me behind him.

"They can take care of themselves," he said. He jerked his head at Eric who made his way to our side.

"Don't go, my dark knight," Niamh called after our backs. "You're going to miss the best part."

The crowd had suddenly turned thick and resistant, not moving aside when we approached. Liam and Eric had to force them out of the way. It was like moving through a bunch of silent, unmoving zombies. They didn't offer us violence, but they also didn't give way easily, simply staring as we forced our way through them.

I looked back, Thomas and the others followed behind at a much slower pace. Niamh's bright gaze met mine, her eyes feverish and anticipatory.

She didn't look like a woman used to being thwarted. Things were going to get ugly. Again, I wished I was a little better armed.

Liam halted abruptly. I twisted to see what had caught his attention.

A white stag stood between us and the path to the cars. His coat gleamed in the moonlight, his antlers lifted proudly to the sky. There was more than one human hunter out there who would have sold his first-born child for a chance to mount the stag's rack on their walls.

He was majestic and proud as he watched us. There was an intelligence there, at odds with what should have been present in an animal.

Liam stilled.

Thomas made an inarticulate sound, coming to Liam's side, his gaze fastened on the stag, rage and yearning there.

Niall stepped from the trees, caught my eyes and jerked his head.

"Run," he mouthed.

I slipped my hand out of Liam's grip. I didn't know why he'd stopped or why he stared at the stag with horror, but the magic was still building. If we didn't get out of here soon, things would go very poorly for us.

"Liam, we need to go," I said softly.

"I don't think you're going anywhere," Sarah said.

She glided out of the forest, her companions by her side. They shone with power, their skin looking even younger and smoother than earlier tonight. There was seduction in their movements, a promise of pain and other things in their gazes.

Sarah tossed her hair over her shoulder as she focused on Thomas.

"What is this?" he asked sharply.

The crowd parted easily for Niamh as she walked toward us. She didn't have to push and shove as we had, the Fae stepped aside as if she was royalty.

She only had eyes for Liam, her gaze possessive, as if she already owned him. The rest of us might as well have been window dressing for all the attention she paid us. She didn't even look at Nathan where he stood with his hands bound behind his back.

Either she was the best actress I'd ever seen or it really didn't bother her to know one of her pawns had been taken off the board. It never seemed to occur to her that she might face any consequences for her actions.

Her lips twisted up in an indulgent smile. "My handsome knight, how you've grown soft in the intervening centuries. Time was you wouldn't have let such a trespass as he intended go unpunished."

There was no doubt who she meant as she glanced at Nathan.

I couldn't hide my shock. She'd as good as admitted she was the one responsible for Nathan's current state. If that didn't give Thomas reason to bring this farce to an end, I didn't know what did.

He seemed to realize it too, his expression turning stormy as power curled around him. "You admit to acting against one us?"

Niamh shrugged creamy shoulders, the gesture negligent. "I broke no treaty."

Her head turned toward the stag and she smiled. "I see you recognize our prey. We can never quite catch him, but it is such fun trying."

Thomas choked, the sound inhuman. Rage was too small a word to describe it. There was a depth of feeling there that shook me, and it should have shaken Niamh.

Liam didn't make a sound, didn't move, his gaze fastened on the stag as he seemed to withdraw even more, becoming cold and unyielding.

Niamh lifted her head, her gaze turning inward. The sigh she gave was almost orgasmic. "The time is nigh."

The Fae hemming us in lost interest, moving off, their gazes fixed and anticipatory.

The magic all around us gave a thrum, changing, twisting.

Everyone shivered. It was hard not to, with the magic whispering to us, coaxing us to join the hunt as either predator or prey. It didn't care which.

Out here, with the night surrounding us and the moon turning Niamh's hair a silvery white, her strange alienness was highlighted. She seemed straight out of a fairy tale, but instead of being the good fairy she was all dark cruelty.

"I'd hoped to give you my gift in private but here will do just as well. Won't it, pet?" Niamh said.

Right then, several things happened at once.

Thomas roared and charged Sarah. There was no fear on her face as she watched him advance, her sister witches spreading out as they raised their hands and started to chant. Their eyes rolled into the backs of their heads as power ripped through the air.

Golems boiled out of the ground, their bodies made of dirt and rock and years of decayed leaves.

Nathan screamed, his back bowing as he writhed so hard Anton and Daniel had no choice but to let him go.

Power shot from Nathan to Liam, wrapping around him like a boa constrictor.

Then the enforcers had their hands full, beating back the golems as the clearing descended into chaos.

Liam sank to his knees, his face pale.

I started for him when strong arms closed around me from behind.

"Easy lass," Jerry rumbled in my ear as I erupted into violence, biting and growling as I thrashed. "There's nothing you can do for him now. She's already got him in her grasp. The enforcer's bite ensured that."

Sure enough, I watched as Liam stilled, slumping to the ground. I didn't know what her poison had done to him; I didn't care. All I wanted at that moment was vengeance.

"You need to run," Jerry rumbled.

I jerked, trying to get free again. I wasn't running. I was going to kill that bitch.

She tilted her head back and laughed.

Jerry spun me around, his large hands settling on my shoulders as he thrust his face into mine. "You need to run. Can't you feel it. The Wild Hunt has begun and you're its prey."

The urgency in his voice broke through and I stopped fighting long enough to pay attention.

Sure enough, the magic that had been steadily building since we got here had changed. It now had a purpose.

I felt it, all around me, crackling through the air as it coaxed and whispered, compelling those present to answer its call.

I looked at where the enforcers still fought.

"They can't help you," Jerry said, shaking me. "Soon they'll be caught in its grasp too."

I shook my head. "They're powerful. They said they can resist."

"Maybe the master can, but Liam has already fallen. Those with a link to him will succumb to its call too," Jerry said impatiently.

As I watched, Liam stood, his face cold and aloof, the lines of it turning cruel. Magic circled him, on his head the faintest shadow of a crown beginning to form.

"The lord of the hunt," I said softly.

Jerry nodded. "Yes. Tonight, he's exactly that, and you're his greatest obsession. His most difficult prey."

That must be the other half of the riddle. What better way to choose a prey than to find what the hunter most wanted.

Along with choice. I could feel it on the air. If I chose to ignore the hunt's call, I could, but Liam would be lost to me.

Niamh held out her hand, a lady of old with her knight. He walked past me as if I wasn't even there, his gaze fixed.

"Liam," I called.

"He can't hear you; he won't recognize you," Jerry said.

Anton and Daniel turned from the golems they were fighting, following in Liam's wake, the same fixed expression wiping out their personalities.

"What do I do?" I asked, never feeling more lost and alone than I did at that moment.

As much as I fought it, as much as I resisted, some part of me must have accepted Liam at his word. That he'd be there when I most needed him, that I'd always have a place with his people. I'd been working toward some type of relationship with the other enforcers, odd though it might have been.

To be isolated now, no recognition on their faces, struck at the heart of me, making me remember what it was like to be the only one I could count on. I'd forgotten how desolate a place that was.

"Make your choice. Then run as far and fast as you can," Jerry said. His face showed strain and I realized for the first time that Liam and the others weren't the only ones caught in the magic of the Wild Hunt. Jerry was resisting for now, but I could tell it wouldn't be long before he lost the battle. "The hunt lasts until the first rays of dawn touch the horizon. Survive the night and you'll have the chance to undo this."

I stared at him. All I had to do was survive until dawn—my greatest nemesis. That was just hunky dory.

The magic had built to a crescendo while we talked. Jerry had been right. I'd met whatever criteria the hunt required. It had chosen me to be that night's prey. I could feel it in my bones, twisting along my veins, the need to run, the need to evade eating at my insides.

"Good luck, Aileen," he said.

Then I was gone, running as fast as I could, my heartbeat thundering in my ears as Thomas's cry followed me. I didn't hesitate. I couldn't be sure he'd resist the magic as well.

Panic and something else beat at me in time with my footsteps. The need to survive at all costs pricked me.

Trees flew by as I fled, the sound of a hunter's bugle following me into the night.

The magic broke over the forest; the Wild Hunt had begun.

I ran as I never had before, with a single-minded focus as I dived deeper into the forest. It reminded me of another time, another forest where I'd fled for my life. During that little adventure, only two wolves had chased at my heels, not more than a dozen spooks intent on my life's blood.

I weaved through the trees, pushing myself harder, abruptly glad both

Liam and Thomas had insisted on human and vampire blood over the last week. Had I been in my former state, this hunt would have been over before it began.

Now, power coursed through me, enabling me to run faster, longer.

Still, even with the boost, it wasn't long before I heard the baying of hounds and the crash of the underbrush as the hunt followed.

As fast as I was, there were so many creatures out there faster and stronger, with better endurance.

A flash of white darted through the trees ahead of me.

I veered away, afraid one of the hunters had gotten ahead of me. The magic caught me up in its grasp, urging me faster. It sang a terrifying song that spurred me to reach deep, my only thought escape and evasion.

Again, the flash of white bobbing in the dark. The stag stepped out of the trees, leaping away as soon as I spotted him.

I don't know what possessed me to follow, but I did, dodging through the trees in his wake as he led me over hills and through creeks.

He came to a stop on a pair of rusted out railroad tracks. He pawed the ground and tossed his head as I hesitated, caught between the urgency of the hunt and reason.

Until now, I'd been mindlessly running, too busy with the need to escape to think. It was a stupid mistake.

Even as I hesitated, the magic tried to grab me in its jaws again and send me thoughtlessly fleeing in any direction. It didn't matter, as long as I ran and didn't stop running, until I was caught or the magic was spent.

The stag stamped his foot and snorted. I struggled to focus, trying to think over the power that threatened to carry me away like a tsunami-sized wave.

Railroad tracks. What was the significance?

The stag began trotting along them—his message clear.

I wavered between answering the call of the hunt and following the stag. Could I trust this creature when he seemed so clearly in Niamh's thrall?

Liam and Thomas had seemed to recognize him, the sight of the stag striking a chord in both men. They'd been upset to see him, but I still didn't know why.

One thing working in his favor, and the reason I hadn't already resumed my flight, was she'd said they'd hunted him many times before but never caught him.

Maybe he was trying to show me how to survive.

Already the sounds of the hunters were nearing. No matter how fast or far I ran I couldn't manage to shake them.

Dawn was still a long way off. If something didn't change, they were going to catch me. And soon.

I turned and followed the stag, trotting along the tracks after him.

The magic's grip eased slightly, and a thought occurred to me. These tracks were old and likely made of iron. Ohio was riddled with the remains of railroads from the last century where people and progress hadn't gotten around to ripping them back out of the ground.

And what hated iron more than anything? The Fae.

"Smart bastard," I said, picking up the pace.

The magic seemed to loosen the longer I stayed near the iron, ebbing and flowing around us as we ran. It made it easier to think for the first time since I'd begun my mad dash.

The stag bounded in front of me, his pale coat practically glowing under the moonlight. If not for the antlers, I'd say he looked like a flippin' unicorn with the ethereal glow he was throwing off.

It was hard to believe he'd survived so many hunts when he looked like a giant glow stick. His passage wasn't exactly subtle.

Still, the baying of some type of dog creature in the distance said his trick had worked. At least for now.

The iron might throw off Niamh's people, but I didn't have a lot of confidence it would do the same for Liam or any of his enforcers.

I slowed down to a fast walk now that the danger of discovery had passed for the moment. Conserving my endurance seemed a better idea than expending all my energy at once. We had hours, and the chances of outrunning pursuit were very small.

The stag seemed of a similar mindset, matching his pace to mine as he picked his way silently over the railroad tracks.

I cast another glance at my silent companion, curious in spite of the dire circumstances. Who was he? How did he get caught up in all this? And what sort of Fae had the form of a stag but the intelligence of a human?

All questions he couldn't answer, so I didn't ask, just studied him closely.

Whatever his species, he was powerful. It lay over him like a mantle, boiling with a quiet ferocity.

There was something else there, gossamer-thin strands wrapped around his antlers, barely visible as they shifted in and out of sight.

I hurried over, looking closer. They weren't just around his antlers. They were everywhere, the rest of his body as well. I'd missed it because they blended into his coat, thinner than any fishermen's net or spiderweb.

Realization turned my insides cold. He was caught like all the rest, bound to Niamh's bidding whether he wanted to be or not.

He looked over his shoulder at me, the odd blue eyes sorrowful as if he'd guessed exactly what I'd seen.

I stepped closer, lifting one hand to touch the strands, half-expecting the stag to shy away. He remained in place, allowing me to touch him without protest. My hand slid through the strands.

Magic, I'd learned, was formed by intent. Shaped by will and then molded by the universe. It was in everything we did, everything we were. In the big moments and the small ones.

Our perceptions influenced how we perceived it. When the sorcerer had taken my eye, it had done something, opened me up to a world that should have taken much longer to access. It left me exposed to possibilities but danger too.

Magic, especially of the type riding the night, was wild and unruly, as likely to burn you up as warm your bones. Mistreat it and it'd break you in half.

Stare too long into the abyss and you might lose yourself to the wonder and terror, the chaotic order.

I'd tried ignoring it, pretending it didn't exist, and it'd gotten me nowhere except fleeing from the people who were my friends.

Time to change the story.

The stag, as if sensing what I was considering, stamped his hoof and lifted his head. He wanted this. Needed it.

"Will freeing you help us?" I asked him.

Normally, I would never consider it, but even if I made it to dawn, I would still be vulnerable. I didn't trust Niamh would obey the rules of her people and let me live. Once the sun crossed that horizon, I would be vulnerable. There'd be nothing and no one to save me.

He moved his head in an up and down motion.

I'd take that as a yes.

"Alright, I'll do my best," I told him.

The world faded around me as I sank into the magic. This left me vulnerable. One of the hunters could approach and I'd never know it. Still, I'd rather go down trying than run until my heart burst and my feet were ragged, only to be shot down like some damn deer.

Niamh's magic had a stranglehold on him. It delved deep into his essence, an insidious web burrowing where it had no business being. It sickened me. Her hold took violation to a whole new level.

It was a wonder he had any independent thought given how deeply her roots were embedded.

His power fluttered at the heart of it all. If I ever freed him, Niamh would need to watch out. His was a bottomless ocean, deep and cool.

I stared into it, losing myself for a moment as I admired its beauty before moving on.

This was no hasty construct like what had been on Hector. It had been reinforced and retooled countless times until there was no sign of weakness, no easy chink to exploit.

I pulled hard on it, calling threads of it to me, stopping when the stag let out a low sound of pain.

"This is going to take time," I told him, fighting dizziness and a headache.

Time we didn't necessarily have.

He grunted.

I prepared to dive deep. A creature stumbled out of the woods just then. It ran on all fours, its nose lifted to the air.

I couldn't say what it was, though it looked vaguely like a wolf, a coat as dark as night and vivid green eyes in a face that was a cross between canine and human.

It lifted its snout to the air and bayed. Answering cries sounded from far off in the distance.

Our time was up. For now.

The stag and I leapt down the small bank of the tracks, abandoning them in favor of the shadowy protection of the forest. Now that we'd been spotted, staying on them was impossible.

Without the iron to dilute it, the magic of the hunt rose with the force of an inexorable tide.

We ran, the sound of pursuit hard on our heels. On the rare instances where we stopped to catch a breath, I worked on the stag's bindings, pulling and plucking any chance I could. My success was minor to say the least. The webbing gave just the slightest bit every time.

He helped as much as he could, pushing when I pulled, but even several hours later, I was still no closer to freeing him, and my reserves were at their limit.

I staggered against a tree, clutching it to keep myself upright as I panted. All around us we could hear the hunters. They were closing in. It wouldn't be long now.

Worse, I was losing time, the magic catching me in its grip for long periods and carrying me off—the forest passing by in flashes as my world spiraled down to survival and running, terror and fear my constant companions.

"Come here," I said.

If I was going to free him, it had to be now. I didn't know if I'd get another shot. No reason we both should die.

He bowed his head before me, resignation in every line. He knew better than I did what our odds were. In this, we were in complete agreement, without a word having been exchanged.

This time I reached deep, summoning that rarely-used power inside, using it to grab the webbing and rip. When I ran out of power I reached deeper, ignoring the throbbing pain in my head or the parts of me that were screaming I was doing too much.

Desperation lent me strength. The bonds were looser than when I started, weaker from all my previous attempts.

From some unknown place inside me, power sparked, giving me a glimpse of what I could do, what I could be given half the chance. Suddenly, reading the magic on the stag was as easy as child's play, a map I'd been born to decipher.

I bore down with my magic, hitting the spell with everything I had left. It crumpled, wisping away like cobwebs.

The stag reared, knocking me down as he screamed a challenge.

Before I could react, he took off, disappearing into the night without a backward glance.

CHAPTER NINETEEN

I pushed myself off the ground, weak and dizzy. Using whatever that power had been, had knocked out the last of my reserves.

And here I'd thought freeing the stag would help me. Turned out it'd had the opposite effect.

I rolled into a depression in the ground, hoping the small spot would shield me from view while I caught my breath, or at least until I summoned enough willpower to stand.

The night was a hazy gray against the darker shapes of the trees, the stars stretched out, so numerous they were infinite.

I didn't know how long I lay there, too tired to move, before a set of purple wings fluttered into view.

Inara landed on my nose, glaring down at me with hands on her hips. "Get up, you lazy fanger. I haven't invested this much time into your survival to watch you give up when you're so close to freedom."

My tongue felt thick in my mouth. "What are you talking about?"

"Get up and survive this and I just might tell you," she snarled.

With Inara pulling at the sensitive parts of me and bitching the entire time, I somehow managed to make it to my feet. For a creature no taller than the length of my hand, she could be surprisingly persistent. Her vicious pinches on my ear and nose kept me moving when I would have faltered.

A blue streak flew by, Lowen's expression frantic. "They're coming."

Sure enough, the sounds of the hunt grew frighteningly close.

Inara cursed.

"You two should go," I said.

They weren't part of the hunt. I could feel it. If they left now they would be fine. Stay and they risked getting caught up in this.

"No, you just need to reach the road," Inara said.

My laugh was grim. "I don't think that's how it works. It's not some magic boundary to keep them off my back."

"No, it's where Caroline waits in a car. You'll be much faster in that than you will be on foot," Inara said flatly.

I couldn't help the disbelief that filled me.

"Why would Caroline be there?"

Inara fluttered in front of me, seeming unconcerned despite the rumble of a threat in my voice. "I called her and told her where to meet us."

"You did what?" I couldn't help the upset in my voice.

"Don't start with me," she snapped. "You were supposed to stop the hunt. Not start it."

"You didn't want Niall or Cadell hunted. I'd say I accomplished that," I shot back.

And boy had I. Maybe I'd done my job a little too well. I'd seen them out here with me, brief glimpses, but it was clear they'd been caught in the same web I had, only they were hunters, not the hunted.

I think one of them had even shot an arrow at me.

"Argue with me when you're safe," she snarled, weaving in and out of the trees as she led me through the forest.

She had a point. After that, I didn't have time to argue as magic clamped me in its jaws once again, sending me mindlessly fleeing, the forest a blur around me as I ran.

Jerry rose from between the trees, his face blank as he raised an ax. I veered away, my heart thundering in my throat as I embraced my instincts, letting them guide me, even as others stepped out of the shadows.

They were herding me, the net growing close.

Dawn and hope lingered on the horizon. The stars above were gradually shuttering their faces and taking the moon with them.

I found myself on my hands and knees panting as the magic eased. It was like the ocean, pulling back only to swamp me with another wave. For the moment though, I was myself again.

Inara alighted on the ground in front of me, concern on her face. "You need to stop letting it take over."

"That's easy for you to say," I told her. "You're not the one caught in its grip."

And I was so tired of fighting it. At least when it took me, I forgot the terror that crouched inside, forgot that many of my former friends were part of the hunt and would be only too glad to end me.

"How much further?" I asked.

Inara looked grim. "More than a mile."

"Still?"

We were no closer than the last time I asked. I couldn't help wondering if she'd lied to me.

When I was human, my best time was a mile in just under seven minutes. Now, exhausted, having been running off and on for half the night, I'd be lucky if I could run a mile at all.

"Yes, still. You keep going the wrong way," she hissed, seeming like her old self. I was glad to see it. This morose woman wasn't Inara. At least I knew what I was getting with the grumpy version.

"I can't help it. The magic grabs me and I just run," I said.

She didn't look appeased. "You're a magic breaker. *You* control its pull, not the other way around."

I lifted my head at that. "Magic breaker?"

She rolled her eyes. "Yes, what do you think you've been doing all this time? You can see the magic, and break it if you wish."

I opened my mouth in question, but the magic grabbed me in its jaws. This time I did as she suggested and resisted. It was like trying to hold back an avalanche, my attempts puny and ineffectual.

Somehow, I managed to retain enough of a sense of self to allow Inara to point me toward the highway and the promise of safety.

Creatures bayed. They were frighteningly close.

Still, I ran, my feet thudding against the ground, tree branches whipping past me. I paid the toll for my passage with blood as their sharp edges left small cuts along my arms and face.

I knew I was leaving a trail a mile wide, but I didn't have time to go softly or quietly. They were too close now.

Whatever advantage the change in my diet had given me was long gone. Exhaustion dragged at me, whispering of a respite from all this.

I pressed on, neither the magic nor my own will permitting me to falter.

I became aware of something shadowing me, catching glimpses of someone running parallel to me. They moved impossibly fast, following when I tried to veer away.

Liam. I'd know him anywhere.

I was acutely aware of the hunter even when the trees shielded him from view, his presence growing until it felt like a thousand shadows weighing me down.

He was playing with me, toying with me as I tried to escape his trap.

The road was in sight and I felt hope leap inside my chest.

Liam flew out of the trees, tackling me to the ground. I hit hard, the breath knocked out of me.

He crouched over me, the hunter in truth, no trace of the lover from last night. His face was just blank. If he hadn't had Liam's face and Liam's scent, I would have said he was a stranger.

My eyes widened, fear catching me in its grip as Liam raised his hand, an old blade in his hand.

Death had come, wearing Liam's form. He was the reaper and angel of death rolled into one. Old magic was in the air, the kind that tasted of the past, of old gods and things best forgotten.

The blade began to descend and I braced for pain, even as I reached for the magic wrapping him in Niamh's will.

Inara had called me a magic breaker. In that split second when death loomed, I embraced it, pulling with everything in me.

The magic came away easily, its weaving looser and more uneven than the stag's. It hadn't had the time to burrow as deep. Darkness crowded into the edges of my vision as small tendrils from the deepest parts of me, the ones that were my essence spiraled up, sucking down the spell around Liam.

The dagger hesitated for just an instant, Liam's face horrified.

He started to mouth my name but never finished it, his eyes wild. The stag barreled into him, his coat glowing like a mini-sun as he trumpeted a challenge.

Then I saw nothing as I lost the battle against myself, sinking gratefully into unconsciousness.

*

Tight arms around me and tears soaking my shirt accompanied me into wakefulness. A chest shook under me.

I opened my eyes, staring up at a ravaged face. Liam looked like he'd just lost his whole world, a wild grief making him slightly crazed.

"It looks like you were only slightly successful in putting the vampire in your thrall," Arlan remarked as he glided out of the trees.

The magic of the hunt still snapped and crackled in the air, though considerably lessened. It clung to him, speaking of wild, untamed things. He didn't just look at home here, with the trees around him and the first of the sun's rays kissing the horizon. He looked like he was born of this place, as integral to it as the trees or land might be.

This wasn't something peaceful or calming. He was wild and fierce, the darker side of nature, the one that relied on death for the circle of life.

Niamh stepped out behind him, a dissatisfied expression on her face at the sight of Liam clinging to me as if he'd lost the only important thing in his life.

Her gaze lifted to the stag, standing close by, and her lips curled in a snarl. Her expression was incandescent with rage.

Arlan began to laugh when he caught sight of the stag, his shoulders shaking as the sound boomed out of him.

"That's impossible," Niamh snarled.

"Evidently not," Arlan said, sounding amused. For being her husband, he seemed awfully elated to see Niamh so upset.

Not a happy marriage between those two, I was guessing.

Liam hadn't reacted to their presence, still rocking me back and forth, looking lost.

"Her death should have cemented my hold," Niamh said.

I realized the two didn't realize I was still alive. Granted, I felt about two steps away from death, my body bruised and beaten, but the pain told me I was still very much among the living.

I remained very still, afraid to call attention to myself.

"That it hasn't, means you are unable to deliver on your promise to put the vampires in this territory under your hold," Arlan said. "What will your master say?"

"Shut it, wildling." Her voice was nasty as she glared at him. "I have not lost yet."

Niamh moved closer to us, her gaze locked on Liam's bowed head. I debated what to do, whether it was better to show my hand or remain still, faking a death she was sure to see through.

I decided to stay pliant in Liam's tight grip. Dawn wasn't far. The sun was minutes away from cresting the horizon. The hunt was all but at an end.

Liam's head lifted, his gaze locking on Niamh's. "You did this."

The rage in his voice was enough to make me flinch. Any sensible person would have fled.

The skin on his face had thinned, releasing the monster I'd only caught the briefest glimpses of. My heart gave a painful thump. Even knowing that look wasn't intended for me, it was hard not to react.

It wasn't just anger there. No, he was every god of wrath and revenge given form. Almost primal, as he looked fiercely at Niamh with the kind of emotion I hadn't thought he'd ever feel for me.

He didn't just want her dead. He wanted to bathe in her blood, to draw out her ending and make it as long and painful as possible.

To her credit, she didn't flinch. Instead, her smile turned seductive as she brushed her hair back from her face.

A glint of purple and blue shimmered from above.

Lowen and Inara looked down at her, their small bodies making their way along the branches as they shadowed her.

I didn't know what they had planned, but from their furtive movements and the snarl on Inara's face, I didn't think it would be good.

Still, I waited, even as the Wild Hunt's magic called the rest of the hunters to the clearing.

Jerry stepped out of trees, his big body surprisingly graceful for such a large man. Ruth and Harry followed, along with several other Fae. Their gazes were all locked on the stag, and me in Liam's arms.

Arlan had a thoughtful look on his face as he glanced around. He looked from me to Liam, cocking his head as he considered. He shut his eyes and breathed in. They popped open, gleaming with surprise and something that looked like awe.

"The hunt's still going," he said softly.

I tensed, waiting for him to call Niamh's attention to that fact. If he did, Niamh would figure out what was going on.

"Very well done, little breaker," he murmured, just loud enough for me to hear.

Niamh didn't react as she glided forward.

He spared her a glance before turning and walking away, gesturing toward where Breandan and Baran waited in the trees. They looked from him to me, fascination on their faces before following.

Niamh didn't notice. The only ones left were the minor Fae and Niamh's followers.

Liam had stilled above me. He didn't throw out threats, though I felt them. Unsaid, just below the surface.

Niamh didn't seem to realize the danger she was in, even as she moved closer.

"There will be other lovers," she said, flicking her fingers in dismissal. "Leave that one there and come along."

I sensed the coiled violence in Liam's body and touched his hand. He flinched, glancing down at me in disbelief. I gave him the smallest of smiles and a wink.

His body shook as he gazed down at me with something approaching wonder.

"The hunt isn't finished," Niamh said, her voice turning threatening when Liam didn't respond. "The stag still lives."

Liam stroked my cheek, a million words there. If I'd doubted what he felt for me, that doubt was gone. The grief when he thought he'd lost me had been real. The rage, even now, wasn't entirely absent, just banked.

Liam set me down, moving cautiously. His gaze lingered on mine, a warning not to move.

He stepped over me, his body hovering protectively over mine. He bared his fangs at Niamh.

"Connor, protect Aileen," Liam ordered, sparing only the briefest of glances at the stag.

Niamh stopped, looking for all the world like he'd just slapped her. Her gaze went from him to me, where I'd raised myself up on one elbow.

I wasn't the damsel in distress type. If he planned to fight, so would I, even if my body protested each and every movement, my muscles trembling from overuse.

Denial was there on her face. "No, she should be dead."

"So sorry to disappoint," I said.

Rage turned her ugly. She didn't stay that way long, her expression smoothing out. "The hunt still goes. Kill her."

The words were a signal. Chaos descended.

Inara and Lowen dropped from above, a net of magic woven between them. Liam launched himself forward, meeting the first Fae with a snarl, breaking its neck and tossing it at those behind him.

I leveraged myself to my feet, determined to fight. As long as we lived, there was hope.

The stag reared, using his hooves to strike another Fae in the head.

From behind us, the howl of wolves rose. Furry bodies poured into the clearing, setting on the Fae and driving them back.

Liam's enforcers were steps behind them. I flinched from Daniel as he wielded his broad sword with wild abandon. Instead of being cleaved in two as I'd assumed, he knocked a Fae out of the air, dispatching it easily.

I sank into my vampire, relying on its instincts to defend us, wrenching apart anything that came close, using fangs and the claws on my fingers to stay alive.

I got lucky. None of those who approached were those I knew.

Not until Jerry ended up across from me, an ax in his hands and murder on his face. He advanced, even as I had enough presence of mind to back away.

"Jerry," I warned. He didn't respond, the hunt and Niamh's thrall binding him too tightly.

I thought I detected a hint of awareness in his expression, regret, even as he kept coming.

I dodged out of the way, aiming a blow at his elbow, then his shoulder. I moved around him, using speed and desperation to stay out of reach while hitting him in the few places he was vulnerable.

Liam roared, coming out of nowhere. The two meeting with a mighty crash.

I turned, surveying the forest. It had more in common with a war zone than it did a forest.

Niamh and her followers watched with gloating glances as the rest of us tore each other apart.

She was the reason for all this. Small threads of magic trailing from her to half those here.

I snapped.

I was before her between one moment and the next, grabbing her throat and wrenching her up before slamming her into a tree.

The shock on her face would have been comical if I hadn't been so damn mad.

Her expression hardened and power snapped up, trying to burn me out. I let it glance off me, unheeding as it poured past me.

The shock in her face was gratifying, and I grinned down at her, my fangs fully lowered. "Weren't expecting that, were you?"

I didn't wait for an answer, burying my fangs in her throat. It was like biting into an electrical outlet. Pure, raw power poured down my throat.

The feeling was indescribable, better than anything I'd ever tasted— with the exception of Liam's blood, but for different reasons.

It was life, bubbly and effervescent. Fire dancing along every nerve at the same time. Like fire, it gave even as it took, scorching those same nerve endings.

But I still couldn't stop. I needed more, even as it became too much. Her power filled me up, threatening to make me burst from my skin. It felt like strapping onto the outside of a rocket, then being shot through the atmosphere.

I fought to stay present, to not get lost. If I did, if I surrendered myself to this never-ending well, I wasn't coming back.

Abruptly, I was in a deep dark space, streams of power all around me. Some small, some no more than a trickle, others vast streams that might have once carved canyons.

I understood, even as I didn't know how, that each of these were Niamh's victims. People and creatures she'd forced under her will.

I could break those bonds. I knew how. Liam and the stag had shown me the way.

A whisper came up from the deep. *They could be yours.*

I saw that Niamh herself wasn't powerful. No, she'd stolen what she had from others, every bond she placed strengthening her.

And every single one of them could be mine. All I had to do was reach out and grab them. No more running from other spooks. No more balancing on a knife-edge between what the vampires wanted and what I needed to survive.

There wouldn't be a soul alive who could challenge me if I took these as my own.

I reached out, fire sparking along my fingertips, burning those threads until there was nothing left, not even ash.

Power wasn't what I was after. It never had been.

Someone jerked me back from Niamh's throat, Liam's frantic face above mine. He said something and I blinked dumbly at him.

He dragged me back several paces, unconcerned as Niamh fell to her knees. She was too drained to give more than a token protest when Daniel grabbed her arm and lifted her up.

All around us the fighting had stopped.

A large blond-white wolf trotted up to me, her tongue lolling out of her mouth. She nudged my hand and gave a happy yip.

"You make such a pretty puppy, Caroline," I said, happily. My lips still felt numb and my head swam with magic.

I wanted to loll on the ground, run naked through the forest and frolic in its meadows.

Liam's firm grip told me none of that was happening. He walked up to Eric and thrust me into his hands.

"Keep her safe," he ordered.

Eric took me with a slightly disconcerted expression, eyeing me like I might turn around and bite him at any moment. I gave him a sappy smile and waved.

"What's wrong with her?"

Liam caressed my cheek before stepping back. "She bit Niamh."

Eric looked startled at that news.

"Drank her down like she was a fucking juice box," Anton said, striding up as he wiped at his face. There was blood all over it. Apparently, sinking your fangs into the throat of your prey, while efficient, was also terribly messy.

"She tasted good," I slurred.

Daniel snorted. "You're drunk."

I nodded. Sure felt that way.

"I'm surprised her brain isn't scrambled," Anton said, looking down at me.

I made a gun with my fingers and pretended to shoot him as I leaned on Eric.

Niamh screamed and staggered to her feet. I didn't even pretend concern as she wobbled toward me. She looked like a newborn colt.

"You drank from me," she accused, her eyes wide, her face pale.

If she'd been human, she'd have been in shock. I'd taken a lot of blood. Not enough to kill her, or any average- sized person, but enough that she would be feeling its loss.

I smiled at her, not caring that my lips were probably rimmed with blood. "Nom nom nom."

She looked at a loss for words.

I sniffed. I thought I was very clear.

A soft laugh came from the trees, Arlan and the twins watching from their shelter.

"I want her dead," Niamh shrieked.

"The hunt is over. Everything that happened during is forgiven," Thomas said, moving into view. His clothes were slightly mussed and his hair just a little disheveled. Other than that, he looked untouched, his expression outwardly calm even as the power in him gave a hint of his emotions.

It waited, crouching deep inside, poised to strike.

I leaned forward and made a small sound of interest. I didn't know it could even do that.

He flicked a look at the men at my back and made a small motion.

"Alright, time to go," Anton said as Eric drew me back.

"She's not going anywhere," Niamh hissed. Her gaze shifted to those Fae who had survived.

The forest was littered with the bodies of those who'd participated in the hunt. There was panic on some faces as the vampires ghosted out of the trees.

I tried to count them but gave up after the third time I had to start again because I'd forgotten what I was doing. It was enough that I knew there were many more of Thomas's people out here than had been present at the beginning of the hunt.

Those who could, fled, leaving behind the injured and dead without a backward glance.

Only a few lingered, Jerry and his couriers among them.

All watched Niamh.

"Kill her," Niamh ordered, pointing at me.

I snickered. She still didn't realize what I'd done.

Niamh blanched, looking around.

My snicker turned into a chortle. Her stricken eyes zero'd in on me.

"What did you do?" she asked, finally realizing something was wrong.

I cocked my head and leaned forward as far as Eric would let me. I gave her a nasty smile. "I took them from you."

She shook her head and just kept shaking it. Gone was the lady of the forest who had gloated in my plight, who had sought to put Liam and the others under her thumb.

"Do something," she cried at her husband.

He shook his head. "The hunt is over. Any action now would break the treaty."

He didn't even bother to pretend at regret.

Baran and Breandan behind him moved through the trees, circling Niamh.

"Such a pity to see the great lady helpless," Breandan said. There was a seductive edge to his voice. "I hope you run fast, my lady."

His twin slid me a look and winked before the two of them turned and disappeared into the early dawn, the forest swallowing them as if they'd never been present.

It might have been my imagination, but I could have sworn I heard a soft voice say, "See you soon, little breaker."

I waited, expecting Thomas or even Liam to do something. They didn't. They stood quietly, watching the Fae with hard expressions.

I straightened, a little of my drunkenness fading. "What are they doing?

Why aren't they doing anything to her?"

"They can't," Eric said, not sounding any happier as he and the rest glared at the High Fae.

My gaze swung toward him, the depths of my disbelief almost comical. "What do you mean they can't? She tried to put Liam under her thrall. She nearly killed me."

"That's exactly why we can't. No one can know she was able to put vampires as powerful as Liam and Nathan under her thrall. It would show a weakness others would seek to exploit. They'll blame everything on the Wild Hunt instead," Anton said, sounding pissed.

I looked back at her. "She's going to get away with everything?"

I didn't want that to be the case. She'd almost broken Liam and damn near killed me. Letting her get off without any punishment offended me.

"I wouldn't necessarily say that," Niall said, appearing beside us.

The enforcers tensed.

Our gazes swung back to the scene as Jerry and the rest of the Fae advanced on Niamh.

Liam made his way over to me, taking me from Eric's hold.

"What's happening?" I asked, still not feeling totally present.

"There will be a hunt of another kind," he said softly.

His insinuation was clear, especially when Niamh blanched and fled into the trees.

"Won't her husband try to help her?" I asked, feeling all trace of inebriation flee with the sounds of the Fae's screams as they gave chase. It was a haunting reminder of my own flight.

Liam drew me close, dropping a kiss on my forehead. "There's no love lost between the two. If she can't escape on her own, he has no need for her anymore."

There was a brief scream and then silence.

I held myself still against Liam, trying not to feel, trying not to think.

Niamh had probably deserved the death she'd received, but the manner of her death, how closely it had resembled the last few hours as I fought to stay alive, pricked at wounds that hadn't even begun to heal.

"I assume you and your people will head home now the hunt is completed," Thomas said.

Niamh might have been taken care of, but the rest of the Fae had been complicit in her plans. Arlan especially, had known what she'd intended, known and done nothing.

Arlan's smile was faint and amused. "I think we will linger." His eyes came to rest on me. Caroline let out a faint growl even as Liam stiffened warily. "I've found something here that interests me."

His gaze drifted to Niall and Cadell and he gave them a meaningful look. "Well done, Lord of the Green. You did not let me down." His focus turned to Cadell. "Welcome to our ranks."

Niall and Cadell remained motionless, not even the flicker of an eyelash giving away their thoughts as Arlan turned and disappeared into the forest, following in the twins' wake.

Cadell's gaze was enigmatic as it met mine. There was an apology there, but no remorse.

My lips parted as shock coursed through me. He'd been the one to mark me. He was the only one who could have. All that time spent wracking my brain trying to figure out who'd gotten close enough and the answer was right in front of me.

It was him. He'd used the excuse of passing me the note to lay the mark. As this night had just proven, both he and Niall were lords of the hunt, perfectly capable of marking prey.

Thomas rested his hands on his hips and bent his head before turning back to me, his gaze alive with irritation.

My mouth snapped shut, and I put aside my suspicions to be examined later when my head wasn't quite so foggy.

I frowned at Thomas. What did I do this time?

I didn't realize I'd said it aloud until Anton choked on a laugh beside me. I looked around to find the other enforcers fighting similar bouts of amusement. My frown grew more pronounced.

My eyes narrowed as a thought occurred to me. "How did you guys slip her thrall?"

In the chaos of the hunt's end, it hadn't really sunk in that they'd been fighting for us rather than against us. Something that shouldn't have been possible because I hadn't broken her hold yet.

"I freed them from her hold in the first thirty minutes of the hunt," Thomas said, sounding vexed.

I blinked at him, my mouth dropping open in surprise. "You did?"

Anton lost his battle with his hilarity, bending over as he gasped with laughter. I bit off a growl as I noticed Daniel and Eric turn away as they fought similar reactions.

"It's not that funny," I muttered. I lost the battle to remain standing and would have fallen if Liam hadn't caught me and pressed me against his side.

"Yes, Aileen, I did. Right after I dealt with the problem of the witches. Something you would have known if you hadn't decided to join the hunt," he said with forced patience.

"What happened to Sarah and the rest?" I asked feeling somber.

Thomas's frown became more severe, but he relented, answering my question. "Most of her disciples are dead. The few who survived have been taken home to be questioned."

"And Sarah?" I asked, already feeling like I knew the answer.

"She escaped." His face was remote, giving no sign of how that must burn.

I left that subject, sensing prying further would only cause consequences I wanted to avoid. I looked around. "So, all this time?"

Daniel nodded, some of the humor dying in his face. "We've been trying to catch you so we could get you to safety."

Ah.

I remembered them amid the trees, chasing me. I'd just assumed they were trying to kill me like all the rest.

"You're pretty fast for someone not even out of your infancy," Anton said.

I ignored the partial complement and craned my head to peer up at Liam. "I guess I didn't free you after all."

He'd certainly done a good job of pretending to still be in her hold. The commitment he'd shown when he brandished that dagger had been very convincing. If he'd been an actor, I'd have nominated him for an Oscar.

He brushed my hair from my face, his expression tender. "You did. Thomas couldn't break her hold over me."

Thomas's frown turned grumpy. "Only because I couldn't catch you."

"And you wouldn't have caught me," Liam said with a meaningful glance. "Not until it was too late."

Thomas didn't argue, conceding the point with a small noncommittal shrug. He looked around, his gaze searching.

What was he looking for?

"Did you see which direction the stag went?" he asked.

"Why do you want to know?" I couldn't help but feel a little protective of the creature. His interference had probably saved my life several times over. There was no doubt in my mind he could have escaped well before the hunters had closed in, if not for my slower self.

"Aileen," Thomas said, a warning in his tone.

I didn't answer, my thoughts turning to another. "Where's Nathan?"

He looked away. The enforcers had grown silent as well.

I pushed away from Liam. "Thomas, where's Nathan?"

"He's alive," he admitted grudgingly. By the way he said it you could almost hear the 'for now' after that.

I narrowed my eyes at him. "Unharmed?"

He looked away.

My eyes widened and a growl slipped from me.

His gaze swung back to me. "Careful. My tolerance only goes so far."

"I see some things still haven't changed," a quiet voice said from the trees to our left.

CHAPTER TWENTY

A man stood there, the early dawn shadows wrapping around his body. They didn't quite shield all the bare skin on display.

He seemed perfectly at home among the trees, as if he was a forest sprite and we were the interlopers.

His hair was nearly white and his skin pale as milk. His eyes were an electric blue, at once familiar and yet strange.

Motionless, Liam and Thomas looked toward the stranger with haunted expressions.

"Connor," Thomas whispered, stepping slightly forward.

My head whipped towards Thomas. Connor. As in Thomas's yearling? The first one? The one who'd disappeared after some argument no single person would tell me about? *That* Connor?

What was he doing here? Now?

I shifted my attention between Liam and Connor. Liam must have known about this. He'd told Connor to protect me during the fight. I hadn't realized it at the time, too consumed with survival. I blinked as realization sunk in. Connor had been the person Liam was looking for when he left. Did Thomas know?

Connor's focus was fixed on me, the expression on his face almost shy. "I wanted to thank you for freeing me."

I blinked at him, having no idea what he was talking about.

"You're welcome?" It came out almost as a question.

"Ah, you may not recognize me without the antlers," he said.

The stag? How? What?

Confusion must have been written on my face because his smile turned wry. "It was Niamh's idea of a joke. A hunt with traditional prey."

More and more, I was finding it hard to regret her death. I didn't know what that said about me.

I nodded. There wasn't much to say after a revelation like that.

"Come, let's get you some clothes," Thomas said, his expression hopeful. "We have so much to catch up on."

Connor dipped his chin in agreement, padding out of the trees, his bare feet whispering over the ground. If he felt any discomfort walking barefoot and naked through the forest, he didn't show it.

It was a quiet journey back to the car. Caroline and a few wolves ranged in front of us, leading the way. Evidently when Inara had said Caroline was waiting, she really meant Caroline and half the pack.

The pack's presence was probably a good thing, considering there were several of us. More cars meant more room.

Given the sun had only strengthened in the short time since the hunt had ended, those vehicles would be desperately needed.

I crawled into the backseat of an SUV, already losing the battle with exhaustion.

Connor, Thomas and Liam joined me in the back of the SUV. Eric and Anton took the front. The rest of those present went with other drivers.

I let my head fall on Liam's shoulder, my eyes shutting under their own will.

I felt his hand brushing my hair back, but didn't move.

"Have you been with Niamh all this time?" Thomas asked.

I didn't hear a response, but there must have been one because Thomas continued talking.

"Why didn't you send word? I would have helped you."

There was a small snort, the same sound the stag had made on several occasions. "You overestimate your abilities. For a long time, I was barely aware that I was more than the stag. By the time I remembered who I was, many years had passed and I assumed you didn't care anymore."

"I will always care," Thomas said, his voice aching.

I didn't know what had happened between the two, but it was clear Thomas felt strong emotions for this man. The hope on his face when Connor had made his presence known had been surprising in the master who normally seemed unflappable.

Liam continued to stroke my hair, the gesture lulling in its comfort, as he spoke to Connor. "Thank you for protecting my heart from me."

My lids lifted enough to see Connor give him a small nod. His blue eyes came to mine in the next minute. One pale hand touched my forehead. "Sleep, *A stóirín*. You've done enough for the night."

After that, I didn't remember much, only half-surfacing as Liam removed my shoes. I fell back into sleep, barely aware as the bed dipped under me and a hard body wrapped around mine.

*

Behind me, Thomas radiated disapproval as I stood in front of the small room that doubled as one of their prison cells. I'd been informed there were silver bars built into the walls, ceiling and floor. The door was also covered with silver and was made of a metal thick enough it would take a tank to punch through.

Thomas didn't like my insistence about meeting with Nathan. He still didn't quite trust him after knowing Nathan had been used as a trojan horse. The bite from Liam's enforcer had opened a small chink in Thomas's defenses. Coupled with the bond between the two enforcers, it had allowed Niamh's compulsion to take hold of Liam. It would probably be a long time before the memory of Nathan's unwilling treachery faded.

Daniel guarded the door, his expression uncertain as he noted my determination.

"How is he?" I asked.

The question triggered a frown as he shook his head. "He refuses to come out. Says he can't be trusted."

"I thought Niamh's thrall ended the night of the hunt?"

When I'd broken it, I meant, but I didn't say it aloud. Liam and Thomas had agreed it was best if no one knew the extent to which I'd been involved in undoing Niamh's bindings on the rest of the hunt's participants.

The enforcers in the room with us during Miriam's questioning might realize I could see through glamours at some point, but they didn't know about all the rest.

I suspected it wouldn't be long, however. Already there were those like Niamh's husband, who had guessed what I'd done. Inara knew as well, since she was the one who'd called me "magic breaker".

My days of keeping that ability under wraps were limited, but I saw no reason to hasten my revelation either.

Based upon the conversation I'd overheard during the trip back to the mansion the night of the hunt, it seemed as if people with abilities like mine were either hunted or enslaved. Given I was still a baby power-wise, I'd delay the inevitable as long as possible—at least until I had a hope in hell of protecting myself.

Given the way the hunt had ended, most people would assume Niamh's death had been responsible for breaking her bindings, not me.

The Fae's hunt had been successful and established the beginnings of a barrow. It just hadn't had the prey Niamh intended. I'm told her ending was not pleasant or merciful. I was just relieved she was dead and we didn't have to worry about her again.

"The thrall did break," Daniel confirmed. "But he planted himself in that room and hasn't come out since. This has hit him hard."

I nodded. I could understand that. For someone at the top of the food chain, it would be difficult to be confronted with your weakness. To be forced into actions that weren't your own. It was a devastating violation.

"Are you sure you want to do this?" Thomas asked. "I'm told he's been quite ugly to others who've tried to talk to him."

I had no doubt about that.

"He's my friend," I said.

That was the only answer I had. In my world, you didn't leave friends to hurt alone. They needed to know someone was there—that someone cared, even when they were in the deepest parts of night.

It might not make a difference, but then again, it might.

Thomas sighed as he studied me. Whatever he saw there must have convinced him of my stubbornness because he gestured at Daniel.

Daniel shook his head but opened the door. "Good luck."

I took a deep breath and stepped inside. Despite the lights, the room still managed to be dark. It was bare of any amenities beyond a simple cot and chair.

Nathan sat in the corner on the ground, his legs drawn up as he stared at me.

I hesitated in the doorway. Now that I was here, I wasn't entirely sure what to say.

"You should go," Nathan said tiredly.

I walked forward and sank down against the wall a few feet from him. I leaned my head back and waited. I didn't say anything as I kept him company.

Sometimes words were ineffectual niceties. When your life has imploded enough that the act of getting up seems like more work than its worth, it doesn't help to have someone whisper meaningless platitudes. It just isolates you further.

Still, there was no reason he had to sit alone.

"This place is a lot nicer than the wolf's cage," I told him, looking around.

For one thing, it didn't look like a cage, even if that's what it was. The surroundings might have been simple, but it looked like a normal room, plain though it might be.

"How long do you plan to hang out in here?" I asked.

He didn't answer. Silence grew between us.

I nodded and went back to staring at the other wall. I relaxed into the quiet. It'd been a long time since I simply sat and thought. My life had become filled with action. There was always something to do, some crisis to solve. It was kind of nice to do nothing for once.

When my butt cheeks got sore, I turned onto my side, stretching out and folding my arm under my head.

Through it all, Nathan remained motionless. I couldn't help but be impressed by his discipline. Me, I'd had to change position a half-dozen times since I got here, while Nathan remained a rock, like one of those ascetic monks who put their bodies through extremes in the pursuit of holiness.

"You're wasting your time," he finally said when it became clear I wasn't giving up.

"It's my time to waste." I sat up and leaned back against the wall. A chair would have been nice right about now.

He bared his teeth at me. "Go."

I snorted. "We both know you're not going to hurt me."

His fangs were at my throat in an instant as his body hovered over mine. My heart gave a painful thump. He'd gotten faster. In all our training sessions he'd never moved like that. It was like watching a snake strike. You could feel it coming but you couldn't get out of the way in time.

I had to wonder if he'd been holding back this entire time, or if this was a side effect of Niamh's tinkering.

I didn't move, refusing to show any signs of fear. That's what he wanted. This was a carefully calculated move to drive me away. As someone who'd perfected such methods against her family, I recognized it for the posturing it was.

"You done?" I asked.

"I can feel your heart racing," he said, his voice silky, a threat on his face that wasn't Nathan. "You can pretend all you want, but we both know I terrify you now."

I raised an eyebrow. "You think you didn't terrify me before?"

He drew back, just the faintest bit, enough so he could watch me through wounded eyes, his expression unsure.

I gave him a sad smile. "All vampires terrify me, Nathan. A vampire just like you killed me, ripped me out of my former life. There was nothing I could do to stop it. Worse, I participated, giving myself over to the pleasure of his bite. Because it felt good. Because it was easy."

He sat back on his heels. There was understanding there. And regret.

I'd take it, even if his sentiments were due to my revelation.

"Thomas may not have been fully in control of his actions because of his curse, but that doesn't mean I don't relive that night again and again in my dreams," I told him softly, as I shared something I didn't like to admit to anyone.

All makings were traumatic, but for Nathan and Liam, and all the rest, the intervening centuries had blunted their memories. For me, the night of my rebirth was still visceral and real. I could close my eyes and be there again, watching as my life drained away, not lifting a hand to stop it.

To make matters worse, my making was more violent than most. I had Sarah's curse on Thomas to thank for that.

"Why are you really in here?" I asked.

He looked away, his jaw tightening stubbornly.

I waited.

After a long moment, he rubbed his forehead. His voice was faint, as if he didn't want to tempt fate by voicing his thoughts aloud. "What if they're wrong? What if there's still some suggestion hidden in there, just waiting?"

Suddenly I understood why he was punishing himself with this place. It wasn't because he felt guilt, although I'm sure that was some of it. It was because he didn't trust himself anymore, didn't trust it was only him driving his actions.

I blinked and took a deeper look at him, searching for any faint shadows or any suggestion of influence that didn't belong.

There was nothing, just Nathan's power fluttering like a banked fire on a cold winter's night.

"You're clear," I told him.

He snorted, a little of the old Nathan coming through. "Sorry, A, but there's no way for you to know that."

I debated how much of the truth to give him.

"I can. I can see magic," I said.

My admission wasn't going to please Liam or Thomas, but if it would help Nathan come to terms with what had happened, it was a secret I was glad to part with.

He gave a short laugh, disbelief written on his face.

I didn't move, just watched him calmly.

The laugh died, then his eyes widened.

"How do you think I knew you were under her influence?" I asked.

He stood, looking down at me with disbelief. "Do you know how dangerous that information is? People would kill to possess such an ability." He ran his hands through his hair. "Does Liam know?"

I lifted a shoulder. "He figured it out a while back."

"And he hasn't told you to keep that little tidbit to yourself?" Nathan snapped.

I smirked.

He rolled his eyes. "Of course, he has. Why are you telling me this?"

I propped my chin on my hand and lifted my eyebrows, silently telling him to guess.

A stunned look crossed his face.

Now he was getting it. I stood and walked over to the door.

"You're worried you could still be under her influence. Don't be. You're not. I can guarantee it," I told him. "All of us will be waiting, when you're ready to leave this place. Do me a favor and don't keep me waiting too long. You know patience isn't my strong suit."

He watched me open the door and step out, without making a move toward me.

That was okay. He needed time to heal. I understood that. I'd be here when he was ready. Until then, I thought it was important he knew he didn't have anything to worry about.

"Aileen," he said, stopping me in the doorway.

I waited.

"Thank you."

I lifted a shoulder. "What are friends for?"

His smile held a shadow of his old self. "If Liam hadn't already staked a claim, he'd have heavy competition."

That wiped the smile off my face, turning it into a scowl. His laughter followed me as I walked from the room, the door shutting behind me.

*

I rounded the corner, my shoes squeaking along the linoleum, the bear I'd bought clasped in my arms.

I'd timed my visit to the hospital well, I hoped. My parents were busy at home and Jenna had just left to get a change of clothes. It should give me time with my niece without the drama of everything else.

Linda was still sick. It turned out Niamh really hadn't had anything to do with her illness. I'd been forced to accept sometimes bad things happened to good people and that children do get sick.

Life threateningly so, it seemed. The doctors still weren't sure what was causing her to throw up blood, but there were whispers of cancer.

At her door, I composed myself, practicing a smile a few times before taking a deep breath. The last thing Linda needed was to see fear on my face when I went in there. The mind was the most powerful part of the human body. If she believed she would get well, then there was a chance— but not if every adult in her life treated her illness like the coming of the apocalypse.

I stepped inside and drew up short at the sight of Thomas sitting by her bed, Liam standing behind him.

I didn't speak, sorting through scenarios and discarding them.

"What are you doing here?" I asked quietly.

"I'm here to offer you a gift," Thomas said.

My gaze darted to Liam's. He gave me a reassuring nod. I relaxed slightly. I trusted him. In this, I didn't think he would lead me wrong.

"How?" I asked.

"You're here to give her your blood," Thomas said. There wasn't any judgment on his face, no hint of anger.

I shifted, uncomfortable at how well he knew me. I hadn't fully committed to my plan yet. One, because I didn't know all the ramifications. There was still so much that was still a mystery to me about being a vampire. I didn't want to risk screwing Linda up further by giving her blood that might hurt her in the long run.

"Possibly," I said, stepping forward.

Thomas was here with no threats or recriminations. If he was willing to help, I'd take it. Hell, I'd even sell him my soul if it meant Linda would get better. There wasn't much I wouldn't do for that little girl.

"Mine will have a better likelihood of healing her," Thomas said.

I believed him. He was centuries older than I and powerful in ways I was just beginning to comprehend. He was a master while I was just barely a vampire.

Still, I hesitated to accept. I couldn't help looking for the trap hidden in his offer. Because that's what it was.

"Will she be like me?" I forced myself to ask.

I wasn't even sure I would tell him no if he answered "yes". I just wanted her to live. I hadn't realized before now, how deep I was willing to sink if it meant her health.

"No," he said. "I would need to drain her unto death after exchanging blood with her for years, for that to be a real risk."

I frowned. That hadn't been the case with me.

He inclined his head, understanding where my thoughts had gone. "You are a special case. The magic at your core reacted violently to my bite, changing you outside the normal course of things. For her, my blood will simply heal her. She might be a little stronger physically, a little faster, and live a little longer, but one feeding will not have many long-term consequences."

I hesitated still.

There was a reason there were sayings warning one to beware of people bearing gifts. Few things in this world were free. I'd learned that more than most.

"What's the catch?" I asked.

I was doing this. I knew that, but I wanted to know exactly what I was giving up.

"Nothing," Thomas said. "You've already given me more than I could imagine."

Uh huh. I didn't quite believe that.

"Perhaps I just want to show you I'm not the monster you've made me out to be," he said simply.

I didn't know about that. He did force me to drink from a human, even used compulsion to do it. For all his dislike of Niamh's methods, he wasn't above doing the same when push came to shove.

I sighed. Perhaps I was being too hard on him. It was human blood that had probably kept me alive during the hunt, giving me the strength I needed to keep going. Not to mention his concern about toxicity.

Devolution.

He read the acceptance on my face and stood.

The feeding was a simple one. Thomas used a sharp nail to open a line of blood then held it to Linda's mouth.

Watching the exchange of blood was fascinating. The power residing in Thomas flowed down into Linda, pooling in her center before dispersing through her body.

Then it was over and Thomas stepped back, his wound closing.

"That's it?" I asked.

"I'll monitor her. Depending on how she reacts, she may need more," he told me.

I nodded. I tried to keep my hope contained, but it was hard.

Thomas left, and then it was just Liam and me in the room with Linda.

"Thank you for that," I told him. "I know you're a big part of why he volunteered."

"He would have gotten around to it." Liam made a small movement. "Eventually."

But probably not until he'd tried to bargain with me, destroying any chance of an amicable relationship between the two of us.

"What now?" I asked.

He stepped closer, clasping the nape of my neck as he angled my head for a kiss. Desire rose between the two of us. It was quick but potent, as we drew back, panting slightly. The bedside of my ill niece wasn't the place to indulge.

"I think your generation calls it dating," he said with a wicked smile.

I raised an eyebrow. "And if I decide I don't want to date?"

He nipped my chin. "I still have nine nights to convince you to my way of thinking."

"Nine? I gave you at least four," I said, jerking back.

His smile turned dark. "I only asked for the first."

My mouth dropped open in dismay as he stepped around me and sauntered to the door. "You could save me the trouble and just move in with me."

"Not in this lifetime," I snarled.

"Ah well, I'll enjoy the chase." The door closed after him, leaving me almost fuming with anger as I stared after him.

Tricky, tricky vampire. I should have known I wasn't getting off that easy.

*

Later that night, I rolled my bike to a stop in front of my apartment building, surprised at the brand-new stairway leading up to my door. Looked like Thomas had finally gotten around to repairing them.

256

I glanced at the space next to them where the black Escalade had once sat. And looked again. In its place was a Jaguar F-Type, with a burnt umber paint job.

I hesitated in front of it, a sneaking suspicion I knew where it had come from. It was identical to the car Liam had. In fact, it was that car.

I walked past it, undecided about what to do with it and not ready to figure out the tangled web it represented.

To my surprise, the light in Niall and Cadell's apartment was on. They were still here. I thought with Niamh dead and the barrow established, they would have returned to the Summerlands. Not the case. It confirmed my suspicion they had other reasons to linger besides the Wild Hunt.

I put it out of my mind. That was a problem for tomorrow's Aileen. Tonight's Aileen was looking forward to a quiet evening watching Netflix and reading.

"Aileen," my dad said, stepping out of a car that I hadn't noticed until now.

I hesitated, the desire to disappear into my apartment strong. It had been a long couple of days. I didn't know if I wanted to deal with family drama right now.

"Please," he said.

Resignation filled me. This was my dad. As tempting it was to duck him, it wouldn't help in the long run. I propped my bike against the stairs, turning to face him. "What is it?"

"I know you were at the hospital earlier," he said.

I didn't react.

"I'm sorry you felt you had to find a time when nobody else was there," he said.

I stiffened, disliking how he'd made things sound like my fault.

"I'm sorry we made you feel like you needed to do that." He corrected himself before I could.

I didn't know what to say to him. This was the man who had raised me, kissed my cuts and scrapes when I fell, and had been my biggest champion even when I felt like I failed. My dad. The man who'd lied to me my entire life.

"Me too," I finally said.

All the anger had drained from me, leaving sadness in its place.

"Are you going to invite me up?" he asked.

I shook my head. I didn't have it in me to be kind. Not tonight. My home was a safe space for me. I didn't want anger and drama to contaminate it.

"Say what you need to say."

He nodded, his face turning unbearably sad. "I guess I deserved that."

"It's been a really long couple of days. I'd like to go to bed," I said when he didn't speak.

"Your mother doesn't want me here," he confessed.

That didn't surprise me. The bigger surprise was that he was here even without her blessing. He'd always deferred to her, letting her run the show. Not because he was weak, but because my mom was comfortable taking charge and he loved her enough to let her.

He held out his hand, a manila envelope in it.

"What's that?" I asked, not taking it.

"Information about your biological father," he said. "I kept it. Your mom doesn't know I have it, but I thought you might need it someday."

I didn't take it from him. I couldn't. All my life he'd been my dad; taking that envelope from him threatened to negate that.

His eyes were red and his voice clogged with emotion as he shook it at me. "This doesn't change anything. I'm still your dad. You're still my daughter. I don't care that we don't share blood."

I reached out and took the envelope from him. Hiding from the truth wouldn't help me, and it wouldn't heal wounds that were a lifetime in the making. Sometimes the best thing to do is to rip the band-aid off and hope for the best.

"Your mother loves you, you know that, right?" he asked.

I nodded. "Yeah, I do. I just wish she accepted me too."

He didn't have anything to say to that, defeat overwhelming him. His shoulders slumped as he shuffled back to his car.

It was painful to watch him go, the envelope clutched in my hand as he drove off, the bitter taste of too many things still left unsaid in my mouth.

My phone rang.

I dug it out of my pocket and looked at the screen. Jerry calling.

I hit the answer button and grabbed the bike before climbing the stairs. "This is Aileen."

"I never did say thank you for what you did," he said.

I contained my surprise at his thanks, something Fae normally avoided saying as it implied a debt they would have to repay. I suppose, though, he hadn't quite said it directly, skirting the sentiment skillfully.

I unlocked the door and let myself in. "Seems to me, you freed yourself."

His chuckle was a low rumble. "Funny thing that. None of us could do anything against her even without the hunt. Not until you bit her."

"Blood loss has a way of weakening a body," I said, throwing my keys on the table.

"Did you know the Fae tell stories of a creature, one able to see magic—more importantly, one able to break magic?" he asked conversationally.

I stopped what I was doing and straightened, my insides going cold.

"That sounds like a fascinating fairy tale," I said, keeping my voice light.

"Indeed," Jerry said.

"Is that why you called? To recite a fairy tale?"

"No, I called to offer you a job," he said.

The doorbell rang.

"You said you can't rehire people."

I opened the door to find an irate sphinx standing on my landing. "Where have you been? I've been waiting for you for days!"

I held up a hand, halting his emotional outburst.

"I'll make an exception for you," he said.

It was a tempting offer. My old job, one I knew how to do.

"I appreciate the offer but a new opportunity just knocked on my door," I told him. I hung up the phone.

The sphinx waited, his face unhappy.

I looked him over and smiled. "First, we're going to agree on terms. Then we'll talk about me finding your missing scroll."

I stepped back and let him into the apartment.

Later that night I picked up the envelope my dad had given me, laying each piece of paper on the desk in front of me. It wasn't much. Just a few photos, a birth certificate and a name.

Bryan Volsk. My biological father.

DISCOVER MORE BY T.A. WHITE

The Broken Lands Series
Pathfinder's Way – Book One
Mist's Edge – Book Two
Wayfarer's Keep – Book Three

The Dragon-Ridden Chronicles
Dragon-Ridden – Book One
Of Bone and Ruin – Book Two
Destruction's Ascent – Book Three
Shifting Seas - Novella

The Aileen Travers Series
Shadow's Messenger – Book One
Midnight's Emissary – Book Two
Moonlight's Ambassador – Book Three

CONNECT WITH ME

Twitter: @tawhiteauthor
Facebook: https://www.facebook.com/tawhiteauthor/
Website: http://www.tawhiteauthor.com/
Blog: http://dragon-ridden.blogspot.com/

Visit tawhiteauthor.com to join the hoard and sign up for updates regarding new releases.

ABOUT THE AUTHOR

Writing is my first love. Even before I could read or put coherent sentences down on paper, I would beg the older kids to team up with me for the purpose of crafting ghost stories to share with our friends. This first writing partnership came to a tragic end when my coauthor decided to quit a day later and I threw my cookies at her head. This led to my conclusion that I worked better alone. Today, I stick with solo writing, telling the stories that would otherwise keep me up at night.

Most days (and nights) are spent feeding my tea addiction while defending the computer keyboard from my feline companions, Loki and Odin.

CPSIA information can be obtained
at www.ICGtesting.com
Printed in the USA
LVHW082150140220
647003LV00012B/262

9 781791 884802